Kate Hatfield was born in London, where she still lives, and after working as an interior designer, became an editor for a London publishing house. She started writing full-time in 1986 and is the author of several acclaimed historical and crime novels under another name. *Angels Alone* is her second novel as Kate Hatfield, her first, *Drowning in Honey*, is also published by Corgi.

Also by Kate Hatfield

DROWNING IN HONEY

and published by Corgi Books

Angels Alone

Kate Hatfield

CORGI BOOKS

ANGELS ALONE
A CORGI BOOK : 0 552 14285 9

First publication in Great Britain

PRINTING HISTORY
Corgi edition published 1996

Set in 11/13pt Monotype Plantin by
Phoenix Typesetting, Ilkley, West Yorkshire.

Corgi Books are published by Transworld Publishers Ltd,
61–63 Uxbridge Road, Ealing, London W5 5SA,
in Australia by Transworld Publishers (Australia) Pty Ltd,
15–25 Helles Avenue, Moorebank, NSW 2170,
and in New Zealand by Transworld Publishers (NZ) Ltd,
3 William Pickering Drive, Albany, Auckland.

Reproduced, printed and bound in Great Britain by
Cox & Wyman Ltd, Reading, Berks.

In memory of
Hilary Goodwin

Acknowledgements

The author would like to thank Mary Carter, Linda Evans, Joanna Goldsworthy, Claudia Johnson and Jennifer Kavanagh for suggestions, advice, information and much support.

Stone walls do not a prison make
Nor iron bars a cage;
Minds innocent and quiet take
That for an hermitage;
If I have freedom in my love,
And in my soul am free;
Angels alone, that soar above,
Enjoy such liberty.

Richard Lovelace
'To Althea, From Prison'

Chapter 1

Lavinia's job was the in-laws. Disliking horses, she was no good at organizing gymkhanas, seeing that the children came to no harm out hunting, or even just giving a hand in the stables. Her education had not fitted her to help any but the youngest children with their homework, and there was nothing she could do for the family concerts since she could neither sing nor read music. Her cooking was thought to be too elaborate and painstaking for the big family gatherings at Christmas and in the summer holidays. But everyone agreed that she was a godsend with tricky outsiders.

The Medworths told each other that it was because she was generally 'good with people', giving the words mocking inverted commas whenever they used them. But in fact there was more to Lavinia's talent than they had ever understood. In the fourteen years since she had married Tom Medworth she had absorbed enough of their myths and traditions to be able to explain them to newcomers, while still being sufficiently detached herself to understand why some people might find them hard to take.

Eight days before Christmas she was helping to make up beds and wishing that the family did not disapprove quite so much of both domestic help and duvets. Having hauled up one corner of a heavy double mattress to shove a folded triangle of three blankets underneath, she let it drop and stood up straight with both hands clamped to the small of her back. The ache there sharpened into pain for a moment as she stretched.

Her husband's sister, Sasha, who was very tall but did not seem to be affected by the repeated stooping and lifting, looked up from a perfect hospital corner with a hint of impatience in her narrow brown eyes. She was an attractive woman in her early forties, thinner than Lavinia and more carelessly dressed. Her brown corduroy trousers had obviously not been pressed after their last washing and her beige-flecked sweater was covered with snags and loops of pulled wool. Unlike Lavinia's dark hair, which was smooth and expensively cut with a deep fringe to accentuate her big grey eyes, Sasha's looked almost unkempt as it hung straight down either side of her bony face.

Despite their fourteen-year relationship, the two women had never achieved any great intimacy. Lavinia had spent most of her marriage living in North Yorkshire with occasional forays to London, while Sasha and her husband, Philip Wold, had been working in Africa. They had brought their children home on leave every other year, but they had always been in great demand then, dividing their time between their friends, the Medworths and Philip's family, and Lavinia had had little opportunity to get to know either of them.

She knew quite a lot about them, though, for the Medworths were great letter writers and news had always flown from one branch of the family to another with almost telegraphic speed. She had often heard the story of how Sasha, who had been working in the Foreign Office when she met Philip, had decided to resign when they married so that she could go wherever his famine-relief work might take him. Her elder sister and both her brothers had disapproved of that, but her generosity had been well repaid for she had built up a remarkable career as a freelance specialist in African affairs with a large and lucrative list of international clients. Her work had dovetailed neatly with Philip's until a series of increasingly dangerous illnesses had forced him out of Africa for good.

'Isn't bedmaking hard on the back?' Lavinia said casually as she disentangled her engagement ring from the edge of one of the blankets.

'Only because you put in such a lot of effort; far more than you need,' Sasha said with a cool superiority that made her seem dauntingly like her sister, Frida Collingham. 'If you lean into it as you lift the mattress and bend your knees, you won't put nearly so much strain on your spine.'

Lavinia had often wished that the Medworths would learn to control their urge to tell other people how to improve themselves, but she knew how difficult they would find it. They were massively gifted, all of them, and could never bear to watch other people doing things badly, even something as prosaic as bedmaking, without passing on some helpful advice.

'I expect you're right,' she said, looking up at Sasha with what she hoped was a pleasant smile. 'How many more have we got to do?'

Sasha pulled a list out of the pocket of her baggy trousers. 'Three more adult doubles and . . .' She paused, counting the names on her list, 'singles for John Hogarth and Great-aunt Elfrida, and four of the children's two-bedded rooms, although it's absurd to call Georgina and Julia children these days.'

'They still count as children as far as sharing bedrooms at Saltley is concerned,' said Lavinia drily. She was only nine years older than her eldest niece-by-marriage. 'Your mother made it clear long ago that no one gets a room to herself until she's married or thirty, whichever is the sooner.'

Sasha laughed and looked much more human. 'True.

13

It's odd coming back after all these years to find everything exactly the same and yet not the same at all.'

'It must be weird,' agreed Lavinia, shaking the pillows for her side of the six-foot-six bed and stuffing them into their starched linen cases. When she had laid them on the bed, she put her hands to her spine again, holding the ache into her back. 'Was it awful having to leave Africa after so long?'

Sasha looked as though she were trying to decide how much to admit. In the end she shrugged and pushed her lank hair back from her face. 'In some ways it's been hell.' She sighed and then produced a mechanical smile and said more briskly: 'But once it became clear that Philip couldn't stay, I had no option. And there are plenty of bonuses. For one thing, the children are getting a chance to pick up all the traditions we couldn't keep up on our own out there.'

Lavinia did not think that her expression had changed as she watched Sasha crumple the list back into her pocket, but it must have done for she tightened her eyebrows and said: 'Do you know, I am beginning to think that rather more goes on behind your placid exterior than one might think. You looked positively amused just then.'

'Did I? I suppose I do sometimes laugh a bit, but only in the most affectionate way, I promise you.'

'Mockery is nearly always an effective distancing mechanism,' said Sasha judiciously. 'It's probably been as good a way as any for dealing with your sense of exclusion.'

Lavinia nodded, easily hiding her disappointment. After years of trying to pretend she did not mind, she had recently been letting herself admit that she detested the Medworth habit of analysing – and judging – everyone else's emotions. She was coming to believe that far from helping them understand other people, it cut them off and damaged the kind of relationships that she privately thought were what made life worth living.

'Come on, Lavinia. You're daydreaming and there's a lot to do. We must get on.'

'So we must. *En avant*. Who next?'

'Aubrey and Caroline in the green room, because . . .'

'He's the senior Medworth son,' said Lavinia, laughing openly and feeling the better for it.

Sasha looked annoyed for a moment and then smiled reluctantly, saying: 'Do you really think our traditions are so absurd?'

'Ah, Sasha, anyone could tell that you'd been away for years. None of the others would even think of asking something like that.'

'Perhaps not. Do you mind?'

'No, not really,' said Lavinia after a pause. She laughed uneasily. 'After all, I'd hardly live up here within sight of the family stronghold if I did, now would I?'

'Perhaps not, but I'm not sure how much real choice you ever gave yourself. I doubt if Tom would have had even his modest success if you hadn't run the constituency for him.'

Lavinia, unable to think of the right – or even an acceptable – response to that double-edged compliment, walked round the big bed and took her sister-in-law's arm. The Medworths had always disliked casual physical contact, but Sasha did not pull away and together they went next door, into a large oak-panelled room dominated by a four-poster hung with tattered green-and-gold silk hangings.

There was a story that Queen Elizabeth I had slept in the bed soon after the house had been built, and, according to the old account books Lavinia had studied, the room had always been known as the Queen's Chamber. When old George Medworth bought the house in the nineteenth century, he quickly had it renamed. No Medworth had ever been interested in royalty and all of them despised any kind of social snobbery.

Lavinia stripped the heavy embroidered-silk coverlet

from the mattress and draped it over the nearest chair while Sasha picked up the pillows and shook them vigorously. Feathers flew out of a gap in one of the seams.

'Oops,' said Lavinia, glad to be offered something that she could do as well as anyone else. 'I ought to deal with that.'

Somewhere in each of the spare bedrooms there was always a pottery dish, probably made by one of the children, crammed with needles and thread, pins of all types and sizes, suede brushes, bottles or sprays of instant dry-cleaning fluid, buttons and hooks. Lavinia found the green room's version on a large oak chest between the two centre windows. Pushing aside all the things she did not want with her forefinger, she found a packet of sharps and some strong, cream-coloured thread and proceeded to whip together the gaping edges of the pillow's seam.

'There. That'll hold for a year or two,' she said, biting off the spare thread.

They finished the last of the beds an hour and half later, by which time Lavinia was longing for a restorative glass of wine. But the family never drank alcohol at lunchtime and she knew she would have to make do with water. Feeling mutinous but not showing it, she went downstairs to the cavernous, old-fashioned kitchen, where her widowed mother-in-law was in charge that morning.

At the age of seventy-six, Flavia Medworth was still as commanding as she had been at the height of her hugely successful psychoanalytical career. All her four children and their innumerable cousins still accepted her rule without question and if their husbands and wives occasionally tried to rebel they would be quickly whipped into line. Any stubborn disagreement would be put down to neurosis and ignored. It went without saying at Saltley that Flavia knew all there was to know about the workings of the subconscious and therefore understood more about the people around her than they could possibly know. She never hesitated to explain them to themselves or to hide her contempt for any who did not share her views.

She was only an inch or two under six foot, with a larger frame than either of her daughters' and woollier, wilder hair, which had been completely white for several years. Like Sasha and Lavinia, she was dressed in corduroy trousers and a heavy sweater and she moved fairly easily about her huge kitchen.

Before she married, Lavinia had assumed that she would automatically like Tom's parents and that, if she behaved herself, she would be liked in return. She had had no difficulty with his father, who had been kind if remote, but Flavia had made it clear from the start that she was a disappointment and unworthy to be married to Tom.

At first Lavinia had believed that she would be able to overcome her mother-in-law's dislike, but it had turned out to be an impossible task. Eventually she had given up trying and had retreated behind a mask of impersonal politeness. Flavia's expressions of disappointment had quickly turned into direct hostility. Lavinia, whose only way of dealing with that was to pretend not to notice it, was still not sure what she had done to deserve it.

When she and Sasha reached the kitchen, Flavia was shaking a colander full of sliced carrots over the sink while Sasha's children, Pippit and Peter, laid six places at one end of the big scrubbed deal table. They were classic Medworths: tall but narrowly built, with straight dark hair and brown eyes set rather close to their aquiline noses. They also had the family's confidence and a sophisticated vocabulary that made them seem much older than their actual years.

Throughout lunch Lavinia listened with bemused envy as they talked to their grandmother, treating her as an equal, not impertinently, but with absolute certainty that their opinions would be valued, as indeed they were. Lavinia herself contributed little to the conversation and

17

longed for the arrival of Tom and her own three children.

Pippit and Peter had gone back to the stables to help the groom who worked there all year round, and the three women were debating whether to have coffee or not, when there was the sound of a car crunching on the gravel outside the back door. A moment later a tall, fit, amused-looking man with a magnificent head of rich brown hair walked into the kitchen.

'John,' said Flavia, rising with only the smallest hint of stiffness from her chair and holding out her arms. 'How good to see you! How was the drive up?'

He let her embrace him and then stood back. 'You're looking stunning as usual, Flavia. I can't imagine how you do it.'

'Hunting twice a week and plenty to do,' she said briskly. 'Have you had any lunch?'

'Not yet. But I'd better unload before I fall on the remains of your . . .' He craned round her ample shoulders, saw the other two women and grinned at them. 'Your shepherd's pie. I've got a boot full of goodies and some of them'll spoil if they're not fridged at once. The traffic getting out of London was vile or I'd have been here at least an hour ago.'

'We'd better give him a hand, Sasha,' said Lavinia as she stood up, feeling infinitely happier for his arrival. 'We don't want to wear him out before the festivities even begin.'

'Poor, decrepit old man that he is,' he said, hugging her. He bent to kiss her white neck above the rough edge of her Guernsey. 'And how are you, my lovely?'

'Fine, as always, John. It's nice to see you. Here's Sasha.' Lavinia pulled away so that her sister-in-law could have a chance to greet the most favoured outsider of them all.

Fifty-four-year-old John Hogarth was no blood relation of the Medworths, but he had known them ever since his mother had died at the end of the Second World War. His father had married one of their distant cousins, Rachel, who had spent the war at Saltley after her first husband was killed in the Battle of Britain.

'You look astonishingly like yourself up here,' John was saying as he held Sasha by the shoulders and examined her face before bending gracefully to kiss her too. 'Quite, quite different from your London self.'

'What on earth do you mean? I am myself wherever I may be.'

'Oh no you're not,' said John, hamming it up like a pantomime villain. 'You're all sophisticated and important in London, but up here you're just the same clever, exasperating baggage you were when I was growing up. It makes me feel all young and quivery. Lovely!'

Keeping one hand on Sasha's arm and looking mischievously at Lavinia, John went on: 'I'll never forget a time when I was about sixteen. Sasha must have been six, I think, and she embarrassed the whole clan by piping up in the most prissy voice: "Of course John and Patrick won't ever be Medworths. They're only Hogarths. They haven't any real Medworth genes in them at all."'

He laughed, but a faint blush was visible on Sasha's high cheekbones. Lavinia felt uncomfortable, but she did not intervene. John must have known what he was doing. He had had more than enough experience in dealing with his step-family.

John, who believed that he knew more about Lavinia than any of the others and felt she needed help with them, turned so that his back was to both Flavia and Sasha and winked at her. 'Come on then, girls,' he said cheerfully. 'All hands to the pump.' He led the way out to his Volvo and opened the boot, which was stacked with boxes of food.

'Nicko's bringing all the wine this time. He's decided that my taste for big, fruity Australian reds is too low for words. Arms out, Lavinia.' She obeyed and he carefully laid a large, shallow cardboard box across them.

'Be careful of that,' he said. 'Some of it's breakable.'

'You know, John,' said Sasha, who was peering into the back of the car, 'we do have food shops up here in Yorkshire.'

'I know you do, my little chickadee,' he said, patting her corduroy-clad bottom with a familiarity no-one else would have risked, 'but I always like to make my contribution to feeding the five thousand. As your mother would no doubt say it's probably some kind of a compensation for my own childlessness.'

Sasha grinned at him, but she said nothing as she carried a deep box of imported vegetables towards the house.

'How are you really, Lav?' said John as soon as Sasha had gone.

'Really fine,' she said. 'Although I must say it is absolute and utter heaven to see you. Last Christmas was a bit of a slog without your supporting presence. Your brother isn't nearly as much fun. Not the same at all.'

'You always were good for a chap's confidence, Lav. I shall preen myself on that for weeks. You know the bugger's gone and swiped my latest inamorata?'

'What, not Gisela? Oh, no, John; how miserable for you! I wondered why you were down for a single room on Sasha's list, but I didn't like to ask. What happened?' She quickly added: 'Don't tell me anything you don't want.'

'Here she comes again. I do want to tell you about it, but not in the middle of all this. Have you still got your room in the tower?'

Lavinia nodded. 'On the other hand, you could be an angel if you felt like it later and drive me back to the Dower House. I walked this morning.'

'Brilliant idea! Just yell when you're ready and I'll extract myself from whatever they've got me doing.'

When they had finished unloading his car and Flavia

had overseen the stowing away of all the food in the larder, fridge or freezer, John sat down to the end of the shepherd's pie while the others had their coffee.

Between the caffeine and the pleasure of John's arrival, Lavinia got through the afternoon's tasks cheerfully enough, but she was relieved when at last she was free to make her private preparations for her own part of the family.

John drove her home, telling her all about his gradual discovery that his latest lover had fallen for his elder – and much richer – brother, Patrick.

'Don't tell any of the family,' he said at last. 'I couldn't bear them to explain my deathwish when it comes to women. Whatever it is I'd rather not know about it.'

'Don't worry, John. I know precisely what you mean, and I wouldn't dream of sneaking. It's sweet of you to have driven me back. D'you want to come in for a drink?'

'Aren't you a bit busy?'

'I've got time for a quick one, and I've got a lovely bottle of nice undemanding Australian red, which I like too, whatever Nicko says about it.'

'You always did know how to get under my defences, Lavvy-lugs,' John said, following her into the house. 'Gosh, this place is glorious after that freezing great barrack up on the moor.'

Lavinia smiled in real pleasure. When Tom had been elected as Member of Parliament for the local constituency after his dismal failure at the Bar and needed to find somewhere to live, his mother had offered them a wing of Saltley itself. Lavinia had known at once that she would not be able to bear such close proximity to her mother-in-law. To the surprise of the Medworths, who had always assumed that she would be thoroughly malleable, she had refused the offer and asked instead whether she and Tom could have the old Queen Anne dower house that

21

stood at the edge of what was left of the estate.

Her choice had caused much amusement in the family because the little house had been a virtual ruin. The roof had caved in ages before and a large ash tree had been growing up through it. But it was more sheltered than Saltley, being backed by a belt of Forestry Commission trees, and she had always thought it not only prettier but also a more practical size. None of the others would have dreamed of putting money into such a hopeless prospect, and none of them had grudged the shell to Tom and Lavinia.

She had used most of her inheritance from her father to put on a watertight roof, have the walls repointed, new floors and windows put in, and damp-proofing and central heating installed. Then, during the long, lonely winter evenings when Tom was in London during Parliamentary sittings and the children were in bed, she had set about painting and making curtains.

Unlike Saltley Hall, which was always cold, the Dower House was warm, and the rooms she had decorated were bursting with colour and light. There were no ancestral portraits or collections of ancient weapons on the walls, but the chairs were soft with down cushions and the draughts were all stopped.

Lavinia sighed with relief to be back, lit the study fire, and opened the bottle of cabernet sauvignon she had promised John.

'Here's to a good Christmas,' he said, raising his glass.

'Fingers crossed,' said Lavinia quickly.

'You seem very jumpy,' said John as he stretched his legs out towards the hearth. The flames were already flickering up against the old fire-back and their reflection sparkled on the well-polished brass fender. A pocket of resin leaked out of one of the pine logs and sizzled in the heat. 'Did something particularly awful happen last year?'

At the sympathy in his voice Lavinia felt herself

22

weakening dangerously. Shrugging and trying to make light of her memories, she said: 'Oh, just the usual, but for some reason I found it harder to take.'

'Why?'

'I'm not sure. Tom had just been promoted in the reshuffle and I was excited about it. Perhaps that stopped me being as careful as usual. Or perhaps I was too cross that the rest of them couldn't bring themselves to be pleased about it. They had to keep reminding me that he was still only a very junior kind of minister and that at forty-six he ought to have been in Cabinet if he was ever going to make it.'

'Poor Lavvy.'

'No, no. Anyway, whatever it was, something seemed to irritate Flavia even more than usual and she had a real go at me.'

'Beastly for you.'

'But not that serious in retrospect. I should have had more gumption, but I let it get to me and then Rory got upset and tried to defend me but didn't know how; he wanted to be a proper Medworth but at the same time wanted to be on my side. It was awful. Eventually he clammed up completely with everyone, even me.'

'Twelve-year-old boys do, you know, Lav; and they don't always tell their mothers everything.'

'No, I know they don't, and there's no reason why they should.' Lavinia stared into the fire, trying not to remember the sight of her elder son's tight unhappy face and her useless attempts to comfort him.

'Didn't Tom help?' asked John after a while.

Lavinia nearly laughed. 'I don't think he even noticed what was going on. He was tired, of course. He always is at the end of a session.' She shook her head to get rid of the memories. 'I'm probably making much more of it than there actually was, but I must say I did keep wishing you were here.'

'Well, I am now and you know I'll do my poor best to protect you.'

'Dear John. I know. But there's no need. It was a whole year ago and Flavia's been perfectly normal ever since. It's silly to drag it up again.'

'I'm not sure that "normal" exactly describes the She-Wolf of the North.' John drained his glass and grinned at Lavinia as he put it down on the table beside his chair. 'I'd probably better get going or she'll rip me to shreds for paying more attention to you than to her.'

'Don't tell me you've got a castration complex now,' said Lavinia to make them both laugh and show that none of it mattered at all really.

'Naughty!' John held her chin so that he could kiss her goodbye. 'You know, apart from Flavia, all of them, even the most Medworthy Medworths envy old Tom for having found and married you. They've come to realize what an asset you are.'

'Thank you, John.'

She stood on the doorstep, waving him off, and wondered whether he had been trying to give her some of the comfort for which he himself always ached. She had often thought of him as a child fighting for a place in the Medworth clan. His need to match up to them had driven him to singular success as an architect, and he had recently won an important prize for a building on the south bank of the Thames.

She pushed the cork back into the wine bottle and went to make up beds for her three children and unpack their school trunks, which had been sent in advance. As she rearranged the battered old toy mongoose on top of Rory's duvet she sighed.

If it had not been one of Tom's most strongly held convictions that children needed the experience of going away to boarding school, Lavinia would have kept hers at home and sent them to one of the local day schools.

As it was, she had yielded and allowed him to send the boys away at eight and Tammy at ten. That autumn term had been the first for both Tammy and Charles, and Lavinia was afraid of what the three months away might have done to them both. Rory, at least, had had four years to get used to his prep school and seemed to be well able to cope with it.

She straightened the tail of the balding mongoose, made sure that everything was as he liked it, and went on to Tammy's room. Decorated with a dazzling mixture of orange and yellow with a few touches of scarlet, it always made her smile. She did not much like Tammy's colours, but it was important to her that the children should learn about themselves and their tastes without being hammered into anyone else's moulds too soon.

The telephone rang as she was shaking Tammy's pillow into its yellow-spotted case and she looked down at her watch. Seeing the time she knew that it must be Tom at the other end of the telephone and sprinted down the passage to her own room to answer it before he rang off and tried the number of his mother's house.

'Lavinia? Tom here. Your school-run arrangements worked perfectly. All three have been safely delivered to West Square and we'll be with you tomorrow. How are you?'

'Fine,' she said, controlling her breathing with care so that he could not be irritated by her anxieties about his and the children's safety. 'And you?'

'Not so bad. Looking forward to a proper break and a bit of hunting. I feel horrendously stale after this last session. How's the weather?'

'Fairly good. A bit of frost at night, but probably not enough to interfere with the scent. You should be all right.'

'Good. I hope my mother hasn't been wearing you out getting everything ready for the hordes?'

Remembering John's new, irreverent nickname for Flavia, Lavinia nearly laughed. 'No. It's been fine.'

'Good. Now look, my love, here's Rory pining for a word. I'll put him on.'

There was a short silence and then a high young voice said eagerly: 'Mum?'

'Yes, darling, it's me. How are you? I've loved your letters. Terrific news about the last match. The team really has done well this term.' Lavinia settled back in her chair to re-establish contact with each of the children in turn.

Chapter 2

Lavinia had completed most of her own preparations in the Dower House by half-past five the following day. The Christmas tree was planted in a big Chinese porcelain pot at the left of the fireplace in the hall, where it looked magnificent against the white panelling and the black-and-white floor. She had decorated the dark-green branches with gold baubles, clove oranges she had been making throughout the autumn, and a few shiny red bows to pick up various reds in the old Dutch painting of a bucolic feast that hung on the chimney breast.

Piles of presents, wrapped in red paper and tied with gold ribbons, were heaped around the big pot. A brass bowl full of holly sprays and trailing ivy stood in the middle of the oak chest where the rugs were kept, and a red-flowered standard camellia stood in another Chinese pot beside the front door.

There were fires alight in the hall and in the study, scenting the whole house with the smell of burning apple logs. The clove-studded oranges were releasing their intriguing scent in the warmth, and the pine needles added an extra spiciness to the whole effect.

Thankful that she had been stubborn enough to refuse Flavia's offer to house them all up at Saltley, Lavinia looked round her house with satisfaction and went into

27

the kitchen to set about one of the last important meals she would be allowed to cook for weeks. They were going to have chestnut soup with bits of crunchy bacon on the top, because it was Rory's favourite, baked ham with red cabbage and apple, because they all liked that, and pancakes, because Tammy loved tossing them and Charles had once said that he liked the crunch of lemon-soaked sugar between the softness of the folded pancake. Tom, like a true adult Medworth, ate modest amounts of whatever he was given and appeared to have few preferences.

When the ham and the red cabbage could be safely left to simmer at the back of the cooker, the chestnut soup was ready to be reheated and the batter was standing in the cool larder, she poured herself another glass of wine and took it upstairs to drink as she bathed.

By the time she heard the sound of the car turning off the road, she was wearing a simple terracotta dress and putting a pair of small gold studs into her ears. Running out to the landing window, she pulled aside the heavy curtain and looked out just as the beam of the headlights swung round and rested on the three curved white stone steps up to the front door. The front passenger door opened and Rory emerged, lankily clumsy as usual. He pushed aside his hair and looked up.

At the sight of his mother waiting in her accustomed place, he raised a hand in a casual wave and then quickly went round to the back of the car to help his father with the overnight suitcases. The two younger children were released from the back seat and raced each other for the front door. Lavinia went down to meet them.

Tammy had already started talking to her mother even before the door opened and she did not draw breath for the next ten minutes. Lavinia sat on the edge of the fender as she listened. Charles sometimes joined in, capping Tammy's experiences of school with his own, but she never listened to him. Lavinia watched them both, smiling

28

in her huge relief that they were all right and apparently unchanged by their three months' incarceration. Every so often she looked up over their untidy heads to include Tom and Rory in the reunion.

'There's an open bottle of red in the kitchen,' she said as Tammy tumbled from one story of what happened in the dorm to the next. Tom nodded and went to the kitchen.

When he came back with two glasses, he put them and the bottle on the hearth and put a hand on his wife's shoulder. 'Shut up for a minute, Thomasina,' he said and, when she was quiet, kissed Lavinia's cheek. 'How are you? You look tired.'

'Do I? It's probably just the bedmaking. Sasha and I did beds for twenty-eight yesterday, and that's a lot of bending and stretching. I kept telling myself that there are women who pay fortunes for aerobics classes to be put through just what we were doing.'

Tom laughed but before he could say anything, Rory interrupted, asking: 'When's everybody coming? I know Pippit and Peter are already here and Bendy's going to get here tomorrow because we've got to practise for our solos.'

'Yes, he is due tomorrow,' said his mother, 'with Jocelyn and Meg obviously. And both the Collinghams . . .'

'They don't matter; they're too old,' said Tammy dispassionately. 'When is Georgina going to get married? She's twenty-seven: far too old to be single. I wonder why she's so bad at forming relationships. Granny-Flavia's really worried about it.'

Lavinia flinched, hating the way Tammy picked up her grandmother's opinions and repeated them parrot fashion. It was bad enough within the family, who would at least know whose words she was using, but what if she said that sort of thing to other ten-year-olds? Or even to their parents?

'Tammy's only bothered because she wants to be a

bridesmaid again like she was at Dominic and Olivia's wedding,' said Charles, sticking his tongue out at his sister. 'Flowers in her hair and a pouty little smile on her fat face. Bridey, bridey, bridesmaid. Bridey . . .'

Tammy punched him in the stomach and he doubled up, gasping. Tom sighed as his two younger children started to fight in earnest. Lavinia felt hugely relieved at the normality of it all. That was how ordinary children behaved.

'It must be a bit like Prime Minister's Questions,' she said to Tom when she had separated them. There was the hint of a real smile in his eyes at last.

'Upstairs with your cases, you three,' Lavinia said sternly. 'Daddy needs a minute or two's silence. All right?'

'Come on, monsters,' said Rory, nodding to her. 'Race you.'

At the clatter of their feet across the black-and-white marble of the hall floor, Tom frowned again.

'Headache?' said Lavinia gently. 'Shall I get you an aspirin?'

'No. I'm all right. Just shaking down after the drive, really. It's the strain of all those headlights bumping across one's eyes, I think. And the little ones have been snarking at each other for the last eighty miles or so, which always gets me down.' He sighed. 'It's good to be back, Lavvy.'

Pleased that he had reverted to the old nickname of their first ecstatic time together, Lavinia moved closer to him, but she did not risk any overt gestures of affection and spoke in the matter-of-fact voice that she always tried to use when he was irritable or tired.

'Good. When we've eaten we can pack them off to bed and have some peace to chat in.'

He nodded and drained his glass of wine. 'That'll be nice. Have I time for a bath?'

'Whatever you want. The timing of supper's as flexible as you need.'

'You're a wife in a million, Lavinia. Thanks.' He rubbed her shoulder and went slowly upstairs, leaving her to watch his hunched backview and wonder what had happened. He was nearly always preoccupied and often irritable when he first got home, but there seemed something more than usual worrying him.

He might tell her later or he might bottle it all up and keep her away from whatever he was thinking. She had taught herself not to mind that, but it had taken a lot of effort. Sighing silently, she went back into the kitchen to lower the heat beneath the pots and pans.

When the children came downstairs again, she took out a pack of cards and played one and a half rubbers of bridge with them on the kitchen table until Charles, who was dummy, got up in the middle of a game, saying: 'I'm starved. What can I have to eat?'

Reluctant to let him fill himself up with biscuits, Lavinia looked at the clock and saw that it was already half-past eight.

'Perhaps Daddy's gone to sleep in the bath. Do you want to go up and see?' she said, neatly finessing the jack of diamonds.

'Do I have to?'

'No, of course not, but we're not going to have supper until he's ready and so if he's gone to sleep that means we'll all have to stay hungry until someone wakes him up. It might as well be you.'

Charles attempted to look martyred, then blew like an angry old man and finally stumped off upstairs.

'He was asleep,' he said cheerfully as he came back to the kitchen a few minutes later, 'but he's going to come down now – in his dressing gown to save time.'

'And he's very sorry for keeping you all hungry,' said Tom, coming in to stand blinking in the bright light. He was still tying the cord of his old Shetland checked dressing gown. He looked better.

'We'll finish the rubber later,' said Lavinia. 'Leave the cards face down and we can start again after supper or tomorrow.'

She got up to pour soup into the bowls that had been keeping warm beside the cooker. Having sprinkled bacon shards on top of each bowlful, she looked over her shoulder.

'Tammy, will you carry those into the dining room for me? Thanks. I'll follow you in a minute.'

Charles was nearly asleep by the time they had finished the pancakes and so Lavinia sent him and Tammy up to bed while she and Rory did the washing up. Tom switched on the kitchen television for the ten o'clock news and sat in one of the creaking old basket chairs to watch it.

Rory started to talk about school as he dried the cutlery. Lavinia longed to hear anything he was prepared to tell her, but she saw the irritable twitch of Tom's shoulders from the reflection in the dark window over the sink and said quietly: 'Better keep it until I come and tuck you up, Rory. Dad's trying to concentrate on the news.'

She was glad to see no sign of resentment in her son's face as he accepted what she said. He was old enough to understand everything she had told him about how burdensome a politician's life could be and what a difference his family's behaviour could make to it.

When they had finished the clearing up, she sent Rory up to have a bath while she locked all the doors and dealt with the fires. When she heard him emerging from the bathroom, she followed him upstairs. 'Shall I come in and have a chat or would you rather be on your own?' she asked as she stood in the doorway of his bedroom, watching him take off his dressing gown. He looked very slight and young in his red-and-blue striped pyjamas. She longed to take him in her arms, but she did not move.

'Oh, no. Do stay,' he said, frowning slightly. 'If you don't think Dad needs you more.'

Lavinia nearly gave in and hugged him then, but she

restricted herself to a brief ruffle of his hair in deference to his probable embarrassment. 'You are such a good boy, Rory.' She settled herself on the lumpy cushion in the windowseat, where she used to sit cuddling her babies, and had a moment's regret for the easy intimacy of those early days. 'Now, tell about the science master. He does sound quite tricky.'

'Well, he is a bit,' said Rory, sliding down under his duvet. She noticed that he had pushed the once-loved mongoose unobtrusively on to the floor and hated the thought that he was having to be toughened up as he got older. 'I suppose it's just because he's got sort of stuck in the anal-sadistic phase.'

He lay on his back, staring up at the ceiling and chewing at his bottom lip. Lavinia watched him, aching for him and wondering if anyone else would feel as worried as she did at the thought of a twelve-year-old boy's dealing with his fear of a bad-tempered schoolmaster in such a way. She knew that Rory's diagnosis must have come from Flavia and wanted to explain that such psychoanalytical theories were just ideas and not necessarily infallible truths, but she could not think of a way of doing it that would not make him feel that she was at war with his grandmother. She had seen how miserable he had been when he believed he had to choose between them, and she could not bear it to happen again.

'I just wish I knew why he hates me so much,' said Rory, sounding much more natural.

'Are you really sure he does? Perhaps he's just bad-tempered with everyone, or ill or worried about money or something.'

'I suppose he is. But he shouts at me all the time.' Rory sighed heavily and muttered into his duvet: 'I hate it, Mum.'

'I'm not surprised. I think it's horrible, too.'

Rory turned over on to his left side so that he could

33

look at her. She smiled at him, trying to give him all the confidence she herself lacked. After a moment he shut his eyes and then, flinging himself on to his back again, he said with determined cheerfulness: 'Anyway, it was great when we beat St Vincent's.'

'Yes, it must have been. Didn't you say it was the first time in twelve years that they hadn't won?' said Lavinia, conscientiously retrieving the details he had given her over the telephone.

'Yeah.'

'That's brilliant,' she said, managing to get some real enthusiasm into her voice. 'Did you get badly mashed up in the scrum?'

'Not too bad, although one of them did stamp his studs into my hand. Luckily it was the left so I didn't have any trouble writing my test papers next day.'

'That must have hurt.'

'A bit.'

'Good. And what about choir? How's that been going?'

As she listened, seeing his face grow more relaxed again, Lavinia herself felt happier. Despite his fear of the angry science master, it sounded as though Rory was coping with school as well as any of his cousins. For the fiftieth time, she reminded herself that the Medworth recipe had produced a great many winners since old George Medworth had bought Saltley Hall and plenty more since Flavia had grafted her psychoanalytical ideas on to the old traditions. There must be something right about them.

She thought about her own smaller and much less stellar family and asked herself what had been so wonderful about their ideas of child-rearing that she should fight to impose them on her own children. The fact that she would probably have had to emigrate to an igloo in the North Pole before she could get her three away from Medworth influence only made her smile. Tammy and the boys were all right, she told herself. They would continue to be all right. And peace at home between their parents, and between herself and Flavia, was surely more important than almost anything else except the fact of her own unconditional love for them.

'You'd better get some sleep, Rory. There's lots to do tomorrow.'

'OK,' he said through a sigh and then grinned at her. 'I am quite tired actually.'

Taking a small risk, she bent down to kiss his forehead as she passed his bed on the way to the door. He did not pull away as he had often done, and, as his head sank down on to her arm, she let herself feel a second's pure happiness.

She pushed the hair away from his forehead, managing to stroke his face unobtrusively as she did so. 'Sleep well, Rory. And if you need anything, come and wake me up.'

'Night, Mum.'

She switched off the light at the door. When she reached the kitchen she found Tom asleep again as the local news relayed its usual tale of sporting triumphs, farming disasters, petty and not so petty crime. Waking him carefully, she said: 'I've just put Rory into bed and it looks as though you need the same treatment. Come on, Tom.'

He sat for a moment, looking up at her in just the same way as Rory had. At that moment the likeness between them was extreme. His eyelids began to close again.

'Come on, Tom,' she said more loudly. 'You'll be more comfortable in bed. Don't sleep down here. It'll make you stiff.'

He hauled himself up and stood, swaying. 'I'd better lock up.'

'Don't worry. I've already done it.'

Together they went up to bed. He slept almost as soon as he had turned off his reading light, but she stayed awake for longer, putting her mind through its usual exercises.

'Yes, we care about each other,' she told herself silently.

'Tom may say what's bothering him in due course or he may not. If he doesn't, there's no need to feel aggrieved; I don't tell him everything either. It doesn't matter. We share a lot already: the children, this house and the constituency. No-one could expect the kind of blissfulness we both felt when we first knew each other to keep going for more than a year or two. What we've got ought to be enough for anyone. Neither of us is ever deliberately unkind, even if we sometimes make mistakes. We never lose our tempers. Provided neither of us asks too much of the other we'll be all right. It is love of a sort even if it's not quite the sort I once envisaged. It *is* love and that ought to be enough. It's more than most people have.' Eventually she too fell asleep.

Chapter 3

Lavinia woke the following morning at eight o'clock when her two younger children burst into the bedroom, yelling: 'Rise and shine, Daddy. Rise and shine. We're building jumps for the hunter trials today. Come on. Up with you.'

Lavinia, groggy with sleep, pushed herself up against the bedhead and saw that Tammy and Charles were already dressed in their second-best jodhpurs, brown-leather jodhpur boots and much-darned, dark-green sweaters.

'Shush, you two,' she whispered furiously. 'Daddy needs to sleep.'

But it was too late. Tom was already awake. He turned to her. 'Don't worry. They're right. The Medworth Christmas Hunter Trials are very important, and there's lots to be done yet.'

'I know. Chicks, why don't you go down to the kitchen, put on the kettle and start laying breakfast? We'll be down soon.'

When they had gone, Lavinia took Tom's hand and was glad when he squeezed hers. 'Listen, Tom. I know that all the old Christmas-holiday traditions are important, but your health matters even more. I don't think I've ever seen you quite as tired as you were yesterday, and you ought to rest while you can. There's bound to be some crisis

37

that makes one of your civil servants need to get hold of you before the end of the holiday. There always is. Give yourself a chance to recuperate before it happens.'

'I'm fine, Lavinia, and a bit of fresh air will do me good.' Tom looked at the clock beside his pillows. 'Heavens above! I've had nearly nine hours. That's enough for anyone. You know they've now discovered that too much sleep is as dangerous as too little?'

She clamped her lips together for a moment and then smiled. 'I'm not going to nag. But at least promise me you'll take time over breakfast and wait until . . .'

He kissed her forehead briefly as he was pushing back his side of the duvet. 'I'll be fine. Come on. Up with you. It's the first day of the Christmas holidays and we've a lot to cram in.'

Lavinia followed him out of bed and went to wash and clean her teeth. When she came back he was in the dressing room, almost ready. 'I promised Edgar I'd do the constituency surgery this afternoon. It's Helmsmoorside today, isn't it?' he said as he bent down to take the wooden trees out of his old, much-cherished boots. 'D'you mind if I usurp your role for once? He was very anxious that I put in an appearance when we spoke on the phone the other day.'

'I don't mind at all, and the constituents will love having you for once. But I probably ought to come with you and tell you what's been going on. There are one or two quite tricky cases at the moment and you'll need briefing to avoid putting your foot in it.'

Stamping his right heel into the boot, he turned his head sideways to watch her as she sat at the dressing table to arrange her hair. 'You know, Lavinia, you are just about the ideal wife for a politician. I can't think of anyone else who does so much while making so little fuss. Do I exploit you horribly?'

'Certainly not.' She pushed her fingers up through her

38

newly combed fringe to make it fall as it should, leaning towards the mirror to check the effect. 'For one thing, you pay me for what I do. For another, I enjoy it. I like having a share in your job.'

'It's a big share.' He frowned and then looked up at her again, saying slowly: 'I know we don't get much time for ourselves these days, but that's how it goes once half of any couple gets a ministerial job, even one like mine. There's just so much paper to process, apart from everything else. And if I ever do get as far as the cabinet . . .'

'I know. Don't look so worried, Tom. It's all right. I took it all on board when you were first made a Parlie Charlie, let alone an actual minister. And I like the fact that you're doing so well. I'm sure you will get a Cabinet job eventually. Don't worry about it. I don't.'

'Sure?'

'Yes. I'm sure. What's brought all this on? You don't usually fret like this.'

He pulled up the other boot, reached for the sweater that she had laid ready over his chair, pulled it over his head and then came back into the bedroom. 'I suppose I've just been wondering lately how much of it all has been worth doing.'

'Is it the hunting vote that's got to you so badly?' Lavinia asked, trying to hide her surprise. 'Or is there some new horror you're having to deal with at Environment?'

Tom wrinkled his nose and then strode to the window to pull aside the curtains and look out. The view across the moors was magnificent: wild and empty of everything but the black stalks of the heather and the dark purplish-grey clouds. Lavinia had always found it consoling when she had come back after a stultifying visit to London and she could imagine that it must be heaven after the aggressive crowds of the House of Commons.

'I suppose it's partly that,' Tom said as he rubbed a patch of condensation off the window pane with his sleeve. 'The antis have mobilized a hell of a lot of support and rather too many people I respect have been eyeing me with distaste – contempt almost.' Tom laughed unhappily and added with a casual air that did not convince her: 'I've never been very good at dealing with contempt. I'm not sure why.'

Lavinia watched him, saying nothing. From the back, he was looking splendid in his breeches and boots: tall, spare and thoroughly in control. But when he turned she saw that his face was unhappy and his dark eyes looked almost afraid.

It struck her that his enemies might have tried to blackmail him into voting for the ban on hunting by threatening to reveal something about his life in London. If that were so, he could well be agitated by the stress of waiting for it to happen. Somehow, without speaking of blackmail, she would have to show him that she was not going to cause trouble if there were any revelations to come. She had coped before; she could do it again. It seemed to her to be part of the unspoken deal that they had made many years earlier.

'Aren't you two coming?' Tammy shouted up from the kitchen. 'The kettle's boiled and the toast's getting cold. And the others'll all be waiting for us. Come *on*, Daddy.'

Tom shrugged. 'When Tammy calls, all must obey, eh?'

'Probably,' said Lavinia, wishing that her energetic and determined daughter had given them just five more minutes. She longed to surround Tom with the sort of warmth that she sensed he needed and that she terribly wanted to give him, but when she had tried in the past it had all gone wrong. At the beginning she had thought he had simply not noticed what she was offering; later she came to the conclusion that he had been deliberately obtuse.

'You go on, Tom. I'll follow when I've tidied up a bit.

Don't worry about it all too much. There's nothing that, between us, we can't mend or deal with.'

'You've excellent bottom along with all the rest,' said Tom with an effortful smile. 'See you later.'

When he had gone, Lavinia propped her elbows on the dressing table and rested her head in her hands for a moment, gathering her strength. Then she sat up straight and made up her face.

'Rory still asleep?' she said as she walked into the kitchen a little later.

'I think so. But it doesn't matter,' said Charles, lavishly spreading butter on his burned toast. 'He's not building jumps with us because he's got a solo for midnight mass. There's a rehearsal with Aunt Frida at eleven. You will wake him in time, won't you, Mum? No forgetting accidentally-on-purpose. It's important.'

'Yes, I know it is,' said Lavinia, just managing to be amused at the idea of being given orders by her eight-year-old son. 'But how do you know what Rory's supposed to be doing? Has somebody been sending you all timetables?'

'Yes,' said Tammy, looking surprised. 'Granny-Flavia. Didn't you know, Mum?'

'No, I didn't.' Some of Lavinia's irritation must have shown because Tom said quietly: 'It helps co-ordinate such large numbers. That's all. It's not meant to control anyone.'

Oh, yes, it is, she thought, and to make it plain just who is excluded, but she smiled and buried her annoyance in her coffee cup.

'Are you driving or walking?' she asked when she had put the cup down.

'I thought we might bike actually,' said Tom. 'I think the rain'll hold off.'

'OK. Then I'll bring Rory up in the car later on. I ought to put in a bit of work on the Saltley papers anyway.'

41

'Come on, Daddy,' said Tammy, cramming the last of her toast into her mouth. Through it, she added: 'You're so greedy, Charles. You don't need another piece.'

'Yes, I do. Don't be so bloody bossy, you old cow.'

'Charles! And Tammy, please don't talk with your mouth full.'

'Sorry, Mum,' said Charles as Tammy swallowed a half-chewed piece of toast and opened her mouth to say something else. 'I forgot. We all swear all the time at school.'

'Maybe, but I don't want you doing it here. It's very unattractive.' Lavinia scowled horribly at him and then straightened her face to add with what she meant to be excruciating sweetness: 'Particularly when it comes from an angelic-looking child like you.'

'Oh, Mum. Don't be disgusting! "Angelic". Yuk!'

'I'll take them away and wear them out with the ponies,' said Tom, laughing as he brushed the crumbs off his lap and stood up. 'See you at lunch.'

'Yes. Have fun.'

'We will.'

When they had gone, the two children still quarrelling and exchanging increasingly petulant insults as they wheeled their old-fashioned, second-hand bicycles out of the shed, Lavinia tidied their breakfast things away and made herself some stronger coffee, which she drank as she read the day's newspapers.

She woke Rory at ten so that he would have plenty of time for breakfast in his dressing gown before getting ready for his singing practice. His mood had changed overnight and he said very little as he ate the breakfast she had cooked him, picking up the news section of *The Times* as soon as he sat down and apparently reading his way through it as steadily as any adult. Lavinia suppressed a sigh and continued to skip through the other papers.

Before they left, she collected one of Tom's tweed

suits, a suitable shirt, tie, socks and shoes so that he could change before they left for the constituency surgery. Rory locked up the house for her and chatted with almost aggressive confidence as they drove along the wild, bumpy road across the moor to Saltley. There were no fences, just the narrow tarmac-surfaced road, a thin strip of grass and a ditch on either side and then the heather. A few wind-tormented trees punctuated the skyline, and some scraggy sheep could be seen on one of the few green patches on the hills way off to the right. Eventually they came to the beginning of the long grey stone wall around Saltley itself and fifty yards later turned in through the gates that had stood open for so long that their hinges had rusted into uselessness.

'Thanks, Mum,' Rory said as she stopped on the gravel square outside the house. He leaped out of the car, calling back over his shoulder: 'See you at lunch.'

'Sing well,' she called, but he had already gone too far to hear her.

She watched him run up the shallow steps to the projecting porch in the middle of the E-shaped façade, thinking how much she preferred the outside of the house to most of its rooms. Unprotected by any trees, apparently unaffected by the violent winds that rushed over the rolling moor, which stretched for miles in front of it, the house had all the dash and confidence of the newly rich Elizabethans who had built it at the end of the sixteenth century. With its two jaunty octagonal towers, gryphon-decorated frieze, fantastic chimneys, and the big many-paned windows that caught the light and sent it glittering back, the outside had a gaiety that was not matched by anything inside.

Lavinia eventually switched off the engine, locked the car and followed Rory into the hall. Apart from the kitchen, the huge stone-flagged hall was the most used part of Saltley, and summed up everything Lavinia most disliked about the house. She knew that when it had

43

been built its interior would have been decked out with plenty of bright colours, but there was none left. The effect was of portentous gloom.

The walls were panelled in heavily carved oak to a height of about ten feet and above that were hung geometric arrangements of pikes, guns, swords and helmets, interspersed with uncleaned portraits of long-dead Saltleys. An oak refectory table, big enough to seat the entire extended family, took up the centre of the hall. Ranged against the panelled walls were chests of varying ugliness and antiquity, mainly holding parts of damaged croquet mallets and unwanted bits and pieces of other games. A pair of handsome chairs covered in dull yellow cut velvet stood on either side of the enormous stone fireplace, and the only other bit of colour was provided by the torn maroon damask curtains that hung at the side of each of the four big mullioned windows.

There was no-one in the hall when Lavinia arrived, but she could hear voices in the kitchen passage beyond the carved oak screen at the far end. She quickly turned right just inside the front door, making for a small, twisting staircase in the corner. The stairs were steep and by the time she had climbed to the top of the right-hand tower she was breathless. But it was worth the effort when she opened the door into her study and saw its comforting mess of papers, pens, computer disks and reference books.

For some time she had been organizing the papers that had been in the house when old George Medworth had bought it from the last of the Saltley family at the end of the 1850s. He had been enriched by his share of the profits from a family wine-shipping business and had bought the enormous house with everything in it. Having no interest in the records of the family he had displaced, he had merely left them where they were, stacked higgledy-piggledy in the tower room. One or two Medworths since his time had poked about among them, but no-one had made any kind of systematic study until John Hogarth had suggested it to Lavinia one summer when she had admitted to feeling under-occupied among her energetic relations.

No-one had objected, not even Flavia, and so Lavinia had set about the work of reading the papers, filing those that were undamaged and setting others aside for professional conservation. Over the two years since she had started the work, she had grown so interested in what she was discovering that she had started to read widely in her search for the background to the Saltleys' own history, sending for books from the London Library almost every week and subscribing to various historical journals.

Had it not been for a comment from Frida that the Saltley papers were providing Lavinia with a nice substitute for a university education, she would have been entirely happy with what she was doing. The previous year she had floated the idea that the documents might give enough of a picture of life at Saltley to make it worth trying to interest a publisher in a chatty history of the house. Flavia had expressed some doubts, as had Frida, but Tom and his elder brother had been enthusiastic. Aubrey had been particularly encouraging and had told Lavinia to start work at once. He had been confident of being able to persuade his mother to sanction the project in the end.

Lavinia, touched and grateful for his support, had often thought it a pity that she had happened to overhear the words he had chosen to use. 'I shouldn't worry about it so much, Mother,' he had said. 'One or other of us can check anything that goes out to a publisher, but it'll probably be all right. After all, Lavinia's reasonably intelligent even though she's almost completely uneducated.'

'But she's so inarticulate,' Flavia had protested. 'It's an absurd idea and it'll be thoroughly humiliating for her. Although that is probably why she wants to do it: to prove to herself and all of us yet again that she's inadequate.'

'She may well be better on paper. Lots of people are.

Don't you think it might be good for her to have a project? After all, we can always pay one of Frida's students to rewrite it if necessary.'

Shutting the study door with a snap, Lavinia reminded herself that the Medworths could not help it and that it really did not matter how patronizing they sounded.

The tower room was octagonal, with windows in four of its sides. There was no fireplace and without the fan heater she had introduced it would have been far too cold to sit in, let alone do any work. She bent to switch the heater on and gratefully warmed her frozen hands in its comforting blast.

Every available piece of wall was lined with shelves on which were stacked the ancient bundles and boxes of papers, and the estate account books dating back almost to the year the house was built. Lavinia's large, flat-topped desk sat in the middle of the room, covered with heaps of paper restrained by outsize, brightly coloured, plastic clothes pegs.

Mindful of the fact that Frida, Aubrey and probably several of the Medworth cousins were likely to ask her polite questions about her progress, Lavinia took out the papers she had been working on for the years 1810 to 1815, when one of the Saltley sons was killed at Waterloo, and turned on her computer.

Chapter 4

Lavinia had been at work for just over an hour when she was disturbed by a knock at the door. Surprised, she pressed the keys necessary to save the new notes she had made and called out: 'Come in.'

The door opened and Sasha's husband, Philip, stood framed in the carved architrave. Lavinia, who had not seen him since the summer, was surprised by how well he was looking. He seemed to have got over the after-effects of his illness at last. His face was no longer at all yellow and he had filled out.

Although he was dressed in the Medworth holiday uniform of trousers and sweater, Lavinia thought that no-one could have mistaken him for one of them. His hair was thick and the kind of greenish-brown with highlights that overtakes some blonds in maturity. It was just long enough to curl up where it met the ribbed neck of his jersey, and it slipped attractively over his forehead. There were deep crescents either side of his mouth and radiating wrinkles from his eyes to his hairline which suggested that he smiled a lot, even though there was neither amusement nor pleasure in his expression at that moment. He looked angry.

'Philip!' Lavinia exclaimed as she stood up. His face suggested that there had been a scene of some kind downstairs and she assumed that someone had sent him up

47

to her for soothing. She set about it with all her usual practicality. 'How nice to see you. Come on in. How are you? You're looking very well.'

'I'm fine, thank you,' he said, leaning against the door post and apparently fighting to control his harsh breathing. 'But I thought I was fitter than this. I won't stay. I only came because Flavia asked me to warn you that lunch is to be at twelve forty-five today. I hadn't realized it was such a climb up here. I can't think why she didn't send one of the children.'

Lavinia could not completely hide her amusement that it was Flavia who had sent him up to the tower, but she did her best and quickly cleared the only available chair of its load of discarded computer printout. She dumped the pile of paper on the floor beside her desk.

'Come on in. Don't stand in the doorway like that, letting in the draughts. It's freezing. Sit down for a minute or two and catch your breath.'

'What's making you laugh?' he asked abruptly as he came in at last and shut the door.

'Nothing,' she said, deciding that Philip was still looking too irritable to take in the fact that he had been sent to her for comfort. She was mildly curious to know what the row downstairs had been about but was quite happy to wait until she was told. 'I hadn't realized you'd never been up here before. Would you like a drink? I've no ice-making equipment, but there's a bottle of undistinguished French red wine or sherry or vermouth. And there's some whisky too, I think. What'll you have?'

'Medworths don't drink in the middle of the day,' he said in exactly the kindly tone the family always used to explain their rules to outsiders.

Lavinia laughed out loud and was glad to see the lines on his face disappearing into a smile. 'I know. But, not being one of them, I keep my own rules up here. What would you like?'

'A glass of wine then, thank you.' He looked around. 'You've made this eyrie cosy.'

'It's rather a mess, I'm afraid, but then it nearly always is – not least because there's such a vast quantity of paper. I don't much like working with the real documents in case I fling coffee over them or something, and so I photostat them. I rather dread the thought of one of the family offering to come and help me put it all in order. I'm not sure I want to be told why I need such chaos around me.'

Lavinia exaggerated her natural shiver, watching Philip to make sure that he was getting the message she was trying to deliver. 'I can just imagine the reasons they'd dream up. Here.'

He took the glass of claret she was offering him.

'Thanks. What is it you're actually working on?' he asked, apparently not wanting to join in a conversation about how fascinating or difficult the family could be. 'Something to do with the Saltleys, Sasha said.'

'Sort of. I'm by way of producing a history of the house. I want to get it as chatty and personal as possible so I'm tracking through all their letters for useful titbits.'

'Interesting?' said Philip, making a question of it. 'Or just another chore?'

'Fascinating. It was never a chore, and once I got to know the letter-writers as . . . well, as people, I suppose, it became fun. Some of them have become quite vivid, almost part of my life.'

Philip watched her in silence for so long that, slightly embarrassed, she raised her eyebrows in a question.

'Are you so very lonely?' he said at last.

'Good heavens no! Not in the least. That isn't what I meant at all. I like reading the letters because they're teaching me so much.'

'Really? Like what?'

Lavinia looked at him carefully to see whether he was

49

genuinely interested or merely collecting ammunition for a sneer.

'I suppose the most important thing is how much changes with time,' she said and then, thinking how silly she must have sounded, quickly added: 'I mean, when you think how sure people have been in the past about things that turned out not to have been true at all, you begin to look at current certainties in a rather different light. I quite like that.'

She hesitated, but Philip was smiling at her in a way that she found encouraging enough to add: 'D'you see what I'm getting at?'

'Oh, yes, and I can quite see why it appeals to you. It must give you considerable satisfaction as you listen to the Medworths laying down the law on everything anyone says anywhere near them.'

Lavinia raised her glass to him then, laughing. 'You've probably hit the nail on the head,' she said when she had drunk her toast. 'I suppose that is what I meant even though I've never put it as clearly as that to myself.'

'How long have you been married?' asked Philip abruptly. 'I can't remember.'

'Fourteen years last October. A couple of years less than you.'

'So you have. We came back for your wedding, didn't we? Silly of me. Was it rough for you – getting to grips with them all while being so much in the thick of it?'

Lavinia shook her head. When she had swallowed some wine, enjoying the taste as it trickled over her palate, she said: 'All marriages entail adjustments. I don't suppose I've had to make more than anyone else.'

Philip did not answer and she thought that he was disappointed. Remembering various things people had said about him, his broken career and his possible envy of Sasha's dazzling professional success, Lavinia said carefully: 'One of the trickiest bits for me has always been trying to be graceful about this business of being so much *less* than all of them.'

'That's absurd.' He definitely sounded angry then, and she quickly did her best to placate him.

'Not really. It would be much sillier not to admit it. I just am less educated, less successful, less musical and so on, and I always will be. That needn't matter, and most of the time I don't mind it at all. Not much anyway. But it was quite hard at the beginning when I was so dazzled by the lot of them.' She paused, watching Philip's revolted expression and then added demurely: 'I was very young.'

'Perhaps that explains your quite unnecessary humility.' He drank some more wine and then said abruptly: 'You found something very funny when I came in. What was it?'

'It's just that no-one is sent up here unless they've shown gloom or rage downstairs,' she said casually. 'Flavia knows perfectly well that I know lunch is at twelve forty-five. She must have had another reason to make you climb all those stairs. Signs of rebellion against some family shibboleth seemed much the likeliest.'

Philip put back his head and laughed. In the circumstances it was a wonderful sound. 'Oh, how superbly practical! That's lovely. I thought it might be something quite different. Sasha . . .' He broke off to finish his wine and then leaned forward to put the glass on the edge of Lavinia's desk, adding: 'I hadn't realized my irritability showed. I hope I didn't upset Flavia. Although I can't be too sorry even if I did since it led me up here. You know, Lavinia, you're quite different from what I'd assumed. I can't think why I've never seen you properly before.'

'What can you mean? I know we haven't spent much time with each other, but . . .'

'I suppose it's just that I've been hearing about you for

51

years and assumed I knew exactly what you were like and didn't really want to know any more. Think what I've been missing! Serves me right for not making my own judgements.'

'What did you think I was like?'

To her amusement Philip looked slightly uncomfortable and shook his head. Lavinia was even more intrigued, but she could not persuade him to say anything more. Eventually she gave up trying and bent down to turn off the heater. 'Time for lunch. We won't be forgiven if we're late.'

Philip stood up and put a hand on her arm, saying: 'Thank you for this half hour. I feel considerably more human. Do we take the glasses down with us?'

'No. There's a little sink down one flight of stairs. I'll deal with them there later. You know, Philip, any time the whole bunch of them get too much for you downstairs, just come up here. If I'm not about, make yourself at home.'

'Don't you lock up when you leave?'

'There's no point. None of them would dream of invading or spying around my papers,' Lavinia said. 'Don't misjudge them just because their certainty . . .'

'Arrogance.'

'Oops. You *are* cross with them, aren't you?'

'Not particularly; but I am generally bad-tempered and tetchy at the moment.' He broke off and looked at her, his mouth curling again at the edges. 'And damn glad to have found a bit of the house where normality reigns.'

'Thank you for that. But come on now. We must show our faces and do our bit.'

They heard the sound of the family growing louder with every step they took down the narrow staircase, but neither of them could pick out any individual voices, not even those of their own children, until they reached the bottom. Fresh from the quietness of the tower, Lavinia felt assaulted by both the noise and the cluttered movement in front of her. She tried to distinguish her children from the crowd.

Tammy, still in jodhpurs and boots, was helping some of her older cousins lay the long oak table. Near her, piling logs into the gaping fireplace, was Aubrey. He looked very like Tom, although he was greyer and craggier. Some of the dignity of his judicial role seemed to cling about him even when he was doing something as menial as stoking the fire. As he straightened up, he said something to his mother, who was sitting in a tapestry-covered chair to the left of the fire. She laughed, looking almost happy, and started talking to him with unusual animation.

Watching them both and occasionally joining in was Great-aunt Elfrida, who had retired as head of an Oxford college in 1986 and chaired a series of quangos ever since. She had had a hunting accident fifteen years earlier and spent almost half a year in Stoke Mandeville hospital, since when she had been confined to a wheelchair. Despite her disability, she coped astonishingly well with the practicalities of life, and even the noise of several competing adult conversations and roistering children all round her did not seem to worry her. Lavinia smiled as Elfrida caught her eye and waved, and then looked away, still searching for the rest of her own brood.

She saw Charles at the far end of the hall, happily fighting with Aubrey's younger son, Benedict, who was easily his favourite cousin. A moment later she discovered Rory, standing beside the heavy brown leather curtain that was supposed to keep out the draughts from the porch. He was talking seriously about something to Frida and Julia, her younger daughter, who were the most musical of the Medworths and had presumably been organizing the rehearsals in the chapel that morning.

About to step into the clamour, Lavinia looked back over her shoulder at Philip. 'Can you bear it?'

'Probably. You?'

'Oh, yes. I always get used to it quite quickly.' She saw Benedict's mother waving to her and blew her a kiss across the crowd. Caroline looked surprised and rather embarrassed, but she smiled.

'I must say hello to Caro – and Aubrey come to that. I haven't seen either of them since they got here. See you later, Philip.'

Before Lavinia could get far into the crowd, sixteen-year-old Sarah Flemming stopped her, saying shyly: 'Hello, Cousin Lavinia. How are you?'

Lavinia kissed her warmly and stood back to look at her. Descended from old George Medworth's eldest daughter, Sarah had all the familiar family features and yet there was something about her that set her apart from her cousins. Her parents' relative poverty did not affect her appearance, because no Medworth ever spent much on clothes and hers were no different from the rest. They had probably been handed down from Georgina or Julia. Lavinia was almost sure that it was only Sarah's inaccurate but devastating certainty that she was stupid which made her seem different, and she always tried to encourage her.

'I'm fine, Sarah. What about you? You look wonderful. I think the shorter hair is terrific. It suits you.'

'Really? Thank you. I've been wanting to thank you for your letter as well. It helped such a lot coming just before my retakes like that.'

'Good. Look, we'll get a chance to talk about the exams properly later. It's all a bit noisy in here, don't you think?'

Lavinia believed that Sarah was quite as clever as the rest of the family, but something had gone wrong and she had come a cropper over her GCSEs the previous summer. None of her cousins had so much as mentioned her results to her, let alone taunted her about them, but she had felt her failure acutely. And her parents had been appalled, however carefully they had tried to hide it from her.

'Tell me,' said Lavinia, tucking her hand into the crook of Sarah's elbow, 'are you involved in the play this year? I haven't heard anything much about it yet.'

'Well, yes I am. But look: there's Mummy and Aunt Frida with the food. Hadn't we'd better give them a hand?'

Their offer of help was accepted immediately and Lavinia was directed to fetch a vast oven dish of baked potatoes from the kitchen and distribute them among the waiting plates. She did as she was told, glad of the opportunity to warm her hands on each potato as she took it from the dish. The huge fire did not yet seem to have made much impression on the temperature of the hall.

When she had distributed the potatoes, Lavinia propped the dish against the edge of the hearth and went to sit down next to Dominic Flemming, Sarah's uncle.

Despite having just as many Medworth genes as Tom, Dominic had somehow escaped the familiar aquiline features. His hair was blonder than his cousins' and his eyes were distinctly blue. He was rounder in the face, too, but he had all the Medworth brains and confidence in his own importance and ability. Unlike Sarah's father, Gerard, who had gone into the church, Dominic was rich from his years in a successful merchant bank. Lavinia had often wondered whether it could have been Gerard's rigorously suppressed resentment of his elder brother's wealth that made him so hard to like.

Seeing Sarah hovering behind the chair on her right, Lavinia smiled and pushed it back. Sarah took it gratefully and sat down.

'Good to see you, Lavinia,' Dominic said from her other side as he shook out his napkin. 'How've things been in the constituency?'

Lavinia checked that Sarah was happily talking to John Hogarth on her other side and turned to answer the question. 'So, so. Why d'you ask?'

'I can't help thinking that if the government doesn't start paying attention to what's happening in the country soon and manage to do something visible to prove that they care about it, they'll lose the next election. And then what will poor Tom do? We're all rather worried about it. Has he said anything to you?'

One of the four large dishes of stew reached him and he ladled some out on to his plate before handing it on to Lavinia.

'No, he hasn't. You know, I wish you wouldn't call him "poor Tom" like that,' she said, taking the dish. She did not believe that she would ever be able to change the family's contempt for what Tom had achieved – which anyone else would have taken as a considerable success – but it annoyed her.

'Do you think there's any hope of his keeping the seat?' Dominic asked.

'I'm sure there is, but you're right: something's got to change before the election. People are so frightened now. They used to be too scared to rock the boat, but I think they're beginning to feel that even swimming in shark-infested waters might be safer.'

Lavinia ate some of her stew and reached for the pepper pot. She longed to add some Worcestershire sauce or soy or anything to give it some real taste, but there was nothing but kitchen salt and ready-ground white pepper. 'What's Julian banging on about down there?' she asked suddenly, hearing Frida's husband talk increasingly loudly, overriding everyone near him.

Julian Collingham made campaigning documentaries for television and was often enraged by what he saw as deliberate obstruction from officials whose failings or procrastination he was trying to expose, but his voice seemed to be expressing more personal fury than usual.

'Lord knows,' said Dominic, sounding amused. 'His temper's getting worse and worse. I don't know how poor

Frida puts up with him, to tell you the truth, although I suppose her work is quite a distraction and they do seem to lead virtually separate lives these days.'

'I think it was very sensible of you to marry a cousin, Dominic,' Lavinia said sweetly, watching him.

He turned sharply and glared at her, but after a moment he started to laugh. 'I've never heard you sound bitchy before, Lavinia. What's up?'

'Nothing really. Just the sort of knee-jerk reaction I have when I hear one of you despising one of us. But perhaps it wasn't fair. How is Olivia? She's not looking very well. Is it overwork?'

Dominic shook his head and, lowering his voice, said: 'We're having a baby. She's only ten weeks gone and is still feeling pretty sick.'

'Oh, poor thing. But it doesn't last much longer. What marvellous news! You must be so happy.'

'Yes, we are. We're not telling the whole outfit yet, but I know she wants to have a word with you. She's . . . well, apprehensive and as it's so long since she was afraid of anything she doesn't know quite how to go about dealing with it. Will you talk to her?'

'Of course I will. But not this afternoon. I'm going to today's surgery with Tom.'

Seeing that she was the last to finish, Lavinia hurriedly ate the remains of her stew and gave up her plate to Sarah.

Dominic had turned to talk to Caroline on his far side and so Lavinia sat back and listened to a lively conversation about rainbows between Philip, Benedict and Georgina. They were sitting at the opposite side of the table from Lavinia and clearly getting on very well. As Sarah and her sister, Josie, brought them all plates of baked apples and packet custard from the kitchen, Philip said: 'What would you say is the most interesting thing about the rainbow, Bendy?'

'It's got a crock of gold at the end,' said Benedict, flashing his best smile at Lavinia when he noticed her listening to him. He added with manifest satisfaction as he began to squash the few sultanas into the white foam of his apple: 'And in fairy tales it's always the *younger* son who gets it.'

Philip and Lavinia laughed, but Sarah, who was having a lot of difficulty dealing with her younger sister's recent successes, stopped pouring custard over her own apple and said earnestly: 'Does he? Why?'

'I don't know, but he always does. What do you think is the most important thing, Uncle Philip?'

Philip reached out for the sugar. 'The different – and equally legitimate – ways people have of deciding how many colours there are in a rainbow,' he said, looking at Lavinia. Hearing echoes of their talk up in the tower, she smiled at him.

'How d'you mean?' asked Sarah.

Philip reluctantly stopped watching Lavinia's glinting dark-grey eyes and softly curving lips and turned to explain himself to Sarah. 'Well, schoolchildren are taught that there are seven colours, as though that's a fact like . . . oh, like our need to breathe oxygen. But really, you know, it's only one way of looking at it.'

'That's a little misleading, Philip,' said Frida from beyond Benedict's chair. 'Newton discovered that when light is split through a prism there are seven different angles of refraction. Therefore there are seven colours. It is a fact.'

Before Philip could answer, Olivia suddenly got up from her place at the far end of the table. As she put her right hand to her mouth and swayed, Lavinia pushed back her own chair. Dominic put a hand on her knee to stop her getting up and murmured: 'She'd much rather deal with it by herself. Don't worry. She's getting used to it.'

'But she looks frightful.' Lavinia glanced across the table towards Philip, wondering whether to ask him to look after

Olivia, who was obviously rushing out to be sick some-where. He had not noticed her departure and was talking to Frida in a voice that was hard enough to make Sarah screw up her eyes and press herself back into her chair.

Lavinia sat back in her chair, having missed a lot of the argument about the rainbow. She watched Frida scoop up the last of the tough skin of her baked apple and doggedly chew it. Like all Medworths, she disapproved of waste and tended to make that clear whenever she saw other people indulging in it.

'But you and I would never be able to look at one and agree where each colour turns into the next,' Philip was saying.

'No, I suppose you wouldn't,' said Lavinia, joining in at last as she remembered a snippet from the art history course she had taken after school. 'Isn't the wavelength continuous from red to violet? Presumably that's why Leonardo da Vinci thought that there were only four colours.'

'There you are,' said Philip before Frida could inter-vene. He caught Lavinia's eye in a private exchange of smiles, which made it possible for her to listen to Frida's crisp lecture on the physical properties of light without feeling as though she were being trampled into the mud of her own inadequacy.

Chapter 5

Tom took the wheel as they drove down into Helms-moorside that afternoon and Lavinia sat with a file on her knees, telling him about the constituents she had seen recently and the problems that she had been trying to solve for them. He seemed unusually irritable, dismissing their complaints and anxieties as trivial. He started to say 'Oh, for God's sake, Lavinia' so often that she was eventually forced to point out that the complaints were not hers and that she was merely giving him the background to what he was likely to face that afternoon.

'Yes, I know,' he said with a sigh. 'Sorry. All right: waiting lists, community care, invalidity benefit, environ-mental health officers. What else am I going to get? Anti-hunt protesters? I wish there hadn't been so much wretched publicity about the hunting debate, though that's past praying for, I suppose.'

'No-one's ever even mentioned hunting to me and everyone up here knows you're pro. I don't think that'll be a problem.' Lavinia looked at him for a moment, feeling a mixture of real sympathy for his difficulties and fierce exasperation about some of the things he and his senior colleagues had done since the last general election. They seemed to have not only inadequate pity for the distress some of their policies had caused, but also an inability to grasp the extent of it. 'It's mainly fear that makes people so irritating,' she said quietly, trying to make him understand so that he would not be impatient with the constituents. 'You have to make an adjustment when you come up here, shift gear and become the local protector of individual people instead of the burdened London minister.'

'Yes, I know. Oh, God! I wish . . .'

'What?'

He looked at her for a second. 'Just that life was a bit easier.'

Lavinia longed to ask which bit of his life was troubling him so much, but direct questions had always tended to push him into himself. She knew that she was likely to learn more if she waited until he could bring himself to tell her.

'I suspect it's easy only when it's dull,' she said eventually, hoping to comfort him.

'That sounds all too likely, but just at the moment I could do with a spot of dullness. Here we are.' He pulled up outside the grey stone school building just before the square. 'Can we park here? I can't remember.'

'No. But you go on in and talk to Edgar. I'll find a space.'

She handed him the file, wished him luck and drove on to the old market square, wishing that Helmsmoorside were not such a magnet for tourists. It was a pretty town with neat grey stone houses set well back from the road. In the old days it had always seemed serene and elegant in a homely way, but the hordes of tourists had taken away some of its straight-forwardness and made it coy. There were plenty of other attractive towns near by, but everyone seemed to want to come to Helmsmoorside. The square was always full of cars and buses, except on Wednesdays when there was still an actual market, and the stepped plinth of its stubby cross was usually littered with chocolate wrappers and ice-cream cartons.

61

The little town's popularity was good for trade, of course, and for local employment. The two old pubs did very well and there were several profitable shops selling gifts, country clothes and the sorts of bits and pieces holiday-makers liked to buy. But Lavinia looked back nostalgically to the days when the only shoppers were locals and parking spaces were plentiful and free.

She found one in the end, bought her ticket, and made her way back through the crowds towards the constituency office. When she got there, she stopped outside the door, feeling excluded from the one part of Tom's working life that was normally available to her. Minding more than she had expected to, she decided not to sit in the waiting room with all the other supplicants and turned aside to the nearest café. She bought herself a cup of tea and went to drink it at a table in the window so that she had a good view of the constituency office. Luckily she had a half-read novel in her handbag and consoled herself with that.

When Tom and his agent emerged on to the street and looked around for her one and a half frustrating hours later, Lavinia thought they both seemed remarkably pleased with themselves. She left the café and walked across the road to meet them. 'You two look as though it went well.'

'It did,' said Tom. 'I wish there were more I could actually do, but given the limitations it was considerably less traumatic than I'd suspected. The worst was Jennie Whatsit and her baby.'

'Nightingale,' said Lavinia, silently angry that he could not bother to remember the actual name of the woman whose last baby had been born with only one eye. She knew quite well that Jennie would probably have been enchanted by the serious way in which Tom had listened to her problems. 'Can you get someone to look into her case and the other two over near Leeds in case they've been caused by some sort of pollution? Did she tell you about them?'

'Yes, she did. But no: there's not a lot anyone can do. Lavinia, don't look like that. Statistically those three babies are insignificant. We can't go spending taxpayers' money on an investigation whenever there's a little cluster of birth defects. There always have been since long before modern chemicals were invented. It's tragic but it happens.'

She turned away, knowing that he was right but angry all the same. She felt his hand on her shoulder.

'Lavinia, I know that blaming someone makes people feel less aggrieved, but encouraging a sense of grievance is not a sensible way to run any country.'

'It's not that. It's just this way you have of seeing people as units or examples of some theory that I find so hard to take.' Hearing the irritation in her voice, she smiled apologetically. 'But, look here, we'd better be getting back. I'll see you after Christmas, Edgar.'

The agent, who had been looking embarrassed as he gazed at a tattered poster on the door in order to avoid their quarrrel, turned back and shook her hand.

'Sorry, Tom,' she said as soon as Edgar had left them. 'I shouldn't have lost my temper, particularly not in front of him.'

'Oh, don't worry. It was hardly a massive rage. And it was justified anyway. But there isn't anything I can do. That's what's so damnably frustrating. I used to think that once I became a minister I'd be able to change things. But no-one can; not really. That's why I've been wondering what the point of it all is. At my gloomiest I think I should have been a journalist.'

Lavinia stared at him.

'I know, it's ironic, isn't it? But they seem to be almost the only people who can get anything done. Stirring people up to fever pitch does eventually change things. It's infuriating.'

'Have you had some particularly awful row with the Secretary of State recently?' Lavinia put Jennie Nightingale to the back of her mind in the interests of what she had long seen as her principal job: helping Tom to keep going.

'In a way. I've been trying to stand firm on something that I think matters. I can't tell you about it yet. I wish I could. As soon as I can I will.'

'Don't worry about that,' she said, feeling as though a heavy rucksack had been lifted off her back. If it were a political fight that had been making him so edgy then enough was probably still all right between them to keep the whole thing viable. She let her hand brush against his as they walked towards the carpark. For a second she thought she could feel his hand turning towards hers, but then he moved it right away.

'God I'm tired. Do you think you could bear to drive back?'

'Of course.'

They walked slowly through the town and stopped for a moment at the river, leaning on the edge of the bridge and looking down at the shallow, swirling water.

'I wish we had time to walk up to the abbey,' Tom said after a long silence.

Lavinia looked at her watch. 'It'll be dark in half an hour. We could go tomorrow. Oh, no. It's the children's hunter trials. Well, the day after. Oh, Tom, do let's sneak some time away from the ponies and all the Christmas doings and have some time to ourselves. It would be heaven to be just you and me for an hour or two.'

He did grip her hand then and she laughed in delight.

'It's good to be out with you, Lavvy,' he said before he let her go. 'A proper walk together is a nice idea, too. Let's make a firm date for the morning of the day after tomorrow.'

'Right. But we must get back now.'

'Yes, I suppose so.' He sounded reluctant, which increased her pleasure. 'What are we all supposed to be doing after tea today?'

'Decorating the tree, making fudge for Christmas Eve and cheese straws for the party. I've got hold of one of the timetables and so at last I know what's going on.' Even the thought of Flavia's all-controlling arrangements could not disturb Lavinia's pleasure in the reassurance that Tom still cared about her. 'Oh yes: those with major parts in the play are having another rehearsal, while the costume team fit the clothes on them so that we seamstresses can finish the hems and the final alterations tomorrow. But as far as I can remember you're free of it all.'

'Good. I could do with a spot of freedom.'

When they reached the car, he lay back in the passenger seat and was asleep in minutes. Lavinia drove up the familiar road towards the moor, enjoying the gradual greying of the light and revelling in her release from several anxieties.

It had shocked her to discover only a year or two after her marriage that the Medworths, who were unimpeachably honest in all their business dealings, who would never break a law even as trivial as parking on a yellow line or driving the wrong way down a one-way street, did not believe that fidelity in marriage was at all important.

When the tabloid newspapers had broken the story of Tom and his secretary a couple of years earlier, Aubrey, Frida and Sasha had each written to Lavinia to explain their philosophy and urge her not to make a fuss. Since she had never planned to do so, their assumption that without their letters she would have tried to ruin Tom's career was a lingering annoyance.

She looked at his sleeping face for an instant, noticing that the lines around his mouth were deeper than usual and the texture of his skin was almost papery. Lavinia reminded herself that it usually took several days before he could properly relax in her – or anyone else's – company. All she could do was wait and be as gentle and subtle as possible.

After tea Lavinia collected Sarah Flemming and together they went to the kitchen to make cheese straws. They found Caro already there with her daughter, Meg, organizing ingredients and equipment for fudge.

Lavinia had always liked Caro, but they had rarely confided in each other. Of all the people who had married Medworths, Caroline had been the one who seemed most at ease with them. She had been qualified as a solicitor before she met Aubrey, which had helped, and her wide circle of friends had included people of whom the Medworths approved. Like Lavinia, she tended to dress rather more elaborately than they did, but she had never been subjected to one of Flavia's barrages of contempt for it.

With her greying blond hair cut in a smooth, chin-length bob with a half fringe, and her grey trousers and jersey protected by an enormous butcher's apron, Caro looked perfectly in command of her end of the long table. Meg, who shared many of her expressions but had her father's features and colouring, was much less tidy. She had tucked a damp drying up cloth in the neck of her loose red sweater and tied another round her minute waist.

Most of the fudge they were making was destined to be eaten by the family, but the cheese straws were for the party that was held every year on 27 December. Lavinia would have preferred to make them on the day they were to be eaten, but the entire kitchen was needed then for the preparation of a buffet supper for nearly sixty guests. She was sieving a pound of plain flour into a large bowl and directing Sarah to cut twelve ounces of butter into small pieces when Caroline looked up from her saucepans and said almost as impatiently as Frida might have spoken: 'I can't think why you insist on making all

66

that pastry by hand. It'll wear you out and it's absurd. The mixer does it perfectly well.'

Sarah flinched at the irritability in her voice, but Lavinia was not afraid of Caro and merely smiled sleepily as she pressed the last lumps of flour through the fine mesh. 'Yes, perfectly well, but it's never quite as good.' She caught Sarah's eye as she added: 'It may be no more than the effect of my sweaty fingers, but whatever it is makes the cheese straws taste better and so I'll carry on doing it my way.'

Sarah tucked her chin down into her neck and concentrated on cutting up the cold butter into little pieces, but she was smiling.

'There's more to life than efficiency,' Lavinia added. Thinking about it later, she was not sure whether she had been trying to provoke Caro or to reach some kind of understanding with her.

'That's what Jocelyn always says,' Meg contributed from the pan of molten toffee-like mixture that she was whipping into fudge at the other end of the huge scrubbed table.

'Of course there is.' Caroline's voice was still hard with impatience. 'But, as I endlessly tell him, without efficiency there isn't enough time left for the more important things.'

'Is there anything I can do to help?' said a cheerful masculine voice from the doorway.

Sarah looked round and pushed her brown hair out of her eyes. 'Hello, Cousin Philip. You can help me by grating the Parmesan if you like. It's a horribly tough job.'

Lavinia smiled at Philip as he came towards them. 'What are you making?' he asked, peering over her shoulder.

'Cheese straws. Haven't you seen it marked down on your timetable?'

'I haven't been given one of the celebrated timetables,' he said a little tartly. 'I don't seem to have any role in all these preparations.'

67

As though scenting disapproval of her mother-in-law's arrangements, Caroline frowned as she removed one pan of boiling fudge mixture from the hob with both hands and said: 'Flavia knows how tired you must be, Philip, after battling with all your patients. I expect she didn't want to make you do more than your health will allow.'

'Tired?' he said. 'Nonsense. I'm long recovered from all that. Still, it's kind of her to be concerned. Where's the grater, Sarah? It'll do me good to excoriate a block of unyielding cheese against a whole lot of sharp steel spikes.'

Giggling, she finished beating two eggs and fetched a large, flat plate, a cheese grater and a craggy hunk of Parmesan, dumping them beside Lavinia's place at the table.

'Thank you,' Philip said, looking at the cheese and then at his own hand. 'And what are you going to do while I wear out my finger joints on this, young woman?'

'I'll do the Cheddar,' said Sarah, gleefully pretending to sound languid and exhausted. 'It's so much softer that it doesn't damage one's delicate hands.'

He laughed and set to work just as Lavinia tipped the butter pieces into her sifted flour and started rubbing them in. It gave her real pleasure to hear them teasing each other and she smiled warmly at Philip.

Caroline ignored the frivolity at the far end of the table. She lowered a sweet thermometer into her vat of vanilla fudge and when the mixture reached the necessary temperature she took the heavy pan off the stove and stood it on a trivet at the far end of the table. Taking a rotary whisk she started to beat the translucent liquid until it turned opaque. Then she poured the contents into a shallow tin, washed the pan and returned a minute or two later to mark the fudge into squares. That done, she pushed the tin further down the table to cool, greased another, and was soon back at the stove to test the temperature of the next pan, in which she was boiling the ingredients for raisin fudge. She had to wait only two minutes before that, too, was ready to be beaten.

'That's a remarkable display of time-and-motion efficiency,' said Philip. Caroline looked up from her work for a moment and then her face relaxed. Seeing the pleasant expression, Lavinia wished that she would smile more often. 'It's just years of practice. I've been making the fudge here ever since I married Aubrey and that's . . .'

'Twenty years,' said Meg, looking up from her chocolate mixture. 'You'd been married for three by the time I was born.'

'So we had.' Caroline took a list out of her apron pocket, ticked off each flavour of fudge that had been completed. 'Then it's on to the mince pies and that's my lot for today. Who's cooking supper tonight?'

'Granny-Flavia and Cousin John,' said Sarah, watching Philip struggle as the lump of Parmesan dwindled to the hardest part near the rind. 'With Bendy, I think, as their runner.'

Lavinia caught Philip's eye and felt that for the first time in years there was someone at Saltley with whom she felt completely at ease.

Caroline hauled a catering-sized Kenwood mixer out of its cupboard and on to one of the worktops, where she proceeded to make three pounds of short-crust pastry in a very short time. In fact, Lavinia was still rolling out her first batch of rich, cheese-flavoured dough as Caroline was pressing the bottoms of her pies into the tartlet tins that her daughter had been greasing for her. As each tin was lined with pastry, Meg filled it with a precisely measured spoonful of mince and returned it to her mother, who laid lids on the little pies. They were given back to Meg for glazing with milk and caster sugar and taken to the heated ovens in batches.

'There, Philip,' said Lavinia, pushing her pastry board towards him. 'Would you cut that into strips about two inches long and a third wide?'

'Certainly,' he said. 'And do what with them?'

'I arrange them on trays for freezing,' said Sarah, fetching a flat metal spatula and standing over him. 'And then tomorrow I bag them up. We're not as quick as Cousin Caro and Meg, but we manage a sort of time-and-motion thingy too.'

Lavinia washed out her bowl, dried it, and started the whole process again, beginning to enjoy herself. The scent of the spiced mincemeat reminded her of childhood Christmases and the sensation of the pastry forming between her fingers was pleasant, but, more than either of those, she was revelling in Philip's company.

They were still finishing off the last batch of cheese straws when John Hogarth arrived with Flavia and Benedict. Lavinia finished what she was doing and started to clear her part of the table. As she was wiping up the crumbs of uncooked pastry she looked at Benedict and saw a bruise on his face. 'Are you all right, Bendy?'

'I'm fine. I walked into a door.' There was something in his twinkling expression that told her he had lied.

'Did you? Or did Charles hit you again? I saw the two of you whacking away at each other before lunch.'

The ten-year-old grinned up at her, intelligence and awareness blazing in his dark-brown eyes. She watched him, trying to decide what message he was really giving her.

'I suppose you're not going to tell me what really happened,' she said, laughing. 'But are you really all right?'

'Yeah. And it wasn't Charles's fault because I'd been teasing him.'

'What about?'

'Oh, I couldn't tell you.' Bendy wrinkled his snubbed nose. 'Honestly. It wouldn't be fair. You don't mind, do you?'

'Lavinia, if you don't understand your own children by now, you never will. You can collect reports on their activities later if you must,' said Flavia with savage contempt, 'but do try to concentrate on what you're supposed to be doing and let the rest of us get on. We've a meal to cook for twenty-six and we need the space.'

Lavinia blinked. Even Flavia usually moderated her criticism when there were children around to hear her. Bendy stared at his grandmother and Philip took a step forwards and opened his mouth.

'I say, Flavia,' John Hogarth began before Philip said anything, but Lavinia shook her head to stop them both speaking and said quietly:

'We'll be as quick as we can.'

She ruffled Bendy's short, dark hair, smiled at Sarah who looked as though she might burst into tears, and finished the rest of her clearing up as quickly as she could.

'How about a drink?' said Philip as he and Lavinia left the kitchen with Sarah five minutes later. 'Do you have drinks yet, Sarah?'

'Sometimes, but I promised to find Jocelyn,' she said, sounding breathless. 'We thought we might play chess.'

'Right. Have a good game.' As soon as the girl had gone, Philip turned to Lavinia. 'That was outrageous. Why didn't you let me or John say anything?'

'It only makes it worse when someone defends me,' she said. 'In the old days when I was first married, Tom's father used to sometimes and it always led to a more ferocious attack later when he wasn't around.' She sighed. 'He once told me she didn't know her own strength, and I always remind myself of that when she has a go at me. Sometimes I think she really doesn't know what it sounds like. At others I wonder why she should dislike me quite

71

so much. I know she thinks I'm stupid and not good enough to be a Medworth even by marriage, but neither of those seems enough to justify the things she says to me.'

'Somebody ought to stop her treating you like that. No-one should have to live with it, whatever the reason.'

'I don't think anyone can stop her without risking something much worse for all of us. But it doesn't matter that much. Except at Christmas, I hardly see her these days and I just ignore it.'

Lavinia pushed open the door of the yellow parlour, where the evening drinks tray was always put, and switched on the lamps. 'Good. No-one else here. We can relax.' She shivered and bent down to light the fire, which someone – probably Aubrey, who had a patent method of arranging the logs – had laid earlier in the day.

'What'll you have?' said Philip, frowning at her as though he still could not understand why she was not prepared to fight back.

'Wine if there is any,' she said, sitting down in one of the high-backed chairs at the side of the fireplace, holding out her hands towards the fire. She sighed as warmth began to reach them. 'I've always liked this room.'

Philip, who had poured himself out a weak whisky and water, looked around in surprise. 'Yes, it is cosier than the others, isn't it? Though I suppose that might be just the low ceiling.'

Lavinia looked at the worn yellow damask on the walls of the long, low room and the greenish-blue tapestry that covered the thick squabs under the mullioned windows and shook her head. With its old oak bookshelves, piled with novels that one member of the family or another had read and left behind, the pleasant watercolours, and the deep sofa with its load of cushions covered in shabby velvet and faded petit point, it was a much less formidable room than any of the others, and more welcoming.

'I think it's more than just that. There's something easy about its atmosphere. I sometimes think that a particularly sympathetic Saltley woman might have used it once upon a time and sort of stamped her personality on it.'

'Goodness, Lavinia, that's rather sentimental, isn't it?' said Frida from the doorway. The other two looked round and Lavinia achieved a smile, but she did not trust herself to comment.

'A little sentiment is no bad thing,' said Philip, defending her too vigorously.

'Even if it goes a long way,' contributed Tom from behind his sister. He looked cheerful. He had changed out of his suit again, but he was not wearing his riding clothes. Instead he had on a pair of grey-green corduroy trousers that were not his own and a loose, black ribbed sweater that Lavinia did not recognize either. She realized that he must have borrowed them from either Aubrey or Julian and wondered why she minded that more than Flavia's attack. Tom was obviously much more comfortable than he had been in his suit and that was all that mattered.

'Cheese straws all done, Lavinia?' he said.

'Yes,' she said, noticing the effort he had made to remember what she had been doing. 'And we've worked so hard we thought we'd have a touch of unauthorized frisko.'

At Lavinia's use of Medworth slang for alcohol drunk before the proper time Tom looked slightly embarrassed, but Frida's lips tightened in distaste. In her view even fourteen years of marriage to Tom did not entitle Lavinia to use the family's private language. Frida flexed her nostrils and turned away to begin mixing drinks for herself and Tom without even asking him what he wanted or checking whether the others needed their glasses refilling.

'Thanks,' said Tom as she put the tall glass in his hand. He drank. 'Ah, that's better. No-one else can make a Tom Collins like you.'

They smiled at each other and then, deliberately enough to make it seem clumsy, Tom turned away to talk to Philip about famine relief and the pros and cons of international aid for Third-world countries. Frida watched them for a while before cross-examining Lavinia about her work on the Saltley papers until the rest of the adults arrived for their evening drinks. It was all most uncomfortable.

Chapter 6

Up in her tower the following morning, Lavinia found herself unable to work and could not think what the trouble was until she realized that she was waiting for Philip. Luckily his knock came before she had wasted too much time.

'Is this really all right?' he said as he opened the door, holding a pile of papers between his left arm and his ribs. 'I haven't come to disturb you, but it's all a bit noisy downstairs and you did say . . .'

'Of course it's all right. Come on in. D'you need desk space?'

He shook his head and lowered his long, well-muscled body into the arm-chair, dropping his papers on the floor.

They worked for an hour or so in silence, an easy silence that held no strain for a long time. It was Philip who first grew restless.

'How did you manage to bear Tom's affair?' he demanded out of the quietness.

Lavinia sat quite still for a moment, then pressed the buttons to save her document and eventually swung round on her chair so that she was facing him. 'I didn't realize that you could get tabloids in Africa,' she said, playing for time.

'I never read them anyway. But you must have realized that tendrils of the family grapevine would stretch much further than merely the Sahara.'

'I suppose so.'

'How did you bear it?' he asked again. 'And how do you manage to stay with him now and seem so affectionate and so . . . so untroubled?'

Lavinia heard a note of urgency in Philip's voice and decided that he would not have asked the question unless he needed her answer. In that case, however reluctant she was, she would have to talk about her feelings. She just hoped that it would not stir up the thick sediment of misery that had sunk well below the surface of her life.

'I minded it all right, but . . .' She broke off, trying to find the right words. 'Oh, it's hard to explain.'

'Try.'

As she looked at him, she saw that for once there was no amusement or even friendliness in his eyes at all, only something that looked remarkably like a plea. All sorts of trivial comments made about him by members of the family came back to her and she began to wonder whether he had just learned of some new affair of Sasha's. If so, it could well have explained why Flavia had sent him up to the tower in the first place. Feeling as though a releasing switch had been thrown in her mind, Lavinia found the words quite easily after all.

'By that stage I'd already got used to something else I'd found so difficult that the affair itself seemed less important.'

Philip was frowning. After a moment, he asked her to explain what she meant.

Lavinia picked up a pencil and started drawing on the edge of a photocopy in front of her, making row after row of small, neat, grey herringbones. 'I've decided,' she said after a while, drawing a double box around the herringbones, 'that there are stages in any love affair, marriage, what-have-you, and that if you don't accept that you just mess things up.'

She paused but Philip said nothing. Setting out on another boxful of herringbones, she went on: 'I hadn't realized, you see, when I fell in love with Tom that the first sort of excited recognition and delight wasn't all there was to it. And when it began to change and he got more and more – disapproving, I suppose – I panicked. I thought he must be going off me because he'd got to know me better and found out that I wasn't what he'd wanted. I began to think he must share Flavia's view that I'm altogether useless.'

'That doesn't seem very likely. You are so demonstrably useful to him, quite apart from everything else you are.'

Lavinia tried to smile. 'Perhaps. But it was clear that something had gone very wrong. Being with him wasn't easy any longer – or even particularly happy. Quite the opposite, in fact. I still loved him like anything, but I felt as though he couldn't stand me. It was horrible, as though I was on the edge of a cliff with the ground crumbling under my feet. I pulled back. And not just metaphorically, if you see what I mean.'

'Yes, I think I do,' said Philip gently.

'It wasn't for ages that I realized he might have felt rejected, too, by what I was doing to protect myself. Perhaps I'd even been doing it for longer than I thought; you know, as though we'd both been doing much the same to each other. When I did begin to understand, I tried to get us back to the first stage, and it was a disaster. The more I tried, the further away he got, and the more of a failure I felt.'

Philip nodded when she paused. She started drawing again and then put her pencil down and looked towards one of the narrow windows. The wind had strengthened overnight and was bowling the bright white clouds fast across the thin-looking sky. She wished that she were more articulate, not realizing that, for Philip, the very clumsiness of her piling up more and more words was carrying its own conviction. 'At least that's how it seemed to happen,' she said eventually, letting some of the sadness out. 'We kept hurting each other – by mistake, I think – and annoying each other terribly. There was a stage when neither of us could say anything without causing trouble of one sort or another. Then I started Rory and Tom got elected and so we . . .' She laughed without amusement: 'As my grandmother used to say when we stuck out our tongues, the wind changed and we got stuck like that.'

She looked at Philip from under her long fringe. Something she could see in his face made her add: 'It's much better these days now that we've got on to the third stage: civilized and affectionate but fairly separate for most of the time. I minded a lot about that, but I've come to terms with it now.'

'And it was the separateness, was it, that made the affair less awful?'

'Yes. I'd been through a certain amount by then and I'd learned . . .' She found she could not go on.

'Tell me,' he said, leaning towards her.

'I'd learned not to expect too much, I suppose,' she said eventually, breathing carefully as she felt the sediment starting to rise and cloud her mind with some of the old misery, 'and so I was armoured when the bombshell fell. Sorry, that's a bit dramatic.'

'But expressive. I don't know that I can be as tolerant as you. I'm just so bloody angry about Sasha's affair.'

'You don't show it.'

'Don't I? I can't think why not. It's boiling about in me like lava.' Philip shuddered and, looking directly at her, added: 'It makes me want to hit someone – I'm not sure which of them.' Lavinia thought her face had not changed, but he quickly said: 'Don't look like that. Obviously I'm not going to hit anyone. But it's what I feel like.'

'So what will you do?' she said after a long silence.

Philip made an odd grimace; his nose wrinkled, his mouth hardened and his eyes tightened into narrow slits. After a moment a kind of resignation took over and his features relaxed into their normal shapes. 'What you did, I suspect, though not perhaps as gracefully. I'll wait for it to end; do my best to pretend . . .'

In sudden exasperation, he added: 'Oh, God knows what I'll do! Perhaps I'll just take the crashing hint, leave her to it and try to start again with someone else. I don't know. One can be too damned sensible, too disgustingly forebearing.'

'I know.' Lavinia wished that she could laugh at his self-mockery, but the atmosphere seemed much too heavy for that. 'But whatever happens, Philip, try not to forget that the Medworths don't take this sort of thing at all seriously. I don't think they have a clue about what we feel – how much it hurts. They can't change, Philip. You'll only make yourself unhappy if you don't find a way to accept that.'

He sat thinking about it in silence and then asked: 'Is it public knowledge, what Sasha's doing at the moment?'

Lavinia remembered all too well the humiliation that he must be feeling. That, at least, she could help to remove. She shook her head. 'I hadn't heard a thing. It was only something you said this morning that made me realize why you might be asking questions about Tom's past.'

'She says that the children don't know.'

'Then I think that's probably true. Medworths don't lie. That's another of their great strengths. They have lots. They are hugely admirable. You know they are. And we love our particular ones for a reason.'

'They don't need to lie,' he said with a bitterness that shocked her because it seemed so unlike him, 'because they don't care twopence what anyone else thinks of them, least of all those of us who have married them.'

'It will end, Philip,' said Lavinia, hurting for him. 'It always does, and usually quite quickly. Don't tear yourself apart over it. She'll be back. Just be as nice to her as you can while you wait.'

'Easier said than done.'

'Philip, listen. You'll only be miserable if you try to have all of Sasha. They can't let us have that much of themselves. And why should we want it? Doesn't the word "have" sound beastly? After all, do you want to be completely had?'

'I think I have been,' he said with a gleam of the old humour. 'Had for a mug. And so perhaps have you.'

'Ah, don't,' she said suddenly, and a lot of well-hidden pain escaped in that word.

Philip reached out towards her. Wanting the reassurance of his touch almost more than she could bear, she forced herself not to see the gesture. Instead she looked at the clock over the door. 'Come on. Lunch. We'd better not be late. It's the children's hunter trials this afternoon.'

'Must we eat again? There are times when I feel so bloody angry with them all that the thought of swallowing their food makes me retch.'

'No; no-one has to eat. But if you don't, you'll look sulky, which would be a pity.' At the sight of his face, she smiled, feeling more comfortable as she slipped back into her familiar semi-maternal role. She had played it with Sarah's mother, Polly, once long ago even with Julian Collingham, and with the spouses of several of the other cousins.

'So I must hide my humiliation and my rage behind a calm face?'

'No. All you have to do is take Sasha's affair as lightly as she does. It would be barmy to turn into great huge tragedy something that they think of as a pantomime. Now, what about a drink to stiffen your sinews?'

'No. Let's go down and eat nursery stew and drink good, honest, Yorkshire water and show that we're tough enough to take anything.'

'Good for you, Philip. You go on ahead. I'll quickly finish this document and switch everything off. I won't be far behind.'

He stood looking at her, his brows sharply raised above his eyes, which for once were showing hurt instead of entertainment. But then he grinned and she realized that there was something else they shared. Despite their superficial air of acquiescence, they were both fighters, and survivors, too. They might forget that themselves sometimes, but the underlying obstinacy would always return to save them in the end.

'You don't want us to look as though we've been conspiring, eh?'

'That's it, Philip. Chin up.'

'I'll see you later.'

She watched him go, switched off her computer and gave him ten minutes' start before she followed him downstairs.

After lunch, dressed in her warmest trousers and sweater, gumboots, a Barbour, gloves and a heavy scarf, Lavinia accompanied most of the other adults out to the course that Tom, Frida and Aubrey had laid out for the children's hunter trials. Olivia had retired to bed and Dominic had decided to read in the library, as had Philip, but everyone else was on parade.

Any child aged sixteen or less was eligible to ride and all nine of those belonging to the house were ready in their best breeches and hacking jackets. The girls had their hair neatly tucked into nets beneath their crash helmets. Only the two Flemming girls had rubber boots; the rest wore full-length hunting boots or jodhpur boots, well-kept but ancient and usually inherited from their older siblings or sometimes even their parents.

They were joined by a dozen children from neighbouring families, most dressed as they were. A few were wearing smooth polo-necked jerseys instead of hacking jackets. There was much noise and jostling as they tried to keep their ponies under control while they greeted old friends they had not seen for months. Some of the visitors were coming back from walking the course and there was much discussion about the number of strides between the logs and the bank.

Meg, who had been promoted to steward in her first year of non-eligibility, handed out cotton squares with large black numbers on them which the children tied around their waists as she noted down the names that went with each number. Everyone concerned was taking the competition with great seriousness.

Lavinia, standing shivering with Polly and Gerard Flemming, was glad to see that her three children all looked reasonably happy. Tammy had groomed Cupcake to a state of gleaming perfection but Charles's pony, Sid, looked a little rough still. Rory, in good control of the excitable Marbles (who had been called that because he had so few), was chatting to Josie Flemming as they waited. He had been picked to go first.

Eventually Meg rang the old ship's bell for him to begin. While Aubrey at the start and his mother at the finish got their stopwatches ready and the other judges stood alertly by their fences, Rory collected Marbles and headed him off towards the oil drums.

Lavinia held her breath. Marbles sailed over the jump, only clouting the drums with one of his back hooves. The dreadful noise did not seem to worry either the animal or its rider. Lavinia stood up on her toes to watch them round the rest of the course, biting her tongue at each fence. As Rory reached the end of the round, she could not help sighing in relief.

'It's horrible, isn't it?' said Polly fervently. 'Waiting for something to happen and being absolutely powerless to stop it.'

Lavinia nodded. 'They all love it. The ones who come off always seem to bounce like little rubber balls. But I can't help worrying.'

'And when they're out hunting?' asked Gerard over her head. He was well over six foot and even thinner than the rest of the family, which made him seem taller still. 'Don't you worry about them then?'

'Oh, yes.' Lavinia looked up and smiled as she shrugged. 'But I don't see how I can stop them doing something they apparently love so much just because I go nearly mad at the thought of what hunting falls do to people.'

She shivered and, seeing the familiar disdain creeping on to Gerard's face, added: 'Let's talk about something more cheerful. How's Sarah done this term?'

'Reasonably,' said her mother, frowning. 'It's hard for her that Josie has just got a major scholarship. Poor Sarah hates the fact that we're still having to struggle to pay her fees because she muffed the senior exam as well as the entry scholarship. Honestly, without Dominic's help, I don't think we could have managed it.'

Polly glanced up at her husband with a mixture of exasperation and affection and added: 'It's lucky one of you went in for merchant banking.'

'There goes Bendy,' said Gerard, ignoring her as he always ignored her when she made any comment or asked any question that had to do with money.

Benedict seemed to be having some trouble controlling Jolly Roger, a dark bay pony who had always gone reasonably well for Rory before he had grown so much that he had had to take over Marbles. So far Bendy and Jolly Roger had not managed to get on good terms with each other. The boy's cheerful face looked tense and his lips were clenched. He urged the pony over the oil drums successfully enough even though they landed badly and had to scramble a bit as they set off for the tree trunks. Bendy looked over his shoulder, patted Jolly Roger and urged him on. He was going quite well until he reached the tree trunks. Then, apparently deciding he did not like the look of them, Jolly Roger refused at the last minute.

Since he was often hunted, he could have refused only out of spite. Bendy, knowing that, hauled on the reins, whacked the pony once, and turned back the way they had come. He then took enough time to lean forward over the saddle and chat reassuringly into the animal's right ear before straightening up to have another go.

'Good boy that,' said Gerard as the three of them watched. 'He takes after his father. Aubrey always did have much more patience than the rest of us, even as a child.'

Jolly Roger set off again with Bendy talking to him, riding him carefully, beginning to look more relaxed in the saddle. They jumped the tree trunks quite easily and rode on at a spanking pace. As they reached the laid hedge, Jolly Roger hesitated slightly but Bendy leaned over his withers, urging him on, and they cleared it without trouble. Lavinia let out the breath she had been holding. Even at that distance, she could see that Bendy was smiling at last. Jolly Roger raced on to the bank, dug his toes in and shot the boy right out of the front door.

It looked horribly as though Bendy's fall might be going to be different from the usual tumbles the children all took in their stride. The assembled adults were running forwards even before the boy had hit the ground. Meg efficiently caught the frightened pony and kept him out of the way of the others, soothing him and walking him round and round in circles. Sarah, the eldest of the competitors, took one look at her cousin's heaving, gasping body and automatically assumed command of the others and led them all as far away from the bank as possible and set them to practising half passes and extended trots before going on to flying changes.

Aubrey, already running in the opposite direction, shouted that he would fetch Philip, while Caroline flung herself on her knees beside her youngest child. He was winded and whooped terrifyingly as he tried to get his breath. She took his left hand between both hers.

'Breathe carefully, Bendy. It's all right. It'll come back. Don't fight it. No, don't try to move yet.'

'I'm sorry I let go the rein,' he gasped. 'I'm sorry.'

'I know. Don't worry about it. You weren't hunting, after all. Uncle Philip will be here in a minute. Daddy's gone to get him.'

Flavia reached them then, carrying the rug she had had wrapped round her knees as she sat at the end of the course. 'Here. Cover him with this,' she said to Caro, who looked up, longing for reassurance. 'He'll be all right, Caroline,' she said firmly. 'Don't fuss.'

Lavinia thought that the boy's right arm might be broken and feared from the way he was lying that he had done some damage to his back, but even she took some reassurance from Flavia's certainty. At the sound of running feet, they all turned and saw Philip pounding along several yards ahead of the boy's father.

'You've taken a nasty purler there, haven't you?' Philip said when he had got his breath back. 'But don't worry about it. We'll soon have you a bit more comfortable.' He ripped open the Velcro straps of a neck collar he had brought with him and, with infinite care, eased it around the boy's neck.

'There. Well done, Ben. I'm going to give you something now, to help the pain, and then we'll deal with the rest. OK?'

'OK, Uncle Philip.' His breathing was better, but his colour was still terrifyingly abnormal and he was clearly in considerable pain and very frightened. Philip neither ignored nor minimized the seriousness of any of it, but he talked as though he were certain that everything would be all right in the end.

'Dominic has rung for an ambulance,' he said later when Bendy was breathing slightly more easily. 'It'll be on its way now. With a broken arm like that, you'll need to go to casualty. D'you ever watch the series?'

'Sometimes. I like it.'

'So do I,' said Philip cheerfully before explaining to Bendy exactly what the paramedics would do when the ambulance arrived and what the doctors in casualty would have to find out before they could send him home again.

Lavinia could see that his calmness was having as soothing an effect on Caroline and the other adults as it was having on her son. His face was still mottled white and mauve from shock, but he smiled up at his uncle and managed to answer questions.

'Shouldn't we get him somewhere a bit warmer?' whispered Aubrey.

'No,' said Philip, still talking at an ordinary pitch. 'Better to wait for the paramedics. They've got all the right sort of stretchers and Bendy'll be far more comfortable on those than if we shift him ourselves. Even if it is a bit cold out here.'

'What about the others?' asked the boy, his voice high with strain. 'They'll miss out. Sorry, Granny-Flavia.'

'They'll be perfectly all right,' she said to him, smiling down with more kindness than Lavinia had seen in her face for years. 'Sarah's got them doing dressage exercises at the other end of the field. Jolly Roger's all right, too. Meg's walking him to cool him off. He's got a bit of a bang on one of his knees, but it's not going to be a serious problem.'

When the ambulance eventually arrived Bendy was lifted into it and driven away with his mother. Flavia briskly set about restarting the competition while Lavinia went to find

Philip, who had gone back into the house after telling the paramedics how he had treated Bendy.

'Has he damaged his back badly?' she asked.

'I don't think it's broken, but it's impossible to tell exactly what the damage is without X-rays. He's a brave child.'

'They all are. Very brave.'

'I know.' He looked at her with a kind of helplessness that seemed quite at odds with the confidence he had shown Bendy. Then he grabbed her hand and burst out: 'I hate seeing children in pain.'

She was about to answer when they both heard running feet behind them. Philip let her go and they both turned to see Tammy.

'Come on, Mum. You must watch,' she said urgently. 'You promised and it's going to be my turn next.'

'I'm coming. Philip?'

'Yes, all right.'

Together the three of them walked back to the start of the course, and Lavinia and Philip both tried to forget what had just happened as they conscientiously watched the rest of the trial.

Rory ended up the winner and was soundly congratulated by his grandmother, who handed out the prizes, but he hardly seemed to notice. Even Tammy, who had managed to come fifth, which was her best-ever result, was muted in her triumph. At tea the long refectory table was much quieter than usual. Flavia talked almost normally to the visitors on either side of her, and at the opposite end of the long table Great-aunt Elfrida, who looked as though she were in the middle of a nightmare, did her heroic best to crank up a conversation about ancient winter solstice celebrations, but the general mood was lugubrious.

The visiting children got up with manifest relief as soon as their parents talked heartily about 'getting going', and the remaining Medworth relations hung about in groups, waiting. Charles kept asking whether he could ring up the hospital to find out what was happening to Bendy, but Philip told him he must wait, adding gently: 'Caroline will ring us as soon as there's news. You'll only take up important time and manpower if you try to ring the doctors before they have the results of the X-rays. We just have to hang on.'

'But it's Bendy,' said Charles, screwing up his face to hide his distress. In the shock of what had happened he had ridden badly, but he seemed quite untroubled by that.

'I know, old chap,' said Philip. 'And I know how hard it is to wait. But I'm afraid it's the only thing to do.'

'Let's go out to the stables and make sure Jolly Roger's still all right, shall we?' said Tom, holding out a hand to his younger son.

Charles gripped his lips together and nodded. The two of them went out hand in hand. Lavinia, for want of anything better to do, started to clear the tea table, loading the sliding piles of sticky crockery on to trays she had fetched from the kitchen. Sasha saw what she was doing and brought her children to help. As she and Lavinia followed Peter and Pippit down the kitchen passage, she suddenly said: 'It's good of you to field Philip like this. He needs your brand of common sense just at the moment.'

Lavinia raised her eyebrows, but she said nothing. She was afraid that she would not have been able to prevent herself asking unanswerable questions if she had opened her mouth.

'I hope it's not being too tiresome for you,' said Sasha, frowning.

'Anything for peace,' Lavinia managed to say lightly, hiding the reality of her feelings behind the familiar phrase that seemed to come in useful in most circumstances. 'Besides, he's a nice man. I really like him.'

'Oh, so do I.'

Lavinia was not surprised, but she wanted to say: well,

if that's true, why are you putting him through so much misery? But she knew there was no point and so she carried on to the kitchen in silence and loaded plates and cups into the bigger of the two dishwashers while the children washed up the knives and emptied the tea leaves out of the three large pots. Sasha put away the remaining food and then consulted the timetable on the wall to check whose job it was to cook supper.

'Oh, Lord! It's Caro's turn. I'd better do it. She can take over my next stint if Bendy's all right.'

'Good idea,' said Lavinia. 'Look, if you'd like help, I can certainly chip in. I don't think I'm down for anything else except the remains of my costume-sewing for the play.'

'No, don't worry. The other adult's Polly, and she'll be fine.'

The door was flung open and Sarah stood there, a wide smile on her face. She was breathing faster than usual. There was some colour in her cheeks and her hair was wild. For once she looked magnificently sure of herself.

'Cousin Caro's rung from the hospital. It's all right. Bendy hasn't broken anything except the arm. They've set that and they're keeping him in tonight, but he'll be home in the morning. No riding for a while. Physio for his back for several weeks, but he'll be all right in the end. And there won't be any wheelchairs or anything like that. And we're going to have sticky toffee pudding after the fish pie tonight to celebrate.'

Dizziness forced Lavinia to sit down at the kitchen table as Pippit and Peter shrieked and started a wardance at the sink. Bubbles of foam floated in the air as they waved their washing-up brushes in front of each other's face.

'Does Charles know?' Lavinia asked Sarah, who nodded. 'And Great-aunt Elfrida?'

'Yes, and she's looking much less tortured now. You know, I was thinking at tea that maybe she was even more afraid than Cousin Aubrey.'

Sarah suddenly pushed both hands over her face, rubbing her eyes as though she had just surfaced from underwater and then looked up again.

'Anyway, it's all all right now. Bendy's all right. Oh, and by the way, Uncle Tom said if you're not busy would you like to have a drink in the yellow parlour? He's got Charles with him there.'

Lavinia ran down the stone-floored passage to her favourite room. Charles got up from the stumpwork stool in front of the fire as soon as he saw her and threw his arms around her, clinging tightly. After a moment, delighted by his spontaneous affection, she pulled back a little way so that she could stroke the fringe back from his forehead and examine his face. The simple relief in his tear-swollen eyes warmed her.

'It's wonderful, isn't it?' she said, unspeakably glad that Charles's affection for Bendy was so straightforward and so obviously important to him. 'You must have been very frightened.'

'Yeah. But it's OK now. And Dad says I can go with Uncle Aubrey to fetch Bendy and Aunt Caro tomorrow morning, even though I ought to be helping with scene painting.'

'Terrific!' She turned her head. 'What a good idea, Tom.'

'Thanks. Now what about a spot of unauthorized frisko, Lavinia? I think we all deserve it after that.'

'Yes, perhaps. If there's any wine, I'll have that; otherwise vermouth or sherry. Dry, please.'

Tom put down his own whisky and soda and pulled himself out of his chair.

'Thank you,' said Lavinia when he handed her a glass of Rioja. 'That's lovely. How was Jolly Roger?'

'No real harm done. All in all, we've been let off lightly, eh, Charles?'

'Yes.' He blew and then grinned at Lavinia, looking more like a normal small boy than ever.

'How about joining the others now?' said his father. 'They're roasting chestnuts on the hall fire with Great-aunt Elfrida.'

'OK.' Charles walked obediently to the door but he stopped there and turned back. There was a mulish expression on his pink face. 'What's for supper?'

'Fish pie, I think,' said Lavinia. '*And* I heard someone say something about sticky toffee pudding as an extra treat to celebrate the good news.'

'Excellent. See you later.'

'He's all right,' said Tom when the boy had shut the door behind him.

'Yes; it was a good idea to take him away to the stables.' Lavinia rubbed her forehead. 'But it was a nasty few hours, wasn't it?'

'All of that. I hope it hasn't put new terrors in that over-maternal head of yours.' Tom drank some whisky and looked at her over the top of the glass. Lavinia raised hers to him in a silent toast. 'I know you have nightmares about the children hunting as it is.'

'No worse than usual.'

'Good. Oh, by the way, I said I'd go out tomorrow morning with Frida, Aubrey and Sasha. We thought we'd sneak in an extra day since they're meeting at Salt Farm and it's so handy. You don't mind, do you?'

Lavinia, thinking with regret of their planned solitary walk to the ruined Cistercian abbey above Helmsmoorside, shook her head and produced her nicest smile. After a moment she felt she could trust her voice and said: 'No. I hope you have a good day. I can't quite remember what I'm supposed to say. Isn't it: "I hope the scent lies breast high"?'

Tom reached out for her hand and kissed it. 'A wife in a million, Lavvy.'

'Good.' She leaned back, watching him. 'It's nice to be alone for a minute or two.'

Before Tom could answer, if he had been going to, the door was pushed open and Aubrey ushered in his mother. Tom got to his feet at once, plumped up the cushions in his chair and offered it to Flavia. She sat down with a wonderfully regal air and watched her sons dispose themselves about her. Then she put her feet up on the stumpwork stool and waited to be entertained. Lavinia reminded herself of Flavia's kindness to both Bendy and Caro and tried to believe that she was fundamentally benevolent.

Failing, Lavinia made herself remember something else Tom's father had said to her, just after his final illness had been diagnosed when Flavia had been particularly ferocious: 'Try to be patient with her. Her temperament sometimes makes her more exigent than she understands, but her needs are many and real, especially now. Be kind to her if you can.'

Lavinia tried to do as he had asked, but it did not work. Flavia either ignored what she said or dismissed it with a bitingly contemptuous phrase before turning back to her sons. Once again Lavinia had to face the fact that she had only two options: to go on ignoring Flavia's inexplicable hostility or to tackle her about it and demand an explanation, if not an apology. But Lavinia was reluctant to start something that might lead to even worse trouble, particularly in the middle of the family Christmas, and so she sipped her wine in silence.

Chapter 7

By Christmas Eve Bendy was well enough to join in most of the quieter indoor activities. He was still shaken and moved with careful deliberation, but he was definitely on the mend and regaining more of his cheerfulness every day. His arm was plastered and he carried it in a sling for most of the time, but he could sing all right and that seemed to be what had worried him most.

The actors in the play knew their parts and their moves, the scenery was painted, the costumes were complete and all possible advance preparations had been made both for the Christmas food and for the huge buffet supper on the evening after Boxing Day.

Lavinia had long ago insisted that her part of the family should have dinner alone together at the Dower House on Christmas Eve. It was thought eccentric of her – and rather unfair on her children – but since there were no particular traditions attached to Christmas Eve until midnight mass in the chapel no-one made any great fuss about it.

She did not go up to Saltley at all that day and so missed the arrival of the last of the family, Nicholas Medworth, great-grandson of old George Medworth's youngest son, who had inherited the management of the family wine business. What had once involved a sprawling and expensive organization with *negoçiants* in Bordeaux, vineyards in both France and Germany, bottling plants and vast cellars in Bristol, had evolved into a small but highly profitable chain of distinguished wine merchants.

Nicko, as he was known throughout the family, did some of the buying himself, but his main work was overseeing the business and he had a satisfactory sideline writing scholarly articles in the most upmarket of the wine journals. He and his wife, Loveday, who was a surgeon, had no children. Taking no part in the play or the Christmas music, they never appeared at Saltley until lunchtime on Christmas Eve and left immediately after breakfast on the day after the party.

Lavinia, having done all she could at the Dower House by noon, was feeling underemployed and lonely. She knew perfectly well that it was absurd to feel left out since it was she who had insisted on not joining the others, but even so she did.

Almost on cue the telephone rang. She reached out to pick up the receiver. 'Hello?'

'Lavinia, it's Philip here. How are you?'

'Fine,' she said when she had controlled the sharp pleasure of hearing his voice. 'And you?'

'A bit at a loose end without you, to tell the truth. I was wondering whether you felt like a walk at all? Not a long one, but enough to stretch our legs and work up an appetite for yet more wholesome food.'

'Oh, I'd like that. But, having made such a fuss about not coming to Saltley at all today, I'd feel a fool to turn up at the front door now.'

'Don't worry about that. I'm not actually there at the moment. I'm in a phonebox on my way back from York and I thought I'd drive up and collect you. Would that suit? I suppose it'll take me fifteen minutes at most.'

'That would be perfect. I'll be ready.'

She went upstairs to change into warmer clothes, singing

tunelessly to herself, secure in the knowledge that there was no-one with perfect pitch or even a good ear to hear her and wince.

In the mirror she saw a new brightness in her eyes and colour in her cheeks and picked up the mascara to stroke a little black on the lighter tips that made her eyelashes look shorter than they were. Blinking to make sure she had not smudged her eyelids, she had a sudden sinking realization of what she had been letting herself do.

'You fool,' she said aloud as she laid down the mascara brush and stared at her face in the mirror. It looked much prettier than usual, pinker and more alive. She wanted to slap it in exasperation.

'Remember how old you are and stop being such an idiot.'

She scrubbed the mascara off her eyelashes and cleaned her face with astringent lotion, almost glad when it stung her eyes. There was a knock at the front door before she had finished. Making a rude face at her newly pristine reflection, she walked slowly downstairs to admit Philip.

'Thank you,' he said as he unwound the scarf from about his neck and unzipped his jacket, adding as he looked round the small, square hall: 'This is gorgeous . . . much more glamorous than I'd expected.'

'Glamorous?' She laughed.

'Yes, it is,' he said looking appreciatively around him. 'There's absolutely none of that high-minded, dusty shabbiness we've come to know so well up at the Hall.'

When he stopped admiring the house and concentrated on Lavinia's face, blood started to thud in its little tubes all over her body. She met his eyes with difficulty, trying to ignore the physical sensations that were at once humiliating and heavenly.

'Would it amuse you to see the rest of the house?' she asked, managing to sound almost calm.

'I'd like that very much. And then where would you like to walk? I don't suppose we've got time to get as far as the abbey.'

'Not if you're going to be back for lunch. As you ought to be. You'll only cause an upset if you're not.'

Her mind was saying completely different things to him and she was half afraid and half hopeful that he knew what they were.

'Ah, but I'm out on licence.' He smiled. 'I told them I'd probably be away all day. No-one thought it at all odd. I'm known to be behaving badly just at the moment. They were probably just relieved to see the back of me.'

'Don't let's talk about them any more this morning,' said Lavinia quickly. 'We'll only start moaning and that would be a waste.'

'Would it?' Philip took a step towards her and then checked himself.

Lavinia knew that she ought to do something to stop the unspoken conversation that was starting to run between them. 'I think so,' she said aloud, almost sure that he knew that she knew. She had to turn away from the sight of his face then. Perhaps, she thought, if I show him the house where I have spent so long with Tom and the children we've had together, this absurd, delectable, dangerous feeling will go away. I hope it doesn't. But it must.

She pushed open the door to the kitchen, saying casually: 'This is where we spend most of the time. It's a bit untidy, but I'm fond of it.'

Philip looked towards the long windows that gave on to the garden at the far end of the kitchen, and sighed with pleasure. It was a glowing room, and it seemed to him to express everything about Lavinia that made her such easy company. It was practical, attractive, straightforward, colourful, and intelligently laid out. It also looked very comfortable.

'Quite frankly, I think Tom must be completely bonkers to spend so much of his time away from here.'

Lavinia, revelling almost as much in the easy slang as in his approval, thanked him and opened a door at the far end of the long kitchen, ushering him into the formal, cream-panelled room that ran along the garden side of the house and joined the kitchen to the drawing room.

He admired the old glass in the Chippendale corner cupboard and the one painting Tom had been allowed to remove from Saltley, a seventeenth-century Dutch still life of oranges with a lace handkerchief, a Delft bowl and a pewter jug. Lavinia had liked it the first time she had seen it and had been touched that Tom had remembered her spontaneous cry of pleasure when they came to furnish the Dower House. She still did not know what he had said to Flavia about it or why she had been prepared to hand it over, but one Friday evening when he appeared unexpectedly from London, he was carrying it under his arm. They had hung it together over the fire place, and whenever she looked at it Lavinia remembered the trouble he had taken for her. For a long time it had been her symbol of the strength of the bond that she was sure still existed between them.

Relieved to have been reminded of the bond, and of how important it was to her, she pointed out to Philip all the glories of the picture, particularly the way the unknown painter had managed the different sorts of shine on the oranges, the glazed pottery and the pewter.

'It's got a splendidly domestic kind of elegance, hasn't it?' he said, noticing precisely the quality she had always valued in it. 'Unpretentious, comfortable . . . warming.'

Lavinia had to turn away once more.

'What's the matter?'

Looking out of one of the two deep windows at the bleak winter garden, she held her hands tightly together and tried to speak casually: 'It's just that that's how

I've always thought about it. You like exactly the same things I do. I'm not used to that.' She looked at him, wanting to be able to breathe properly again, to feel ordinary. Eventually she said rather desperately: 'Come and see the drawing room.' She pushed open the third door in the room and shivered. 'We don't use it much, which is why it seems a bit chilly.'

'And, no doubt, why it's all so clean.' Philip looked at the pale-grey carpet, the ice-like chandelier, the spindly, expensive-looking Regency furniture, the white sofas, pink-dragged walls and formal grey-and-pink chintz curtains. He had a sudden horrible doubt.

'It's very impressive,' he said politely, 'but I must say, I like the kitchen better.'

'So do I.' Lavinia sounded heartfelt. 'And the study. You haven't seen that, but it's better than this: not so like the inside of a glacier. I went a bit over the top in here, trying to do something smart enough for constituency entertaining. You know, to impress possible voters. But it's not really me at all – or Tom, come to that. Come on.'

She could feel Philip relaxing as she took him into the red study and smiled at him over her shoulder. He did not smile back, but after a moment, he said: 'Yes, this is much more like you.' He came to stand very close behind her and she knew that she had only to lean back a little way and she would find herself supported. The prospect of not having to hold herself upright any longer was nearly as alluring as the thought of his touch on her skin. She stiffened all her muscles so that her back was very straight and her knees felt tightly gripped.

'Upstairs is just bedrooms and bathrooms,' she said as briskly as she could. Trying to gather her thoughts and control her sensations, she added: 'We'd better walk now. I'll go and get my boots. Could you put the guard in front of the hall fire for me?'

She left him on his own in the resinous emptiness of

the hall and returned a short time later with her feet encased in thick socks and boots, carrying her dark-blue Barbour and a scarlet scarf. He took the jacket from her and held it out so that she could slide her arms into it. When he had lifted it over her shoulders, he let his hands rest there for a moment.

Lavinia, still feeling as though she would not be able to breathe or think properly if she did not put some space between them, found that she could not move away. After a moment Philip turned her as though she were a child and zipped up the jacket for her, tucking the red scarf between the points of the corduroy collar.

'You look wonderful in that colour.'

'Thank you. Philip, we . . .'

'Don't say anything. Not yet. Let's just . . .' he hesitated and then frowned: 'Let's just walk.'

When she had locked the front door, they set off uphill behind the house towards the open moorland, in the opposite direction from Saltley and walked in silence, enjoying the stiff pull of their calf muscles and the wind in their faces. Lavinia had to work hard to keep up with his much longer legs, but out in the open air everything else seemed easier. She even managed to feel amused at the thoughts that had been doing such odd things to her senses. As they reached the flatter ground at the top of the long hill, she stopped and turned her back to the strengthening wind.

'One could almost lean back on it,' she said. 'Oh, I do love it up here.'

'What is it that pleases you so much?'

She looked at him, suddenly afraid, but she saw that he was only asking because he wanted to know, not because he wanted to use her answer as either ammunition or evidence for some new theory about her character.

'The openness and the emptiness,' she said. 'It makes no demands. It is what you see, and you can see it all.

There's nothing hiding behind corners ready to ambush you. I like that.'

'I know what you mean,' he said easily, taking her comments at face value. 'Quite different from an empty London street after dark.'

It was all right, Lavinia realized, and perfectly safe. She had been making a ridiculous fuss about a rare but perfectly simple kind of friendship. In her delight that they could have had the feelings that had been filling them both in the house and yet find that everything was still normal between them, she flung her arms wide and breathed in great draughts of the cold, rain-smelling air. She felt the wind biting at her teeth.

'You look like some ancient spirit of freedom with your arms spread out like that,' Philip said and something in his voice told her that it was not all right after all and not at all safe.

She let her arms drop to her sides at once. 'Up here, I always do feel free, although of course that's fantasy,' she said when she could speak normally. 'There's no real freedom for any of us. Oh, Philip.' Almost instantly, she added: 'Sorry.'

'Don't say that. It's here. It's us. I don't think we should apologize to each other.' He laughed briefly. 'Even though we both keep trying to stop the other talking about it as soon as one of us starts.'

'We do, don't we?' In her relief that they had started talking about the real thing, however obliquely, she smiled at him. 'Which is probably wise because it's all so frightfully unsuitable. I was incredibly happy about it until I saw what was really happening, and then today I thought we could still enjoy being happy while just ignoring the reason, but now that doesn't seem possible. And I don't quite see what we can do to put things back to where they were.'

'Must we?' he asked with a tenderness that she could hardly bear because she wanted it so much.

'Yes, we must,' she said with a huge effort. 'And I'm afraid that the more we say the more difficult that will be. Yet I long to talk to you about it. I want . . . Oh, I find I terribly want to know just exactly what you do feel and why and tell you . . . Oh, you know.'

He gripped her arms just above the elbows and made her look at him.

'It is real, isn't it? I wasn't absolutely sure that you felt it too, until just now. But you do, don't you?'

Lavinia nodded. 'But the feeling can't be for doing anything with,' she said inelegantly. 'Philip, it really can't. We must stop it here and now and not talk about it again. Sort of bury the feeling up here on the moor before we go back down to the family. We must.'

'But why?' He breathed deeply and, still looking at her, added more coolly: 'They do it all the time. We both know that. Why shouldn't we?'

Lavinia turned her head away, wondering if she could ever have had enough self-control to keep the whole thing unspoken and wishing that she had.

'Because for us it would be a betrayal,' she said at last, still not looking at him. Then she found some courage, faced him and said what she really meant. 'At least it would for me. It would mean too much. I couldn't take it as frivolously as they do and I don't know where it would lead us. And it seems that we're alike enough for me to think it would be the same for you. Perhaps there'd even be a bit of revenge added. I'd hate that, and I think you would, too. Or wouldn't you?'

'I don't think', he said carefully, watching her, 'that what I feel is any desire for revenge. It's much more fundamental than that. It's a recognition. I feel just at this moment as though I've always known you. I can't think why I didn't wait until I'd met you.'

'Philip,' she began and then could not go on. She felt as though she were suffocating.

101

He waited, still holding her arms, until she had worked out how to breathe normally and which words went with her thoughts.

'It's been too quick to be anything real. It's too pat. It has to have something to do with the fact that you and I are so different from them and yet so like each other. After all, just now both of us are needing something that we're not getting from them. It can't be more than that.'

He looked at her and once again she saw his tremendous obstinacy. She recognized it easily because it was hers too, not often used, usually forgotten, but always there at the base of her pliancy.

'It's a fairy tale, Philip,' she said, still trying to convince them both. 'We're not children to be taken in by one of those.'

'Even though you're the princess in the tower and I know I could rescue you?' he said whimsically, taking off his glove and touching her neck, sliding his fingers between her woollen scarf and her ear, pausing just below it and then running his fingers on until they reached her chin. His touch left a wake of tingling nerve ends under her skin.

Lavinia, feeling a sensation of immense relief that he had touched her, let herself stand still for a moment and accept it. There was such a strong current of communication flowing between them that it seemed as though neither of them would ever be able to misunderstand the other. In that moment words did not matter at all. She tried to persuade herself that everything that seemed so real was in fact illusion. It had to be. But she knew that it was not.

'That feeling was real, Lavinia.'

'The feeling may have been,' she said, clinging with difficulty to what she had to believe. 'But that doesn't mean that we can let ourselves have it again.'

'You don't believe that, though, do you?' His tone made it clear that he was not asking a question and she did not answer. 'Not really.'

He put a hand in his pocket and held out a small package wrapped in scarlet paper and tied with navy-blue ribbons. Lavinia felt a sudden panic as though some moving stairs under her feet had started to run at five times the normal speed, threatening to buck her off and mash her between their hidden cogwheels.

'It's all right. You don't need to look like that. I haven't remortgaged the house to buy you diamonds. It's nothing lavish, but I wanted you to unwrap it away from prying eyes. Do you mind so terribly that I'm giving you something?'

'No, of course not,' she said, reverting to her social voice. 'It's very kind of you. I'm just rather troubled because I haven't anything for you – apart from the family present, I mean, and that's just a . . . a kind of token.'

'Here.' He held the package out to her and she eventually took it, reluctant for all sorts of reasons to accept anything concrete from him.

Since he clearly wanted her to open it, she did so, revealing not the jewellery she had feared but a small piece of polished glass nestling in a bed of cottonwool. Puzzled, she pushed aside the stuffing and took the glass out. It was heavy and wonderfully smooth. Turning it between her fingers, she understood at last. It was a prism.

'If you keep it on your desk with your reading lamp shining through it, you'll always have a rainbow.'

'Yes.' She looked up at him, quite unable to say anything else.

After a long moment, he added: 'It'll be there to remind you that however certain they are that their ways are the only possible ones, yours are just as real, just as valuable.'

'Oh, Philip, I can't tell you . . .' Lavinia said, breaking off in her usual search for the right words. He looked worried and that spurred her explanation. 'I just can't tell you how much you've done for me.'

'And you for me.' His eyes were unfocused and she

103

wondered what he was thinking. Then he looked at her properly. 'You know, I'm beginning to think young Benedict might have been right about the rainbow, after all. I am a younger son, you see, and look what I've found.'

'I've never been called a pot of anything before, Philip,' said Lavinia laughing with him and grateful for the slackening of the tension between them. 'But thank you.'

'Do you talk to Tom like this?' he asked in a detached tone.

'No. Do you to Sasha?'

'I used to try, but it was as though I was talking in some language she did not understand.'

'Tricky, wasn't it?'

'So you tried as well.'

'For a while.' Lavinia paused, remembering the days of exaltation and terror that had been her experience of being in love with Tom at the beginning.

Philip held out his ungloved hands. She looked at them, noticing their strength, and her eyebrows jumped in shock before settling tightly across her face. Her teeth were hard against each other and she swallowed. To take his hands seemed to imply a declaration of some kind.

After a time he turned them over so that they became enquiring instead of demanding. When they started to quiver, she stuffed the box containing the prism in her pocket with the crumpled paper and the untied ribbons and put her hands in his. Not knowing what she wanted to do with them she stood stiffly in front of him. He guided all four hands to her waist and held her there.

Chapter 8

Returning to the Dower House alone, Lavinia felt as unsafe as a small boat with a dragging anchor. It was as though storm clouds were massing on the horizon, the swell was beginning to strengthen, and she had no purchase on the sea floor.

She wandered about the house, trying to fix herself back in her real life. Tom got in soon after five, as tired as the three children after their day's activities. They all decided to have baths and then a snooze to prepare them for the late night ahead and so she was left alone again, trying not to think.

When the children emerged from their beds just after eight and straggled downstairs to help lay and decorate the dining-room table, they seemed more serene than at any time since their arrival from London. Lavinia began to feel a little safer as she put the celebration food on the table and lit the six red candles in their Delft sticks.

For once Charles and Tammy did not fight, but competed instead in telling stories of riding triumphs and disasters as they ate. Rory forgot his seniority and his forthcoming solo and smiled pinkly in the soft light as he sat between his two parents, facing the younger children, and capped their stories with his own. Even Tom produced some of the latest malicious witticisms from the whip's office, and when Lavinia laughed he seemed to smile directly at her, as though he minded that it was she laughing with him and not anyone else.

When he reached out for one of the dishes ranged along the table to help himself to more prune-stuffed carp, she felt as though her anchor was beginning to grip again. Even though she knew it was absurd to see in Tom's approval of her food anything beyond simple pleasure, she could not help taking it as a sign of something more. She felt nearly as comforted as she would have been if he had told her everything that had been bothering him and let her in to the self that he kept so zealously apart from her.

For that moment she felt as though she did, indeed, have all of him. Her patience – and her deliberate suppression of the truth whenever she had felt irritable or unhappy – seemed to have been worthwhile. She felt her muscles relax and, looking down the table, saw that Tom was raising his glass of wine to her in a toast. It seemed like a reward for refusing to give in to the feelings Philip had been offering her that afternoon.

Gilded with unexpected happiness, Lavinia told the younger children to collect the dirty plates and, while Tom fetched cool Sauternes from the cellar, she and Rory brought in the pudding: individual dried-apricot and amaretti mousses with caramel tops.

They sat on over grapes, nuts and coffee and then, at eleven o'clock, set off for Saltley, to be ready for the sung mass that always began at half-past.

The small panelled chapel, which ran at right angles to the great hall, had apparently not been used for many years before Gerard became a priest. Until then, long deconsecrated, it had been used as a kind of boxroom, full of unwanted furniture and pictures that had split or needed reframing. Practising Christians among the family had always gone to the parish church in Helmsmoorside. But, soon after his ordination, Gerard had asked Flavia and Peter whether he could arrange to have the chapel consecrated again.

Once that had been done he had conducted private family services whenever he was up at Saltley. All the children born after the reconsecration had been christened in the chapel, and Dominic and Olivia had had their wedding there. The tradition of the Christmas midnight mass had been well established by the time Lavinia married Tom, and it was assumed that everyone staying in the house would attend. For the years when Gerard had been unable to get away from his duties at Christmas, Flavia had almost always managed to find an Anglican priest staying somewhere nearby who was prepared to take his place.

When Lavinia and her family got to Saltley, the chapel was lit only with candles and Gerard, wearing the ancient white-and-gold vestments that had been in the house for centuries, was waiting at the altar steps. Julia was playing the miniature organ as she had done ever since her fifteenth birthday, when she had taken over the responsibility from her mother.

When they were all settled Bendy sang the first verse of 'Once in royal David's city' from one of the choir stalls instead of processing up the short aisle as usual. But everything else was done as it always had been. As Rory lifted his face and began to sing his solo, Polly turned from her seat in the front pew on the right of the aisle to nod appreciatively to Lavinia. Rory sounded so certain, so perfect as he sang the plainsong Gloria that, unmusical though she was, Lavinia was extraordinarily moved. Tom leaned a little nearer so that his arm touched her shoulder.

This *is* where I belong, she told herself, despite what Philip and I felt today. My language may be different from Tom's, and there may be separateness between us, but that doesn't matter. I have a place here.

Ten-year-old Peter Wold was the thurifer that year and, taking his duties with complete seriousness, he released small puffs of pricklingly fragrant smoke into the atmosphere at all the right moments. Pippit had the bells and rang them with the requisite firmness at the Sanctus. No-one made any mistakes in the familiar ritual or in the complicated music and all those who had been confirmed fell in behind Flavia as she went up to the altar rail to take communion.

Lavinia, uncertain how much of it all she could believe, nevertheless followed them, telling herself that it was courtesy and a wish to ally herself with those who did believe, rather than hypocrisy. She did not know how much any of the Medworths really believed either. Sometimes she thought it was merely Gerard's profession and the existence of the chapel that made any of them even think of going to midnight mass at all; at others, she thought they might be searching for some certainty beyond even those that they already had. At her most cynical she had even wondered whether their adherence to the High Anglican rituals might be the result of wanting to keep their footholds on as many different professional ladders as possible.

But that night she was not feeling at all cynical. As she knelt at the rail between Tom and Polly, she wanted to believe in everything she heard and said. Remembering the words of the collect they had recited at the beginning of the mass, she found herself begging to be let off her feelings for Philip. Tom waited until she was ready and they walked back down the short aisle together.

Afterwards Dominic, who had a fine baritone, sang the first verse of 'Three kings from Persian lands afar' and then everyone else who could sing joined in. Lavinia merely listened and enjoyed the sound. She noticed that Sarah and Jocelyn were both mouthing the words but not letting out any tuneless singing that might draw criticisms down on them later. Lavinia was glad that neither she nor her two unmusical children felt the need for such pretence.

At the end of the service, when Gerard had spoken the blessing, they stood in silence as they did every year, while Pippit took the long candle snuffer to put out the flames around the altar. Then, once again led by Flavia, they walked out of the chapel. Pippit came last, snuffing out all the remaining candles and leaving the chapel dark except for the red sanctuary light.

Congregating at last before the fire in the Great Hall, they stood exchanging chat and ideas as loudly and excitedly as though they had all been parted for the previous seven days rather than cooped up together. Aubrey and Caroline brought in jugs of mulled wine from the kitchen while Frida and Julian followed with cocoa for the youngest children, and Meg and Jocelyn handed round the big trays of fudge. Tammy had announced that she was old enough for mulled wine, but having taken her first sip she surreptitiously handed her glass to her father and substituted a comforting mug of sweet cocoa.

'Hey, Meg, is it safe to eat the muscovado this year?' she called out with her mouth full of vanilla fudge.

'You little rotter! I only burned it once. It's delectable this year if you really want to know.' Meg laughed at her young cousin's cheeky face and added: 'So is the raisin, actually. I didn't make that, but I think it might be the best. Try some.'

Tammy needed no more urging and stood at Meg's side, peering at the round tray to find the biggest piece of fudge. Charles, Bendy and the two Wold children joined her and they soon seemed to be competing to see who could eat the most without feeling sick.

It was all so familiar and so safe and so pleasant that Lavinia began to feel secure again. When she found herself near Philip, she smiled at him easily and at Sasha, too, and anyone else who came to talk to her.

That night, back in the Dower House, Lavinia and Tom made love for the first time in months and she fell asleep knowing that the weird, wild, frighteningly desirable feelings that had threatened to swamp her as she stood with Philip's hands on her waist did not matter. What was important was the bond with Tom, and even Philip could not threaten that.

Philip would be all right in due course when he got over the shock of learning that Sasha wanted someone else as well, just as Lavinia herself had learned to be all right again. There was nothing, after all, to fear. A bit more warmth in the family could do nothing but good. Provided she and Philip did not step over their private frontiers into actual betrayal, what they felt for each other was neither wrong nor dangerous. She went to sleep happier than she had been for some time.

Disapproving so much of the acquisitiveness engendered by Christmas, the Medworths had made sure that none of their children had grown up expecting stockings, which meant that there was never anything to wake them early on Christmas Day. After their musical exertions, not to speak of the midnight feast of fudge and cocoa, they tended to sleep late. That year was no exception and Lavinia was able to take a tray of toast and coffee up to her bedroom for a peaceful breakfast with Tom without having her concentration on him diverted by any of the children.

He kissed her as she handed him a big cup of strong coffee and hot milk, and she smiled. When things went well between them they went very well. That had always been so and it made up for all the rest.

'I've got a public present for you downstairs, but I thought you ought to have a private one, too.' Tom put down the big blue-and-white cup, which they had bought years ago during a trip to Denmark, and reached into the drawer of his bedside table for a small package. 'Here.'

Lavinia took it with a feeling of familiar reassurance and none of the reluctance she had felt when Philip had offered her his present. This was appropriate, normal and exactly how Christmas should be between a husband and wife. Smiling, she picked off the Sellotape that held the edges of the shiny blue paper together and revealed a flat black leather box about four inches square. She pushed its clasp and the lid sprang open.

Inside was an antique bracelet. With its delicate leaf-shaped diamond links, it was one of the most beautiful pieces of jewellery she had ever seen. It made her feel sick.

She knew exactly what a present of such magnificence meant. Tom had often given her jewellery, but it was usually modest. Antique diamonds were something quite out of the ordinary. They seemed to suggest a mixture of guilt and gratitude. She could not bear to think that he had bought her something so beautiful and so obviously expensive as a kind of payment for her outwardly calm acceptance of his London love affairs or – worse – a bribe to persuade her not to make a fuss about some new one that was about to break.

Coming on top of her own turmoil and the peaceful resolution she had felt overnight, Tom's guilt-present seemed even more horrible than its few predecessors. Lavinia pushed the lid of the box down again, looked up to smile at Tom and thanked him, adding: 'It's quite magnificent.' Hearing the flatness in her voice, she made a greater effort and added more brightly: 'I've never seen one quite like it. Where did you find it?'

'A little shop in Edinburgh when I had to go up there last month. I wanted . . . I thought you deserved a proper present. I don't often say . . .'

'It's all right, Tom. You don't have to say anything. It's very kind of you to give me something so splendid.'

He twisted round so that he could kiss her again and she let him do it. After all her lectures to Philip about the best way to take Medworth infidelity, she could hardly start shouting and throwing things. As she had told Philip during one of their conversations in the tower, she had chosen her job of making Tom's life as easy as possible. No-one had forced her to take it. Gracefully accepting over-lavish or unwanted guilt presents was simply part of that job. Besides, she had her pride and she could not bear the thought of begging for something that Tom could not – or did not want to – give her.

The strong coffee helped as it usually did and she was able to greet her children with most of the cheerfulness they expected at Christmas. After their late, and deliberately meagre breakfast, they loaded the still-wrapped presents into the back of the Volvo, strapped themselves in and waited to be driven to Saltley.

'Will you drive?' said Lavinia, zipping up her Barbour as Tom locked up the house.

'Sure. Are you all right? You seem a bit subdued.' He seemed concerned and genuinely unaware of any reason for her to feel less than exuberant.

'I'm fine,' she said and then thought of an accept-able excuse. 'I must have slightly overdone the mulled wine last night. I've got a bit of a headache. But as it's self-inflicted it doesn't count.'

'Maybe, but you ought to take something for it. It's going to be noisy and frenetic today. There's no point suffering if you don't have to.'

Not wanting to play the martyr, she went back upstairs to take a couple of aspirin, telling herself that she was being irrational as well as sentimental. Tom's affair must be over, since the lavish presents came only afterwards, and therefore the time to have been feeling kicked in the face had gone. He never made love with her when he was in the process of an affair with someone else. Last night must have been as much a signal that he was back with her as was the bracelet.

112

He greeted her with a smile when she emerged from the house and treated her with all his usual consideration for the rest of the day.

She spent most of it concentrating on the surface things, seeing that the vulnerable cousins were all right; trying not to notice Flavia's increasingly sharp gibes; watching Philip sometimes and testing her resolve to stick by her marriage; doing everything she could to keep the day smooth and everyone happy because that was the only way to keep the anger and the hurt inside herself.

Everything went off quite well. All the presents seemed to please their recipients, the traditional Christmas food was well cooked and pleasant, fights broke out only between Tammy and Charles and Pippit and Peter, and they were soon reconciled. Every tradition was respected. Lavinia played her part as well as usual, accepted compliments and returned them, ate reasonably well, laughed at suitable moments, took her part in the afternoon charades and once even made Flavia herself laugh with a neat joke.

And all the time, running through Lavinia's head was the question: am I being a coward or just sensible?

She knew that she had a good life and a very civilized one and asked herself what point there would be in making a fuss. She also knew that she did not want to leave Tom, even though she did not know why, and she was not arrogant enough to believe she had any right to try to change him.

Just before supper the effort of pretending that everything was all right grew too much for her and she slipped away from the noise to climb up to the tower. She turned on the desk lamp and put her prism underneath it, trying to decide what she ought to do and how best to start.

She was still standing there, twisting the heavy glass this way and that, watching the rainbow form and disappear and reform, when Philip appeared in the doorway. He said her name gravely.

113

Looking up, she said: 'Hello.'

'What's happened? You seem quite different. Is it my fault? I didn't mean to make life any more difficult for you. That's the last thing I wanted.'

'I know. And you haven't. This is nothing terribly new.' She had been determined not to tell him anything about it, but he looked so worried and apologetic that she had to reassure him.

'Tom just gave me this.' She held out her wrist and the bracelet fell from beneath the cuff of her sweater, one of the diamonds catching on the rough wool before it let go and fell over her wrist bone, glinting in the light.

'Guilt?' said Philip after a long pause.

'I think so. I'd half suspected it at times, but I told myself I was being unnecessarily paranoid. Then when I'd got all relaxed and cheerful – whang! Down it came again. Or up or whatever. Sorry, I'm not making much sense, I know.'

'Does it change things for us?'

She half-closed her eyes and looked away, shaking her head. 'It ought to be so unimportant,' she said eventually. 'And yet it isn't. I can't quite think why. I've had plenty of practice. Nothing is any different from what I said to you yesterday, and yet and yet . . .'

'Would a hug help?'

'Probably,' she said, beginning to smile. He took her in his arms and she leaned against his broad chest. He made no attempt to kiss her and they stood leaning against each other's warmth.

Neither of them heard the footsteps on the stairs and did not realize that they were not alone until Tom said: 'Oh, I'm sorry. I didn't mean to interrupt.'

Philip took his arms away and stood beside Lavinia, part champion and part embarrassment.

'What is it, Tom?' she asked with difficulty.

114

'I just came to see if you were all right, that's all. And since you clearly are, I'll go down again.' Tom smiled at her, looking as though he were taking particular care to be polite.

'No, don't go. Philip, I'll see you later.'

'Are you sure?'

She nodded. When he had had time to get down the spiral stairs, Tom said: 'That was a poor moment to have chosen to come up. I'm sorry.'

'I wish . . .' Lavinia began and then stopped.

'Can I help?' He sounded diffident. 'I'd like to.'

'I know,' she said. 'That's what makes it all so hard. We all want to help each other and none of us can because we look at things so differently.'

'I'm not sure I understand.' Tom was frowning in a way that made him look almost like a stranger.

'That's what I mean. Philip and I are both feeling a bit bruised at the moment because of what's been going on in the bits of your and Sasha's lives that we can have no part of, and we were exchanging a bit of simple comfort just then.'

'Ah. But there isn't anything to make you need comfort,' said Tom, coming into the room and holding out a hand. Lavinia took it as she always did accept any overture he made.

'Perhaps not,' she said in her most reasonable voice. 'But do you know? I find I want to make a great huge screaming scene.'

'Why?'

'Because . . .' She broke off, reluctant to start something whose end she could not see. Then, having started, she thought she had to try to get it out for once. 'Because I'm jealous of whoever she is – or was – and because I don't like being bribed or rewarded for good behaviour.'

'It wasn't a bribe,' he said very seriously. 'Or a reward. If you're talking about the bracelet, that is.'

'Yes.'

'I saw it in Edinburgh. I knew that it would suit you – as it does. And I wanted to give you a major kind of present, for all sorts of reasons. There wasn't anything sinister in it.' He frowned again and she saw that he was actually hurt, which seemed ironic and really rather unfair. 'The last thing I wanted to do when I bought it was to distress you, Lavinia. The very last.'

'Tom, I never ask this kind of thing, but do you still sleep with Teresa?'

'Not for some time.' He spoke abruptly, sounding angry. She wondered if he felt that she had invaded his privacy and decided that he probably did.

'Anyone else?'

'Sometimes. Not at the moment.'

'Why?' At the sight of his expression she shook her head. 'No, it's all right. You don't have to answer that. You've told me before and so have all your siblings, and your mother, too.'

'But why do you mind?' He sounded so reasonable then that she did her best to bury her anger, trying to find an acceptable answer. After a while, she picked one feeling out of the swirling sediment that was clouding her whole mind.

'Because it belittles me.'

'Not in my eyes. Nothing could. You know that I think you're wonderful.' He smiled, but he still looked hurt. 'I keep telling you that.'

'But clearly I'm not quite wonderful enough.'

'Oh, don't take it like that.' There were hints of patiently restrained irritability in his voice that made him sound like a kinder version of Flavia herself. Lavinia tried not to hear it. 'It isn't so.'

'This doesn't get us anywhere,' she said in frustration, knowing that she was hurting him nearly as much as he had hurt her and yet quite unable to find a way for either of them to escape it. Helplessly, blaming both herself and him, she added: 'I knew it wouldn't. I can't think why I started it. Talking's always a mistake. We'd better go back down.'

'Not while you're this miserable,' he said, holding out his arms. 'Can't I comfort you since Philip's not here any more?'

With difficulty Lavinia stood her ground. She could not bear the thought of covering it all up again and pretending that everything was all right. It was not. 'No, I don't think so, thank you. Not just now.' She turned and switched off the desk light, quenching the rainbow. 'Let's go down.'

'I do love you, you know,' he said as she passed him on the way to the door. 'And respect you and admire you and like you.'

'Yes, I know you do.'

'Isn't that enough for *you*?'

'Not quite,' she said when she had managed to absorb the shock of his sarcasm.

'Then what more can I do?' There was definitely anger in his voice then, a kind of reined-in exasperation that almost made her lose her hold over herself.

'Be faithful, perhaps? No, that's not quite right.' She thought of her conversation with Sasha over the bedmaking eight days before and added lightly: 'I don't want you to struggle for it. I suppose what I want is for you to *want* to be faithful to me. It's all right, you don't need to look like that. I know it's asking far too much.'

'Why now? Why this time? I don't understand. You've never talked like this before and nothing's any different now.'

Except perhaps, she said to herself, that Philip has shown me the possibility of the kind of life that I always thought I'd find with you because I loved you so. It would be much easier to love him because he means the same as I when he uses the words I use. His language is my language. Yours is strange. He's stirred up the tricky feelings I thought had sunk out of reach and I find that they're all still there after all, as fresh as ever. Damn it: I want you to see me as I am and value me for what I am and not what you think I should be. I want you to give yourself up to me as I have given myself up to you, and you won't. Can't. And there's nothing to be done about it. There's no point talking about it. If I want you at all, I've got to accept you as you are. If I can't accept it then all that effort and misery was for nothing. And that would be too much to bear. Perhaps *that's* why I want to stay married to you.

'Don't worry about it all so much,' said Tom kindly as he followed her down the steep, twisting stairs. 'Christmas is an odd time. It makes us all a bit irrational and over-emotional.'

'Perhaps that's it,' she said aloud, slotting neatly back into her appointed part: reasonable, accepting correction, well behaved.

'You'll be all right tomorrow. The headache probably hasn't helped. I'll get you some more aspirin.'

Chapter 9

Lavinia woke the following morning to see Tom inching out from under the duvet beside her and creeping across the carpet to his dressing room. Not wanting to talk while she still felt so muddled, she lay pretending to doze and waited to see what would happen.

Half an hour later he returned, dressed in his white hunting breeches, socks, shirt, gold-pinned stock and waistcoat, carrying a breakfast tray. When she saw what he had put on it, she looked up at him helplessly.

He had taken great trouble, brewing strong coffee in the smaller of their two espresso pots and heating milk to go with it. On one of the best plates was a warm, napkin-wrapped croissant. He must have foraged in the freezer for it and taken the trouble to heat up the oven so that he could defrost it. A square of unsalted butter and a heap of her favourite greengage jam filled matching shell-like silver dishes. A clean white linen napkin was folded at the side of the tray. In one of the pockets at the side of it was an envelope. She reached for the envelope as he laid the tray over her knees.

'Don't open it yet,' he said quickly. 'We'll be off in a while and leave you in peace for a decent rest. You can read it while we're out.'

'All right. Thank you for this, Tom. It looks gorgeous. I hope you have a good day. You will . . .'

'Take care of the kids? Of course I will. But you really needn't worry too much. They all ride well and they're used to hunting now. None of us will be in at the kill; we rarely are. We'll all be fine. You spend the morning in bed and have a long bath and then you'll be fine again too.'

He smiled at her from the door, but his eyes were not focused on her. When he had gone she drank her coffee slowly, savouring its bite and strength. All the children looked in to her room before they left to show off their hunting gear. She thought they looked wonderful, as they nearly always did on hunting days. Even Tammy was immaculately tidy, her boots gleaming and her usually rough hair neatly netted under her velvet cap.

Lavinia reached for her dressing gown and got out of bed to wave them off. Tom, by then fully and magnificently dressed in his red coat and mahogany-topped boots with their steel spurs, blew her a kiss and advised her to go back to bed, finish her breakfast and recover her strength. Smiling, she called back her thanks, and watched them drive off. As she went back upstairs, she muttered: 'But I am not an invalid. Like Philip, I'm angry and I'm damned if I want to be made to feel that it's my inadequacy that's caused the trouble. It is not.'

Back in bed, she poured a second cup of coffee and opened Tom's envelope to read:

My dearest Lavinia,

I am horrified that you should be so miserable – and about something as unimportant as the past interlude. You never seemed to mind any of them before and it never occurred to me that you were hiding such a ferment of distress. Finding myself hurt by the amount you've been concealing, I am tempted to ask why you never told me,

120

but I suspect that would need a fairly complicated answer. All I can say is that I am sorry.

I have always loved you. Just as I have always wanted you to be happy. I thought that you were – apart from your exasperation with my failings. I hope you will be again. I really do want you to be happy. Believe that, please, Lavinia.

Tom

Forgetting that she had already watched the car leaving for Saltley, Lavinia flung back the duvet and in her nightgown and bare feet ran back downstairs calling Tom's name. There was no answer.

In the kitchen she pulled out a chair and sat down, rereading the letter over and over again. It seemed extraordinary. The idea that he should have thought her exasperated with him completely threw her. She had spent a large part of the past fourteen years trying to be what he wanted and subduing herself in an effort to avoid crowding him with her needs. How could he have felt anything so different?

Shivering as the cold of the quarry-tiled floor bit into her bare feet, she returned to her bedroom to dress. The sight of the remains of the lavish breakfast tray he had brought her was almost too much and she seized a pad of paper and a felt-tipped pen Tammy had left by her bed and sat down to write an answer.

It took her all morning. She produced draft after draft that had to be ripped up and thrown into the kitchen bin. By noon, dressed at last, she had probably written nearly three thousand words, words that had dragged her thoughts out of her mind, exaggerated them, muddled, and ultimately clarified them.

Eventually she simplified the outpourings and edited them down to two pages, which she believed contained nothing ambiguous and yet explained some of her most ambiguous feelings. On rereading it, she felt that the letter was very cold, but she could not think how to warm it up without fudging the things that had to be said. And, having reached the stage at which they were at last exchanging words about their real feelings, she could not be anything other than completely frank.

Tom,

You asked why I have never told you that I disliked your London love affairs. It did not occur to me that you would think I might feel anything *but* dislike for them. I thought you knew but needed them more than I disliked them.

Also, I don't think that I believed the dislike was really justified until Philip told me how he felt about his situation with Sasha and whoever it is she's with at the moment . . . Much the same as me, you see, which has made me realize that perhaps it's reasonable to feel like that. It sounds weird, but I have put so much energy into trying to be as much like your family as I possibly could – and then into not minding that I was not managing to be very like them at all – that I tried to share your ideas about infidelity, too. I thought that my misery about it all was because I was being weedy.

I think I was also afraid of what I might be told about myself if I let anyone see how much I minded.

I can't imagine why you should think that I have ever felt exasperation at anything like a 'failing' of yours. Tom, the only anger I have ever felt has been when my feelings have been taken wrong or belittled (oh, that word again! Perhaps I'm just vain and mind because of that).

We both seem to have been misunderstanding each other. Perhaps we could try to talk now and sort it all out. Will you try?

Lavinia reread her draft and decided that, inadequate though it might be and possibly hurtful, there was nothing more she could do to improve it. She understood why Tom had not wanted her to read his letter until he had left the house. She would have hated to stand over him while he read hers. It seemed important that he should have time to think about what she had written and work out what his response should be before either of them said anything.

She was astonished to see that it was already nearly one o'clock and she tried to remember whether there was anything she ought to have been doing up at Saltley. As far as she knew there was nothing until her share of the tea-making for the returning riders. The emptiness of the hours until then frightened her and she tried to think of a way to fill them. Basic housework seemed the easiest and so she cleaned the entire top floor of the Dower House before walking over to Saltley.

By four o'clock everything but the teapots, the soup, the garlic bread and the eggs was spread out on the table in the great hall and a huge fire was sending crackling, spitting flames up the chimney. Loveday, who hated hunting, had defrosted the scones and set out dishes of butter, jam and honey; Philip had carted traysful of cups and plates from the kitchen to the Great Hall; and Lavinia had turned two long brown loaves into sandwiches filled with cream cheese and chutney, cold turkey and cranberry sauce, and curried egg mayonnaise. The basket of eggs to be boiled was waiting beside a pan of simmering water and slices of bread and cheese lay ready for toasting near the grill. The garlic bread was already in the oven and the huge stockpot full of soup waited to be heated at the back of the cooker.

The first Medworths to appear were Caroline and Bendy, who had followed the hunt in one of the Landrovers. He was full of frustration at not having been able to ride. At the sight of them, Philip said he would make the first pot of tea and went off to the kitchen. Great-aunt Elfrida, sitting in her wheelchair by the fire with Olivia beside her, asked wistfully how the day had gone.

'Not too bad. A bit fast and furious for us to see much. They found very early,' said Bendy and launched into an enthusiastic and highly technical description of every view and check he had seen and every hedge and gate he had watched being jumped.

'Did anyone come off?' asked Lavinia when he drew breath.

'Lots of people,' said Caro. 'No-one was hurt as far as we could see.'

'Jolly muddy, though,' said Bendy through a mouthful of scone, cream and honey.

'Benedict!' said his mother. 'You ought to wait until everyone here is ready to start.'

'Sorry, Mum. I was hungry.'

Before anyone could comment there was a gust of cold air followed by Jocelyn, Sarah, Meg in dreadfully muddy breeches with her hair all over the place, and Nicko.

'Goody! Tea. I'm frozen stiff,' said Meg.

'And bruised by the look of you,' said Loveday over her shoulder as she went to greet her husband, who had a long scratch down his right cheek and a tear in one of his expensive boots.

'Better?' he asked her.

'Much. I had a marvellously long sleep after lunch. You all right?'

'Couldn't be better. It was a terrific day. Are there any eggs?'

'Oh, lord yes,' said Lavinia. 'I've been forgetting my duties in all the excitement. Five minutes. Have some sandwiches first.'

'On the other hand, I might bath,' he said, 'and take advantage of the hottest water.' He grabbed two sandwiches and took them off upstairs, chewing as he went.

'I'll go and do the eggs,' said Loveday kindly. 'I know you'd rather wait for your brood.'

Lavinia blew her a kiss just as Philip whispered into her left ear: 'Solidarity of the in-laws.'

She had to wait until nearly five for her children, who came chattering in with their grandmother and Josie. Charles looked completely exhausted despite his excitement and Rory had splashes of mud around his eyes, which merged in with the scoop of blue-grey shadow that tiredness had painted under them. But Tammy was as wide awake and voluble as usual. Her hairnet had been torn and a funny-looking stiff bunch of hair was pushing out of the hole, there was a lot of mud down the left side of her breeches and coat, which suggested that she too had come off, but she looked undamaged.

She caught sight of her mother and darted across the room to stand in front of her, stinking of horse, scarlet-faced with cold and excitement, and filthy. She lifted her chin to tell excitely of the wonderful moment when Cupcake had cleared an absolutely enormous gate.

Lavinia listened in pleasure to Tammy's enthusiasm, occasionally looking away from her bright face to check that the two boys were all right as they recovered themselves with food and liquid. When Tammy had at last sucked all the triumph and drama out of her moment of glory, Lavinia stood back for a moment to look at her. 'It sounds utterly staggering,' she said with enough emphasis to satisfy even Tammy. 'Did Dad see?'

'No. He was somewhere else. I haven't seen him for ages.'

'Didn't he come back with you?'

'No. Granny-Flavia brought us back.'

Suppressing a sharp but wholly absurd terror, Lavinia looked around the big room. Her shoulders relaxed a little as she noticed that there were still several important gaps. John Hogarth was not back, nor was Frida. Julian was chatting to his two daughters, who still looked splendid in their full hunting kit, despite having sweated off most

125

of their elaborate make-up and being nearly as splattered with mud as the rest, but there was no sign of Aubrey or Gerard and Polly. It was not surprising that the two Flemmings were still out. They could not afford to hunt anywhere except at Saltley, where Flavia provided horses for all the family, and they always tended to stay until the very end. It was not unknown for Tom to let his children ride without him, but it was odd enough to work on Lavinia's agitation.

'Mummy, you're not eating anything,' said Rory, coming over to her with a plateful of sandwiches.

'That's kind,' she said. 'But I haven't been making myself hungry over all those hedges and walls and gates and things. Besides, I nibbled all afternoon while I was making the sandwiches.'

'They're great, you know.'

'Good. Did you enjoy the day?'

'It was excellent. Although old Charles was a bit of a clot.'

'Was he? What did he do?'

'He'll tell you. Better than me sneaking.'

'All right. What happened to Dad?'

'I don't know.' Rory did not look at all anxious, which reassured Lavinia. 'He was talking to Uncle Aubrey at the meet and they set off together and I sort of tried to keep the little ones out of his way and, you know, keep an eye on them so that he could have a good fast day without worrying about any of us. I heard him telling you he needed lots of fast runs.'

'Yes, he did. But it's getting late. Oh, there's Aubrey. I'll be back in a minute, Rory.'

She left him by the fire, eating the sandwiches he had meant for her, but by the time she reached the great doorway, she saw that the newcomers were only Aubrey and John Hogarth.

'Where's Tom?' she said at once.

126

'Give us a minute, Lavvy,' said John Hogarth. 'We're aching and frozen and fiendishly hungry.'

'Are you worried about him?' said Aubrey, stripping off his gloves. 'Why?'

'A bit. I'm not sure. No-one seems to have seen him for ages. Rory saw him riding with you at one stage but . . .'

'Lavinia, Tom's been hunting this country on Boxing Day ever since he was seven and a half. He's not going to get into trouble.'

'Then where d'you suppose he is? Nearly everyone else is back.'

'In the bath, I expect, at the Dower House so that he gets plenty of hot water. We all know that only the first three or so get it anything but tepid here.'

'I didn't even think of that. Oh, thank you, Aubrey. Sorry to be hysterical.'

'It's not like you. Has something happened?'

Thinking of the letter Tom had left her, Lavinia was tempted to say 'yes', but she did not want to betray him to any of his analytical relations and so she shook her head briefly and returned to the tea table. Loveday was peering into one of the four brown teapots.

'Do we need more water?' asked Lavinia brightly.

'Yes, but you don't need to come. What's the trouble?' asked Loveday.

'I'm not sure. I've got the most awful feeling that something horrible has happened, but I've no evidence for it. Aubrey thinks I'm loopy.' Lavinia suddenly wondered whether her fears were simply the result of a hangover from the first major anger she had ever expressed to Tom. That was possible. She breathed more easily.

'Are you worried about the children?' Loveday, having none of her own, was not particularly conscious of which child was where.

'They're all safe and sound. It's Tom. I'm just going to ring home. Oh, no. If he's in the bath, he won't get out to

127

answer it. Oh, Loveday . . . No. Let's get the kettles and hope.'

'You're all over the place. Hadn't you better have some whisky to calm you down?'

'I hate it.'

Lavinia went to telephone the Dower House, deciding that if she rang over and over again without waiting for the recorded message on the answering machine, Tom would realize that she needed an answer and get out of the bath to find out whether there were an emergency. But nothing happened. On her sixth attempt, she merely dictated a brief message into the machine and then went back to join the others. Philip came to stand beside her. 'They tell me you're worried about Tom.'

'Yes, I am. It may be silly, but I've hardly ever known him let the children come home without him, and it sounds as though no-one's seen him for hours.'

'Rory's older now. Tom may have thought he could escort them safely. Wait until Polly and Gerard are back and then panic.'

'I'll do my best.' Lavinia put a hand to her aching forehead.

'Eat something and you'll feel better. Even if you're not hungry, it'll help. Come on. Cake or brownies or one of your own sandwiches?'

Chapter 10

By eight o'clock even the Medworths were beginning to worry. Aubrey suggested that Tom might have ridden home with a Mrs Anlaby, with whom he had been seen several times during the day. It was quite possible, Aubrey said lightly, that Tom might have accepted an invitation for a drink or decided to make sure she got home safely since she was out with the hunt for only the second time since moving to Yorkshire and lived not far from Saltley.

There was something about the way Aubrey looked as he mentioned Mrs Anlaby's name that made Lavinia think she might be more than simply a hunting acquaintance of Tom's. She glanced at Philip, whose hazel eyes were full of sympathy. Sasha watched them both without showing any emotion of any kind and then turned back to Aubrey to say: 'I know Sally Anlaby. Why don't I give her a ring and find out?'

'Would you? That'd be great,' said Lavinia, trying to deal with her unpleasantly gyrating emotions. Making a great effort, she did not follow Sasha to the telephone and hover while she made her call, but she could not stop herself rushing forwards when her sister-in-law emerged from the little telephone room off the hall. Sasha was frowning.

'Well?' Flavia demanded from her chair by the fire before Lavinia could say anything.

129

'Sally says she lost sight of Tom after Drover's Ditch and never caught another glimpse of him. He's certainly not with her.'

'Well, that's not particularly surprising,' said Aubrey heartily. Behind his forced smile, he looked so worried that Lavinia could hardly bear to watch his face. 'It was so fast and such a big field that anyone might have got mislaid.'

'I saw Daddy later than that,' said Tammy, coming to stand close to her mother and pressing against her thigh. She looked up, trying to reassure Lavinia, who leaned towards her gratefully. 'He showed me how to make Cupcake not be fazed by the wall at High Mill, and that was much later than Drover's Ditch.'

'Was it? Oh, thank you, Tammy,' said Lavinia, kissing her netted hair. 'And after that? Did you see him again?'

'No.' Her eyes grew rounder and her mouth tighter as she tried to remember. 'No, I don't think so.'

'What time were you at High Mill?'

'I don't know.'

'About three,' said John Hogarth, reaching out to touch Tammy's head in languid reassurance. She looked up at him gratefully.

'Did anybody see him after that? I didn't.' John's eyes were shut as he concentrated on the past few hours. 'No, I'm sure I didn't see him after he jumped the wall at the south boundary of Salt Farm and that was before Tammy's encounter.'

No-one else could remember seeing Tom after that either. Flavia started to speak and then stopped. Lavinia saw that her face was much paler than usual and her eyes looked blank. For once she had nothing to say. Sasha disappeared back into the telephone room and returned twenty minutes later, saying that she had rung up all their friends and no-one had seen Tom later than Tammy when he gave her the impromptu lesson at High Mill.

Then they all turned as they heard the front door flung open and moved forwards, but it was only Rory standing there, his face pale-grey under the mud splashes and his eyes wide open. He was panting and there was sweat on his face as he tried to speak. 'I went to the stable in case there was any sign, and Henchman's there,' he said when he could make his voice work.

'In the yard?' said Aubrey at once. 'Loose? What about the tack?'

'He was still saddled . . . sweating and foaming. Janice took him into the box, but I thought you ought to see before she did anything else.'

'Good for you. That was sensible,' said Lavinia, sounding almost calm. But she reached the doorway before anyone else. 'Show me.'

They ran side by side, slipping over the cobbles in the yard, dreadfully cold but not even noticing it. 'There he is, Mum,' said Rory, pointing towards Henchman's box and clearly all too aware of the implications of the horse's return. 'Dad must have come off. He'd never have left Henchman out in the cold in this state. Never. However tired he was or . . . anything.'

'No, I know,' said Lavinia, watching Janice, the groom, running her hand down the big bay's legs. Steam was rising from the animal and he was breathing fast, tossing his head and making the bit jangle. 'Is there anything on the saddle or the stirrup leathers to show what might have happened?'

'Nothing, Mrs Medworth,' said Janice as she straightened up. 'He must have just come off somewhere.'

'But he wouldn't have let go his rein, Mum. He just wouldn't,' said Rory.

'No, I know.'

Henchman was clearly both distressed and frightened, but even when he kicked out sideways, she did not move away. Rory, holding the reins just above the bit and

131

stroking Henchman's nose, murmured comfortingly, trying to keep the big bay as calm as possible. Janice moved out of the way as a group of Medworths arrived. Lavinia also yielded her place, which was taken by Aubrey.

John Hogarth wrapped a coat he had brought with him around her shoulders and hugged her. She shivered violently.

'He'll be all right. As Aubrey said, he knows this country well.'

'But something's happened to him, John. We must find him tonight. If he's unconscious – or just immobile – he can't stay out there in this cold. Oh, God, and now it's snowing!'

The first few flakes settled on them and danced before their eyes. 'We have to get a search going.'

'I agree, Lavinia,' said Aubrey, emerging from the relative warmth of the box. 'Janice will unsaddle Henchman and see to him now. We'd better go back into the house and discuss with my mother what's best to do. Come along, Lavinia. You were right to be anxious. But don't worry too much. We'll get him back.'

'Yes,' she said politely, although she knew quite well that even Aubrey could not possibly guarantee his brother's safety.

Back in the Great Hall, John pushed the tea things down the table to make space for a large-scale Ordnance Survey map that Flavia had fetched from her study, and Philip weighted the edges with knives and spoons so that it would lie flat.

'Here's where we found first,' said Aubrey, pointing.

'Then we galloped off towards the north,' said Tammy, leaning over his arm and putting her face between him and the map.

'Yes, but pipe down now, will you?' said Aubrey with reasonable kindness. Even so, Tammy quickly stepped back and looked as though she had been sent off the field by the Master for some dreadful solecism. She cast a scared look at her mother, who did her best to smile reassuringly.

Aubrey put the point of a pencil against the map, saying: 'That's the wall where I last saw him. We went on to Drover's Ditch and Salt Farm, but no-one saw him after Tammy's wall here at High Mill. I propose that we take the Landrovers and storm torches and see what we can find there.'

'What about the police?' asked Philip.

'No,' said Flavia with much of her old force. Her colour was better, but her eyes still looked worried.

'I think that's premature, too,' said Aubrey. 'The police know he's up here, of course, and as soon as we ring they'll pull out all the stops, but I think we should see what we can do first. Tom wouldn't thank us for over-reacting if he's merely come off and got stuck somewhere, perhaps with a broken ankle. The last thing he needs now is any extra publicity about his hunting. If we make a fool of him over this and it gets into the press, he'll be out of the government at the next reshuffle. I doubt he'd get another chance and we can't do that to him. Now, who's coming with me?'

'I certainly am,' said Lavinia. She understood and agreed with what Aubrey had said about publicity, but she wanted to do whatever could be done and quickly. 'No, Rory, I think you should stay here with the other two.'

'Oh, Mummy, must we stay?' wailed Tammy. 'Why can't we come? We know the country better than you. You've never ridden over it. You don't know anything about hunting or horses. You weren't even there today. We were.'

'That's exactly why, Thomasina. You've had a long day already,' said Flavia with the automatic assumption of authority that Lavinia had so often resented. For once she was grateful.

'I'll be staying and you can keep me and your Aunt Olivia company,' Flavia went on, 'and so can Jocelyn and Bendy, and Sarah and Josie, too.'

Tammy scowled and moved away to kick the nearest wall with her muddy boots.

'Thank you, Flavia,' said Lavinia warmly as soon as Tammy was out of earshot. 'I'd never have persuaded her to give in without the most tremendous fuss. I'm really grateful.'

Flavia looked her up and down with an expression of the utmost disdain. 'It's perfectly simple to organize children when they respect you and impossible if they don't.'

Lavinia turned away without a word. She told herself that Flavia could not have meant to sound quite so insulting. It was possible that in her obvious anxiety for Tom she was not even aware of the implication that her contempt for Lavinia was shared by Tammy and the other two children. But it took Lavinia several minutes to regain enough self-control to concentrate on what was happening around her. Eventually she realized that Aubrey was giving a series of efficient orders to his rescue team.

He divided them up between the three Landrovers, deputing Sasha, Julian, Dominic and John Hogarth to ride. There were enough fresh horses for them and he decided that there might be places inaccessible to the vehicles that ought to be searched. Caroline went off to fetch the powerful storm torches that were kept in the games room, Frida hurried to the kitchen to heat up some of the leftover soup and pour it into a vacuum flask, while Philip assembled an emergency medical kit.

'Lavinia, what about boots and waterproof gear?' he said as he was checking his stocks of morphine and syringes. 'Have you got any here? You mustn't go out like that in this weather.'

'No, but . . .'

'There are plenty of spares in the cloakroom,' said Sasha. 'Why not find some that fit?'

Muffled against the cold, equipped for every foreseeable event, the fourteen of them set off and only a short time later, Lavinia was being bucketed over the moor, hanging on to the edge of her seat with one hand and Philip's knee with the other. The Landrover's headlights shot up to light the falling snow one minute and plunged downwards into the heather the next. She was too frightened for Tom to feel sick and only wanted Aubrey to drive more recklessly. He stopped just short of the wall where he had last seen Tom and ordered his passengers out.

'If he came off here, the last thing we ought to risk is driving over him. Take a torch each and spread out, about an arm's length apart and we'll comb the country, going Nor, nor, east.' He took out his compass and, having checked the direction, hung it around his neck. 'If only it weren't so curst cloudy, we'd have enough moonlight to pick a landmark to steer towards. As it is . . .'

He caught sight of Lavinia's white face and firmly set lips and stopped himself. As each of the other Landrovers came up, he gave the passengers their orders and told Dominic to wait by the wall for the riders. They were to stay there with him until Aubrey returned with fresh instructions.

'Now, is everyone clear?'

'Yes. Come *on*,' said Lavinia. 'He may be just out there.' She pointed into the thick blackness.

'All right. Calm down. You won't see or hear anything if you're in a panic. Now, no talking, everyone. Follow the illuminated patch on my Barbour. I'll call out every so often to Tom and I want you to be as quiet as possible while we wait for his answer. OK?'

None of them protested and they set off, sometimes tripping over loose rocks in the heather, peering forwards into the blackness, shivering as snow found its way down the necks of their sweaters and melted against their warm skin. Despite their matter-of-fact behaviour, they all knew what a night out on the moor in snow could do to a man with a disabling injury and inadequate clothes.

By midnight, when the walkers had covered nearly four difficult miles and the riders much more than that, Aubrey called off the search. They were all tired and hoarse by then. The batteries in the storm torches would not last much longer. They had checked all the likely hazards and called Tom's name, shining the light into every dip in the ground where he might have been lying. Apart from their own footsteps and increasingly ragged breathing there had been no sounds at all. Even the animals and birds seemed to have taken silent refuge from the cold. There did not appear to be anything living except for themselves for miles and miles and miles.

'If Tom had been here, conscious, he'd have seen the torches and heard us call,' said Aubrey at last. 'The light shows up well. He'd have been able to make his presence felt somehow.'

'And if he's unconscious?' Lavinia answered her own question the minute she had said it. 'There's nothing more we can do until daylight. We must ring the police now. We really must, whatever his possible embarrassment or the repercussions from publicity.'

'Yes, I agree,' said Aubrey. 'Back to the Landrovers.'

That night, back in the Dower House with her children at last, Lavinia slept very little. Aubrey had sent her home, telling her sternly that he was quite capable of dealing with the police and that she would not help any of them by wearing herself out. By then she had been so tired and so desperate that she had just done as he said. He had promised to ring her up if there were any news of any kind, and for much of the night she lay open-eyed in the darkness waiting for the sound of the telephone bell.

She did fall asleep occasionally but woke at any sound. Once she slept long enough to dream that Tom was shouting to her and woke herself in terror. Half still in her dream, she got out of bed and ran to fling up one of the tall windows. Kneeling on the padded windowseat, she put her head out into the darkness, calling to him. Snow fell on her hair and cold seemed to freeze her hands on the window ledge. Her nipples hardened violently and hurt as they touched the brushed cotton of her nightdress.

She called again, and waited. No-one answered and there were no sounds of walking or running or even breathing. There seemed to be no noise at all, not even the usual soughing of the wind. Reluctantly, by then thoroughly awake, she shut the window and fetched a towel to rub the thick snow from her hair.

The feel of the snow on her hands and bare neck made it easy to imagine how cold it must be out on the moor. There would be little hope for anyone, disabled or otherwise, in the open on such a night.

Tom had been wearing his normal hunting clothes. They were pretty warm but not designed to keep his body temperature high enough to prevent hypothermia if he were out all night. It might even have been the lethargy of the later stages of that killing condition that had prevented him from reacting to their lights and voices earlier in the night.

Lavinia's fears for his safety were difficult enough to deal with, but she had other fears, too, and she could not bear to think of them at all.

Almost worse than the cold would be the wet, she told herself in an effort to keep them at bay. As the snow fell on him while he was still faintly warm, it would melt, drench his clothes and then later, as his body temperature dropped, it would freeze. There was almost no shelter on the moor and the snow was not nearly deep enough to dig into for warmth as survival manuals for climbers recommended.

Lavinia tried to loosen her muscles as she walked back to bed, but they ached with stiffness from the involuntary clenching that was stronger than any conscious wish to relax. Lying down, rigid and nauseated, she knew that if she did not sleep she would be vague and stupid all the next day. The only thing left that she could do for Tom was to be alert and ready for anything once morning had come. To achieve that, she would have to sleep.

Once or twice more before dawn her eyes closed and her mind stopped tormenting her, but it never lasted long and by the time the light came again, she was longing to leave her bed. Tired to a point where even the thought of lifting her arms to brush her hair seemed nearly impossible, with smarting eyes and a hollow aching head, she nevertheless flung back the duvet and got up.

She dressed quickly and took time to write a note for the children, telling them that she had gone up to Saltley and would either fetch them later or send one of the relations to them. They were to put on warm clothes and take whatever they wanted for breakfast. She knew that they would not wake for hours. Hunting always tired them out in any case and they had not got to bed until after one o'clock that morning.

Moving as quietly as possible, she made sure that the front door was secure behind her, and drove up to the big house.

Aubrey was already up, as were his mother and Caro. They were drinking coffee in the kitchen and it was obvious that none of them felt much like eating. Someone, Caro probably, had cooked bacon and eggs and they lay congealing in a dish at the edge of one of the cookers. The smell added to Lavinia's nausea.

'Coffee, Lavinia?' said her mother-in-law, getting to her feet. She, too, looked as though she had not slept and she moved stiffly, almost awkwardly, looking much older than usual. Lavinia tried to feel sorry for her, but the memory of what she had implied about Tammy was too fresh for that. 'I'll make another pot. This is cold.'

Lavinia could not even bring herself to speak to Flavia and so she turned to Aubrey. 'There's been no news then?'

'Nothing yet, but there's no need to be hysterical. The police are searching the moor and there are still plenty of possible explanations for Tom's absence.'

'I'm not hysterical,' Lavinia said with enough determination to make Aubrey raise his eyebrows. 'But I just can't think of anything that could possibly have happened that doesn't include harm to him. Oh, listen: that must be the police now.'

'I didn't hear anything,' Caro was saying, but then they all heard it. Footsteps were crunching on the gravel outside the kitchen door. Flavia reached it first. A youngish man in a civilian suit, flanked by two uniformed police officers holding their caps in their hands, stood on the back step.

'Mrs Medworth? I'm Chief Inspector George Hexham. This is Sergeant Susan Pleasington and Constable Roy Blackburn. May we come in?'

'Is there any news of my son?'

'Not yet, but we should hear something soon.'

As Lavinia automatically took Flavia's place at the cooker, waiting to make the coffee, Aubrey introduced himself to the police and once again took charge. He repeated everything he had said to Hexham's colleagues the night before when he had first reported Tom's absence, describing accurately where Tom had last been seen, when it had become clear that something had happened to him, and what steps they had all taken to find him.

'Right, sir,' said the plain-clothes officer when Aubrey had come to the end of his concise report. 'And who else has been informed of Mr Medworth's absence?'

'No-one – except your colleagues and those of our friends we telephoned yesterday evening in case he had stopped off with any of them. My sister, Mrs Wold, who did the telephoning, can give you a list if you'd like. She'll be down soon.'

'We've been making a search of the moor since first light. There's a chopper there, too,' said Hexham, 'and we should be getting some news very soon.'

'And if they don't find him?' said Flavia. 'What then?'

'Special Branch will be sending people up from London. If we don't find him, they'll take over the operation.'

Lavinia brought a large cafetière to the table and then fetched more cups and a bigger jug of milk.

'I beg your pardon,' said Aubrey, smiling at her. 'Chief Inspector Hexham, I should have introduced my sister-in-law, Mrs Thomas Medworth.'

'Don't bother about that,' said Lavinia without looking at him. 'Chief Inspector, would you like to bring your coffee next door? There are some things that I need to ask you.'

For a moment it looked as though Aubrey was going to protest or follow them out of the kitchen, but Caro grabbed his wrist and hung on to it so tightly that he had to look at her. She shook her head violently and, with an expression of astonishment, he sat down again. She let his wrist go.

Chief Inspector Hexham, watching everything but commenting on none of it, said impartially to all of them: 'Certainly, and in the meantime I'd like my constable to go to the stables, have a word with the groom, take a look at the horse – Mr Thomas Medworth's horse.'

Chastened, Aubrey managed not to say anything, although he did nod. Lavinia left it to Flavia to give

140

permission. After all, it was her house and she was the eldest person there.

'Thank you. Now, Mrs Medworth, I'm all yours.' Lavinia led the way to the yellow parlour and invited both him and the young sergeant to sit down.

'There were no marks on the horse, you know,' Lavinia said. 'At least nothing except the usual scratches and things of a fast hunting day or whatever they call it. I mean, I don't think he can have fallen badly enough to stop him getting home. That's why I'm so worried – and why I want to talk to you.'

'Falls can be funny things,' said the senior police officer carefully. 'If your husband wasn't attending and the horse put its hoof in a rabbit hole, perhaps, he could have come off, knocked himself out briefly, come to later without the horse and set off home, only to find himself lost. He could be out there somewhere and still perfectly all right.'

'Or there could be quite another reason.' Lavinia bit her bottom lip.

'Such as?'

She could hardly bring herself to mention it, but since she had dragged Hexham away from the family for just that purpose, she had to do it. 'It seems worse than silly, but the memory of the horse's unmarked legs keeps making me think that Tom might have gone on purpose.'

It was clear from his expression that Hexham, too, had considered that possibility. 'Is there anything particular that makes you think that?' he asked calmly.

Lavinia swallowed. She was not sure how much she ought to tell a local policeman about Tom's anxieties or about his mistresses. A Special Branch officer accustomed to the lives and stresses of ministers would be different. On the other hand if Hexham did not have all the facts, he would be hamstrung in the search for Tom. Old, familiar terrors of spoiling his career by an incautious word or action returned to her so powerfully that for a moment she could not speak.

'I definitely got the feeling that he was anxious about something serious to do with his work,' she began at last. 'But he hadn't given me a clue what it was.'

'I see. Was that usual? Him not speaking about it, I mean?' There were no overtones in the quiet, polite voice, but Lavinia felt humiliated by what he must have been thinking.

'Yes. It was. Mainly because anyone in his sort of job has to keep quiet about it all, and . . .'

'Of course he does,' said Hexham when her voice dried up. 'What about other anxieties? Perhaps personal. Did you know of anything that had been upsetting him that might make him feel he could not go on as he was?'

Lavinia's eyes closed. 'I can't believe he would have run away from anything,' she said at last, aware that she was contradicting herself. Opening her eyes again and seeing that Hexham was smiling in apparent reassurance, she added: 'However worried or upset he's ever been about anything, he's always stood and faced it. That's the kind of man he's always been. I can't believe he would run away. Not from anything.'

'Fine. I have to ask these things to get them clear. There'd be nothing sillier than ignoring a question that might lead to something useful just because it could be painful,' Hexham said, not looking at her.

'No, I do see that. And it's true that he's . . . we've . . .' To her complete shame, Lavinia burst into tears, covering her face with her right hand and trying not to make any gulping or snivelling sounds.

Without waiting for an instruction or even a signal from her boss, the sergeant moved forward and offered Lavinia a clean, impeccably ironed handkerchief. She took it.

'Sorry,' she said, having blown her nose and managed to contain the tears. 'I didn't sleep much last night and the mixture of that and all the anxiety is what's making me so stupid. What I was going to say was that my husband has been talking a lot about the need for freedom since he got up here the week before Christmas. On the other hand, thinking about it more calmly, I don't think he can have . . . because . . . um . . .'

She had to break off to regain her composure, but, with her teeth clamped around her lip, it did not take long. To her relief the police officer neither urged her to take her time nor interrupted her struggles with reassurance.

'Because I don't think he would have done anything to damage the children, and just to go off like that without an explanation would have hurt them. D'you see what I mean?'

'Yes,' said Hexham. 'It's quite clear. And it makes sense.'

The unemotional approval in his voice made Lavinia look at him gratefully. She blew her nose again and then pushed the handkerchief into the pocket of her cords.

'I'll get it back to you clean in due course,' she told the sergeant.

'Please don't worry about that. There are plenty more where that came from.'

'Standard issue to comfort weeping women?' suggested Lavinia, sounding tougher to herself and feeling glad of that at least. The young officer shook her head.

'Now,' said her superior. 'There is just one more point that we need to cover at this moment. Men in your husband's kind of position naturally make enemies. It must go with the territory.'

'Yes, it does.' Lavinia had herself in hand again and there was nothing beyond polite co-operation in her voice.

'Anyone or any group in particular?'

'Lots,' she said and even managed to smile. It was much easier to talk about Tom's enemies than the hypothetical sorrows and fears that might have made him need to escape from the life they had been leading. She described some of the people who might have had reason to resent Tom. The sergeant took notes of everything Lavinia said.

'I see,' said Hexham at the end. 'Is there anything else that you think I ought to know?'

Lavinia shook her head. 'No, but could I ask one thing? Could I give you my telephone number at the Dower House? That's where he and I live with the children. And then you could telephone me there when you get any news.'

'Not here?'

Lavinia's shoulders sagged. 'Here too, I suppose. If it's in the day, I probably will be up here. But at night I go home. What I mean is, would you tell me first rather than any of the others? Please?'

'Give Sergeant Pleasington the number while I find Constable Blackburn. I'll do my best to speak to you personally. Thank you for your help, Mrs Medworth. If you do think of anything else, give me a ring.' He scribbled a number on the back of an old envelope he had taken from his pocket. 'That'll always find me.'

'Thank you. Both of you. You've been kind. I'm sorry to have broken down. I . . . I would be grateful if you wouldn't pass on to the rest of the family anything that I've told you.'

She saw that he was looking surprised, and even felt a bit surprised herself, but there was nothing she could do about it then.

'Very well. It's a worrying time for you, Mrs Medworth. Of course, your husband may simply turn up. That's the likeliest eventuality. Don't forget to let us know in all the celebrations if that happens.'

After Lavinia had dictated the telephone number to the sergeant, they talked for a while about Tom and the kind of man he was and then at last she was left alone, pressed into the back of the chair. She was ashamed of having made a fool of herself, desperate with anxiety for Tom and full of a restless longing to do something to find him.

Eventually she reached for the telephone that stood on a little round oak table beside her chair. She wanted to ring the Dower House to make sure the children were all right, but when she picked up the receiver it was to hear Aubrey's voice telling someone what had happened.

'Who's that?' he said sharply.

'Only me: Lavinia. I wanted to ring the children. Who are you talking to, Aubrey?'

'My name's Benkitt, Mrs Medworth,' said a vaguely familiar voice. 'I'm the Attorney General. We met at Number Ten last month. May I say how much I sympathize with your anxiety?'

'Thank you.' Her eyes closed. The Medworth machine was being cranked into action. And a very good thing, too, she said to herself, adding aloud into the telephone receiver: 'I'll say goodbye now, Sir Kenneth.'

'I won't be long, Lavinia,' said Aubrey as the Attorney General reiterated his sympathy.

Five minutes later Aubrey appeared in person in the doorway of the yellow parlour. 'All done now. But it was necessary that someone in the cabinet knew and most of them are away. Benkitt will hold the fort until we've more evidence of what's happened and then if necessary he'll inform whoever else has to know.'

'I see.'

'You're not alone in this, Lavinia.' Aubrey sounded stern. 'We're all . . .'

'I know. He's your brother as well as my husband. I know that.'

'It's not so much that.' Aubrey's face, so like Tom's except for its certainty and its deeper lines. 'I meant that we're with you. You don't have to feel that you need to do everything. There are lots of us up here and between us we have some very useful contacts. Everything that can be done, will be.' He hesitated and then delivered one of his most charming, sparkling smiles: 'There are some compensations to marrying into a big family.'

Lavinia nodded and managed to thank him, wanting more than anything for him to go. Since there was no genuine comfort to be had, she did not want to be soothed with meaningless kindness. When Aubrey had gone, she rang the Dower House. Tammy answered.

'Are you all up?'

'Yes. Is Daddy back yet?'

'Not yet. But a friendly policeman has just been talking to me and he says there are lots of his officers up on the moor going over all the ground where you hunted yesterday. And they've got a helicopter. Have you had any breakfast?'

'A bit. Orange juice and toast. We didn't want anything else. Mummy, what's going to happen?' For once Tammy sounded tentative, almost afraid.

'I'm not sure. But the best thing is for all of us to carry on as well as we can until Dad's back, and so I think I'll nip home now and pick you all up in the car and bring you here to be with the others as we planned.'

'All right.'

'Good. Tell the boys, will you? And I'll see you in about ten minutes.'

'OK.'

Chapter 11

The children were waiting for Lavinia on the steps of the Dower House, sensibly muffled up against the snow.

'Good,' she said as she got out of the driving seat. 'Got everything?'

'Yes.' Rory was speaking for them all. 'And I've made sure the cooker's off and the kettle too, and I've locked up. It's all quite safe, Mum.' He held up the keys in his gloved hand. Half saddened and half impressed by his assumption of family responsibility, Lavinia touched his cold face and then hustled them all into the car. Rory took the seat beside her and looked over his shoulder to check that the younger two were putting on their seatbelts. When he was sure that they were safely buckled in, he turned to his mother and said seriously: 'Have there been any developments?'

'Not yet. But the police were at Saltley all morning, and . . .'

'Why the police? Dad hasn't done anything,' said Charlie from the back.

At the note of hysteria in his voice, Lavinia looked at him in the mirror and said: 'No, of course he hasn't. But whenever anyone's missing the police are best placed to see to the search. They can ask anybody everything in a way that not even Uncle Aubrey can, besides getting a bigger search party together than anyone else.'

Charles said nothing. Lavinia switched the engine on again and manoeuvred the big car out of the gates. The wheels slid on the impacted snow on the road and the tank-like car felt terrifyingly light and uncontrollable. She changed gear and slowed.

'What's happening about the play and the party?' asked Rory in the unhappy silence.

'I don't know,' said Lavinia, switching on the wind-screen wipers as more snow started to fall and clogged her view. The wind blew the big white flakes in different directions, making it almost impossible to see. She put on her headlights and slowed down to about five miles per hour, peering forwards to find the turning up to Saltley Hall. 'I'd forgotten about it all.'

'There's all those people coming to tea and supper,' said Tammy. 'We can't stop them. Not now. It wouldn't be fair. Besides, what about the play?'

'And all that food everyone's been cooking,' said Charlie mournfully. 'We can't waste it, and we'll never be able to eat it all ourselves before it goes rotten.' He had slumped right down on the back seat, and Lavinia could only just see his face in her mirror.

'What is it Great-aunt Elfrida always says?' she asked as cheerfully as she could manage.

'Don't give up till you've got to the end – or the end will never come,' chanted all three children in unison. 'If the end doesn't come, it was all for naught, and YOU WILL BE UNDONE.' The last four words were shouted in full voice as was customary, and Lavinia was relieved to see that some colour had come back into Charles's doughy cheeks.

'Here we are. Good. Oh, look, Charles. There's Bendy, waiting for you.' Lavinia switched off the engine and released the central locking to let them out. Rory sat on beside her in the car as the two younger ones rushed forward to meet their cousin.

'What do you think's happened to him, Mum? Really?'

'Rory, I just don't know,' she said, putting her arm around his shoulders and laying her cheek on his hair for an instant. It felt soft, slippery. 'There are so many possibilities. Some of them are horridly worrying and some hardly worrying at all. Since we can't know which the true one is yet, I think we've just got to do our very best not to get in a fuss. There may not be anything to fuss about, you see.'

'Yes. I do see.' He thought a while. 'Can you actually manage not to be afraid?'

Lavinia decided that only honesty would do. She let Rory go and put her hand lightly on his arm. 'No, I can't,' she said. 'But I do try, because that's the only bearable way of carrying on. We mustn't make up terrible stories of what might have happened. Stories like that frighten us but don't help Dad one jot. There's no point in it.'

'No, I see. Right. Yes. Thanks.'

'OK. Are you all right, Rory?'

'Mostly.'

'Then I think we'd better go in. I want to be near the telephone in case anyone rings up with news.'

'Oh, sorry, Mum.' Rory was already scrambling out of the door as he spoke. 'I didn't think of that.'

The first person Lavinia saw when she walked into the Great Hall a few minutes later was Philip. He was talking to Rory and there was no sign of the others. Philip held out a hand without pausing in what he was saying to Rory, and Lavinia took it. There was none of the delirious-making excitement she had felt on Christmas Eve. His touch held only friendliness and comfort.

'Has there been anything since I was out?'

'No. Not yet. Rory's been telling me what you said to him. Inspired common sense.'

Lavinia smiled and removed her hand. Philip nodded and told Rory that he thought there was a last-minute run through for the play up in the Long Gallery. When the boy had gone, Philip said: 'You look all in.'

'I didn't sleep much, but that's not exactly surprising. I hate having to wait like this. If only . . . But there isn't anything I can do.'

'D'you mind that they're going ahead with this great shindig today?'

'In some ways, yes, I do mind, but it would be tricky to put everyone off – and that, too, would hardly help Tom.' Seeing doubt in Philip's steady eyes, she nodded. 'I loathe it, to tell you the truth, but it doesn't surprise me to hear that they're carrying on. They always do. Part of the family myth is that nothing short of some kind of total wipeout would stop a Medworth in its tracks. But I do wish that they could have given something up for Tom. They'd all say that was my sentimentality coming out, but . . .'

A shrilling, old-fashioned bell stopped either of them saying anything else. Lavinia ran for the nearest telephone, which happened to be in Flavia's study. The ringing had stopped before she reached it, but she picked up the receiver anyway and was puzzled to hear a cool, unaccented male voice saying: ' . . . cassette in the phone box at the north-east corner of the market square in Helmsmoorside. That'll tell you all you need to know.'

One possible explanation of the statement hit her. 'Who is it?' she burst out, not knowing which of her relations was at the other extension.

'All in the tape,' said the voice before cutting her off.

'Who is it?' she said again into the buzzing receiver.

'It's Flavia here. We're all in the kitchen, Lavinia, with the police. Please come and join us now.'

'We must get that tape first.'

'Chief Inspector Hexham will do that. The police will need to see all the evidence *in situ*.'

'Oh.' On the point of running back out to her car, Lavinia had to control the impulse, calm her breathing and let the adrenaline dissipate throughout her body. 'What did you hear before I came on the line?'

'Very little, but come to the kitchen now and you will hear everything.'

Feeling a hand on her shoulder, Lavinia whirled round, but it was only Philip. She leaned against him and felt his hand on her head, holding in all the terror for her. When she had stopped shaking, she pulled back, saying: 'It sounds like kidnap of some kind. There's a tape in a telephone box. Flavia wants the police to fetch it and me to present myself in the kitchen.'

'Then we'd better go,' he said, putting an arm round her waist.

'It's unimaginable,' she said, trying and failing to think of any words to use since she did not even know what she wanted to say.

'Come on, Lavinia.'

They walked in silence through the door at the far end of the Great Hall, down the dark, stone-flagged passage to the kitchen which seemed to be even more full of people and noise than usual.

John Hogarth and Aubrey got to their feet as soon as Lavinia appeared in the doorway and she nodded to them. The three police officers looked round. Chief Inspector Hexham took a few steps towards her. 'We're retrieving the tape now as discreetly as possible in case the box is being watched. My officers will bring it here at once,' he said, gesturing to his radio. 'We'll be making house-to-house enquiries in the area as soon as it's safe. And we're trying to trace the call, but they've probably blocked it.'

Lavinia, who had stupidly forgotten that he would be in touch with his entire team, breathed more easily. Other people, better-equipped people, were responsible for getting Tom back. She blinked and licked her lips. 'What do you know so far?'

'Very little, I'm afraid, Mrs Medworth.'

'Now come and sit down, Lavinia,' said Flavia almost kindly. 'And drink some coffee. You didn't have any of the last pot and you look very pale.'

Philip pulled out a chair for her between Aubrey and Nicko, and Flavia poured her a cup of coffee. Hexham explained that she had not missed much of the call Flavia had answered. The man had not identified himself but had said merely: 'We have Thomas Medworth. He is unharmed. There is a cassette . . .'

'I heard everything after that,' Lavinia said, feeling stupid and useless. 'So there's nothing we can do until we hear the tape.'

'That's right. It should be here within half an hour.'

'Flavia's right,' said Philip, who was still standing behind her chair. 'You ought to eat something.'

Lavinia shook her head. The pictures of Tom's body lying broken and frozen on the moor were being replaced with others, just as frightening.

'You need it. I'll do you some toast.'

There were some cold slices in a tarnished silver rack on the table, which Philip rejected. Without saying anything, he cut several thick slices from a newly defrosted white loaf and put them under the grill. When they were toasted he spread two with butter and marmalade and put them in front of her. 'I know you don't feel like food,' he said, understanding her expression of revulsion. 'But you must try to eat.'

With a faint smile, Lavinia looked up at him.

'What you really mean is "Get that down yer neck, damn you",' she said.

Philip and the police officers all laughed. The others stared at her, surprised by her frivolity, or perhaps by her deliberately coarsened voice. But it was the tiny spurt of amusement that helped her to deal with her unruly throat and force down some toast.

'Where is everyone?' she asked when she had finished

both slices. Grateful to Philip for his insistence, she felt less sick and much less faint. He started to butter two more pieces of toast.

'Georgina and her father have got everyone remotely involved in the play up in the Long Gallery rehearsing again,' said Caroline, who was sitting beside Aubrey. She sounded astonishingly gentle and she seemed to exude a kind of wordless sympathy that lapped around Lavinia's terrors. 'It seemed best that they should be occupied.'

'Oh, thank you, Caro,' said Lavinia with much more fervour than seemed suitable to Aubrey, who looked at her in astonishment.

They all lapsed into silence, waiting for the tape. Lavinia ate a little more of the toast and then left the rest at the side of her plate.

It was in fact only about twenty minutes before a young police constable brought it into the room. He looked surprised to see so many people and took a step backwards so that he could wipe his feet more thoroughly on the mat.

'Come on, come on,' said Aubrey, holding out his hand palm upwards and shaking it at the young man. The young, pink-cheeked police officer looked towards his superior, who asked whether the tape and its box had been dusted for fingerprints.

'Yes, sir. It's clean.'

'Right. Give it to Mr Medworth, then.'

Lavinia, trying to keep her mind on the facts in order to stop her imagination flashing its horrific pictures through her mind, noticed that Aubrey was struggling with some idea or problem. She thought with another blessed spurt of amusement that he was probably having to force himself to remember that it is the police officer in charge and not a judge on holiday who takes precedence in a criminal investigation.

He slipped the tape into a radio cassette player that he had brought down from his bedroom and they all listened to the mechanical clicks and hissing of the machine. They were followed by the same, accentless, unemotional voice some of them had already heard.

'This is LAFE – the Liberation Army for the Foxes of England. We have Thomas Medworth in custody. He will not be harmed.'

Lavinia sighed and covered her face with both hands.

'But he will not be released until a statement has been issued by the Prime Minister that all hunting with hounds will become a criminal offence forthwith. This statement must be made in *The Times*, the *Guardian*, the *Telegraph*, the *Independent* and the *Sun*, and on each BBC radio station at precisely one o'clock. They will all be monitored. Mr Medworth will be released as soon as the statement has been made. Here he is now.'

There was a short pause and then Tom's voice sounded from the small black plastic box on the kitchen table, shocking them all with its familiarity and with its hint of a tremor. 'This is Thomas Medworth. I am in the custody of LAFE. They will tell you what they want.'

There was another pause, long enough to make Aubrey reach out for the stop button, but Hexham stopped him and in a moment Tom's voice sounded again: 'In order to convince you that this is no hoax or manufactured tape, I am required to state that I was removed from the Saltley Hunt at Blackbird's Bank half a mile from High Mill. My horse, Henchman, a bay 16.2 gelding, was kept concealed until the field had ridden on and was later released. From what I could see, he did not appear to have any serious marks on him. Please do not worry. Lavinia . . .'

The voice stopped and there was only the hissing of the tape against the machinery. Lavinia took her hands away from her eyes, but she could not look at any of the others as she tried to contain her feelings. The overriding emotion was relief that LAFE, whoever they might be, had promised not to harm Tom. Her imagination had had him dead so many times since the previous afternoon that even that small reassurance seemed wonderful.

'It's not so bad, Lavinia.' Aubrey's voice was gentle. 'At least we know he's alive and unhurt.'

She looked at him and nodded, trying to smile. 'I know. It's just too hard to deal with straight away.'

As she spoke she became aware of another huge – and selfish – surge of relief that Tom had not run away from her, or worse, and that he had called out to her at the end of the tape. He had not wanted anyone else, only her.

'Now the police have got something real to work on,' Aubrey was saying, 'they'll be able to get somewhere.'

Lavinia blinked and tried to stop thinking about her own feelings. Chief Inspector Hexham had taken his sergeant out of the room, and the other two police officers were standing in silence, watching the Medworths. Apart from Philip, they were all talking to each other about what ought to be done next. Lavinia drank the last of the tepid coffee in her large cup. Her mind sharpened a little.

'They must have known a lot about us all,' she said, bringing several other conversations to a stop. 'I mean, they must have been sure that Tom would be out hunting yesterday and had pretty complicated plans to get him away from the rest of the field. They were probably quite a big gang. Someone must have noticed something. It would have taken more than one or even two to overpower a man as strong as Tom on a horse as big as Henchman.'

'Unless it was someone pretending to be hurt or in trouble,' suggested Caro slowly. 'I can't imagine Tom riding by without stopping to see if they needed help even if lots of other people do.'

'That's true,' said Lavinia, even more grateful to her. It seemed important that people should be reminded of everything that was good about Tom. 'But, Caro, d'you really think that someone who hunted would do something

155

like this? Could anyone who was a committed anti actually go out with the rest of you?'

'It has been known,' said Sasha, watching her with a mixture of compassion and something else that Lavinia could not understand. 'But it needn't have been one of the field. There was the usual gaggle of followers and sabs at intervals all through the day. There were quite a few scuffles. It could have happened during one of those. I mean, for instance, I saw Sally Anlaby threaten to take her crop to one spotty yob who was dragging on her reins, but she yelled out that she was all right and said she didn't need any help.'

'What do you know about her?' asked Philip suddenly. 'She's new to the area, isn't she? And several of you said she was riding with Tom before he disappeared. Could she have been involved – at least as much as providing some sort of distraction like a scuffle with a sab so that other people could decoy Tom without being noticed?'

'Absolutely not,' said Sasha in a tone that Lavinia remembered well from her early marriage. It was made up of irritation, immense superiority, and an upsetting suggestion of distress that anyone who mattered at all could be so tiresome. The sound of it made Lavinia feel cold in her very bones.

'Really, Philip,' Sasha went on in the same voice. 'Idiotically ill-informed suggestions are not going to help.'

He put his hand on Lavinia's shoulder, which steadied her, but before he could answer Sasha or demand evidence for her certainty Chief Inspector Hexham returned. 'I have been asked to request from you a list of all the people you are expecting this afternoon and evening,' he said to Flavia. Turning to Aubrey, he added: 'And a list of everyone who was out hunting yesterday. Naturally we shall also ask the Master, but I should be grateful for anything you can tell me.'

'What about the car followers and the sabs?' asked Aubrey. 'It's not likely that anyone planning a kidnap like this would advertise his sabbing activities, but, as my sister has just suggested, they could easily have been among the foot followers. There were even some on mountain bikes. And I don't for one moment suppose all of those were recognizable to this family.' He looked at Sasha, who nodded.

'You're absolutely right. Caro, you were following – did you recognize many?'

'No, but then I only see them once or maybe twice a year. You'd need a real local, Chief Inspector, not a visitor like me.'

'It's in hand.' He turned to Lavinia and smiled at her. 'Now, a team from Special Branch will be up here shortly. They will, of course, want to talk to you, but there may be other things they have to do first. I've been asked to say that a senior officer will be here probably later this afternoon or early evening. By then he'll be able to tell you a great deal more than any of us can now.'

She stood up and held out her hand. 'Thank you. You've been terribly kind.'

He took her hand and shook it firmly. Then he looked around all of the others.

'In this sort of case news management is crucial. The Special Branch team will be organizing that and they want to make sure that no-one else says anything to any interested journalist, so may I suggest that you don't tell any of your visitors what has happened? It is important that the kidnappers get as little publicity value as possible from what they've done, but even more crucial that they're not tipped off about any stage of our investigation.'

'That's sensible,' said Aubrey, nodding. 'We will hold our tongues and await Special Branch then.'

'I can't say precisely what time the officers will get here, but they'll be discreet if your guests are already

157

here.' Hexham looked at Lavinia's white face and added gently: 'It is encouraging that they have not threatened to harm him, Mrs Medworth, or forbidden you to contact us. That in itself makes this look more like a publicity stunt than anything else. Try not to worry too much.'

'Thank you,' said Lavinia fervently.

'All right. I'll say good bye now but we'll keep in close touch.'

As soon as the door had shut behind him and his subordinates, Flavia fished in her pocket for her copy of the holiday timetable.

'Right,' she said briskly: 'Caro, you and I and Sasha had better get going on the turkey stew for tonight. Lavinia, your cheese straws . . .'

'They don't come out of the freezer until after the play,' she said, glad of at least one minute piece of certainty in her shaky world.

Her first relief at Tom's relative safety was beginning to be overtaken by new fears. However reasonable the LAFE spokesman had sounded, there was no guarantee that he would stay reasonable when it became clear that the government was not going to yield to blackmail. The kidnap might have started as no more than a publicity stunt for the anti-hunt activists, but it could easily turn into something much more dangerous. The thought of what frustration – or fear of retribution – might make LAFE do to Tom if the stunt failed was sending new and ever more horrible pictures through Lavinia's mind.

'Nor they do,' said Flavia, breaking into her fears. 'Then you'd better start chopping onions and bacon for the turkey stew. And then you can mash garlic and butter for the garlic bread. It'll be better for you to work than to sit moping.'

Philip looked at Lavinia as though to ask whether she wanted him to intervene in her defence. She touched his hand briefly and said: 'Good idea, Flavia. I'd like

158

a job. What happens about family lunch today? I can't remember.'

'Ham sandwiches.'

'Of course. Ham carving's Tom's job, isn't it? Philip had better do it and then when I've done my chopping John and I can assemble the sandwiches as usual. You can wield a carving knife as well as a scalpel, can't you, Philip?'

'He's not a surgeon, Lavinia.' Sasha sounded sharper than usual. Lavinia frowned, unable to deal with other people's anger on top of everything else.

'No,' said Philip easily, 'but I can carve. Come on, Lavinia, we'd better clear this table and get on with it.'

She was genuinely grateful to be allowed to chop the four pounds of onions. Tears streamed down her face and she did not need to be either ashamed or afraid of embarrassing anyone else. At one moment, running her hands and the knife under bitterly cold water to remove some of the acrid juice, she remembered an Everly Brothers song about crying in the rain and nearly laughed at herself.

'All right?' asked Philip quietly. He had been slow in carving the ham because he needed to check her face between almost every slice that he carefully laid on a great Delft charger.

'Yes,' she said with a smile, but she did not explain. There were too many other people around.

A moment later she caught Sasha's eye and watched her palely tanned face flush, which seemed peculiar. Looking back down at the large, damp pile of minced onion, Lavinia tried to work out what could have made Sasha's colour rise like that, but it was not until some time later, when she had moved to the Great Hall to join John Hogarth in making almost fifty ham sandwiches that she discovered any clue to Sasha's feelings. By then Philip had been sent up to the Long Gallery to bring the actors and stage managers down to the hall for lunch and the two of them were alone.

'You've really rocked Sasha, you know,' said John, sounding not only amused but also malicious.

'Look, I don't want to spoil your fun, but now is not the time for cryptic comments. I can't think about anything except Tom and what they're doing to him. If you want to say something, John, say it straight out. Don't play games with me. I just haven't the oomph to deal with them.'

John looked hurt but quickly disguised it with his familiar mask of amusement and busied himself spreading butter on the pile of cut slices of bread so that she could add mustard and ham.

'I only meant that Sasha's noticed the effect you're having on Philip and it's upsetting her.'

'What?' Lavinia knew that she sounded both tired and impatient. She assumed John had been trying to cheer her up and merely picked the wrong method. She pushed her fringe away from her forehead and realized that she had left a trail of mustard on her hair. Taking a napkin from the pile lying ready at the end of the table, she cleaned her fringe.

John continued: 'To see Philip switching all his affections and concern to you over the last few days has made her go all quaggly.' He paused, his buttery knife held high above the next slice of bread. 'I know how she feels actually.'

'A few days ago,' said Lavinia, deciding to switch from mustard to chutney for the next batch of sandwiches, 'you were telling me off for not working hard enough to cheer Philip up. I don't think it's fair to tease me about it at the moment.'

'It's gone a lot further than that, though, hasn't it, Lavvy-Lugs?' John said, peering round to look into her face. 'Old Philip isn't just being cheered up; he's being given a taste of true love at last.'

'No, he isn't.' Lavinia wanted to swat John's peering face as she might have swatted a mosquito she wanted to kill. His suggestion, with its implication that she, too, might have found truer love with Philip than she had ever had during her difficult years with Tom, would have been upsetting at any time. Just then it was unbearable.

She made a deliberate effort to remember how fond she was of John and manufactured a smile. 'I expect you're trying to perk me up, but please don't. It's too silly. For one thing, what's happened to Tom makes everything else so unimportant. For another, there's nothing going on between Philip and me. For a third, even if there were, Sasha would hardly be in a position to object, considering what she's up to at the moment.'

At that John laughed and patted her shoulder. 'Sorry, Lavvy, but that's really naïve. And you're not usually that, whatever the others say. You can't imagine that Sasha wouldn't be jealous if her husband starting playing around, can you?'

'She'd have no reason to be. Think of everything they've said to all of us about how unimportant fidelity is.'

'Human nature never is logical. You ought to know that by now, even if Flavia's right about your terror of emotion.'

Lavinia dropped her knife. It hit the chutney jar, which overbalanced and crashed into the mustard. A mixture of the two glutinous sauces dribbled out on to the scarred oak of the old table and began to drip off the edge on to the flagged floor. She watched them oozing, decided to ignore them and simply walked away without a word, leaving the mess behind her. She heard John's anxious voice calling after her as she climbed the stairs to the tower and thought: he actually sounds worried.

Lavinia knew that she was behaving badly, even child-ishly, but she decided that she was simply not prepared to put up with anything else from anyone. In a detached way she wondered who would be sent to fetch her down, or if she would be left to sulk in private.

Up in the tower, she opened one of the windows between

161

the bookshelves and stood, feeling the full blast of the cold wind and staring out over the thick white landscape. It had stopped snowing and the air was as clear and stinging as antiseptic. The sky was the hard, bright blue of eighteenth-century enamel and the sun was refracted off the snow crystals in bursts that were almost painful to watch. The whole landscape looked more ravishing than she had ever seen it, hard but glamorous, glittering and artificial, like very expensive costume jewellery.

She could see for miles. Tom could be anywhere. In the time since he had last been seen he could have been smuggled on board a boat at Hull and taken who knows where, to Scandinavia perhaps. Or he could have been forced to assume another identity and be in the air, on the way to the other side of the world. She could not bear to imagine what he must be feeling or what might be being done to him.

It seemed essential to hold on to the certainty that he would be found, and found soon, but at that moment with all the dazzling space in front of her Lavinia could not imagine how it would happen. She knew it was silly even to hope that the Prime Minister might give the undertaking the kidnappers had demanded. He could never be seen to give in to terrorism. The British don't. She leaned against the freezing stone. There was a knock at the door. Half-turning, she called: 'Come in.' Then she saw Sarah, standing with a tray in her hands.

'We thought you might like a bit of lunch.'

'Thank you. That was very kind.'

'We all knew you ought to eat,' said her niece, setting the tray down on top of the emptiest part of the desk. Lavinia saw that there was a plate with two of the ham sandwiches, a glass of red wine, and a banana on the tray, beside a tiny glass bowl of chocolates. She wondered who had suggested the wine.

'I'm behaving badly,' she said dispassionately and saw

Sarah shake her head vigorously. 'No, you're not. Has there been some news of Cousin Tom?'

'What did they say when they asked you to bring the tray up?'

'Cousin Caro just said that you were a bit upset and wanted to be by yourself for a while. She told me to bring it and . . .' Sarah looked away, blushing. 'She told me not to ask you any questions, but I like him so much. I . . .'

'Don't worry, Sarah. The police are doing all they can to find him. It will come out all right in the end. Where are my children?'

'They're with Meg, helping her to lay out the make-up tables for the play, I think. Mummy decided to send Julia up there with lunch for them. Only Jocelyn and I are going to have it downstairs with the grown-ups.'

'Right. Thank you for bringing mine. I'll be down as soon as I've finished it. Quite soon. Don't be too frightened.'

Sarah left with reluctant obedience and Lavinia did her best to eat the sandwiches. She did not want to finish even the first but she made herself choke it down, sipping the wine in between each mouthful. Then she took the other sandwich and, carefully tearing it into small pieces, laid it out on the windowsill. She shut the window again and watched. Within three minutes there were two blackbirds and a thrush pecking at the bread and meat. It was lucky, she thought, that Sarah had brought her one of the sandwiches that had neither mustard nor chutney in it.

Eventually Lavinia returned to the kitchen to discuss with Aubrey and Flavia how much they ought to tell the children of what had happened to Tom.

Chapter 12

The first batch of guests, the most favoured ones, started to arrive at half past three. For once the Medworth women had exchanged their shabby trousers for more formal clothes. Flavia was wearing an astonishing scarlet robe that John Hogarth's brother, Patrick, had brought her back from Rajasthan. With her commanding height, strong-boned face and wild white hair, the dramatic dress suited her, and it certainly cheered up the bleak decoration of the hall.

Elfrida had chosen a full-skirted suit of dark-blue bouclé wool with big gold buttons, which had been her winter celebration outfit for the past ten years at least. Lavinia was wearing her terracotta dress and gold jewellery, and the others varied between Caro's dark-blue mid-calf dress, Sasha's black wool crèpe trousers and long, yellow knitted tunic and Polly's Monsoon skirt and quilted waistcoat, which Lavinia well remembered seeing on Olivia nearly a decade earlier. Only Lavinia and Caro had put on make-up.

As usual, Meg and Jocelyn were on coat duty. Having put away the damp coats, scarves, gloves and boots that the guests shed, one of them would escort the newcomers into the Great Hall while the other waited for the next knock at the door.

Inside, in front of a colossal fire, Flavia and Elfrida poured tea and cut Christmas cake and chocolate log. With so many of the family already talking to each other there was none of that cool, stilted beginning to a party that Lavinia knew too well from constituency functions. The buzz of conversation soon rose to a roar.

A few of the people who had been hunting the previous day and knew something of their anxieties asked after Tom, but the family held the line they had finally agreed and said merely that he had been called away unexpectedly. It was clear that not everyone believed the cliché, but they were far too polite to question it.

Lavinia had argued that her own children at least would have to know what had really happened and could be trusted not to tell anyone else. To leave them believing that Tom might be dead or badly injured and dying of exposure somewhere out on the moor would be more cruel than telling them the truth and swearing them to silence. When Aubrey had looked as though he were about to disagree with her, Lavinia had held on to her emotions as tightly as she could and pointed out that her children were old enough to listen to the radio and often did so at night in their bedrooms. If anything were to be said on the news before the children had been told everything the adults knew, they would feel betrayed by the very people on whom they most depended. 'And that,' Lavinia had said, looking directly at Flavia, who seemed quite unabashed, 'is one of the worst things that can happen to any child.'

To her astonishment, Flavia had smiled condescendingly as she said: 'That is a reasonable point, Lavinia.' Flavia had then ignored her completely and turned towards Aubrey to discuss with him what the other children should be told.

Throughout tea, Lavinia kept an eye on her three and could not help feeling proud of them. There had been tears from both Charles and Tammy when they first heard the

165

news, and they were still red eyed, but they seemed to have control of themselves. Rory had merely asked a few pertinent questions about the kidnap, done his best to comfort his mother and said nothing more about it. He was moving among the guests, chatting and refilling cups with an air of ease that belonged to a much older boy. But every so often, Lavinia would see him close his eyes and breathe deeply. She thought that he was having to work hard to keep his feelings so well hidden. Whenever he looked at her she smiled with as much reassurance as she could and made as many opportunities as possible to talk to him.

At exactly four-fifteen Georgina spoke to both her parents and then collected her cast and stage-management team to take them quietly away from the hall. Fifteen minutes later, Frida began to marshall the audience and led them up the three flights of stairs to the Long Gallery, where rows of chairs had been arranged in a half-moon around the improvised stage.

When Lavinia had first heard about the Medworth Christmas play, the year before she had married, she had dreaded an embarrassing amateur fiasco. But all generations of the family took the plays so seriously and worked so hard at them that every performance she had seen had been interesting, and some of them had been startlingly good. Julian had produced them with the utmost professionalism ever since his marriage to Frida and for the last ten years he had written them himself. The family had been surprised when he had announced earlier that year that he had decided to hand over the responsibility for the writing to his elder daughter.

Despite her curiosity about how Georgina's first play would turn out, Lavinia was too worried about Tom to pay proper attention that afternoon. She saw figures moving about on the stage and heard voices, but she could not keep her mind on them for long enough to discover what any of it was about.

At one moment she looked beyond Flavia, who was sitting in the centre of the front row of chairs, to Philip. His serious-looking face gave no clues to his thoughts, but suddenly he looked up and saw Lavinia watching him. For a long moment they stared at each other and then she looked away.

She did not know what she wanted of him any longer. His affection and the easiness she always felt with him had made her extraordinarily happy, but Tom's disappearance had changed everything. Because of what had happened she could no longer let herself rest in the warmth Philip had given her.

As she understood that, Lavinia had a moment's sharp fear for him, wondering whether he would feel her withdrawal as yet another rejection. She looked back at him and saw that he was still watching her. A singularly reassuring smile banished the gravity from his expression and she felt better.

A few minutes later she was shocked out of her thoughts by a spatter of clapping, which quickly swelled as the audience burst into enthusiastic applause. She saw that the curtains were shut and realized that the whole play must be over and she still had no idea what had happened. Annoyed with herself, she clapped as hard as anyone else and hoped that no-one would ask her any detailed questions about the acting or the play itself.

The curtains parted again, as Rory and Jocelyn ran to hook them back, and the cast formed up to bow to their by-then thunderously appreciative audience. Smiling, the lines of adults and children parted in the middle and Georgina walked forwards to take her bow. The clapping grew still louder and she waited, looking towards her parents. Both Julian and Frida joined in the applause with enthusiasm and Georgina's pale face flushed.

She was wearing a plain, short, black stretch-velvet dress, matte black tights and flat shoes, and she had on a flamboyant necklace of scarlet, black and white perspex discs. Her dark hair was tied back, and she looked slight and much younger than her twenty-seven years as she fluently thanked her audience and all her collaborators.

When she had finished, she bowed her head slightly and signalled to her two unseen helpers. The curtains swung down again. A babble of talk burst out among the audience as they stood up and stretched. Some of them walked away from the rest down the Long Gallery, pointing out favourite portraits to friends. Others clustered near the stage, ready to congratulate the author and her cast as soon as they emerged from the makeshift dressing rooms.

Lavinia found herself alone, staring at the fat, satisfied face of an eighteenth-century Saltley in a portrait by Reynolds when she heard John's voice, unusually tentative, from behind her. 'Lavvy?'

She turned and, seeing his anxious face, quickly said: 'Don't look like that. I'm sorry I lost my temper, John.'

'You mustn't be. It was all my fault anyway. I don't know why I had to needle you like that. Flavia could no doubt explain it to me but I'm not sure I want to hear.' He grinned and looked more like himself. Lavinia could not help smiling back. 'I'm sure that makes sense to you.'

'It does ring a teeny bell,' she admitted.

'I thought it might. But it was cruel. I know what Tom's disaster must be doing to you and I can only think it must have buggered my judgement. Will you forgive me?'

'I already did.' She put her hand on his elbow. 'Let's go down. Someone ought to lead the way and the rest of the invasion's due in about half an hour. Golly, yes: I ought to get the cheese straws into the oven. Coming?'

As they walked down the broad, polished stairs, not talking but reasonably peaceful again, Lavinia was surprised that she could even think about the cheese straws, let alone worry about them. But her unextravagant common sense told her that it was only by holding the line on the small things of normal life that she could keep any kind of sanity. As she had said to Rory, it simply would not help Tom for her to get into a great fuss or panic. And at least worrying about things like cooking gave her respite from her lurid imaginings of what might be happening to him.

'What time did Hexham say the Special Branch people would get here?' she said suddenly as they reached the hall. 'Surely it ought to have been by now. It's well after six.'

'God knows, but I don't think you should worry about it,' said John. 'They'll know that we can't tell them anything that we haven't already told the local cops, and the less time they waste reassuring us the more they'll have for finding Tom.'

'True, but . . . Hell!' She blew her nose. 'I wish there was something practical I could do.'

'There'll come a time for that. But at the moment we've all just got to wait. Don't worry too much. Hexham did say that the Branch officers wouldn't get round to us until this evening.'

'So he did,' said Lavinia, but she could not stop herself opening the front door to look for them.

Sure enough, there was a large well-kept black Rover with two men sitting in it parked just beyond the steps. The man in the back seat appeared to be talking into a mobile telephone. After a moment he put it down. The rear door opened and he emerged, revealing himself to be of middle-height, brown-haired, extremely compact in his dark suit, and surprisingly young. He looked to be not much older than Lavinia herself. He moved towards them, saying: 'Mrs Medworth?'

'Yes. You must be . . .' She broke off, not wanting to risk making a fool of herself if he were not from the police.

'Superintendent John Chorley,' he said as he reached her side. He pulled off his right glove and shook hands with her.

'This is my husband's cousin, John Hogarth.'

'Sir.'

'Do come on in out of the cold. I hope you haven't been waiting long. We've all been upstairs and can't have heard the bell.'

'No, I haven't been here long. I didn't ring. I'd been told there'd be no-one around until six. Still five minutes to go.'

'Is there? Sorry. Come in now, and tell me what's been happening.'

'Thank you,' said Chorley pleasantly. 'It's a worrying time for you, Mrs Medworth.'

At that understatement Lavinia smiled. Having asked John to take over her responsibilities with the cheese straws, she took Chorley into the yellow parlour and explained the card tables that had been laid out ready for the party. As they sat down at either side of the fire, she said: 'What's going to happen? I mean, I do realize that there's not going to be a statement banning hunting as they've demanded. And so . . .'

'We'll find him. That's what I came to tell you. I gather that when Chief Inspector Hexham was here this morning he asked you all to avoid talking to the press.'

'Yes. And to our friends.'

'Good. I must stress the importance of it. We shall tell the media whatever's necessary when they need to know anything. Can you manage to say nothing at all?'

'Sure,' said Lavinia, almost amused. 'I detest talking to the press.'

'How sensible of you! Now, I understand that you were not hunting yesterday?'

'That's right. I don't hunt at all.' Lavinia felt horribly inadequate. 'I'm afraid I can't tell you anything about what actually happened to my husband.'

'That's all right. There are plenty who can. What I need from you, Mrs Medworth, is information about him. I met him once and I know about his career and

170

his public personality, but I need some input from you about how he's likely to be taking this.'

Lavinia frowned.

'For instance,' said Chorley carefully, 'do you think he might panic at all? Any history of claustrophobia?'

'Oh no.' Lavinia was relieved by the precision of the last question and spoke decisively. 'None at all. And he's not scared of the dark or mice or any of the things there might be in a cellar – if that's where they've got him. But Hexham said that this is probably just a publicity stunt for the antis.'

'It could well be. In fact we think it probably is, but we have to proceed on a worst-case basis. We'll know more when we see what their next move is – probably to tell the press what they're demanding.'

Trying not to think what the worst case might be, Lavinia took extra care to speak calmly. 'You wanted to know if Tom's likely to panic. I shouldn't have thought so. He's sensible, obviously, and he'll know that you're pulling out all the stops to get him back. They've promised not to . . .' Her voice cracked again and then steadied once more: 'not to hurt him. But if that should change, I don't know how he'd react. Physical pain isn't usually something he makes a great fuss about. No-one who hunts could. They're always coming off and breaking bones. He's not a physical coward.'

'That's helpful. And what about his inter-personal skills? Is he likely to be able to form some kind of relationship with his kidnappers? That could be quite important.'

'It depends what they're like. What sort of people, I mean. Idealists? Thugs? It would make a big difference.'

'We think they're probably amateurs, youngish and pretty impressionable. Possibly quite well educated. We've got psychologists working on a profile at the moment and when we know more I'll tell you. How does he generally respond to other people? Aggressively ever?'

Lavinia thought for so long that Chorley put his question again, worded slightly differently. Looking at him, she tried to assess both his intelligence and his trustworthiness. Eventually she decided that he must score high on both qualities to have reached his rank in an important part of the police force.

'I'm only wondering,' she said eventually, 'if a kind of well . . . arrogance that he usually tries to hide might show up too clearly.' Lavinia smiled painfully and, not wanting the stranger to think she was criticizing Tom, particularly at such a time, added: 'He has bags of charm, as I'm sure you know, but he can be impatient with people who aren't as clever as he is or don't share his tastes. And these people won't do that, however clever they may be.'

She paused, thinking of the occasions when Tom had let his irritation show. There was a curiously alert expression in Chorley's eyes, which worried her. 'Also he hates being insulted or criticized. If his kidnappers started to do that he might not be able to make a joke of it like a less clever person might. In fact I think he might find criticism worse than a bit of sort of . . . well, physical bullying.' She broke off, having to exert all her self-control to keep her terrors at bay. After a moment, she added: 'But then until something happens you don't know how even you'll react, let alone anyone else.'

'True. What about a sense of humour? Has he got much?'

About to say, no, not very much, Lavinia thought back to the early days and felt her lips stretching into a much more real smile.

'I see that he has,' said the superintendent kindly.

'In a way. It's been driven to earth a bit recently,' she said, 'but he can be really funny when something gets him going.'

'Excellent.' Chorley went on to ask her various other questions and neatly sidestepped the things she asked him about whether or not the police had informers among the hunt saboteurs and the various animal rights groups who might have had a hand in the kidnap. It seemed to her highly likely that there would be some police or security service agents planted in the major groups.

'When we find them,' said Chorley at last, 'and find them we certainly will . . .' – Lavinia looked at him gratefully, but she did not interrupt – ' . . . how do you think your husband might react to the kind of rescue action we may have to mount when we've found him?'

'Can you give me some idea what you're talking about?' She thought of films she had seen and novels she had read. Trying to avoid melodrama, she made her voice light, almost frivolous: 'I mean, would it be the SAS rushing in with machine guns? Or what?'

'It will be police, Mrs Medworth, armed police. It's possible that the SAS may be brought in to advise, but it will be police officers who conduct any action. I can't go into any details now since they'll depend very much on the precise physical surroundings, but, for example, should we have been able to place a bug of some kind, will your husband be alert enough to give us useful hints when he talks to them?'

'About their own guns and things, you mean? Yes, probably. As I said, he doesn't panic easily, and he *is* very clever.'

'And if we should break in and shout instructions to him – to lie on the floor or to move to a particular spot, that kind of thing – would he be able to obey?'

'Almost certainly,' she said without even thinking about it. 'He has a lot of respect for the police.' She considered the idea more carefully and added with some of her own humour showing: 'And he's well used to treating the Master like a god when he's out hunting. I should think that shouted instructions are the absolutely first thing he would obey.'

'It all sounds most promising. Now, Mrs Medworth, you must try to keep calm. You can help your husband best by living as normally as possible. The kidnappers may well be watching you for clues to what we are doing, and it's vital that they don't get any. All right?'

Lavinia nodded, unable to trust herself to comment. He bared his remarkably white teeth in another formal smile. 'Don't forget that the statistics are all on our side. Most kidnaps end within five days and the vast majority of hostages are returned unharmed.'

'Physically,' said Lavinia before she could stop herself.

'Indeed, but most make a full recovery in every way. And there are plenty of people qualified to help him at that stage. We'll keep you as closely informed as we can, but you must understand that we won't be able to tell you very much until it's all over. Chief Inspector Hexham will be your liaison with us. All right?'

As she nodded, he stood up and told her that he and his team would be based at Hexham's office for the next day or so.

'Is that all?' She, too, stood up, but she did not move towards the door. The thought of letting him go seemed awful. It was as though his knowledge of kidnaps and terrorism was her only link with Tom. 'There must be more things you need to know.'

'Yes, indeed.' A kindly smile drove the intentness out of his dark eyes. 'But they're things that only people who were on the scene yesterday will be able to tell me.'

Lavinia nodded, feeling patronized yet again but still accepting the sense of what he said. 'Silly of me.' Her voice was much cooler than it had been. 'Thank you for what you're doing. Would you like to stay and have some food with us this evening? As I said, large numbers of hunting friends will be here and it could even help you. No-one need know you're from Special Branch, and you might overhear something useful. Lots of the people coming were out with Tom yesterday. I suppose it's even possible that someone we know is involved.' She shuddered.

'Why do you think a friend might be involved?' Chorley said, sitting down again. Lavinia subsided on to the stump-work stool. Her hands closed together in her lap. 'Just because whoever did it must have known about the family routines, about the hunt, and about the country around here. His hunting friends come into all those categories.'

'Yes, I see. Well, thank you very much for your invitation,' he said, standing up again. 'I'd like to stay.'

'And what about your driver? Will he be all right? It must be freezing out there. Hadn't he better come in, too?'

'Don't you worry about him. I'll nip out and have a word with him and he can come back and pick me up later.'

Lavinia showed him the way back to the front door and ran to the kitchen to find that John had dealt perfectly well with the cheese straws. He was already putting the fourth batch into the oven, along with trays of half-cooked sausages. Charles and Bendy appeared in the doorway with empty plates and Lavinia ruffled her son's hair, grinning at Bendy over his head.

'They all like them, Aunt Lavinia,' said Bendy cheerfully. He put his plastered arm back in its sling. 'Just as they always do.'

'The next batch will be ready in ten minutes,' said John. His face was red from the heat of the ovens and his hair was wild.

'I'll take over, John. You've done wonders,' said Lavinia. 'Go and join the party.'

'OK, Lavvy. See you later.'

When she eventually followed John into the noisy throng in the Great Hall, she was not surprised to see the Special

175

Branch man talking earnestly to Aubrey in one corner of the room, well away from everyone else. She left them to it and did her best to banish reality to the back of her mind so that she could at least look as though she were unworried. The thought that someone in the huge room might know where Tom was being held, might have been involved in taking him, horrified her, but it also made her even more determined to show nothing of her feelings. In a relatively short time she felt confident enough of her voice and her bright smile to play her part.

She greeted old friends and acquaintances first, moving from one group to another, fielding commiserations on Tom's absence 'due to pressure of work, you know'. The more she talked, the easier it became. When she went to talk to one of the local farmers, whose problems with Set Aside she had discussed at one of her surgeries, he introduced her to a Colonel Trewhitt.

She thought that he must have retired from his regiment at least twenty-five years earlier, for he looked to be well into his seventies. Remembering the kinds of things her own father used to enjoy discussing, she asked him what he thought about the latest army cuts. He answered politely but perfunctorily and in turn asked her what she thought of the recent fertilization and human embryology bill on which Tom had spoken in the House just before the disastrous hunting vote. Surprised that someone who looked so conventional should want to talk of such a subject to a strange woman, Lavinia answered carefully.

Fifteen minutes later they were still hard at it and she had stopped trying to disguise her strong views. They were not all the same as the colonel's but he seemed quite untroubled by her disagreement. Looking up at one moment to search for the precise words that would explain what she thought, she saw Philip edging towards her through the crowd.

He touched her shoulder, smiling politely at the older

man. Lavinia introduced them and sketched the development of their discussion. Philip joined in at once, obviously finding the colonel as intriguing as she did. They might almost have been the same age as they talked, Lavinia thought, instead of being separated by at least thirty years, if not more.

'I know that my wife would very much like to meet you both,' the colonel said at last. He smiled first at Lavinia and then at Philip. 'May I fetch her?'

'That would be lovely,' said Lavinia, still mentally reeling in surprise at Colonel Trewhitt's broad-mindedness and easy familiarity with modern scientific discoveries and feminist thought.

He showed his age as he moved, having to rock backwards and forwards to get his legs working properly and, even then, showing signs of stiffness. When he had gone, she smiled up at Philip, ready to take issue with one or two of his opinions.

'You keep up a magnificent front,' he said before she could speak. 'If I didn't know what had happened, I'd have thought you were completely serene. It's extraordinary.' He frowned. 'A bit unsettling, too.'

'It's just a knack, acquired with difficulty and polished up with practice,' she said lightly, trying to remove the faint unease set up by his last comment. Seeing that he was neither convinced nor comforted, she did her best to explain. 'Endless constituency jollies and London parties have taught me that you can't think of your own worries when you're on show. It loses votes. Hiding oneself becomes second nature.'

'All I can say is that it's astonishing in the circumstances.' Philip stopped and when he spoke again his voice was quite different. 'Lavinia, are you all right? Fundamentally, I mean?'

'No. But I will be, especially if I don't have to talk too much about Tom.' She lowered her voice. 'My job is to hang on with as much self-discipline as I can muster until he's back, help the children bear it and not make a fuss that will embarrass him when he has to face everyone again. It may not be much but it's taking everything I've got.'

'It's a lot. And look, Lavinia, I don't want to trivialize what's happened by banging on about myself,' said Philip unhappily, 'but I must tell you that I know everything between you and me has got to wait until he's home. If there's anything I can do to help – anything – you must ask. I don't want you to be afraid that I'll want some kind of pledge in return.'

Lavinia swayed as though she were tempted to lean against Philip's strength. He put out a hand to hold her up in case she overbalanced, but she did not. 'Philip, that is the most generous thing you've ever said to me, and you've said plenty. Thank you.'

'I mean it. Don't forget. All you have to do is tell me what you want and if it's within my power I'll provide it. OK? Deal?'

'It's a deal,' she said, putting out her right hand. He shook it vigorously just as the colonel returned with his wife in tow. She, too, looked as though she were in her seventies, with white hair, faded blue eyes and slackening skin, but it was obvious that she had once been beautiful. He introduced her as Elizabeth Trewhitt, and they resumed the interrupted conversation with surprisingly little constraint. Lavinia was relieved to be able to distract herself from all the emotions that were churning up inside her.

Mrs Trewhitt's voice was much stronger than her fragile appearance would have suggested, and her opinions were as independent as her husband's. Lavinia liked her immediately and was impressed with the way she seemed prepared to take issue with things her husband said, without betraying any of the petulance or anger so many long-married couples resorted to when they could not agree. They seemed more at ease with each other than any husband and wife that Lavinia had ever encountered. She found herself smiling much more naturally than before and even enjoying herself.

As Lavinia listened to them, she had a sudden vivid memory of herself in the tower earnestly explaining to Philip the three stages of marriage as she had understood them. For the first time it occurred to her that there might be yet another stage beyond the laboriously manufactured peace she had achieved with Tom. Before she could even begin to work out what it might consist of, Mrs Trewhitt put a fine-boned, liver-spotted hand on Lavinia's wrist and said gently: 'We really shouldn't be monopolizing you like this. Please don't think that just because we're strangers up here you have to take care of us. You must want to talk to your friends.'

Realizing that she had been standing in silence and probably with dulled eyes and drooping mouth, Lavinia thought of her earlier boast to Philip and blushed as she made herself concentrate on the present. 'To tell you the truth, talking to both of you is one of the nicest things I've done for days,' she said frankly. 'I was wondering why we haven't met before. Have you just moved up here?'

'Oh, no. We live in London,' said the colonel. 'But our daughter's recently rented a house near here and we're staying with her for Christmas. It's splendid of your mother-in-law to have included us in her invitation. Quite unlooked-for civility. Really made Christmas for us in a way, hasn't it, Liz?'

'Do I know your daughter?' said Lavinia tentatively. She did not want to insult them, but she could not place them at all.

'Sally Anlaby, her name is,' said Mrs Trewhitt. 'We're still not quite sure why she chose the north when she decided to move, but it's certainly magnificent country up here – and good hunting, too, which matters to her.'

Lavinia felt suddenly cold and then hot and then very

cold again. She was afraid she knew just why the unknown Mrs Anlaby might have chosen Medworth country.

'I was talking to her a little earlier,' Philip said casually enough, 'but being rather a new arrival myself, I hadn't realized she was new too. Was she based in London before?'

'She's had a flat there for some years,' said the colonel, 'although she hates London.'

Lavinia, who had disliked the idea of Sally Anlaby ever since Aubrey had first mentioned her, could not think of anything polite to say. Philip rescued her by asking whether the Trewhitts had any other children.

'Alas no. And Sally has none either, which leaves us short of young in the family.'

Managing to dig some manners out of her unhappy preoccupations, Lavinia smiled at them both. 'Then it's even more impressive that you're both so amazingly well briefed about things that . . .' She broke off, realizing that there was no polite way of finishing what she meant.

'That wrinklies don't generally talk about?' suggested Mrs Trewhitt with a glinting smile. 'Ah, but London and our friends keep us up to the mark. Will you come and see us when you're in town? I should hate to lose the chance of knowing you properly now that we've met.'

She seemed sincere and Lavinia, whose liking for her could not be changed by any suspicions of her daughter, nodded. It would be good to have London friends who were nothing whatever to do with politics, and friends with whom she might be able to be herself rather than an honorary Medworth.

'And you, too, Doctor Wold,' said the colonel. 'When are you going back to town?'

'Tomorrow, alas,' he said. 'At dawn so that I can be back to relieve my long-suffering partners.'

A muscle in Lavinia's eyelid fluttered as she tried to deal with the shrieking protest in her head. Not to have

Philip to lean on, to look to for comfort, seemed nearly unbearable. When he had gone, she would have no-one.

Nonsense! she told herself. There are the children, as well as the family. I don't need anyone else.

'I'm sorry?' she said, realizing that the colonel had been talking to her again.

'I was merely saying that I think old Mrs Medworth is signalling to you,' he said.

'Oh, dear. I'm getting vaguer and vaguer. It's probably all that Christmas food weighing down my brain. Thank you. I'd really better go and see what needs doing.' She smiled at both Trewhitts, more grateful than she could have said for their interest and apparently spontaneous liking. 'When I come to London I will take you up on that invitation.'

'Do, please,' said Mrs Trewhitt with warmth. 'You go on now and I'll give our address to Doctor Wold for you.'

'Thank you,' Lavinia said, smiling back over her shoulder as she made her way to where Flavia was standing.

It seemed that Flavia wanted her to talk to one of Tom's more influential constituents, who had a problem but felt that he was too important to queue up at a surgery. Not sure whether she was more irritated by his arrogance or by Flavia's assumption that she could be insulted one day and relied on the next, Lavinia smiled sweetly and invited him to tell her all about what was troubling him.

Later, when she had managed to pacify him, she found Philip again and asked him to point Sally Anlaby out to her. Lavinia was not surprised to discover that Sally was ravishing and beautifully dressed. As tall as a Medworth and with the taut, slender body of someone who took her riding seriously, she had short, feathery blond hair and a vividly expressive face, beautifully made up. The small solitaire diamonds in her ears sparkled as they caught the light and gave her face a startling radiance. There were five men surrounding her who seemed completely absorbed in what she was saying, but there were women, too, who looked equally entertained. It was irritatingly apparent to Lavinia that Sally was interesting as well as devastatingly attractive.

Convinced on no evidence at all that Sally had been Tom's latest mistress, Lavinia made quite certain that she never went near her all evening and tried to mock herself out of her pettiness.

Chapter 13

Philip left at dawn the next day. He passed the Dower House and stopped to slide a letter under the front door, but he did not try to wake Lavinia. He thought that she needed every moment of rest she could get. If she had not heard the car's engine he was not going to do anything else to disturb her.

Driving down the moor to her house, he had been fantasizing about the sight of her looking out of a window as he drew up. He had had her running down the stairs in her dressing gown and, perhaps worried about his long journey, persuading him to come in while she cooked breakfast. He was aware enough of his own feelings to laugh at himself and he did not even look in the mirror as he drove away again.

Lavinia heard nothing. In fact when she did wake she found, surprisingly, that she could not make herself get out of bed. There was usually so much to be done that she hated lying about in a curtained room once the night was over. But that morning there was nothing. She did not want to face the day, her thoughts, her family or her obligations to keep smiling.

She turned over and tucked a pillow around her head, but she could not force herself back into sleep. Flopping on to her back, she stared up at the dark ceiling and tried to keep her thoughts at bay. Failing, she said aloud, 'Was it Sally Anlaby?'

There was nothing but circumstantial evidence to suggest that the tall blond, beautiful woman Lavinia had seen at the party had been Tom's lover. She knew she was being childishly stupid in even trying to identify her rival and then thought up a legitimate reason for her curiosity.

LAFE had probably been planning to snatch Tom ever since the much-publicized Commons vote on banning hunting had been announced at the beginning of the last session. They could easily have drafted Sally Anlaby to seduce Tom, found her a house near Saltley to rent, ordered her to join him at the Boxing Day meet, ride at his side and lure him into their trap.

As Lavinia thought about it, she realized how easy it could have been. All the woman would have had to do was entice him into a borrowed horsebox for some illicit love-making. Lavinia had heard enough hunting gossip over the years to know how often that sort of thing happened. She had been given several rhapsodic descriptions of the cosiness of the straw and the horse rugs, the excitement after a particularly good run, the smell of horse, and, above all, the thrilling naughtiness of it all.

'You can hear the Master cursing,' she had been told by one youngish wife towards the end of one hunt ball when everyone had drunk too much, 'the music of the hounds and the wail of the horn, drumming of hooves, yells from the huntsmen. Your blood's up from the terrific run you've just had, and there's this incredibly good-looking, brilliant rider you've always adored with half his clothes off doing the most delectable things to you, and you're absolutely hidden from all your friends and enemies only a few yards away. It's wicked and it's secret and, to be quite frank, darling, it's the greatest fun ever. I don't think Donald would mind even if he knew what I'd been doing. After all, he's always done it. Why shouldn't I?

And it's so much more interesting than boring old married sex. Let's face it, Lavinia darling, that does pall after a bit for both parties, doesn't it?'

Lavinia sat up and violently shook her head. It was absurd to treat what had happened to Tom as though it were part of a thriller. And yet she had no other way of dealing with it. The combination of misery and terror, her longing to do something constructive, and her familiar detestation of the things hunting seemed to make ordinarily delightful people do was making her desperate.

Thinking that fresh cold air and bright light might help, she got out of bed to open the curtains. Bright light seemed too much to expect. The sky was veiled with grey clouds, which made the dead garden outside her window look even more depressing than usual. When she pushed up one of the windows, thrusting hard as the swollen, frozen wood of the window frame stuck against the architrave, she got a blast of icy air in her face.

Leaving the window open, she went back to bed and piled all four pillows up behind her so that she could see out over the gloomy wreck of the garden to the moor beyond. She tried to think and then she tried not to think. Both were painful. She was saved at last by the sound of muffled voices outside her door and then, before she could call out, a gentle knock.

'Come in, darlings,' she said, sharing out the pillows into a soft bank along the whole of the headboard. The door opened and all three heads peered round.

'Really?' said Tammy.

'Yes. It's lovely to have you.' Lavinia flung open her arms and Tammy bounded across the room and up on to the high bed, hugging her mother before clambering over her body and snuggling down at her side. Charles followed just as enthusiastically, although he did not attempt to hug, but Rory walked slowly and got under the duvet at the extreme edge of the far side of the bed.

185

Lavinia reached out across the untidy heads of the other two to stroke Rory's face. He flinched as her hand touched him. Hurt, she bit her lip and decided not to ask him if he were all right until they had a chance to talk without the others.

'Did you sleep?' she asked them all.

'Yes, but I had nightmares,' said Tammy at once and proceeded to tell her dreams in all their ghastly detail. There were foxes' bloody masks and severed pads, bolting horses, prisons, spiders, people chasing her and all sorts of fairly predictable horrors.

'What about you, Mum?' asked Rory as soon as there was a gap in the torrent of words. He sounded as though he minded what the answer might be.

'Not too bad, although it took me quite a while to get to sleep. I don't suppose I'll have a really good night until Dad's safely back with us.'

'Do you think he will be?' asked Charles, his face contorted into a scowl. Lavinia knew that it was to prevent tears leaking out of his eyes.

'Yes,' she said with a conviction that surprised her as much as any of the children. 'We have one of the best detective police forces in the world. They'll find him. I'm sure they will.'

She did not know whether that was true, but it sounded reassuring, and she had no evidence to suggest it was not.

'They really will get him back and he'll be all right again,' she said firmly. 'In fact the policeman I was talking to yesterday said that nearly all kidnaps end within five days, so we can hope that he'll be back even before term begins.'

The two younger children relaxed and moved closer. Rory looked at her from under his lashes. She could not interpret his expression at all and the need to talk to him began to seem urgent. Putting an arm tightly round

Tammy, she said: 'As a treat, shall we have breakfast in bed?'

'What, all of us in here with you?' she said, her reddish face creasing into a smile. 'Coo-ool, Mum.'

'I thought it might be nice, and we need to keep our spirits up. It won't help Dad if we mope around. So, why don't you and Charlie go down and start getting things going? Put on the kettle for my coffee and quite a lot of milk so that you can all have hot chocolate. There are *pains chocolats* in the freezer, and . . .'

'*Pains chocolats*, too? Excellent!'

'You'll manage, won't you? And you can start putting plates and things on the tray and then Rory and I will come down and help and carry the trays up here again. OK?'

Tammy was already clambering over her brothers. Charles took a little more persuading, but at last he went. Rory remained at the outer edge of the bed. Lavinia did not want to threaten him and so she did not move any closer. Not looking at him, she said in as calm a voice as she could produce: 'Is it just the thought of what's happening to Dad, Rory?'

She felt the mattress move and looked quickly to see him shaking his head. He was blushing and his eyes were closed.

'Can you tell me?'

'I . . . Granny-Flavia said . . .' Then to her horror he burst into tears. He had not cried loudly like that, howling and gasping, since he was about three. At the sound of it she did move closer and hugged him. He stiffened, but she did not let go.

'Try to tell me. I can probably help.'

'It's just that it must be my fault,' he gasped, choking.

'Rory, darling, what on earth makes you say that?' Lavinia asked when the paroxysm of coughing was over.

'Well, Granny-Flavia,' he began and then could not go on.

'It's the second time you've talked about her,' said Lavinia, working hard to keep the incipient rage out of her voice. 'What has she been saying to you?'

'Last Christmas she told me . . .' He pulled away, brushed the tears angrily from his face and sat hunched, his face turned away from his mother. In a voice that sometimes faltered he managed at last to get it out: 'I was angry with Dad after we'd had a bit of a disagreement about something, and I . . . She overheard some of what I said to him and later on she told me that I mustn't be afraid of wanting him dead because at my age it was natural to feel jealous of him. She said that I wanted to be in his place with . . . with you, I mean. You know, Mum, sex and all that.'

He sniffed and broke off, keeping his back to his mother. She could see his shoulders shaking.

'I've been thinking about it all night. But honestly, I don't feel like that. And I never wanted him dead. I don't. And the other thing . . . The whole idea is horrible. But Granny-Flavia said I did.'

Lavinia kneeled up on the mattress so that she could put both arms around Rory and she kissed the top of his head. Despite his recoil, she held on to him, determined to free him from the horrible misunderstanding of his grandmother's probably well-meant attempt to explain his feelings to him. She took a deep breath and began. 'Rory, I know that you do not want any harm to come to Daddy whatsoever, and that you have absolutely no feelings like that about me. There's nothing wrong – or peculiar – about any of the feelings that you have for any of us.'

She paused to control her fury and gather the right words. 'I don't think that Granny-Flavia meant what she said quite as literally as it sounded, Rory. She has a lot of ideas about what people's subconscious minds make them feel without them knowing why. But even if her ideas are true, which isn't by any means certain, it doesn't mean that she thinks that what's in anybody's subconscious is that person's fault or what they actually want in real life.'

Lavinia breathed carefully, still hugging her son and leaned her chin on his head. His body already felt less tense.

'I know that you love Daddy and I hope that you love me. I certainly love you, just like I love Tammy and Charles. It's a quite, quite different feeling from the sort I have for Daddy. Rory, you mustn't ever be afraid that the two sorts have to be mixed up together. In some rare, unhappy people they do get muddled, but not in everyone, whatever Granny-Flavia seemed to be saying to you. Do you understand what I mean?'

'Yes, I think so.' He moved his head so that he could glance up at her. 'But why are you so angry?'

She smiled and smoothed the hair away from his worried face.

'Because I hate seeing you made miserable by something that doesn't exist. I'm livid that she made you so unhappy. That's all. I'm not in the least angry with you, Rory.'

He grunted.

'I'm sure that she didn't mean to make you miserable,' Lavinia went on, still holding him. 'I expect that she just wanted to help but got it a bit wrong. All right?'

'Yes,' he said, drawing the word out. Then he turned in her arms so that he was facing her, smiled shakily and nodded, rubbing the back of his left hand under his nose. She let him go.

'You know, Mum, we'd better go down before those two start putting coffee in the milk pan and stuff the *pains chocolats* into the toaster and then try to dig them out with a knife and electrocute themselves.'

Lavinia laughed, admiring his courage.

'You are absolutely right there,' she said, trying to match it. 'In fact, taken all in all, you're not a bad egg.'

He laughed, too, and voluntarily leaned forward, flung

his arms around her and buried his face against her scarlet brushed-cotton nightgown. Then he let her go and leaped for the floor, looking like any twelve-year-old boy who has been let off some frightening punishment.

Lavinia put on her dressing gown and followed him downstairs more slowly, trying to select words that might make Flavia understand what she had done to Rory. Lavinia knew that she should have had the courage to do battle with Flavia years earlier, find out what had made her so hostile in the first place, and work out some bearable way of communicating with her. Lavinia had no illusions about her own imperfections but she did not think they were enough to justify Flavia's unending aggression. She had put up with it for years, but if it were beginning to spill over on to the children, it would have to be stopped.

On her way to the kitchen a few minutes later, Lavinia saw the letter just inside the front door and ran to pick it up, thinking that it might be from the kidnappers with some new ransom demand. When she recognized Philip's writing, she forced herself to calm her thumping heart and perched on the edge of the oak chest to read it:

Lavinia,

Alas, I've got to go back to my patients. You've got the number of the house and my surgery one's at the top of this. Please ring – any time you want me.

I can't tell you how much I wish that none of this had happened to Tom – not for my own selfish reasons, believe me, but because of what it's doing to you. I know something of what you feel for him, because it must be much the same as I feel for Sasha, i.e. a lot of love, a lot of hurt and a lot of rage. But we can't either of us pretend there isn't love.

What we feel for them may not have the easy brilliance of what seemed to be all around you and me on Christmas

190

Eve, but it's there. Don't think I underestimate it, or what you must be going through now because of it.

Remember what I said: anything you want that I can give you is yours. Just ask.

Philip

Blinking, she stuffed the letter into her dressing gown pocket and went to help her children carry trays upstairs.

They had a riotous breakfast in her big bed and by the time they had all eaten and drunk enough there was melted chocolate on the pillowcases, croissant crumbs all down the bed and smears of milk on Tom's table. Lavinia recognized the mood as one of hysteria and a kind of Dionysian excess, but it helped to let out a lot of otherwise inexpressible feelings. Once the children had gone off to their own rooms to dress and she had bundled up the bedlinen for washing and remade the bed with clean sheets, she felt spent and almost too tired to think, which was a blessing.

When she had wiped the smears and stickiness from the bedside tables, she fetched the Hoover. That dealt with the crumbs on the carpet easily enough and the room soon looked normal again. She took off her dressing gown and went into the adjoining bathroom to turn on the taps.

As in most politicians' houses, there was a radio in every room at the Dower House and as soon as her bath was run Lavinia turned it on, just in time to catch the eleven o'clock news on Radio Four. She got into the bath and felt the water swooping up behind her shoulders as she settled back.

'Downing Street have confirmed today that the Junior Environment Minister, Thomas Medworth, has been taken hostage by an animal rights group called the Liberation Army for the Foxes of England. The Prime Minister will be making a statement later today,' said the newsreader calmly before going on to describe the latest horrors in Africa.

191

'Mum?' called Rory from outside her bathroom door. 'Did you hear that?'

'Yes,' she said wondering whether it was the kidnappers or the police who had given out the information. She hoped passionately that it was the kidnappers; that at least would confirm Chorley's view that publicity could be their chief aim. 'It doesn't really make any difference.'

'No. But it sounds worse, somehow, to have heard it on the radio.'

The telephone rang. 'Could you see who it is, Rory?'

She heard him running heavily to the telephone beside her bed. 'Oh, hello, Uncle Aubrey. Did you hear the news? She's in the bath. I'll get her.'

Lavinia heaved herself out of the water. Wrapping a large towel around herself, she hurried back into the bedroom.

'Here she is,' said Rory and handed her the receiver.

'Aubrey? Has anything happened?'

'No. We just wondered when you'd be coming up. There's been a lot of telephoning and the Prime Minister just rang. He asked me to say that he was sorry to have missed you.'

'Didn't you tell him I was at this number?' Lavinia demanded in outrage.

'Lavinia, we could hardly make a man that busy . . .'

'I'll be up in twenty minutes.' Putting down the receiver Lavinia's hands were shaking. She turned to Rory, deliberately smiling. 'Are you all ready to go?'

'Nearly. I'll get the others.'

'OK. I'll dress and lock up.'

All the wild exhilaration of their breakfast had gone. Rory's face was scared and his mother's was set as they left the house. Even Tammy was subdued. They drove between sheets of glittering snow, marked only by the small herringbone tracks of birds' claws and the deeper, rounder marks of small animals.

192

'There's a fox,' said Charles pointing. Sure enough, still, silent and almost taunting, a dog fox stood only twenty yards from the road. The redness of his brush looked magnificent against the white ground and the greyish blue of the sky. After a moment he stopped looking at the car and trotted off over the brow of the hill, leaving his tracks unmistakable in the snow.

If it weren't for that, Lavinia thought, Tom would still be here, safe. Through her fury, she became aware of something moving beside her and glanced at Rory. 'Well at least that one's safe for a bit,' he muttered.

Her face felt as though it were freezing, but she had no chance to say anything as the other two hurled protests from the back seat. When they had fallen into sullen silence again, she said: 'Don't you like hunting?'

Rory screwed up his face as he looked at her. 'I love the riding and the clothes and all the excitement,' he said, 'but I hate the rest.'

'I thought . . . Daddy told me that none of you is ever in at the kill.'

'No. But you know what's going to happen. It's not quite as bad as cubbing though. They cry then, you know, Mum, the cubs. You can't imagine what it sounds like. Babies nearly.' His arms were tightly tucked around his body as though it hurt.

'No worse than a caterwauling tomcat,' said Tammy from the back seat. 'There's one at Salt Farm that howls just exactly and precisely like a tortured baby.'

Lavinia hardly heard her. For all her love, all her attempts to understand and help her children, to leave them free enough to find themselves and yet protect them from as much as she could, she had not managed to understand anything much about Rory; and that in spite of the fact that it was beginning to seem as though he were far more like her than any of the Medworths.

She let her left hand drop from the steering wheel

to his shoulder and gripped it for a second, trying not to feel triumphant delight at the thought that she had passed on some of herself to him.

'Here we are,' said Tammy, her voice rising to a shriek as she added: 'Don't miss the turning, Mum. What on earth's the matter with you?'

They found part of the family having a council of war in the kitchen. Apparently Nicko and Loveday had already left for London, soon after Philip. Olivia, looking fragile but much prettier than usual, was sitting in the old rocking chair next to Great-aunt Elfrida's wheelchair and waiting for Dominic to bring their suitcases downstairs.

'So there you are,' said Flavia, looking, Lavinia thought, as though she were about to dismiss some unsuitable employee.

'There didn't seem much we could do here,' Lavinia said as calmly as possible. 'And so we had a long breakfast. Where are the rest of the young?'

'Up in the Long Gallery with Georgina,' said Caro. Turning to Rory, she added: 'Why don't you take the others up to join them?'

He looked mulish for a moment and then nodded. 'All right. Mum, you will tell me, won't you?'

'I'll come and find you as soon as there's any kind of news,' Lavinia promised him.

'As I was saying, Gerard,' Flavia said as soon as the oak door had closed behind Charles, 'the difficulty may well be with Tom's subconscious desire for an excuse for failing in politics.'

Lavinia gritted her teeth and dug her nails into the palms of her hands beneath the edge of the table. She saw Polly leaning forward as though to say something, but Flavia ploughed on unaware. 'When the police find the hideout, he may do something to stymie their rescue operation. I've explained this to Chorley, but I don't think he completely understood.'

Lavinia looked at her mother-in-law, feeling something much closer to hatred than she was prepared to recognize. Before she could speak, Caro glanced at her and then at Polly, nodded and leaped into the breach. 'I'm not sure that I understand either, Flavia.'

'Don't you, Caroline? How odd! You must know that Tom's always been terrified of failure and, knowing that virtually every politician's career ends in just that, his subconscious has found this way out for him. It's understandable but the implications for his rescue are . . . worrying.'

'That is a quite monstrous thing to say,' said Lavinia, surprised by the venom in her own voice. From the looks of the others, so were they. She stood up and clung on to the edge of the table with both hands. 'I have listened to you ever since I married Tom, and I have tried to believe that you wanted to help people, really to understand them. But now I don't think it's anything like that. I think it's no more than a selfish need to make yourself feel superior to everyone else around you.'

'Lavinia. Steady on.' It was Gerard who had protested, sounding at his most parsonical. She did not even look at him.

'If Tom had been stricken by some vague illness, something no-one could diagnose, then you might have been justified in putting it down to his subconscious. But this? How could you? What sort of a mother are you?'

Something, some barrier, seemed to give way in Lavinia's brain, and words fountained up in it. All the hidden anger, the suppressed resentment at what she had felt to be Flavia's tyranny burst out with a fluency that astonished everyone in the room. She talked and talked, pouring out her loathing of what Flavia had done to her, to Rory and to the rest of the family, not really aware of the words she was saying. Only when she saw her mother-in-law's stricken

195

face looking much older than usual did she stumble, grow unsure again and stop talking.

She gagged then, and put a hand to cover her mouth, while she struggled for mastery over herself. Tears balanced on the edge of her eyelids, raised either by the choking or the shock of hearing herself saying the things she had only thought for so long.

Flavia said nothing at all.

'You're overwrought,' said Frida coldly. She stood up. 'Come along upstairs and lie down. You're not responsible for what you're saying.'

Lavinia obediently went with her and lay on the stripped bed in Olivia and Dominic's room. The ticking of the pillows scratched her neck and the sensation seemed to bring her nearer to herself again. She sat up.

'Lie down, Lavinia. I'm getting you an aspirin.'

'I don't need an aspirin, Frida. There's nothing wrong with me except temper and appalling manners. I must go and apologize to your mother.'

'She'll understand the emotions that motivated your extraordinary outburst.'

At the infinitely superior, soothing tone of Frida's voice, Lavinia remembered every bit of the storm of feeling that had pushed the words out of her, even though she remembered only a few of the words themselves. 'Oh God! Poor Tom growing up with all that,' she said, leaning her elbows on her knees so that she could support her heavy head.

There was a short, barking laugh from Frida as she came back with a glass of water and two small white pills. '"Poor Tom" indeed! He was always spoiled. Aubrey and I had to fight for everything while Tom just eased along in the slipstream, picking up anything he needed instead of working for it. But they saw through him at the Bar. Luckily for him, the House of Commons is rather less demanding. Here, take these.'

Lavinia automatically accepted the glass and the pills

and put them down on the bedside table. 'You sound as though you hate him.'

'Of course I don't hate him. But he's had an astonishingly easy ride. My father always gave him everything he wanted, nearly as much as he gave Sasha.'

That's all you know, Lavinia thought, but she did not say it aloud. 'You and Tom have always seemed so close,' she said eventually. 'I never realized there was quite so much hostility under the surface. What about the others? D'you feel like that about them as well?'

'You've worked yourself into a frenzy, Lavinia. Take the pills, lie down, sleep if you can, and come on downstairs again when you've sorted yourself out.'

Frida turned away, almost with a flounce, and left Lavinia to her thoughts. She tried to remember what it was that Tom had said when she had once, emboldened by his father's sympathy, ventured a mild criticism of Frida. The actual words had gone from her memory, but the sense of them was clear. Tom had been outraged that Lavinia should have dared to criticize a member of his family.

Lavinia asked herself what he would have felt if he could have heard what Frida had said about him that morning. She lay back against the scratchy pillows, sneezing as feathers and dust blew out of another tiny break in the seam, and let her mind loose to look and comment and criticize and feel without any of the internal censors that she usually applied with such rigour. She kept hearing the sound of the telephone ringing in the distance and waited for someone to bring her news.

No-one did and eventually she could bear it no longer and got up, certain of one thing only: she could not bear to spend any more time in Flavia's house at the mercy of the family.

Dizzy with the drama of what she was about to do, Lavinia washed her face in the nearest bathroom, tidied her hair and went downstairs. When she reached the kitchen, she found only Gerard, Aubrey and John there. They looked as though they had been arguing, and all three of them turned sharply at the sound of the door.

'Hello,' she said inadequately. 'I was looking for your mother, Aubrey. I must apologize for making a scene and explain why I'm taking the children away.'

'Yes, I think you should apologize,' he said coldly. 'It was inexcusable. But there's no reason to take the children away.'

'I must. I don't think it'll do any of us any good to have a repetition of this morning's scene. And I'd like your word that if anyone such as the Prime Minister or any of the police working on the case telephones here you will ask them to ring me at home.'

Lavinia waited. When Aubrey did not commit himself, she added: 'If you won't promise, I shall just have to have the calls intercepted by the operator so that anyone asking for me will be given the Dower House number before they even get through here.'

'I say, Lavvy, I'm not sure that's such a good idea.' John Hogarth spoke with none of his usual malice or humour. 'Ever since the radio announcement this morning there've been journalists ringing up for comments and information. We can't take the phone off the hook in case the police or LAFE try to get through, but we can at least deal with the press between us. I don't think you should try on your own. Besides, there'll be all sorts of crazies and loonies trying to get through as well as the media. The last thing you need is any of them having your private number.'

Lavinia took a moment to assess that and then nodded. 'I suppose you're right. We'll have to decide what we're going to do about calls from crazies. Presumably the police will need details in case any of them are giving anything useful away. Are they monitoring them already? They should be. I'd better have a word with Chorley about that.'

She pushed back her hair in frustration.

'You don't have to do anything, Lavinia,' said Gerard soothingly. 'It's all in hand. Now, I know you're upset, but it would be stupid to go and sulk in the Dower House. You'd do much better to move in here with the children so that we can handle everything for you. Aubrey may have sounded harsh, but he's right. And please don't think we're going to criticize you. We know what terrible pressure you're under, and I think we all understand why you flew at Flavia this morning. She does too, and she won't bear any malice.'

'No, of course she won't,' said Aubrey more kindly. 'Gerard's right, Lavinia; don't cut yourself off from us just because you're ashamed you made a fool of yourself this morning. We can help keep you on the rails and shield you.'

'Aubrey.' Lavinia sighed, wondering whether she would ever be able to make any Medworth listen to her and hear the sense of what she said to them. 'I don't think that I can find it in myself to be in this house and listen to stuff such as she produced this morning about Tom. I'd rather face all those bloody tabloids from two years ago all over again than stay here.'

Aubrey was rubbing at the corner of his nose as though he had a spot or an itch there. 'Lavinia.' His voice sounded much less certain; there was almost a pleading tone to it. 'Please don't do anything too dramatic. Try to understand. My mother is desperate, just as worried as you and the rest of us. Is it fair to punish her just because you can't accept some of her odder ideas?'

'And you would go nuts, Lavvy, on your own with the children,' put in John, 'without any of us to help distract you. Fetch some clothes from the Dower House and move in. You can have Dominic and Olivia's room.'

His intervention clearly irritated Aubrey, who frowned. 'I don't think I have ever heard any of you admit that all of your mother's theories might not be right,' said Lavinia slowly. More ideas about the way Tom had grown up were building in her mind. She began to realize just how different it might have been from the perfectly adjusted, wholly understood upbringing he and his siblings had claimed for so long.

'Try not to take your anxiety out on Flavia. Look on your disagreement with her as a challenge,' said Gerard. 'If you accept your anger and offer it up to God as a prayer, you will come to realize that she's simply afraid and tackling her fear in the best way she can. Wouldn't you be, if it were Rory who had been kidnapped?'

Lavinia's head turned slowly so that she was facing him. She nodded, disliking his sanctimonious smile. 'But never, ever, could I have said of any of my children what she said of Tom this morning. I love *my* children.'

Gerard frowned, but Aubrey's face seemed to shrink. It was only an infinitesimal change, but it was enough to remind Lavinia that if Tom had suffered from his mother's emotional autocracy, then so probably had the others.

None of them said anything. The uncomfortable silence was eventually broken by John's saying: 'Well, whatever happens we've got to eat. And there are still twenty-two of us in the house. Someone had better do something about lunch. Will you spud-bash, Lavvy?'

'Yes, all right,' she said, feeling as though she were coming round after an anaesthetic. 'But will we really be that many still for lunch? Gerard, I thought you and Polly were going south this morning with the girls.'

'Not till this afternoon,' said Gerard. He shook himself and then ran both hands through his hair.

'Then you will stay, Lavinia,' said Aubrey, 'for lunch at least? Good. I'll have a word with my mother and ask her not to say those sorts of things to you any more. Gerard, will you come and talk to her with me? John, shall I send you some more hands?'

'That would help. Children probably. Or Caro. She's always been good in a domestic crisis.'

Aubrey and Gerard went out without another word.

'Is it a crisis?' said Lavinia, trying to ignore the physical effects of her turbulent feelings.

'You know it is. Worms turning with a vengeance. I've never seen you like that, Lavinia. It was quite, quite terrifying.'

Wanting to be let off it all, not exactly forgiven but allowed to forget until she could cope again, Lavinia could not help saying: 'What exactly?'

'All the power and eloquence that's been locked up all these years. You shocked the lot of us, particularly when you shrieked at old Flavia that you were not angry because you were in denial but because you were outraged by her twisting the most ordinary anxieties in the world to suit her own sick fantasies.'

'Oh, come on, John! You can't possibly remember everything I said, and I'm sure I wasn't as direct as that.'

He laughed, but he looked more worried than amused. 'There was all that and more. I was so impressed by it all – as well as shocked – that I suspect I'll never forget. You told Flavia that the way she forced her theories on to vulnerable people in distress was a violation and that her whole attitude to the family is coercive and tyrannical; that far from helping people to deal with their feelings, she punishes them for her own miseries and makes them believe that they are mad or wicked.'

'Oh, dear.' Lavinia blew and fiddled with her hair. She thought of the horror into which Flavia had plunged Rory. 'There are times when I have in fact thought a lot of those things, if not quite so exaggeratedly, but I hadn't realized that I'd actually said it all. Poor Flavia. I wish I hadn't.'

'But you haven't actually felt violated, have you?'

'Sometimes. And hated watching her doing it to other

201

people.' Lavinia clamped her lips together then, determined not to tell anyone what Flavia had made Rory think. She opened the larder door and looked in, aware that she was still shaken.

'What am I supposed to be fetching?' she asked as she re-emerged from the cold room.

'Potatoes. There's no time for anything interesting, so we'd better mash them.' He looked at the clock on the wall. It was already half-past one. 'Fish pie, I think. I know there's more bags of fish bits in the freezer, because I put them there.'

In five minutes he had a dozen eggs boiling, four pounds of skinned and boned chunks of cod and smoked haddock defrosting in the two microwaves and an immense pan of water coming to the boil with three peeled onions, several sticks of celery, a cut lemon and a small handful of peppercorns in it.

'What can I do?' said Caro from the doorway. She, too, looked shaken. Lavinia, full of regret for upsetting so many people, walked across the cold noisy flagstones to put her arms around her sister-in-law.

'I'm sorry, Caro,' she said and felt herself pushed away.

'I don't blame you. But it was shattering. I don't quite know . . . Look, let me cook or lay the table. I can't be doing with all these naked feelings. I . . . I detest it.'

John Hogarth gave a snort of laughter as he tipped his defrosted fish into the simmering pan and set the kitchen timer for five minutes. He took another pan and started to melt four ounces of butter in it.

'So do I. In fact I'm still reeling.' Lavinia went on peeling the potatoes as fast as possible. 'You could help with these. We've got to get them sliced, cooked and mashed by the time John's done his roux and peeled his eggs.'

Caroline took a thick chopping board from one of the cupboards and sharpened a triangular-bladed cook's knife so that she could cut up the potatoes Lavinia had peeled. It was not until she had poured the whole pile of slices into boiling water that she said over her shoulder: 'I can't say I don't sympathize. I've felt like saying that sort of thing at intervals for nearly twenty years.'

'Why haven't you?'

Caroline looked at John as though she did not want him to hear and then shrugged. 'For one thing I never felt I had the right. And for another, I didn't dare take the risk.'

'What risk?' asked Lavinia. 'I mean which particular risk?'

Caroline's face crumpled like a child's and then smoothed out again almost at once. 'The risk of what it might do to Aubrey to have those certainties smashed.'

'We ought to have talked, you and I,' said Lavinia after a pause. 'Long ago.'

'You never stop talking, you in-laws,' said John, sounding bitter enough to make the two women look at each other in surprise. 'Huddling in corners, complaining about the family. I've watched you all at it ever since Frida married. At least, no; in those days there was only Julian. He could hardly do it on his own. It started in earnest with you two.'

'And I always thought you were on our side,' said Caro, trying to seem amused and failing.

'I wasn't on anyone's,' he said, beating his white sauce viciously. 'I was half-way between you all, trying to keep everyone happy.'

Yes, thought Lavinia, her senses and sympathies sharply alerted by the emotional upheaval that was shaking her own foundations, you didn't belong in either camp. You must have been lonely too.

Chapter 14

The next morning, after another restless night, Lavinia was woken by the harsh ringing of her front door bell. She pulled the duvet over her head, hating the press. When she had driven the children back from Saltley after dinner the previous night, they had found a thrusting noisy gang of journalists, photographers and television crews camped outside the Dower House. She had run the gauntlet between them, urging the children on and then fumbling with her keys to get the front door unlocked. When she had thrust the children inside, she had turned back on the top step to face the cold, bored, angry pack. Sharp bursts of light had flashed in front of her eyes. The whirr and click of motorized cameras had added to the crunch of gravel and shouted instructions that echoed in the freezing darkness.

'This way, Lavinia. Smile, Lavinia. Look this way,' the photographers had yelled as reporters demanded to know how she felt, what news she had of Tom, what she felt about hunting, and what the Prime Minister was going to do. Eventually they had quietened as they saw that she would talk to them.

'Thank you all for coming,' she had said eventually, doing her best to smile as though she really were grateful. 'I'm sure you're aware that I know nothing more than you. In fact, you journalists usually have so much more information than the rest of us that I'd been hoping you could tell me what's going on.'

There had been a ragged, cynical burst of laughter at that, she was glad to remember, and she had managed to smile more easily at the hungry faces that had come at her, white and threatening, out of the darkness.

'You'll also understand that the whole family is desperately anxious. As soon as we get any news you'll have it too. Until then, please give us as much space and time as you can. Thank you.'

Then, ignoring the whirring, flashing cameras and the insistent voices, she had gone into the house and refused to answer the bell or knocker for the rest of the evening. She had turned on the answering machine so that she could monitor the calls and duck any that were not from the police or real friends. In fact she had ducked the lot.

The front door bell rang once more and she cursed again. Glancing at the illuminated clock at Tom's side of the bed, she saw that it was nearly eight. 'Why can't they sleep in?' she asked aloud as the bell rang yet again.

Stumbling out of bed, she pulled on a dressing gown and ran downstairs in bare feet, silently swearing at the intrusive mob. Leaving the warmth of the staircarpet for the black-and-white squares of the hall floor, she realized how cold it was. With her feet aching and her toes rearing up away from the stone, she hurried across to the mat by the front door to fling back the heavy door. About to launch into a furious tirade, she almost bit her tongue as she saw the postman. Behind him were the journalists already jostling forwards as they saw her. The cameras had started clicking even before she emerged in her dressing gown. Glad that it was floor length and made of firm, thick, dark-blue wool, she ignored them and smiled at the familiar postman.

He said nothing, just pointed his chin downwards. Lavinia saw that he was holding the necks of two vast grey woven-plastic sacks. They rested on the step, rigid with the weight of their contents. 'All for us?'

He nodded. 'And there's as much again for the Hall. More. Sorry to get you up, but I couldn't leave it on the step with that lot ready to tear it all open.'

'No, of course not. Thank you, Fred. I'm sorry you had the bother and all that weight.'

'No call for thanks. It's what they pay me for.' He shifted from foot to foot, opened his mouth, shut it and then managed to say: 'They're right buggers, them antis.'

'Thank you, Fred,' she said again even more warmly. 'I must go in now or they'll rush the place.'

'I get you.'

'And you won't . . . I mean, have they asked you any questions about Mr Medworth?'

'They won't get anything out of me, lass,' he said and heaved the two great sacks over the threshold for her. Then he turned away without another word to trudge back through the crowd to his red van. Lavinia waited only long enough to make sure he was not molested and then shut and locked the front door.

'Are they still out there?' Lavinia turned at the sound of Rory's voice and saw him shivering in his red-and-green tartan pyjamas. He looked very thin and rather scared.

'Yes. But they're basically on Dad's side. They're not our enemies, Rory. We just have to ignore them and when they see that we don't know anything they'll go away. They're just a bore. Nothing worse.'

'OK. Are those sacks for us?'

'Yes,' she said, lugging one of them towards the kichen. 'We're both as mad as each other, Rory. Coming down to all this cold without so much as a pair of bedsocks between us.'

She was glad to see his pinched face soften into a smile. He even laughed. 'You never wear bedsocks, Mum.'

'No, but in this weather it might be sensible. Come on into the kitchen and I'll make us a hot drink to take to bed again. There's no point getting up yet.'

'Aren't you going to open any of the post?'

Remembering John's warning about the sort of people who might try to contact her, Lavinia shook her head and told Rory what John had said.

'But most of the letters must be from friends and things. Otherwise how would they know where to send them?'

'Unfortunately it's not very difficult to get people's addresses these days. And the sort who write to abuse people they hate are used to finding out where their targets live. They had most of yesterday to do it in.' She stroked his head. 'I think it's best if I take the sacks up to Saltley with us when we go. Uncle Aubrey and John can give us a hand sorting the letters out up there.'

'But we'll never be able to carry them out through that lot out there. Couldn't we have a look here? Please. Then if I recognize anyone's writing, we can open their letters. There might even be one from Dad. It would be awful if there was and we didn't find it. Can't I, Mum? Please? It would be something useful.' He looked away, biting his lip and then muttered: 'I need to do something useful.'

Lavinia switched on the kettle, knowing exactly what he meant.

'Please, Mum.' He stood shivering in front of her, his hands clasped together, and his dark-brown eyes wide and insistent. 'Please.'

'All right. But we'll just sort the envelopes: typed ones into one heap; hand-writing we recognize into another; handwriting we don't into a third. OK? And I don't want you actually opening any of them because some may be pretty rude. People do sometimes get very silly when they

207

start writing letters about people like Dad who've been in the newspapers. All right?'

'OK.'

'I'll fetch your dressing gown and slippers. You go and stand by the radiator and warm up a bit. We can start when I get back.'

'Thanks, Mum,' Rory said, already wrestling with the seal on the first mail sack. He gave up after a moment and fetched a heavy knife from the kitchen drawer.

Upstairs Lavinia was waylaid by Charles, who was rubbing the crunchy bits out of his swollen eyes and wanted to know what was happening. He insisted on joining in with the letter sorting and ran down the stairs, leaving her to collect Rory's thick dressing gown and slippers.

When she got back to the kitchen she saw that there were already several heaps of letters in front of both boys. She felt Rory's neck which was almost as cold as the hall floor had been, draped his dressing gown around his shoulders and led him to the radiator. While he was thawing out and stuffing his feet into his slippers, she picked up the pile of typed envelopes and shuffled through them. Recognizing the stationery and the huge type used by Downing Street secretaries, she opened the envelope and read the Prime Minister's formal condolences. At the foot of the letter was a hurried, handwritten postscript: 'Lavinia, I was sorry not to be able to speak to you this morning. I gather you were resting. Please don't be too alarmed. We're doing all we can to get him back. I'll ring Saltley again tomorrow, as near eleven as I can manage. James.'

Lavinia looked at her watch, determined to be in place to receive the call. She knew that she was unlikely to be able to speak to him if she rang Downing Street herself. The wives of junior ministers were not among the people who had an automatic right to speak to the Prime Minister and the telephonist would probably not even put through her call, even in those most extraordinary circumstances. Her mind still mostly on what must be going on at Westminster, Lavinia reached for another letter from the typed pile and slit open the envelope.

That one, too, had been typed on paper that felt expensive to the touch, but there was no address at the top. There were three, perfectly typed lines:

> Thomas Medworth has got what he deserves. I hope they torture him as he has tortured foxes all these years. Nothing is too bad for people like you. You should be torn apart by dogs yourself.

'I suppose that's only to be expected,' Lavinia said aloud, carefully folding up the letter and sliding it back into its envelope so that Rory and Charles would not see what it said. She tried to make out the postmark and was disheartened to see that the letter had come from central London. There could be no help from that.

'What's to be expected?' asked Rory, looking up from a pale-blue envelope he had been studying. 'I say, I think this is from Mr Fowler at school.'

'The science master?'

'I think so.'

Lavinia put out her hand and saw that the envelope had been addressed to Rory himself.

'Shall I read it first?' she asked, trying not to sound as though she were taking any rights from him.

'Why?'

'It's just that some people will probably take advantage of what's happened to Dad to write horrible letters, and I'd hate you to be upset by having to read them. You know, people who disapprove of hunting. I don't suppose Mr Fowler would do something like that, but I could check in case the letter isn't from him but just someone whose writing looks like his.'

'It's all right. You shouldn't read horrible letters either. I'll see what sort it is.'

Lavinia held on to it.

'It's all right, Mum. If it looks awful I won't read any more. You get on with the others and don't worry.'

'All right.' Deeply reluctant, Lavinia let him have his letter and opened another envelope addressed to herself in writing that looked vaguely familiar. It was from a constituent who had heard what had happened and wanted to express his sympathy. She had got to the end of it by the time she heard the rip of paper from Rory and looked up to see him unfolding the letter. He flushed as he read it and then handed it over.

My dear Rory,

This must be a difficult time for you, worrying about your father. I hope that he will soon be back with you and that in the meantime you will be able to keep yourself from thinking too much about what may never happen. You have a strong imagination. That's a wonderful gift. But it is a gift with a disadvantage: it can make you worry more than a less sensitive person would do. Try not to let yourself get sucked into fear. That feeds on itself and then on you until it wears you out.

Your good friend, Simon Fowler

'I thought he hated me,' said Rory, sounding dazed. 'He's always so angry.'

'Well, he obviously doesn't hate you at all. That's a kind and very sensible letter. Will you write back?'

'Probably.'

Lavinia pinned Mr Fowler's letter to the kitchen notice board so that it would not get lost in the growing piles of paper on the table. She could tell from the way Rory was sitting hunched over his heap of envelopes that he was feeling unsettled and she knew exactly why. Everything that had once seemed solid now cracked and shivered around him. Even enmity was no longer certain.

'What are you doing?' cried an indignant voice from the doorway. 'You've been leaving me out again. It's not fair.'

'Tammy,' said Lavinia with a sigh. 'No-one's leaving you out of anything. I just wanted you to get as much sleep as you needed. All these are letters I've been sent. Some of them are nice; some nasty. The boys are just sorting them out into types for me to open. D'you want to join in?'

Tammy was already dragging a chair to the table and brushing her hair back out of her eyes with her free hand. A moment later, she had bent down to grab two overflowing handfuls of letters from the open sack and was shuffling through them. Her lips were pushed forward into an angry pout and she was working hard to make sure she sorted envelopes more quickly than either of her brothers.

Lavinia made coffee for herself and hot chocolate for the children and then gingerly opened such letters as looked safe. Most of them came from old friends, relations, constituency workers and party activists. Every so often she came on another that, although it had looked civilized from the outside, turned out to contain violent invective or disgusting filth.

After reading one series of particularly revolting insults, Lavinia fetched a large pile of plastic carrier bags from the sackful under the larder shelf and began to label them with a freezer pen: 'Anonymous', 'Pro A – D', 'Anti A - D', 'Pro E – K' and so on. The letters could then be thrust into the appropriate bag when she had glanced through them.

'Why are you sorting them like that?' asked Charles.

'Because we'll probably have to answer the nice ones in the end,' said Lavinia. 'And the police may want to see the others in case there are any clues.'

'But there are hundreds. You'll never be able to answer them all.'

'Dad's secretaries will probably help and the party volunteers, too.'

'There's something in this one,' said Tammy, picking up a small padded brown envelope.

'We won't open that now. No, don't waggle it like that. Stop now. Give it to me,' said Lavinia sharply, adding: 'What time is it, Rory?'

'Quarter to ten. Why?'

'I've just got to ring someone up,' said Lavinia, taking the padded envelope with her. Tammy looked mulish.

The envelope was addressed in capital letters and the postmark was smudged. At the door, holding the envelope as far away from herself as she could, Lavinia said over her shoulder: 'I'll be in my bedroom. Don't open any more letters till I'm back. Just sort them into typed and handwritten. And if there are any more with things in them, put them carefully to one side and don't touch them again. All right?'

'All right,' said Tammy with a heavy sigh, reaching down for another bundle from the mailsack.

Lavinia ran upstairs to her bedroom telephone, stumbling over her loose sheepskin slippers. 'Could I speak to Chief Inspector Hexham?' she said as soon as her call had been answered. 'Or Superintendent Chorley?'

A moment later Hexham came on the line. She explained why she was ringing. 'And so should we open it?' she said when she had described the padded envelope.

'It doesn't sound like a bomb, but you can't be too careful. Don't touch it. We'll deal with it. I was coming over to see you today in any case. Are you at the Dower House?'

'Yes, I am at the moment, pretty well besieged by journalists and cameras and things.'

'That's only to be expected, I'm afraid. I'll be with you as soon as I can. Fifteen minutes probably.'

Lavinia used the time to dress and was sitting at her

dressing table, staring at the photograph of Tom that she always kept there when she heard the police car turning into the drive. Once again the camera crews burst into action, but they could not have caught many pictures. Lavinia was waiting by the front door ready to open it the instant Hexham reached the top step. He had Sergeant Pleasington with him and an unknown, tough-looking young man with steady eyes and a hard mouth.

Lavinia took all three of them into the kitchen, where the curtains were still shut so that at least they would not have cameras pointing at them through the windows. Tammy looked curiously at the newcomers and asked them who they were. Hexham introduced himself and his sergeant and then, pointing to the teetering heaps of unopened envelopes on the kitchen table, added: 'And what are you doing with all that?'

'We're sorting the mail,' she said, sounding surprised and as though it should have been obvious to him. 'And those are just letters that look as though they're from crazies and loonies.' Lavinia thought she must have been talking to John Hogarth the previous day. 'Mummy wants to open them herself.'

'She's a brave woman, your mother,' said Hexham and then grinned as he looked back at her standing in the doorway.

'Thank you for that. Shall I show you the other one?'

'It's not in here then?'

'No. Upstairs out of the way.'

'Carry on the good work, kids. We'll be back in a minute. Sergeant Pleasington can give you a hand, eh, Susan?'

'Sure, sir.'

'How are they?' he asked Lavinia quietly as they went upstairs with the other man tagging along behind them. Hexham had not introduced him, which seemed odd.

'Managing.'

'And you?'

'The same. Although my temper's unreliable.' She thought back to the scene she had made at Saltley. 'Frighteningly so in fact. There's the package.'

Hexham looked at the envelope as it lay on her bed and then glanced at his colleague.

'Over to you, Sam?'

'Right.'

'We'll leave you to it then,' said Hexham, standing beside the open door. 'Mrs Medworth?'

Lavinia meekly walked out into the passage. 'What now?'

'We wait. Shall we go downstairs?'

'All right.' Thinking that he might talk more freely without the children present, she took him into the study and switched on the lights. 'Luckily there are shutters in most of the rooms as well as the curtains. We're pretty well protected from the cameras.'

'Yes. But it's depressing to be besieged like this. It won't go on too long. It never does.'

Lavinia did not answer, knowing that it might well go on until Tom was back, and then it would probably only intensify, with everyone wanting his story of what had happened and his reactions to it and his plans for the future. Doing her best not to think about anything at all, she took the guard away from the fireplace, brushed the old ash down through the bars of the grate, laid a new fire and lit it.

The man Hexham had called Sam looked round the doorway, saying: 'It's fine. Just a cassette tape. Nothing sinister.'

'What's on it?' demanded Lavinia, noticing that there were traces of silvery powder clinging to the plastic case. He must have checked it for finger prints as well as whatever else he had done.

'I haven't listened, Mrs Medworth,' he said with a slight smile. 'Not my job.'

'Have you a machine here?' asked Hexham.

'Yes. But I don't want the children to hear whatever it is.' She pulled forward her small dictating machine, turned the volume button low and swapped the tape for the one that was already in the machine and pressed the 'play' button.

As the tape unreeled, she was deeply grateful that the children were safely in the kitchen with Sergeant Pleasington. The contents of the tape proved to be a series of heartbreaking screams. Lavinia had to sit down, longing to block her ears. Hexham listened stony faced. The other man was examining the books in one of the bookcases over her desk, apparently uninterested. Her only comfort as the agony went on was that the screams could not possibly be made by Tom. They were too young, too childlike.

They came to an end at last. Then came the familiar, hateful voice of the LAFE spokesman. 'That's a taste of what Thomas Medworth is listening to all the time. He has films, too, shot during hunts, and still photographs as well, so that he can watch exactly what happens to a fox when hounds rip it apart while it's still alive and screaming like you've just heard. He's beginning to understand what a hunted fox feels like. And he's not taking it too well. In fact, we're not sure how much more he can take at all. Copies of this tape have gone to Downing Street, to the radio stations and, with a selection of photographs, to the newspapers.'

The tape whirred on with no other sound. Lavinia whispered: 'They said they weren't going to harm him. He must . . . Oh, God!'

She felt a large, warm hand on hers, tried to speak and failed.

'It's quite likely, you know,' said Hexham, 'that that's just for your benefit – and for the publicity. Your husband may not be listening to or seeing anything at all. Them

215

sending it to the papers does suggest that this really is a stunt. It's a good sign.'

'All right,' said Lavinia, trying to feel anything but horror. 'Damn! What time is it?'

'Half-past ten.'

'I've got to go in a minute, I'm afraid,' she said, extremely anxious not to miss the Prime Minister's call. 'I'm sorry to sound hysterical, but I'm going to have to get the children dressed and go. Is there anything else you need before you go?'

'Nothing at the moment, although we will have to have a look at the letters.'

'Yes, I suppose you will. But there are hundreds of them and the same up at Saltley apparently. You can't possibly have enough manpower to read them all.'

'It'll take us some time. We're in touch with your brother-in-law up at the Hall about it and as soon as the arrangements have been finalized we'll explain them to you. By the way, I don't think you're hysterical at all. You're bearing up well under the kind of stress no-one is equipped to deal with.'

'Thank you.'

'I'll have to take the tape away with me, and the envelope, but you can have them back if you like.'

'I don't think I want the tape back. Well, perhaps. I'm not sure.'

When Hexham had taken his colleagues away it dawned on Lavinia that she could always ring the Downing Street switchboard and ask them to put the Prime Minister's call through to her at the Dower House rather than Saltley. There really was no need to leave the house and face the press again.

The telephonist took her message without protest and Lavinia sat by her desk in the study waiting for the Prime Minister's call. When the telephone rang, she grabbed the receiver and was disappointed to hear Aubrey's voice. She explained crisply why she needed a free line and told Aubrey she would ring him back.

'I just wanted to make sure you're all right,' he said, sounding hurt. 'The postman told me you were surrounded with press as well when he dumped two sacks of post on you. Are they bothering you?'

'Only if I actually go out.'

'And the letters? If they're anything like the ones we've got up here, you must be upset. We're sorting them out so that we can hand all the hostile ones over to the police; if you bring your sacks with you, we can do yours, too.'

'Don't worry: I can cope. I'll fill you in later, Aubrey. Thank you for ringing. Good bye now.' She put the receiver down without waiting for his permission or even his acquiescence.

The Prime Minister got through at four minutes past eleven and was both gentle and honest. 'You do understand why we can't give in to what they're asking, don't you, Lavinia?'

'Understanding it isn't the problem. You believe that if you give in to this lot, someone'll start picking off ministers every time they want any bit of legislation changed.'

'Good. I'm glad you see the point.'

'Yes, but I can't bear the thought that Tom is to be sacrificed for the protection of other politicians in the future.'

'There's no question of sacrificing him. None whatever. You're not to worry about him. We will get him back. The police are pulling out all the stops. I can't go into any detail on the telephone.'

'No, of course not. I understand that, too,' said Lavinia, thinking of the ease with which bugs could be planted on anyone's telephone line.

'You're taking it all just as I expected you would,' said the Prime Minister. 'Tom will be proud of you.'

'Thank you.'

'I must go now, Lavinia, but I will ensure that you're

217

kept up to date as far as possible. Don't be afraid for him. He'll be all right. I'll speak to you soon. Goodbye.'

'Goodbye, James.'

Lavinia put down the receiver and tried to believe what he had said. When she was sure that her face showed none of her feelings, she went back to the kitchen to make sure the children were not opening any of the letters. She discovered that they had switched on the kitchen radio and were listening to a vibrant masculine voice saying: 'While I don't in any way condone what this particular group has done, you must understand that when legitimate means of changing uncivilized behaviour have been so comprehensively blocked, people who feel as strongly as many animal-rights activists do are often forced to take drastic action.'

Lavinia waited for the interviewer to protest, but she was disappointed with his politely phrased question. 'Is it legitimate, in a democracy, to try to alter legislation by committing crimes?'

'Look at the suffragettes. They tried fair means first, peaceful protest, lobbying and so on, but it was not until they roused the country by smashing windows, causing damage to the propertied classes, and got themselves properly publicized that they had a hope of changing anything.'

'It was the First World War that changed everything that mattered,' said Lavinia.

'It's stupid talking to the radio,' said Tammy rudely. 'You're just so stupid, Mum.'

Seeing that Tammy was looking miserable beneath her truculence, Lavinia turned the radio off and went to hug her. 'I know it is,' she said into Tammy's rough, unbrushed hair. 'But they made me cross. Now, what about dressing? We can finish sorting the letters later.'

'I don't want to. I don't see why I should. There's no point. And it's none of your business what I do anyway.'

218

'Tammy.' Lavinia knelt down on the floor in front of her daughter so that their faces were almost level. The boys had stopped sorting envelopes. Lavinia looked at them briefly over her shoulder and smiled as reassuringly as she could. Then she turned back to Tammy. 'I know that you feel cross and miserable. We all do. But we've got to keep going and behave as normally as possible. It won't help anyone if we're horrible to each other.'

'You're not miserable. You don't even care.'

'I am, but I'm trying to keep it inside as much as possible. There isn't any point going on about it. All that would happen would be that I'd make you three – and myself – feel even worse. Don't you think so?'

Tammy's hot face crumpled and tears seeped out from under her scrunched eyelids. She shook her head violently from side to side. Lavinia tried to hug her again, but she made her body absolutely rigid. Lavinia took her arms away and temporized by stroking Tammy's tangled hair.

'You don't care about what's happening to him,' she shouted, her eyes still screwed tightly shut. 'You hate hunting and you hate us and you hate Daddy. And you'll be glad if he never comes home. I hate you.'

At that Tammy wrenched away and flung herself out of the room. Lavinia, who felt as though she had been stabbed, breathed carefully and stood up to face her horrified sons. They all heard a door slamming upstairs.

'She didn't mean it. She's just in a state. I'll go and calm her down. Are you two all right?'

'Yeah,' said Rory, picking up a heap of envelopes and glaring at Charles, who did likewise. He looked particularly shaken. 'We'll be fine, Mum. Don't you worry about us.'

'Charles?'

'I'm OK,' he said in a growling voice, not looking at her.

Lavinia left them to it, knowing that she could not deal

219

with all three at once. As she followed Tammy upstairs, she told herself that it was perfectly natural for a ten-year-old to say the sort of thing she had.

'She doesn't really believe any of it,' Lavinia muttered. 'She's a child and she's unhappy and not thinking straight. In normal times she must know that I love him – and her.'

Stiffly walking into Tammy's room, she saw the child lying face down on her bed, both hands clenched into fists on her pillow. Her body was heaving with sobs. Lavinia sat on the edge of the bed, but she did not try to touch her daughter.

'Go away. Leave me alone. I hate you. I hate you. I hate you.'

Wait, Lavinia told herself, hoping that the yells had not reached the waiting ratpack outside. She told herself to wait until Tammy was calmer and she herself able to speak kindly. The crying will stop, Lavinia said to herself. It's better that she knows you're here. She's only a child. She can't understand what she's making you feel. And your feelings are not her responsibility anyway. She'll learn to understand later. Wait. Wait.

As Lavinia waited an unregulated part of her brain started to taunt her. Waiting's always been your philosophy, hasn't it? You thought that if you waited patiently enough Tom would start to love you again. But it never happened, did it? Waiting's not enough. And you're not enough either. You've never been enough for anyone.

'Tammy,' she said aloud, ignoring the ideas as well as she could. 'Tammy, don't give in to it like this. You know really that I love you very much and that I love Dad. Come on, darling, try to stop crying. You'll make yourself sick if you sob and gulp like that.'

Speaking as gently as she could, trying not to let her own feelings and terrors make her voice sound harsh, Lavinia repeated her message and her encouragement over and over again. Gradually Tammy grew calmer. Choking, wiping her face and nose on her pillowcase, she eventually stopped crying, but she stayed lying on her front with her face in the pillow. Lavinia stroked her back.

'Well done, Tammy. Lie quiet for a bit.'

The telephone rang. Lavinia did not move. After four rings the sound stopped, to be followed a minute or two later by the sound of running feet and then Rory's voice:

'Mum? Mum? Where are you?'

Lavinia moved and Tammy whirled round and clutched her round the waist. 'Don't go.'

'All right, darling.' Lavinia turned her head slightly to call: 'I'm in Tammy's room. Who is it?'

'Someone from the *Sun*.'

Suppressing an oath, Lavinia called back: 'Will you ask them to ring Uncle Aubrey? They'll have the number at Saltley. Don't say anything else to them, will you, whatever they ask?'

'OK.'

As his footsteps retreated towards the kitchen, Lavinia set about reassuring her daughter.

Chapter 15

Gradually Lavinia and the children got used to the extraordinary life of ever-increasing anxiety and media siege. The first horrible frenzy among the journalists had quietened by the end of the first day but there was still quite a crowd outside the house for several days after that. Questions were shouted at Lavinia and the children whenever they opened the front door. She would not let them leave the house on their own and tried to impress on them the importance of never answering any of the journalists, whatever they said.

Tammy could hardly bear not to respond to the more provocative questions as Lavinia edged the big car through the crowd and sometimes had to be forcibly restrained from opening the car windows to yell insults at the reporters. The boys seemed quite capable of holding her down, but Lavinia wished that she would not fight back so obviously. The thought of the possible photographs appalled her.

She continued to let the machine answer the telephone and spoke only to her closest friends and the police. Philip rang every evening at ten, when he knew that she would be back from Saltley and that the children would be upstairs in their own bedrooms. His calls helped her to keep going. He never said anything more about his feelings or his needs; he just turned himself into an absolutely reliable friend whose affection made no demands on her at all.

It soon became clear that Chorley and most of his team had returned to London and Lavinia's only regular police contact was with Chief Inspector Hexham. He continued faithfully reporting once a day. Usually there was no news at all, but sometimes her hopes were excruciatingly raised. There was one evening when he rang to say that they had found the horsebox in which Tom had been removed from the hunt. But it led nowhere. The horsebox had been stolen hundreds of miles away a week before the kidnap and had been found abandoned in the carpark at a children's hunter trials in Surrey. There were marks on the number plates that suggested it had recently carried false ones, but no-one knew what the false number had been. The only identifiable fingerprints in it were Tom's. And the vehicle examiners had found no useful evidence of where it had been driven or parked: they had found no unusual mud in the tyres, no hairs or fibres, nothing to give any clues at all. The only good news for Lavinia was that there was no sign of any blood.

More often Hexham had nothing to report. He managed to persuade her that everything possible was being done to find Tom, but he was not allowed to give her any details. She just had to use her own imagination, and Aubrey's experience, to give her a mental picture of the operation.

Tapes of screaming fox cubs kept coming to her through the post and she forced herself to listen to them all the way through in case there was a message from Tom in the middle. There never was, but she clung on to her certainty that he was still alive, unhurt, and sane.

But it was hard to keep her terrors under control as days went by without any obvious progress. She continued to take the children up to Saltley after breakfast every day, because even that was better than sitting at the Dower House waiting for news that never came.

On the fifth day after the snatch everyone was even more keyed up than usual, having believed Superintendent Chorley's reassuring information that most kidnaps ended within five days. The tension at Saltley was almost unbearable and after lunch Aubrey suggested taking Lavinia for a walk to relax her. She looked at him as though he were completely mad, saying: 'I've got to stay by the telephone. You go.'

She was glad when he managed to persuade everyone except Great-aunt Elfrida to go riding with him instead. The only good thing that day, Lavinia felt, was that she had a respite from Flavia. Throughout the long, empty afternoon Elfrida said very little, apparently concentrating on her heavy-looking book as they sat on either side of the fire, waiting.

The day dragged itself out with murderous slowness. There was no news. Lavinia telephoned Hexham just before half past five to ask whether anything had happened. She knew perfectly well that if it had he would have rung her at once, but she needed to do something.

He was kind but preoccupied. As she had suspected, there was nothing he could tell her. She put down the receiver, no better off than she had been, to face the rest of the family.

After that day, the atmosphere at Saltley grew even worse. In the interests of peace Lavinia had reverted to her old methods for dealing with Flavia and listened in withdrawn silence to long analyses of the emotions, motivations and probable actions of the kidnappers, Tom, and his fellow politicians. Flavia seemed to have learned nothing from Lavinia's outburst, but she herself had learned a lot and for most of the time she managed not to say anything at all.

When she did answer back, she kept her temper, but to her surprise several of the Medworths lost theirs. Fierce arguments would blow up over their differing reactions to articles about hunting or kidnapping in the various newspapers. There would be childish squabbles over which television programme to watch when there were relevant ones on more than one channel. Meals became a nightmare as the possibilities of civilized conversation disappeared completely. In the old days it had only ever been the youngest members of the family who quarrelled, but soon even Aubrey and Frida seemed unable to say anything that did not spark off a verbal battle.

After one particularly gruesome lunch nine days after Christmas, when most of the journalists had got bored and left or been ordered away by their editors, Lavinia suggested to her children that they might prefer to spend the last few days of the school holidays alone in the Dower House. All three of them looked appalled, although Rory quickly corrected his expression to one of polite blankness.

'But what would we do?' asked Tammy at once. 'We wouldn't have the stables or the Long Gallery for roller skating when it snows or the cousins or anything. And there'd be all that bloody time to fill. Ugh!'

'We could be at home with Mum and help her with the letters and things,' said Rory, watching Lavinia's face. For once she did not even seem to have heard Tammy's swearing. That worried him. 'And there are books and the television,' he went on. 'And we could go for walks. It would be perfectly all right.'

'It would be awful. Television's boring,' said Tammy crossly. 'Stupid. Granny-Flavia's right: it's only people with second-rate minds that watch.'

'There's hardly any of the holidays left and then I won't see Bendy for three months, Mum.' Charles's lip quivered. 'He's helping me with my dressage. It's not fair.'

Rory was still looking at Lavinia with eyes full of anxiety. Seeing it, she smiled at him and hoped it was not despicable of her to feel even more for him than she felt for either of the others.

'It's all right, Charles,' she said, slowly turning away from Rory. 'It was only a suggestion. But don't you all hate the arguments at meals?'

'What?' said Tammy. 'No, of course we don't. It doesn't matter what the aunts and uncles say. We don't even listen when they're snarking at each other. And if we weren't here, who'd exercise Cupcake? Honestly, Mum, you're mad. We must be here.'

Wanting them to have whatever pleasure or distraction was available, Lavinia gave in at once and tried to forget her own loathing of the hostility that bombinated around the table at every meal.

Ancient, incredible resentments began to resurface. Awful accusations were hurled across the table, no less violent for the occasionally gentle phrasing or the patronizing pseudo-understanding with which they were phrased. But the worst scene took place in the kitchen before lunch two days before the end of the children's school holiday. It was set off by an inoffensive remark Sasha made about disliking washing spinach.

'That's absolutely typical of you,' Frida hissed from the table where she was carving the remains of the ham. 'You always shirked your fair share of unpleasantness. That's why you ran away to Africa just when Father was beginning to grow frail and needed you most. You've always shifted your responsibilities on to the rest of us. And no-one ever pulled you up for it. They let you get away with murder from the day you were born.'

As Lavinia watched, Sasha dropped handfuls of huge, yellowing, slug-holed spinach leaves into the sink and turned to face her sister. Different expressions appeared on her face as quickly as light and dark patches fly over a sheet of water when a stiff wind sends clouds scudding across the sun. There was anger, guilt, resentment, misery and even a kind of private satisfaction.

'You always were a bitch,' she said quietly, almost

226

spitting the words out. 'You were jealous of me, weren't you? Even though you had more than I did. You always had all the new clothes and I never had anything but your horrible hand-me-downs, five years out of date by the time I got them.'

'Don't be so petty. You were spoiled to death.'

'Hah! Anyway, why are you so angry about my going to Africa? You wanted me out of the way, didn't you? Could it be that Papa didn't like you any better for my absence?' She affected a laugh. 'That's what it is, isn't it? But didn't you ever think that perhaps he might have realized how much you hated me and thought it unjust? Don't you think that was why he used to take my part when you'd savaged me? Not because he started off preferring me. He didn't: he thought you were wonderful. But you've always had this fantasy that I took him away from you.'

Frida's face whitened and she started to shake. As she opened her mouth to retaliate, Lavinia stepped forwards, thankful that at least none of the children had witnessed the outburst.

Before she could speak, Sasha had taken a breath and started again: 'Isn't that why you're always so angry with me and everybody else? All that jealousy of yours was idiotic, and it ruined my childhood. Why the hell do you think I took the first possible opportunity to put thousands of miles between us? You could have had everything. I didn't take your share. You threw it away.'

At the sight of Frida's face, Lavinia knew she could bear no more. Without giving either of them a chance to do anything else, she said sharply: 'Stop it, both of you. This is only going to make it all worse.'

'It's none of your business, Lavinia. Keep out of things you don't understand,' said Frida, not even bothering to look round.

'It *is* my business. It's my husband who's in danger – terrible danger all the time – and it's my children and me

227

who are affected by what you're all doing. This house is hell at the moment and you're behaving like six-year-olds. Grow up, for heaven's sake!'

The two women stared at her. In their surprise and resentment at her interference, the family likeness between them was exaggerated. All the Medworth haughtiness returned to their angry faces and they even moved a step closer to each other. Frida was taller than Sasha and her hair much greyer, but there was no mistaking their bond – or at that moment their loathing of their sister-in-law.

'All right,' she said with a slight smile. 'Band together against the intruder, just as you've always done. It makes you feel better, but it doesn't change anything. You all try to hide from what you feel behind your mother's psychoanalytic theory and fantasies of superiority. But what's happened to Tom has blown it all apart, hasn't it? You've been forced to face the fact that you do feel things like other people, and it's scaring the lot of you out of your wits. But you won't cure the fear by tearing yourselves apart over it.'

'Lavinia, you're hysterical,' said Frida, looking quite different from the pale, angry antagonist of a moment earlier. 'We can manage here. You'd better go and lie down.'

Lavinia turned and left them to it. She knew that they would reform their sisterly closeness by discussing her inadequacies and they would soon feel all the better for it. She did not mind what they said about her behind her back, or at least not much, but their quarrel told her that once the children were back at school she really would have to get right away from Saltley.

Tom usually drove them back at the beginning of every term. Flavia had decided that in his absence they ought to go by train, but Lavinia was determined to take them herself. She did not say anything to Flavia for a while, in order to avoid an argument, and when she did was faced with the usual explanation of why she simply was not up to the task. For once she stood firm and to her pleased surprise Caro supported her. Aubrey had gone back to London by then, but Caro was staying, as usual, for the entire school holidays, as were Sasha and Frida.

Early on the day before the children were due to go back to school, fifteen agonizing days after Tom had been taken, Lavinia got up after another bad night to make herself some tea and sat in the kitchen with both hands wrapped around the big stoneware mug, not drinking, just staring at the curtained window, seeing nothing.

It was obvious to her by then that the police and whichever arm of the security services had been involved in the search for Tom had got nowhere with their attempts to negotiate with LAFE or with their informers, their interviews with everyone who had been following the hunt on Boxing Day, or their suspects among the known animal-rights activists.

Very near despair, Lavinia heard the heavy thump of the days' newspapers on the front door mat and went out into the hall to fetch them. Reading through them a little later she was appalled to see that there was not a single headline about Tom in either the broadsheets or the tabloids. It seemed a horrible irony to mind so much that the tabloids were ignoring him, since there had been a time when she had cursed their obsession with Tom and his affairs. There was a paragraph in each paper announcing that there had been no more news of him, but that was all. None of the features were about him any longer or even about hunting or kidnapping. 'Hardly even a nine days' wonder,' Lavinia muttered. She turned on the television and there was nothing about Tom there either.

The terror that had been with her all along returned. It must have become clear to LAFE by then that the government was never going to give in to their blackmail, even if they had originally believed it might work. And if their true aim had been publicity for their cause, they must have been watching the dwindling news value of the story with nearly as much despair as she was herself. Lavinia could not bear to let herself imagine what they might do to Tom once they gave up hope of getting what they wanted.

She opened the kitchen curtains a crack and saw that there were only two reporters left, sitting in their fuggy car outside her gates. They did not have a photographer with them. She pulled the curtains right back and opened the window to let some fresh air into the house. The two men in the car did not even move.

It crossed Lavinia's mind then that perhaps Special Branch had had something to do with the virtual news blackout. All along they had said they wanted as little publicity as possible. She began to wonder whether they were trying to push LAFE into taking some action that would betray their hiding place. If so it seemed a terrifyingly risky strategy. Hexham's almost daily reassurances that heaven and earth were still being moved to get Tom back began to seem like so much soft soap.

Lavinia tried to keep a sense of proportion but it was very difficult. She decided that once she had taken the children back to school, she would go on to London and stay there until Tom was found. There at least, she would be nearer the people who had the power to keep up the search for him. There was nothing she could do in Yorkshire, after all, and in London she would at least be able to see Philip sometimes and that might help to keep her disintegrating self together.

It was only then, as she drank her tepid tea that she remembered the children's school trunks. Three of them were too heavy for any car and so she was in the habit of packing them in advance and having them delivered to the schools by a local haulage firm which had a regular run between North Yorkshire and the South-East. But it was far too late for that. Angry with herself for forgetting – and with the children for not reminding her – Lavinia fetched the school lists from her desk and went upstairs to start assembling the uniforms.

When it was a respectable enough time to start telephoning people, she took a break from packing and rang Chief Inspector Hexham to ask him for a number where she could reach Superintendent Chorley. Sounding both surprised and, for the first time, obstructive, Hexham asked if there were anything he could do to help her.

'No thank you,' said Lavinia firmly. 'I need to speak to him.'

'I'll get him to call you,' said Hexham irritatingly. 'Where will you be today?'

'At the Dower House.'

Chorley rang at half-past eleven, when the three children were reluctantly sorting out their tip-like bedrooms. Lavinia shut the study door.

'Thank you for ringing,' she said. 'I thought I ought to tell you that I'm coming to London tomorrow. I'd like to consult you about what's going to happen next. May I come and see you?'

'I should be delighted to see you, Mrs Medworth,' said Chorley sounding anything but pleased. 'But I'm not sure how much point there would be.'

'With your help I would like to make a public appeal for information,' she said, trying to sound as though she knew what she wanted and was prepared to fight for it.

'Mrs Medworth . . .'

'It seems clear to me,' she went on as doggedly as possible, 'that the likeliest way you're going to get him back is if someone betrays the kidnappers.'

'I can assure you that . . .'

'I know you're doing everything you can. But I do not see how an appeal could cause any harm and I want to do it.'

'I must confer with my colleagues on this, Mrs Medworth.'

231

'Fine. I'll be here until about ten tomorrow morning and at our house in London as soon as I've dropped the children. I'm not sure how long it will take, but there is a machine if you want to leave a message. The number is . . .'

'It's all right. I've got the number. I'll be in touch.'

She put the receiver down and tried to nerve herself for another scene with Flavia. All the old feelings of inadequacy in the face of the Medworths surged up in her and for a moment she was tempted just to go away to London without even trying to explain herself. Then the memory of how badly she had already failed Rory by refusing to speak out, and the thought of what Tom must be going through, stiffened her dissolving courage. Leaving the children to their tidying, she drove up to Saltley, found Flavia and announced what she was going to do.

To her astonishment, Flavia just looked at her for a moment and then turned away, saying: 'If you must you must. There's nothing I can do to make you see sense. You've never listened to me. I've given up trying to make you understand anything at all.'

She walked into her study and shut the door, leaving Lavinia staring after her in astonishment. As she left the great house five minutes later she had a moment's purely instinctive terror that some frightful cataclysm would follow her bid for independent action. Then she reminded herself that the cataclysm had already taken place.

Late that evening, after the children had gone to bed and she had washed up the supper things and put the last few things in the trays at the tops of their trunks, she telephoned Philip. It was not until he told her that he thought her decision to go to London perfectly sensible that she realized what she had wanted of him.

'And how have you been, really?' he asked later. 'You've been very reticent about what's been going on in the She-Wolf's lair. Has it been horrible?'

There was exquisite relief in telling Philip everything that had been happening. Lavinia took care not to repeat any of the particular things that Sasha had said or had had said to her, but the atmosphere was describable and she laid it out for him in vivid detail.

'It sounds like sheer hell. I never thought that there'd be anything worse than the Medworths banding together against us, but clearly fragmenting Medworthery is worse.'

Lavinia laughed.

'I shouldn't find anything funny at the moment, but it is such a relief to hear a joke once in a while. It's been grim, trying to keep the children OK, trying to keep my temper, trying not to be too afraid for Tom . . .' Her voice croaked into nothingness and she had to stop trying to use it.

'What is it? Try to tell me.'

She coughed and felt the flesh of her throat rasped and sore.

'Bring your chin back,' commanded Philip down the telephone wires. 'Don't cough. Just bring your chin back into your neck and swallow. Calmly. OK? Now try.'

'Sorry. It's just that it's been so long now. What kind of state is he going to be in? Are they feeding him? Is he freezing in some wet cellar? The weather's getting worse and worse. And if they're playing those hellish tapes to him, or putting him through some sensory-deprivation business, how will he cope? Are they sending him mad? I try not to think about it all, but . . .'

'I know,' said Philip and she was grateful that he did not try to pretend she was exaggerating the dangers. 'But I think he's probably got the strength to withstand whatever they're doing. He really is a tough bloke, Lavinia. And I doubt if they're putting him at real risk. After all, it's in their interests to keep him well and usable. He's the goose and they'll be determined to get their golden eggs.'

'Unless,' said Lavinia, voicing one of her worst terrors,

'they give up and remember that . . . that dead men tell no tales.'

'It's possible,' he said, still taking her seriously, 'but I'd have thought it unlikely. It's quite hard to dispose of a body without leaving any trace – particularly when the weather's this bad.'

'Why?'

'It makes digging such very hard work,' he said drily.

'When's Sasha due to go home?' Lavinia asked, suddenly desperate to change the subject.

'I don't know. I was going to ask you.'

'She hasn't told me.'

'Well, if she's not back tomorrow evening, would you like to meet? Will you be too tired? Not for anything other than friendliness.'

'Oh, Philip, you can't imagine how much I need friendliness just now. That would be lovely, but not out anywhere where we might be spotted. Will you come to the house? Tom's and mine, I mean? There's bound to be some food in the freezer there, and at worst we could always have bread and cheese. There's stacks of the Christmas Eve Stilton left. I'll bring it with me.'

'Perfect. Eight o'clock?'

'Yes. I'll see you then. Thank you.' She put down the receiver and went upstairs to sort out the clothes she would need in London.

All three children spent a large proportion of the journey begging Lavinia to let them stay with her in West Square until Tom was rescued, telling her that she would need them to help get him back. To all their blandishments, and arguments, she said the same thing: 'You can't help Dad except by carrying on as normally as possible.'

'But what about you, Mum?' said Rory at one moment, almost breaking through her defences. 'Will you be all right without us as well as Dad?'

234

He was sitting beside her in the front of the Landrover, looking at her with a concern that seemed far too mature for his narrow face.

'You know I'd much rather have you with me, but I'll be all right. Watch the signs, will you, Rory? We need to turn off at junction eight.' Lavinia eased the battered Landrover back over into the left-hand lane when she had overtaken a crawling truck and looked quickly down at her watch. It was a long time since she had made the long school run south and she had forgotten what a strain it could be. If it had not been for the three trunks, she could have used Tom's car, which would have been far more comfortable.

The boys' school came first on the route they had chosen together and by the time she had dropped Tammy, Lavinia's head was aching and she longed to lie down. The last leg of the journey did not usually take more than about an hour, but she reached the outskirts of London just as the rush hour was beginning. Every junction seemed to be clogged with angry, unhelpful drivers who seemed to take perverse pleasure in blocking her turns, and she did not reach the house in Lambeth until half-past six.

Pulling up the handbrake at last, she sat for a few minutes, just enjoying the stillness and the lack of noise after the long, battering journey. Then, when she was sure that no suspicious characters were lurking on the pavement to jump her as she emerged, she got out, relocked the door, and let herself in to the house.

It was cold but stuffy, as she thought any efficiently burglar-proofed house would have to be. After all, she said to herself, when you can only open the windows an inch or two and only then when there is someone in the room to repel intruders, you'll always have stuffiness. All the old dislike of the locked-in, beleaguered feeling that London had produced in her returned with full force.

At least the house was clean enough. Mrs O'Grady,

235

who came in twice a week and acted as Tom's house-keeper between Lavinia's irregular visits, had seen to that. There was plenty of bread in the freezer next to a pile of ready-cooked meals for the microwave. Cartons of Long-life milk were stacked in one of the cupboards with boxes of tea and bags of coffee. The fridge seemed to be almost full of mineral water and bottles of lager, but there were also a lump of butter, three half lemons that were growing penicillin on their cut surfaces, and half a pound of bacon well past its sell-by date.

Without bothering to unpack, Lavinia emptied the kettle, washed it out and, having run the cold tap for long enough to clear stale water from the pipes, refilled it and made herself a cup of strong tea. She drank it sitting in the old rocking chair in the kitchen and thought how ironic it was that Yorkshire, which had always seemed so safe, should have turned out to be so much more dangerous than the streets of London.

Eventually she set about getting the house ready for occupation again. She herself had not been there since early November when she had gone up to London for a big party at Downing Street and it felt strange and unwelcoming. When she had switched on the boiler and lit the gas-log fire in the small double drawing room, she walked round the room, trying to feel at home in the little house.

As she prowled about the rooms, straightening pictures and plumping up cushions and remembering how happy she and Tom had once been there, she began to think it was absurd that she had ever left it. She had to remind herself how sensible her move to Yorkshire had seemed when Tom had first been elected to Parliament.

It had been obvious to both of them then that the London house would be far too small once they had more than one child. Equally clear had been the fact that some-one would have to spend a lot of time in the constituency, keeping the voters happy and dealing with all the local demands. Tom could not do that if he were to build up the right kind of support at Westminster, and it seemed only practical for Lavinia to take it over. Constituency business could easily be combined with looking after the baby, they both thought, and Tom had assumed that Flavia would be able to help out if Lavinia needed a break.

Lavinia had been more than willing to go, having seen the move as a chance to escape the loneliness that had grown out of her inability to make Tom happy or to be happy with him. It had worked, too. Living in the Dower House and getting it decorated, she had found it much easier to cling to her memories of the good times between them and her hope of retrieving them. Tom had sounded affectionate whenever he telephoned, and when they met at weekends there had always been so much factual news to exchange that they had been able to forget nearly everything else. As she grew to be at ease with her new work, Tom had been visibly impressed with the way she was dealing with the constituents and she had begun to feel that he valued her for that at least.

Their semi-detached life had worked for a long time, but, looking back at it, Lavinia began to see it all quite differently. She wondered whether, if she had stuck it out in London, they might have fought their way back into the sort of marriage she had always wanted. At the very least if she had been there in London with him all the time it would have been harder for him to have slipped into affairs with other women. She looked around the drawing room and wondered how many of them had been entertained in her house.

Her mind went at once to the diamond bracelet and the most ferocious jealousy she had ever known seized her. Her whole body began to shake. Absurdly, she felt that she had to know for sure whether it was the beautiful Sally Anlaby who had been sleeping with him, as though it made any difference who it was. Upstairs in what had once felt like her own bedroom, she turned out the pockets of Tom's suits and jackets as they hung in the wardrobes, but there were no letters to be found. None of the new-looking books dotted about the house had any inscriptions in them, and there were no cosmetics or boxes of tampons in the bathroom that did not belong to her.

Unhappy and ashamed of herself, Lavinia read through the big leather-covered diary for the previous year, which still lay on Tom's desk. There were all kinds of cryptic entries that could have meant anything. But several consisted merely of the letter S and seemed to tell her all she needed to know.

Her old suspicions that Sally might have been implicated in the kidnap returned to torment her and she blushed as she remembered passing them on to Superintendent Chorley. He had looked embarrassed enough to suggest that he knew of a connection between Sally and Tom, but he had convinced Lavinia of her innocence of the kidnap at least. Apparently everyone who had been hunting on Boxing Day had been questioned and Sally had been able to satisfy the police that she had been accompanied by at least one other person throughout the day. Between them the witnesses had given the police proof that she could have done nothing that could possibly have helped kidnap Tom.

Lavinia opened the handsome leather address book that someone had given him and sure enough she found Sally's address and telephone number on the first page. Lavinia told herself that there was nothing particularly incriminating about that. No-one had made any secret of the fact that he knew her. There were addresses for several other women, too, and they could not all have been his mistresses. Almost without meaning to, Lavinia pulled forward the telephone and dialled Sally's number. After four rings a machine cut in. 'Hello!' said a cheerful, slightly throaty voice. 'This is Sally Anlaby. Sorry not to come to the 'phone. I'm a bit busy just now. But leave a message and I'll get back to you as soon as I can. Thank you for ringing.'

Lavinia listened to the bleep, toyed with the idea of leaving a message, and then put her finger on the cradle to cut the connection. Lifting it again to get a dialling tone, she telephoned a local Indian restaurant and ordered some food for herself and Philip and tried to stop thinking about Sally Anlaby.

He arrived five minutes before the delivery from the restaurant and hugged her as soon as she had shut the front door. She rested against him for a while, not speaking, and then took him into the drawing room and poured him a drink.

When the food arrived she left Philip to unpack the spicy-smelling bundles in the kitchen while she went down to the cellar and brought back the first bottle of red wine she had found. They ate at the kitchen table, scooping the food straight from the cartons on to their plates, licking their fingers when they dipped in the sauce and drinking the unsuitable burgundy that they could not really taste because of the spices. They talked of books they had both enjoyed and swapped stories about their childhoods, trying to pretend that they were just two friends casually eating together and unworried by anything at all.

'D'you miss Scotland?' Philip asked, scraping the last bits of sauce from one of the foil boxes.

'Not these days. It's such ages since I belonged up there. My parents are dead, my brother Sandy's in America, skiing at the moment I think. He can't have heard the news or got my letter yet or he'd have been in touch. I know he would.'

'Of course he would,' said Philip.

'Yes, I know he would.' She pushed away the thought of Sandy and the ease with which he had forgotten the existence of his family once he was old enough to travel under his own steam and earn his own living.

'Um. I've still got some cousins in Rannoch and a few old school friends dotted about Scotland, but I hardly ever go up there except for family funerals and weddings. I don't belong there any more.' She looked down at her hands and surprised herself by adding: 'I don't actually think I belong anywhere any more.'

'Lavinia.' Philip put his hand half-way across the table. She shook her head, wanting to understand herself rather than be comforted. After a moment he withdrew his hand and started eating again, but with rather less enthusiasm.

'I was so glad to leave Yorkshire this morning that I thought I'd be all right as soon as I was here,' she said, wanting Philip to understand why she was so edgy and uncooperative. 'But now it's worse and all the feelings I've been trying not to notice keep popping up all the time. This house feels so strange. I've no place here either. I don't know who I am or who I should try to be, or even who . . .' She broke off and looked at Philip. His face was blurred.

'Don't worry about it so much,' he said eventually after an unhappy silence. He left the food on his plate and picked up the cardboard lid of one of the dishes, folding it in half and then in half again and again until it was too stiff to bend any more. 'Things went wonky for you and me on Boxing Day, didn't they, even before Tom was taken? You said he had written to you. Was it his letter that caused the trouble?'

'I think it must have been.'

'Why?'

Lavinia concentrated on dissipating the mental fog that seemed to fill her brain and pinned down something she felt. 'Because it showed me that it wasn't only he who hadn't seen me.'

Philip looked puzzled.

'D'you know what I mean?'

240

'Not completely.' He stared down at the stained and crumpled cardboard between his fingers. Lavinia frowned, unfairly hurt that he had stopped understanding her with such heartwarming ease.

'Then d'you want to read his letter?' she said, trying to get rid of the idiotic – and selfish – feeling of being let down. 'I've got it here. I keep reading and rereading it. It might show you . . .'

'Not much.'

'Oh. Sorry. No, I see. It's just that in it he apologized for things and said that I'd been irritated by his weaknesses.' Lavinia put her right hand over her eyes for a moment and then, as they began to smart, realized that she must still have curry sauce on her fingers. She took her hand away and wiped it on a piece of kitchen paper.

'He sounded so unhappy in the letter that I could hardly bear it. You see, I'd always thought it was only me.' Lavinia's forehead clenched with the effort of understanding and then telling the truth. 'I thought that we were living like that because that's what he wanted, and that it was up to me to put up with it or go. And I always knew . . . I mean, until what happened to you and me happened, I always knew that I didn't want to go.' She looked at Philip and saw from the tightness in his face that he was hurting.

'But now it looks as though he hadn't wanted it like that either,' she said, still wanting Philip to understand. She felt that he might not look so unhappy if he understood. 'All that effort and sadness had been for nothing, but worse than that really. Destructive. D'you see now?'

Philip nodded, but he did not say anything or look at her, continuing to examine the wedge of stained cardboard between his fingers.

'And if something happens now; I mean if he isn't rescued and . . .' Lavinia did not want to say the words. But she knew she had to say them. With an enormous effort, not looking at Philip, she did it.

'If Tom dies, having written that letter, feeling that I had cut him off from me because of failings of his, I . . .' The strain of the last week, the lack of sleep, the terror for Tom, the arguments with Flavia, the wine she had just drunk and the effort of the long drive in an unsuitable vehicle, all combined and poured out of her in a storm of tears that infuriated her, but she could not stop it.

Philip cursed himself loudly, dropped the cardboard and went to take her in his arms.

Chapter 16

Philip stayed in West Square that night, sleeping in one
of the two spare bedrooms. He looked into Lavinia's
room just after seven the following morning to say good
bye, adding: 'I'll ring you this evening to see how you
are and if you need anything.'

She had been awake for more than an hour, thinking
round and round her problems, her regrets, her feelings,
and anything she could do that might help to get Tom
back. When Philip came in, she thought that he was
looking tired but she was relieved to see him smile. She
held out a hand to him. He took it and sat on the side
of her bed, gently stroking her face.

'I'm sorry,' she said, meaning that she had offered
him only the spare bedroom.

'Don't be sorry. It's enough to know that somewhere
in you is a kind of love for me. I'm not wrong about that,
am I?'

'No. You're not wrong at all. There always will be,
although . . .'

'I know. You needn't say it. I've got that message loud
and clear.' He smiled with difficulty. 'I must go now, but
will you promise to ring me if you need anything?'

'Yes. I will. And Philip . . .'

'Yes?'

'I wish it could have been different.'

'I know.' He leaned forwards to kiss her lightly, and then left.

When he had gone, Lavinia did her best to banish the looming depression and the panic that had been in her mind when she woke at half-past five. She dressed and made up her face as well as she could, disguising the bags under her eyes and her pasty-looking complexion before going downstairs to drink a lot of very strong coffee. She forced herself to eat, too, and sat at the kitchen table making a list of all the things she had to do, from having her hair cut to persuading Chorley and his unknown colleagues to let her start fighting to get Tom back.

The Superintendent himself telephoned soon after ten to say that her suggestion of an appeal for information had been discussed at the highest level and that it had been sanctioned. Arrangements had been made, he told her, for a press conference that afternoon. He would be making a short announcement to the assembled journalists, she would then say her piece, and they would both answer questions. 'Although we would like you to restrict yourself to specific answers to any questions about what is being done and what you know of the kidnappers. You may, of course, say what you choose in answer to any personal questions.'

'Fine.'

'Good. We'll run through it with you here beforehand. Could you get here by two o'clock? The press are due to arrive at two-thirty, which will give the BBC plenty of time to get you on to the six o'clock news.'

'Two is fine,' said Lavinia. 'Where do I come?'

He told her and then rang off, leaving her to arrange a hair appointment at half-past twelve. She went upstairs again to change into a formal dark suit and look out some more dramatic earrings. Having packed them in her large handbag with her make-up kit and a tape-recorder, she

244

locked up the house and set off on the first of her private tasks of the day.

The weather was surprisingly good for January, crisp and sunny, and so she decided to walk up to the House of Commons. She went past the Imperial War Museum, smiling at a gaggle of small boys standing staring up at the soaring guns that seemed to guard the building. Ten minutes' brisk walking brought her to Westminster Bridge. She stopped on the bridge itself, shivering in the sharp wind, and looking across the Thames towards the Houses of Parliament.

She felt a sudden intense hatred for the place. Tom had worked too hard there for miserable rewards. He had been vilified in the press. His mother, brother and sisters despised his work, believing that only second-rate people would ever want to be elected to Parliament. Many of his colleagues had treated him as an enemy throughout the acrimonious debate on the banning of field sports. And, at last, he had been kidnapped by a gang who objected to the result of the free and democratic vote. It seemed a cruel repayment for eleven years' devoted service.

A large bus drew up and disgorged a group of excited tourists, who all wanted to take photographs of the gothic façade from the best vantage point. Lavinia realized that she was in their way and hastily walked on.

The policeman at the main door of the building recognized her at once and almost overset her by the directness of his sympathy. But she managed to hold on and was soon on her way up to one of the secretarial offices. It was a small room, rather dark, and there hardly seemed room in it for the three desks, their chairs and the row of filing cabinets. An electric kettle was perched on top of one with a tray of mugs, a jar of coffee, boxes of teabags and a scruffy-looking bag of sugar.

To Lavinia's relief the only person in the room when she got there was the one she had come to see. Teresa

Somercote was no longer working for Tom, but it was clear from the sight of her lined face, reddened eyes and general air of emotional collapse that for her at least their relationship was still very much alive.

'Do come in,' she said in a quivering voice. She was standing behind her desk, clinging to it as though for protection. 'I'm so sorry. I'm really so sorry, Mrs Medworth.'

'Yes, I know,' said Lavinia, trying not to hate her or to ask herself what on earth Tom could have found so alluring in her. Teresa was not particularly pretty, although she was slim and long legged. Under her velvet hairband her mouse-coloured hair was very clean and it had been brightened with artificial highlights. Her eyes were small and a dreary faded blue. Her smile, when it came, was sweet and gentle, but her clothes were positively dowdy.

'Would you . . . ? Would you like coffee or anything?' she asked.

'Yes, please. Some coffee would be nice.' Lavinia counted up the number of cups she had already drunk that morning and quickly added: 'Actually, tea would be better if you've got any.'

'Only rosehip or camomile bags.'

'Rosehip would be lovely. No caffeine at all. Teresa, don't look so worried. I haven't come here to have a row with you.' Lavinia smiled. 'I'd hardly do that after all this time, now would I?'

The other woman shook her head and turned away to switch on the kettle.

'But I gather that you still see quite a lot of Tom, and I know that he's always found you very easy to talk to.'

'Thank you,' said Teresa, gulping.

'I just wanted to ask if you knew who else he's been seeing. It's really quite important for me to know just now.'

Teresa's brimming eyes overflowed, washing mascara down the sides of her nose, and she shook her head. She looked humiliated as well as unhappy and guilty.

'I don't know. I sort of needed to, too, if you see what I mean, but he didn't tell me anything this time. It was the first time he'd ever clammed up on me and it made it all the harder. I didn't mind, you see, that there were others. Well, I didn't have the right to mind since I'd . . . Oh, I'm sorry, I didn't mean it like that. But I did mind when he stopped talking to me about them.'

'I think I can understand that,' said Lavinia, wincing at the dryness of her own voice. It struck her that she was in a position to get answers to a lot of the questions that had tormented her for years.

But before she could find the right words to ask any of them, Teresa poured boiling water over the herbal teabags, put down the kettle and wailed: 'I can't bear not knowing what's happening to him.'

'I'm not sure that I can either,' said Lavinia after a long pause.

Teresa blushed again as she shook her head and then picked up her mug to hide her face.

'I wish I could help,' she said a little later when she had got her colour and her tears under control again. 'But I don't know a thing.'

'Although this place has always been such a hotbed of gossip?'

'I know it has, but not this time. I used to tell myself that it was partly that Tom had to be extra careful once he was a minister, although we do know about lots of their goings-on.'

Lavinia could not quite bring herself to ask Teresa whether she had ever heard of or met Sally Anlaby, and she could not think of anything else to say. Feeling that she had made a fool of herself to no purpose, she sipped the rosehip tea, which was still too hot to drink comfortably, and tried to think of a way of leaving the office gracefully.

'The only thing I do know is that something went wrong,' Teresa said abruptly into the unhappy silence.

'When?'

'Towards the end of the last session, just before the big hunting debate.'

'What happened?' asked Lavinia. 'And how do you know?'

'I'm not exactly sure what it was, but he came here to the office late one evening when everyone else had gone home. He was in a dreadful state.'

Lavinia felt her face beginning to harden. The thought that Tom had wanted to confide in Teresa even though he had broken with her nearly two years earlier was hard to bear.

'But I couldn't help him. He was just as sad afterwards. Oh, Mrs Medworth, don't look like that. I'm so sorry. I didn't mean to say that. But, you see, it didn't seem to matter very much at the time. He was so miserable and he wouldn't talk. It was the only thing I could do for him. But . . .'

Teresa started to cry in earnest. Lavinia, who was having a hard enough time dealing with her own emotions, knew that there was nothing she could have done to help even if she had wanted. She left Teresa and walked back into the mockingly bright sunlight to hail a taxi to take her to her hairdresser off Sloane Street, hoping that a new haircut might give her some much-needed confidence for the press conference.

She decided that she did look better when she emerged with her hair looking even sleeker than usual, but she felt no different as she set off to meet Superintendent Chorley and a young woman from the Scotland Yard press office. They took her through the appeal they had drafted for her and then told her of the sort of questions she would be asked and the answers they wanted her to give. When she had learned the text to their satisfaction, they led her into the press briefing room to sit in the middle of a long table in front of the waiting journalists.

The lights were much hotter than she had expected and she was afraid that her face would begin to sweat through her carefully applied make-up. Surreptitiously she switched on the tape recorder she had brought in her handbag so that she would have a record of everything she said. She knew from experience that she would probably wake in the middle of the night, terrified in case she had said something dangerously wrong. If she could listen to a recording, she might be able to keep her anxiety under control.

At last Chorley started his speech and then he introduced Lavinia. The stills photographers jockeyed for the best position and she did her best to smile in different directions as the press officer had suggested while she repeated her little speech.

Then the questions began. The journalists seemed less aggressive than the ones who had camped outside her house, but the questions were much the same. She declined to answer any that were to do with her views on hunting and confined herself to the prepared answers to all those about the operation against the kidnappers. Hoping that she had done adequately, she glanced at Chorley, who smiled encouragingly just as an unpleasantly familiar voice called from the back of the room: 'And how do you feel about your husband's kidnappers, Mrs Medworth?'

Peering over the heads of the journalists in the first few rows, Lavinia saw the grinning face of Ben Wroot, who had been her chief torment when the scandal of Tom's affair with Teresa had first broken in the *Daily Messenger*.

'Angry,' she said coldly, departing from the prepared text for the first time.

'And how do you feel about your husband now?'

'I love him very much,' she said, hating to have to say anything so personal, 'and I am extremely concerned about his wellbeing. I have no idea where he is being held or in what conditions. As you can imagine, that is a nightmare.'

The press officer stood up then and announced that the conference was over. Lavinia watched Wroot slouching towards the door. She turned to Chorley. 'You will tell me as soon as anything happens, won't you?'

'Of course we will. You did very well indeed.'

'Thank you. Now, may I take it that the embargo against speaking to the press has been lifted?'

'I don't . . .'

'I don't mean talking about the kidnap necessarily. But I do want to give some interviews.'

'May I ask why?'

'Yes, of course. There's so much anti-hunt feeling in so many otherwise sympathetic people that I want to remind them that Tom is a human being and that whatever they think about hunting, nothing can excuse what's being done to him. As far as I can see at this stage publicity about his humanity and decency can only help. You need information about who's got him and where, and we'll only get that if someone who knows something can be persuaded that the kidnappers are not justified in what they've done after all. You don't still think we ought to keep quiet, do you?'

'Not necessarily. Or we'd never have had this press conference. But you will take care, won't you? Don't . . .'

'I don't know anything about your operation,' she said, letting some of the exasperation sound in her voice. 'There's nothing I can give away.'

'True. Well, within reason we won't object to your giving interviews on personal matters.'

'Good. And thank you for arranging this.' She shook hands with both Chorley and the press officer and went back home to start telephoning Tom's colleagues to enlist their active sympathy.

Before she started she listened to her messages and was touched to hear one from Julian Collingham inviting her to dinner that night. He told her that Frida was still up at Saltley for another two days but that he and Georgina would like to take her out to a new restaurant they had discovered. She rang him back at once to accept and then made a start on her list of influential members of Tom's party.

She wanted to make absolutely certain that, whatever their views of bloodsports, they were solidly behind the police effort to find him. All the ones she managed to speak to were superficially sympathetic, but she got the distinct impression from several that they were not altogether unhappy with the idea that Tom Medworth was in trouble. None of them was crass enough to say so, but it was clear that some of them disliked him intensely.

Some of his colleagues were honest enough to admit that they hated hunting and disapproved of Tom's support for it, and Lavinia did not mind that at all. What she hated was the sly pleasure she could hear behind some of the formal expressions of sympathy and the whole air of 'serves him right' that came across from two of his fellow junior ministers.

When she had put down the receiver after talking to the second of them, Lavinia was suddenly reminded of the disintegration of Medworth solidarity in the days before she fled from Yorkshire, and she realized that she had seen a faint reflection of that unpleasant satisfaction in Aubrey, Frida and even Sasha. None of them, she was absolutely certain, wanted real harm to come to Tom, but there had been a hint of excitement in their reactions to his disaster. It had always been quickly suppressed, and Lavinia had not recognized it for what it was until she had heard the more blatant version in the words of the politicians who disliked him.

She had most encouragement from Frank Oxborn, the Home Secretary, who had been elected the same year as Tom and had always been one of his better friends in the House, even though they had begun to see less of each other once Frank was promoted to the Cabinet. When she telephoned his private office at the Home Office to ask whether he had time to see her, she had a long wait before she was told by one of his secretaries that he had wall-to-wall meetings for the next few days, but that he would like her to go to his flat for a drink at seven o'clock that evening.

Oxborn lived in a lugubrious, red-brick block in Buckingham Gate, only minutes walk from the Home Office. The flat did not get much light since the windows looked out either over a courtyard or a lightwell, but that did not worry him too much. He rarely left the Home Office before dark during the week, and every weekend was spent with his wife and children in his constituency in Berkshire.

With his large frame, greying-blond hair and high-coloured complexion, he looked like a bluff, rather stupid man, devoted to healthy, mind-numbing activities in the open air. In fact, he had one of the sharpest brains in the government, his interests were politics, bridge, gothic mausolea, and wine. He loathed everything to do with the country except the fact that its inhabitants voted for him.

He was dressed in white tie when he opened the door to Lavinia and she blinked at his splendour, feeling seriously underdressed in the terracotta dress she had put on for dinner with Julian and Georgina. Oxborn folded her into a tight hug, apparently unconcerned about the effect on his boiled shirt, white waistcoat or carefully tied white bow tie. Lavinia kept her powdered face as well away from them as she could, rather enjoying the fervour of the embrace. It made her feel much more comforted than the diplomatically distant telephoned sympathy of the Prime Minister or the half-concealed *schadenfreude* of Tom's other colleagues.

'So how are you, Lavinia?' Oxborn said cheerfully,

252

releasing her at last. 'Apart from being terrified for Tom and miserable, I mean?'

'Oh, Frank. It is good to be here.' She ignored his question as she sank into one of his comfortable arm chairs. They were covered in cracked brown leather and looked as though they might have been throw-outs from some Pall Mall club.

'Excellent. You look tired. Aren't you sleeping?'

'Not a lot. And to tell you the truth, I feel as though I'm in some extra circle of hell that Dante didn't even know about. I think it's reserved for people who never say what they are feeling.' She saw a shadow of impatience on Frank's broad ruddy face and stopped, smiled and started again in a less emotional voice: 'It's just that I'm desperate to do something positive to get Tom back. Nothing's happened yet despite all the police efforts. As far as I can see, there's no reason for anything to change unless someone stumbles over him by mistake.'

'Or someone responds to your appeal. You did well this afternoon. But you mustn't start thinking the police aren't trying or that we're going to sacrifice your old man. That's quite out of the question.'

Lavinia sighed. 'Good. Some of his so-called honourable friends have given me the distinct impression that they'd like to do exactly that.'

'Have they? Well, the hunting vote raised some ferocious passions in the constituencies as well as the House. You can't blame the beaten for feeling angry, particularly if they've been savaged by anti-hunting constituents during the recess.'

'There's something else though, isn't there?' said Lavinia watching him carefully. 'Some fight that's been going on between Tom and the Secretary of State.'

Oxborn turned away at the drinks table and started pouring out drinks. 'Gin all right for you?' he asked airily over his shoulder.

253

'I'd rather have sherry – or vermouth – if that's not a bore. But come on, Frank, tell me what's been going on.'

'I can't go into that, Lavinia. You must know that perfectly well.'

'But what is it? Tom was cagey, too. I don't mind not knowing things. Heavens! I'm well used to *that* by now. But it might have a bearing on what's happened to him.'

Oxborn came back to her chair carrying an overfull glass of pale sherry. 'You don't have to worry about that. It's something that could not possibly have had anything to do with his kidnap.'

'Unless that's been just a blind to keep him out of the way while whatever it is that he was being obstructive about is shovelled through so that he's presented with a *fait accompli*.'

Frank roared with laughter and could hardly get out any words.

'You've been reading too many thrillers, Lavinia,' he said when he could speak soberly. 'We don't carry on like that. Honestly, there's a hell of a lot more cock-up than conspiracy in our world, I can tell you. Besides, use your loaf. No-one would bag Tom in the middle of the recess if that's what they wanted, now would they? They'd wait until something could be shovelled through, as you put it.'

'Unless they wanted to disguise what they were doing so that it looked like an anti-hunt protest.' Lavinia's voice was dry, but Frank pretended not to have heard it. He shook his head and grinned at her like the middle-aged schoolboy he was pretending to be.

'Far too subtle for any of us. Besides, to be a bit indelicate about it, old Tom doesn't have enough power yet to make anyone need to do that.'

'No?'

'No. He can object all he likes, but all he could actually

254

do is vote against it when it comes to a division, lose his job and probably the whip. Now, let's talk about more cheerful things. We don't see enough of you in London. How are the offspring?'

'Bearing up remarkably well,' said Lavinia, burying the mental pictures of Tammy howling on her bed, Charles battling with his tears as she left him at school, and Rory's white face as he sat on the edge of her bed and told her about his terror that it was his fault Tom had been taken. The sight of Frank's amused frown reminded her where she was and what she was supposed to be discussing.

'We're all keeping a relatively stiff upper lip.'

'Good. Lavinia, I hate to hurry you, but my driver will be downstairs in five minutes. I'm off to a dinner thing at the Inner Temple and mustn't be late because I'm by way of being guest of honour and all that.'

She downed the last of her sherry and stood up. 'It was good of you to see me, particularly now that you're so busy and important, Frank. You will make sure that I'm told everything as soon as it happens, won't you? Chorley and Co. keep saying they'll tell me everything, but I hear very little.'

'That's because there hasn't been anything much to hear. Don't worry so much. We will get him back.' He looked at her and then nodded as though he had made some kind of decision. 'It is true that Tom's particularly uncorruptible integrity has caused some people a lot of amusement and others a strong degree of irritation down the years,' he said much less exuberantly than usual, 'but we've all got used to it by now. In a funny way, you know, he's become a kind of mascot for some of us, as though whatever we're doing must be justifiable because, if it weren't, Tom Medworth would have protested.'

'Really?' Lavinia had not known that she could sound so disbelieving. 'Even though he hasn't any real power to stop you?'

255

'Yes. Bizarre, isn't it? He's often inconvenient, and not much liked by a lot of people, but he's respected. Really, Lavinia, it is inconceivable – literally – that the outcome will be anything but satisfactory. Tom Medworth will be brought back safely from wherever he is.'

'I wish I could be certain of that.'

'You can definitely be certain that everything that could be done is being done to ensure it.'

Something about Frank suggested more sincerity than Lavinia had expected, even from him, and so she smiled before she kissed him. Leaving him to his chauffeur, she hailed a taxi to take her to Julian and Frida's house in Paddington.

Chapter 17

The day after her meeting with the Home Secretary, Lavinia was invited to record a short interview with a local Yorkshire radio station to be sent 'down the line' from Broadcasting House in Portland Place.

Almost as nervous as she had been before the press conference, she presented herself at the pale-grey building behind the pretty church of All Saints, Langham Place, fifteen minutes before the appointed time. The receptionist checked her name against a list and handed her over to a uniformed commissionaire, who smiled and took a key out of his pocket.

Unlocking a polished wooden door, he led her through, into a lift, up several floors, along a silent, carpeted corridor and then stopped outside another anonymous door. He opened that for her, too, switched on a light and left her alone.

Puzzled and at a loss, Lavinia looked round the small room. There was a mass of forbidding equipment on the table in the middle, a set of headphones, a telephone, and a microphone. There were also notices on the walls explaining what she had to do. Some of them seemed contradictory. Eventually, she chose one, read it several times to make sure she understood, lifted the telephone and eventually made contact with the engineers who would connect her with her interviewer in Yorkshire. The engineer told her what would happen and what she was to do. She replaced the telephone and put on the headphones.

'Hello? Lavinia, is that you?' came a sturdy voice through her headphones five minutes later. 'It's Greg Strout here.'

'Yes, it's me.'

'Great. What's the weather like with you?'

'What? Oh, fairly cold.'

'Good. Push the microphone a little further away, would you? Is it still snowing?'

'No. Not any more.'

'That's fine. Leave it there. I'll be back to you within a few minutes. You can hear what we're doing by pressing the switch in front of you. 'Bye for now.'

Lavinia flicked the switch and heard the same voice urging his listeners to tune in again at the same time next week. There was a break for the news and then Strout's voice in her earphones said: 'And now, joining us from our London studio is Lavinia Medworth, the brave wife of the Environment Minister who is being held by a group of animal-rights activists. Lavinia, what do you know of them?'

'Very little,' she gasped, breathing in instead of out in the shock. 'They're called the Liberation Army for the Foxes of England and that's all I know.'

'Have you had any contact with them?'

'No. No, I haven't.'

'What would you like to say to them?' said Strout, sounding slightly strained. Lavinia realized that she was not giving him full enough answers. She smiled to make her voice sound warm, as Julian and Georgina had suggested the previous evening, and concentrated hard to make sure that she did not give away anything Chorley might consider sensitive. She breathed out so that her voice did not emerge as a snobbish-sounding squeak.

'Obviously I would like to ask them to release my husband,' she said. 'Holding him can do them no good; releasing him now can only help their cause. But there are other things I would like to say to other people.' She paused, gathering her strength.

'Who are they?' asked Strout, sounding happier now that she was launched and talking at a more normal pitch. 'And what would you like to say?'

'I'd ask every member of the public who may be listening to this to keep alert and report to the police anything they have noticed that is out of the ordinary,' Lavinia said, making herself speak slowly and distinctly. 'Someone must have seen something unusual somewhere. Even if Tom was moved after dark, he might have been seen being taken out of a car boot or the back of a van perhaps. He might have been bundled up into a roll of carpet or something like that. But someone somewhere must have noticed something unusual. Or some friend or a relation of one of the LAFE people, or even . . .' She broke off and laughed a little. 'Even an old enemy. Someone must have been startled by something. Out there among you must be people who know who has my husband and where they are keeping him.'

'Yes, I see what you mean. That's quite possible, isn't it?' said Strout, making his voice bouncy to keep it interesting. 'What would you say to someone who did know?'

Lavinia tried to concentrate on the idea of a man or woman with the information she needed, ashamed of the information, perhaps, or of the temptation to betray comrades. She spoke directly to that imagined person: 'You can probably understand what my children and I are going through as we wait for news. We desperately want to know where he is, but also *how* he is and what's happening to him. Tom's mother, too. You may not know, but she's seventy-six and the anxiety is doing dreadful things to her.'

Lavinia tried to let some of her real feelings sound in her voice without swamping it in either anger or anguish. She took a moment to gather her strength and then added: 'All I can say to the person who knows something and who could help us is that if you have ever loved another human being, please get in touch with the police or even discreetly with me. Please. I need your help.'

'We'll all do what we can, Lavinia,' said Strout brightly. 'I'm sure everyone will understand your family's feelings. Have you any message for any animal-rights sympathizers who may be listening?'

'Oh yes. Just this: whatever you may feel about hunting or vivisection or meat-eating or any of the other issues that concern us all, how can you justify such cruelty to human beings? Doesn't it make you at least as bad as the people you so despise for any horrors they perpetrate on animals?'

'Thank you, Lavinia. Now, over to Jack Harsent in the weather studio.'

Lavinia eased the headphones off, thinking that she had done badly and wishing that they could start again.

Greg Strout's voice coming over the internal microphone surprised her: 'That was great. Terrific message at the end. I hope you get him back soon.'

'Thank you. I hope . . .' But she could not complete the sentence. Strout's voice had already gone.

Lavinia gathered her things together and left the building to take the tube back to West Square, feeling let down by herself as much as by the media. Sitting in the half-empty train to the Elephant and Castle, she began to toy with a desperate plan.

Knowing how much Tom would hate it, feeling as though it would be like taking off her own clothes in public, she nevertheless decided that she would have to do it. She could vividly remember his telling her after the constituency surgery that the only people who could get anything changed were journalists.

Breathing more rapidly even though it would be some time before she took any real action, she went into the nearest newsagent, bypassed the girlie magazines and the secondhand-car catalogues and picked up a copy of the *Daily Messenger*. Remembering the revulsion she had felt when she had been sent clippings from it during the Tom-and-Teresa scandal, Lavinia could hardly bear to touch it, but she carried it to the small cash desk.

The Asian man behind the counter seemed to look at her as though he could hardly believe what she was buying and she was tempted to explain that it was not because she wanted to read it. She handed over her money, accepted change and left, feeling grubby.

As she walked towards West Square, she turned the pages in search of Ben Wroot's byline. She found it next to a repellent photograph of a nearly naked teenager flaunting her charms at the edge of a snooker table and nodded in cold satisfaction. Wroot owed them all something for the misery he had caused. The time had come for him to pay his debt.

Back in the house Lavinia telephoned the number printed at the bottom of the back page, asked for Wroot, and was amused to hear the wary surprise in his voice when the call was put through to his extension.

'Lavinia Medworth? Can it really be you?'

'Yes, Mr Wroot, it is. I should very much like to speak to you and it's urgent. I don't terribly want to come in to your office; could we meet somewhere? Have a cup of coffee, perhaps?'

'All right,' he said after a short pause. 'There's an Italian-owned bar with a decent espresso machine just across the street from here. Can you give me some idea why you want to meet?'

'I'm sure you know. I'll be with you in half an hour. What's the bar called?'

'Niccolino's.'

'I'll be there.'

Thirty-five minutes later, she saw him, a tall reasonably well-dressed man, edging between the small tables towards her.

'Mrs Medworth,' he said as he reached her side. 'How are you?'

'Surviving. Thank you for coming, Mr Wroot.'

He did not answer, being more interested just then in ordering himself some coffee. Lavinia waited until his attention returned to her.

'OK, so what is it you want?' he said at last when he was settled with a double espresso in front of him and a lighted cigarette between the yellowed fingers of his right hand. He stirred two heaped spoons of sugar into his coffee.

'This is your chance to make up for what you did to me two years ago. I want you to run a series of pieces exposing the worst aspects of the worst hangers-on of the animal-rights movement. Most of all I want you – your paper, that is – to offer a reward for information about where my husband is being kept.'

Wroot peered at her through the smoke he had generated. 'Two years ago I was doing my job. You can't blame me for that.'

'Actually I can. I don't think I've ever seen an exposé of any extra-marital bonkings in a newspaper office, but I cannot believe that they never happen. Why should you pick on politicians for doing what a lot of you do? And don't tell me it's because you object to their hypocrisy – yours is just as bad.' Her voice cracked and she added furiously: 'It's so bloody unfair apart from anything else.'

A reluctant smile tweaked at the edges of his mouth. She assumed it was amusement at her loss of temper rather than an acknowledgement of her point. He raised an eyebrow and said: 'Aren't you taking a bit of a risk here?'

'I'm sorry?'

'By showing yourself so different from the sad-but-perfect wife who forgave her husband and saved his career.'

Lavinia made herself laugh. She knew that it was essential to appear completely in control and utterly confident. 'I never put forward that view of myself. I've never spoken to a journalist on that subject. Or on any other, come to that.'

'That's what I mean. Think what we could do: a swearing virago; hates hunting herself; could this be revenge on an unfaithful husband for past humiliations? Nice shot of you looking angry or sulky. There must be plenty in the files. I've never come across a political wife who didn't look mad or at least boot-faced on some public occasion.' He swallowed most of his coffee in one go and then took another puff at his cigarette.

Lavinia remembered the various dire warnings of what might happen if she ventured to speak to a journalist.

'This gets better and better the more I think of it. I can see the headline now. No legal trouble because we'll put a question mark at the end: "Animal rights or marital fights?" No, perhaps that's a bit sophisticated for the readership, but we could work out something very tasty. I think I could get to like it, and I'm sure the editor'd go for it. A wholly new angle. Lovely.'

'And the fact that you knew it was complete rubbish, wouldn't that worry you?' Lavinia was so interested that for a moment she forgot why she was talking to Wroot.

'Why should it? Our readers – or a large part of them – would love it. They don't care if things are true or not any more than I do; they just like a good story to divert themselves from the deadening boredom of their dreary little lives.'

Lavinia drank her coffee and signalled to the waitress

for a refill. Her curiosity about Wroot's views on truth would have to wait for another day.

'Mr Wroot? More for you?'

'Why not?'

'Two double espressos, please. Now that you've finished amusing yourself at my expense, perhaps we could get down to business.' She took the small tape recorder from her handbag and replayed a little of their conversation as though to make sure that it was working. She had to suppress a smile at the look on Wroot's face.

'Now, you know and I know that the press has a lot of power. We also know that you have often misused it and caused a great deal of mischief – and a lot of pain to people who are not always in a position to protest. This is your chance to redeem yourselves, get up a crusade, whip your readers into a frenzy of righteous indignation and boost the circulation to dizzy heights. Outrage – however synthetic – is one of your prime sellers after the royal family, isn't it?'

'Yes,' he said with a lurking smile in his dark eyes.

'Well then, this time you've a chance to harness it in a genuinely good cause. The very novelty of it ought to excite you.'

He leaned back in his chair, tilting on to the two back legs, watching her all the time. 'It's much easier to be morally outraged by rich bullies on huge horses tearing apart little furry animals while they're still alive and howling.'

The waitress brought their second cups of coffee and Wroot let his chair bang forwards on to all four legs again so that he could shovel the usual mass of sugar into his cup, spilling grains of it all over the polished wooden table.

'Horses don't tear any animals apart,' said Lavinia, mocking his ambiguity with a certain pleasure. 'No, it's all right,' she added, seeing irritated surprise on Wroot's face. 'I know what you meant. Look on this as a challenge then. Come on, there must be some really nasty stories about some of the anti-cruelty people. The very fact that the ones who bomb factories or put ground glass in food – do they do that? I can't remember – risking the lives of humans shows me at least what cockeyed values they've got. Besides, I'm sure I've read somewhere that one of the saboteurs was quoted as saying that he would see nothing wrong in murdering a huntsman. That truly is bizarre, you know, whatever one thinks about "rich bullies on horses chasing foxes". Quite frankly, it's enough to make even someone like me who doesn't much like the idea of hunting into a bloodthirsty fanatic, determined to chase every last fox in the British Isles.'

The journalist leaned back and crossed his legs. He looked completely at his ease and as though he were enjoying her indignation. 'Don't you mind about the cries of the poor, tormented little furry beasties?'

'Has someone been sending you tapes of screaming fox cubs?' asked Lavinia and saw at once that they had. 'So, what about it? A crusade on behalf of a single, powerless individual against an organization that wants to impose its own views on the rest of the world – with force if necessary. That's a pretty undemocratic, not to say uncivilized, way of carrying on, don't you think?' She sipped her coffee, watching him over the rim of the cup.

'I'll think about it,' he said eventually, 'and perhaps take it to the editor. If he goes for it, would you pose for photographs?'

'As what?' Lavinia finished her coffee and put down the cup so hard that it snapped against the saucer. 'Foul-mouthed virago?'

'You minded that, didn't you?' said Wroot, laughing at her openly. 'No, actually, I had in mind more the suffering-but-courageous-little-wife. Lonely Lavinia. Lovely Lavinia. Lost Lavinia. Something like that.'

'All right,' she said, trying not to grit her teeth. 'I suppose I could bear that in the cause.'

'Probably looking windswept and fragile against a background of the House of Commons.'

'Whatever.'

'And some exclusive loving thoughts on your husband?'

'If necessary.' Lavinia felt her teeth grinding together again. 'But I'd need some guarantees from you – about precise accuracy of quotation, approval of your text, and so on – before I said anything.'

'You can't have approval of the text. No-one gets that. As for the rest . . . Is there a number where I can call you?'

Noticing that he had made no real comment on her demand for guarantees, Lavinia wrote her number on a paper napkin as he finished his sickly coffee.

'There's an answering machine if I'm out,' she said as she handed him the napkin.

He took it, wiped his mouth on it and then put it in his pocket, saying: 'Haven't you got a mobile?'

'Certainly not.'

'Pity. We'll need to move fast if the editor goes for it. What sort of figure are you looking for?'

For a moment Lavinia could not think what he was talking about, and then it hit her. She felt blood rushing to her face and for a moment could not speak.

'Good God! I don't want money,' she said eventually. 'You must be mad. All I want is you to offer a reward for information. I haven't any idea what's right for that, but your people must know the market. They can decide. Look, settle with your editor and ring me as soon as you can. I'll probably be at home and if not I'll ring in for my messages every hour or so. You needn't worry about not getting hold of me, Mr Wroot.'

'Why not Ben, since we're going to get to know each other so very well? I must say it'll be easier if you don't want money.'

'Ben,' she said, finding, in spite of her loathing of what he had done in the past, that she almost liked him. 'I must go. Thank you for seeing me. On reflection, I couldn't promise total exclusivity and so on because I have to use every possible avenue to whip up enough public opinion on Tom's side to make someone tell us where he is. But I'll give you a particular clutch of exclusive "loving thoughts" if that's what it'll take.'

'Fair enough.'

She switched off her tape recorder, put it back in her bag and left to stand on the pavement outside the café, looking for a taxi. It was already dark and she did not want to risk walking from the tube station to West Square without being able to see any possible pursuers.

Having paid the driver from inside the cab, made her usual checks for anyone loitering with intent, she went into the house and listened to the messages on the answering machine. There was the usual crop of abuse, but in the middle of it was her brother's voice, sounding slightly American after all his years in the States.

'Lav, it's awful what's happened to Tom. We were at the cabin in Maine without radio or newspapers and only got back today to find your letter. Would you like me to fly over? I can easily do it, if it would help, but I don't want to get in your hair. Call me when you can.'

Feeling irrationally safer just for having heard his offer, Lavinia listened to the rest of the messages. Among the filth and the support from both friends and relative strangers, there was a short message from Philip, saying that Sasha was back in London but apparently going to a concert with friends that evening. He wondered if Lavinia would like to eat with him. There was also a message from Superintendent Chorley asking her to call him and another from Aubrey, inviting her to dine with him and Caro in a few days' time.

Lavinia made notes of the calls she had to answer and then rang through to the machine at the Dower House to get the messages from that. There was a repeat of Sandy's, another earful of abuse, and finally one message that set her heart bumping again:

'I just heard you on the radio,' said a female voice with a Yorkshire accent. 'I didn't want to ring the police because it might be nothing. But I found your number. I don't know if it's anything, but . . . Sorry, hold on a minute.' There was a pause, during which Lavinia could hear subdued banging and voices. She willed the woman to return. 'I don't know if it's useful, but there's a house down the far end of Willerby Road here in Hull that's been empty for years. Number 450. There's been someone there these last few weeks, and I've seen a van. It may be nowt, but now you know.'

Lavinia did not wait for any of the rest of the messages. She replayed that one, taking down the actual words used in her long-forgotten shorthand, checked it and then telephoned the number Chorley had left for her.

He had already gone for the day and so she tried Hexham's office. He, too, had left, but when she gave her name to the constable who had answered and told him that she had something desperately urgent to say, he promised to get through to Hexham at his home and ask him to ring her.

Lavinia sat beside the telephone, not daring to fetch herself any food or drink, or even answer the front door when someone rang the bell. Instead, she twitched aside the curtain and looked out of the window. A young man stood on the step, carrying a large flat plastic basket of polythene-wrapped dusters and dishcloths. He did not see Lavinia looking out at him and so she knocked on the glass. When he looked up she shook her head. He yelled abuse at her and rang the door bell before rattling the letterbox.

The telephone rang and she left the window to pick up the receiver. 'Mrs Medworth, it's Hexham here. What's happened?'

She described the message she had heard.

'Did she leave a name?'

'No. Nor her own address or telephone number. But it must be worth checking out.'

'You're telling me,' he said with encouraging fervour. 'Thank you for letting us know.'

'You will tell me what happens, if . . . you know, won't you?'

'We'll tell you whatever happens. But don't say a word of this to anyone else. Anyone. All right?'

'Yes, of course.'

'Great. I'll be in touch.' He cut the connection without even saying 'goodbye'. Lavinia slowly replaced her telephone and sat, trying not to remember all she had heard about hoax calls. It was a while before she realized that there was no sound except the distant throb of traffic around the Elephant and Castle. The abusive pedlar had gone.

She picked up the telephone again to ring Sandy, checking the time to work out where he would be. His office number seemed the likeliest bet, but she was unlucky. She got through to his secretary, who was warmly sympathetic and promised that Sandy would ring her as soon as he returned from his meeting.

Philip understood at once when Lavinia told him that she wanted to stay beside the telephone to wait for her brother's call and suggested that they might have another Indian meal sent in. 'Unless you'd rather be by yourself this evening,' he added carefully.

'No. I'd love to have you here, if you really don't mind crossing London again.'

'Quite the opposite. I'll be with you as soon as the traffic allows. Order something delicious for me, will you?'

'OK.'

When he came, twenty minutes after the food, which she had put in a low oven to keep warm, he hugged her as usual. 'What's the matter?' he said at once.

'Nothing. Or nothing else. Why?'

'You're tight as a drum.' He pulled back to look at her. 'What is it?'

She shook her head, not prepared to lie to him but equally determined to stick by Hexham's prohibition, even though Philip did not constitute any kind of danger to Tom.

'There's been the slightest hint of a breakthrough,' she said, 'but I'm not allowed to say what to anyone at all — even you.'

'Quite right,' he said after a moment's silence. 'I can smell onion bhajis. What else have you got?'

Grateful all over again for his instant understanding, his undemanding kindness and his astonishing ability to calm her, Lavinia took him into the kitchen, reciting the names of the dishes she had picked for their feast.

'You must be hungry!' he said, laughing at her.

'We'll see. It just all sounded so wonderful when I read through the menu they brought last time.'

The telephone rang just as she was tearing a piece from her Peshwari naan to dip into the spiced sauce of the chicken tikka masala. She dropped the sweet, almond-stuffed bread at once and tripped as she was getting off her chair. But she reached the telephone before the answering machine cut in.

'Mum? It's Rory. How are you? Is there any news? The Head said I could ring.'

'Rory. It's bliss to hear you. No, there isn't any news yet. But I'm sure there will be soon. I'm all right. Much more important, how are you?'

'Not too bad, but people will keep wanting to talk to me about it.'

His tone of disgust made her smile, but she asked quite seriously: 'What, other boys?'

'Yeah, some. But matron, too. And we've got a counsellor who comes. They want me to talk to him.'

'Don't you want to?'

'No. There's nothing they can do to get Dad back, and so there's nothing to say.'

With her heart singing with an extraordinary kind of delight that Rory should be sounding so sure of himself, Lavinia said carefully and with complete sincerity: 'The good thing about counsellors is that they can help one deal with all sorts of tricky feelings. He might . . .'

'I'm just afraid for Dad,' said Rory reasonably. 'And they can't change that. And anyway, I wouldn't want them to. It's right to be afraid until he comes back. Mr Fowler agrees with me.'

'Does he?' said Lavinia, relaxing as she perched on the arm of the sofa. 'I'm glad. How are you getting on with him this term?'

There was a short pause. 'The same, really,' said Rory. 'Even though he wrote me that letter. I mean, he's quite nice to me when he's talking about you or Dad, but he's just the same in lessons as he always was.'

'Just as frightening?'

'Nearly.'

'Oh dear.'

'You mustn't worry, Mum,' he said quickly. 'I can cope.'

'I know you can. You're remarkably strong, Rory. And it's been lovely to hear you talk. But I'd better let you go now.'

Lavinia could almost feel Hexham trying to get through to her, but she could not bring herself actually to tell Rory to get off the line.

'Yes, I ought. The bath bell's just gone. Can I ring you tomorrow, Mum?'

'Of course, you can. Every night if you like. Have you got enough money or shall I send you another Phonecard?'

'Could you? That'd be great.'

'I'll put one in the post tomorrow.'

'Great. 'Bye, Mum. And you will . . .'

'I'll tell you the instant there's any news. I promise that, Rory. When we know something for sure, I'll ring the Headmaster and get him to have you found and told.'

'Thank you,' he said.

'Give my love to Charles. Goodbye.'

As soon as he had gone, she clamped the receiver back on its cradle and waited. There was no sound.

'Shall I hot yours up for you?' said Philip from the round table at the far end of the double room.

'No, it's all right.'

She tried to eat, but all her hunger had gone and she sat in front of the big tray of silver-foil dishes, worried about the waste of all the food.

'If you're not going to eat that naan,' said Philip, 'may I have a bit?'

'Of course. Have it all,' she said.

He tore off a piece and ate it. 'Have something, Lavinia. You haven't eaten anything.'

'I can't. I thought I was hungry, but now I just keep seeing pictures of Tom getting in the way of police guns, or being mistaken for a terrorist, or being shot by them during a raid. I . . .'

The telephone rang. 'Mrs Medworth? It's John Chorley here.'

Lavinia moved to the sofa arm and sat heavily on it. She was afraid that her legs would not have kept her up.

'What's happened?'

'The house in Willerby Road is empty, I'm afraid. There are signs that someone has been there recently and left in a hurry. It could have been LAFE and we'll be following it up at once.'

272

Lavinia looked at Philip and shook her head, forgetting that he did not know anything about the possibility that Tom had been found.

'Mrs Medworth, are you there?'

'Yes, I'm here. Was there anything to suggest that someone might have been kept there – you know, against his will?'

'One or two things. You did a good job on the radio. Keep it up.'

'Thank you,' she said, wanting to ask for more details about what the police had found at the abandoned house but understanding that he could not give anything away over the telephone.

When Chorley had gone after repeating his familiar reassurances that the police were doing everything they could and that Tom would be found, she went back to Philip. She even managed to eat something.

Philip left her at half-past ten, telling her to get an early night. Almost as soon as she had double-locked the door behind him, Sandy telephoned and listened in sympathetic silence until she had finished telling him everything that had happened.

'I'm sorry, Lav. What hell for you! My god, that family have put you through it, haven't they?'

'No, they haven't. What can you be talking about?'

'Come on. This is Sandy you're talking to. Last time I was over you were spitting with rage.'

'Oh, dear! I do sometimes get into a bit of twizzle about them all, but not Tom. He's different somehow.'

'How?'

There was an expensive pause as she tried to think. 'He's just nicer than they are,' she said eventually.

Sandy laughed. 'Or you know him better,' he suggested. 'Look, Lav, I'd better go. I've got a deputation from my attorney's office due any moment and they cost an arm and a leg every second they're here. Would you like me to

273

come over? I could nip across for the weekend if it would help.'

'You're a dear, but it sounds as though you're awfully busy and there's not a lot you could do except hold my hand, and you're doing that jolly well like this.'

'Good. Well, ring me whenever you need a bit of hand-holding, and I'll keep in touch, too. Martha sends her love, and the kids. We've been talking about coming over at Easter anyway, but if you want us any earlier, just tell me. We'll come at once.'

'Thank you. I can't tell you what it means that people – friends and you, I mean – should be so . . . Oh, I can't explain.'

'Still the same gabby, articulate sister I always knew.'

'Pig! We'll talk again, Sandy.'

'If you can think up any words to use. Love you, Lav.'

'Goodbye, Sandy.'

Chapter 18

The first of Wroot's articles appeared two days later under a banner headline announcing the *Daily Messenger*'s reward for information about Tom's whereabouts. There was a large photograph of Lavinia looking soulful on Westminster Bridge against an angry sky and under it were some toe-curlingly embarrassing thoughts about Tom and her misery about what he must be suffering. She hated reading the column quite as much as she had hated dictating the thoughts to Wroot, but if his article was the cost of the paper's campaign, it was worth it.

Tom would understand, she told herself, even though his family clearly did not. The police had sanctioned the campaign, but that did not stop Flavia dictating a stinging rebuke on to the answering machine at ten o'clock on the morning the article appeared and over the next day or two the others also made their displeasure known. Lavinia even began to wonder whether she should offer to release Aubrey and Caro from their invitation to dinner.

Despite the family's disapproval and her own terror of putting Tom in extra danger by talking about him, Lavinia gradually began to feel more confident of what she was doing and her ability to learn to do it well. As the days passed she grew less scared of making a fool of herself during interviews, and her arguments became crisper as her anger was more effectively harnessed. During the recording of one late-night television show, she found herself able to talk almost as fluently as one of the Medworths might have done.

Sitting between an animal-rights activist called Dan Elloughton, who was dressed in jeans, a cloth blouson jacket and white trainers, and a tweed-suited, leather-shoed, sixtyish man called George Ferriby, who turned out to be a fervent and deeply tactless supporter of everything to do with hunting, Lavinia tried to hang on to reason and civility as she silently marshalled her arguments. After the two men had explained their entrenched and violent opposition to each other, she was asked for her views.

'As you probably know I don't even ride, let alone hunt,' she said directly to the camera. 'It takes considerable skill to do that, which I don't have. There are many things about hunting that I dislike, but I cannot agree with Mr Elloughton that any of us has the right to stop other people doing it. After all, is there really something so particularly barbaric about it in comparison with other forms of pest control? If you're prepared to keep a cat, say, to control the mice in your flat, how can you feel so superior morally to someone who hunts foxes with hounds?'

She paused courteously to allow the others to come in, but the presenter stopped them and made her go on. 'If you consider it unacceptably cruel to kill any animal or insect that causes trouble – mouse, rat, wasp, even flea – then I can see that you could reasonably object to hunting, although I still don't see how you could ever justify damaging human beings in your effort to get your point of view across to other people. But if you're prepared to kill other sorts of vermin, pests, it seems to me inconsistent to object to hunting and suggests you may be motivated less by sympathy for the hunted than loathing of the enjoyment of the hunters.'

She turned to smile at the activist, who scowled back at her.

'So what? No animal should be chased in terror across miles of country for the entertainment of bloodthirsty bullies,' he said.

'You've no idea what you're talking about,' snorted Ferriby, obviously determined not to be kept out of the argument any longer. 'It's only because foxes are furry and nice-looking and you used to read about them in sentimental children's books. You know nothing about the country. Every farmer in the land knows that foxes have to be controlled.'

'Then they must use humane means.'

'Such as?'

'Trapping or poisoning.'

'Neither is particularly humane,' said Lavinia quietly. 'Traps can wound foxes badly without killing them and poison leads to an agonizing and long drawn-out death.'

'There are other ways to control them,' said Elloughton. 'Genetic for one.'

'The trouble with ignorant rabble-rousers like you,' Ferriby shouted, not even bothering to pretend he wanted to hear anything Lavinia said, 'is that you don't care a fig for animals; you're just looking for ways of venting your spleen. You're weak and you're a failure and you're trying to get your own back on the world for that.'

Finding herself sandwiched between two furious men whose ideas she detested, Lavinia felt that she had to try to make some kind of peace. Catching the presenter's eye, she waited until there was a gap in the increasingly personal argument and then said: 'Have you ever seen a hen-run when a fox has been in it, Mr Elloughton? Or a field at lambing time?'

'No, but that's not . . .'

'Just what I said, an ignorant townie talking about things he knows nothing about, and a bloody lefty to boot, I

277

should think,' muttered Ferriby over his shoulder, luckily missing his microphone. 'Pig ignorant.'

'Perhaps you should go and see what foxes do,' Lavinia went on, pretending she had not heard. 'They leave scenes of the most frightful carnage. They don't just kill what they need to eat, you see. That's why they are such a pest in farming country. They kill as many animals as they can, perhaps even for the pleasure they get from it.'

'Hen-runs can be better protected and foxes can be controlled by less foul means. Hunting has to be stopped.'

'Because people enjoy it?' asked Lavinia politely.

'No. Because it's cruel.'

'So are a lot of other things that happen.' Her temper suddenly snapped. 'Kidnapping for one.'

'That's a crime,' said Elloughton with considerable satisfaction. 'As hunting should be.'

Once more George Ferriby tried to speak, but the presenter was firm in his determination that Lavinia should answer. Furious with herself for having said anything so ambiguous, she went on steadily: 'What I meant was that I don't think trying to protect animals justifies anything as cruel as kidnapping.'

The activist leaned forward in his leather swivel chair until his face was only a foot or so from hers. Lavinia flinched at the hate in his eyes.

'Unfortunately we have to end it there,' announced the presenter before either of them could say anything. 'I would like to thank my guests, Dan Elloughton, Lavinia Medworth, George Ferriby.'

A moment later the credits were rolled in front of the camera and Lavinia was able to escape.

The following day brought several faxes and telephone messages of admiration and support mixed in with the usual abuse. It also brought a call from Sally Anlaby's mother, Elizabeth Trewhitt, who first congratulated Lavinia on the campaign and then invited her for tea either that day or the following one. 'I know how busy you must be, but I thought that perhaps you might like a little break from all the anger and battling that you've had to do. But if you're too busy, just say. We could meet any time.'

'I've got nothing on tomorrow afternoon that I can't shift, and I should simply love to see you.'

'Good. At half-past four tomorrow then. I'll be alone.'

'Thank you,' said Lavinia. She put down the receiver, smiling at the prospect of seeing Elizabeth Trewhitt again, and tried to think what she ought to do next. It seemed impossible to concentrate on anything except Tom, and yet she knew she had to think about other things, practical things, or she would lose control again.

When she heard the post clattering through the letter box, she went out to fetch it. Shuffling through the pile for writing she recognized, she found envelopes from Sasha and John Hogarth and put the rest on the hall shelf to be read later. She took the others upstairs and opened Sasha's. It was a short, kind note of mild approval, which ended: 'I don't imagine that there is anything you would like me to do that might help you, but if there is, let me know. I would like to see you when you've time and energy to spare.'

Lavinia was grateful, but she did not want to see Sasha. The feelings between her and Philip were complicated enough without that. Lavinia dropped the note and its envelope and opened John Hogarth's. Even the first few lines made her laugh as he described Flavia's changing reactions from horror at 'the vulgar sentimentality' of Wroot's first articles to qualified approval once interviews with Lavinia had started to be published in what even her mother-in-law considered respectable newspapers. John, too, offered his help and she reached for the telephone to thank him.

'Darling Lavvy,' he said. 'You're doing seriously well.

Even Frida approves – or so Julian told me when I ran into him yesterday.'

'Coo,' said Lavinia, trying for the right tone of frivolous astonishment. 'It was sweet of you to write, John. How are you?'

'So, so. I'll be better when Tom's back, as I'm sure you will. Is there really no news?'

'Not yet. There was a ghost of hope the other day but it came to nothing. Frank Oxborn assures me that the police are doing things, but none of it's had any effect yet.'

'It's too ghastly for you. But at least you know the family's all behind you now. That must help.'

'Not much.'

There was a pause and then John said in a quite different tone of voice: 'Behind all that sweetness and co-operation you're a tough little nut after all, aren't you? I don't think I'd quite realized how tough, in spite of the scenes those last few ghastly days at Saltley.'

'No, I'm not tough. Not really. I've just got utterly fed up with their assumptions of superiority. We've all taken them at their own estimation for too jolly long, John, and joined in with it. I'm not prepared to do it any more. That makes me feel better.'

He laughed, but there was a hint of strain in his amusement. 'This promises to be a good new spectator sport, Lavvy. I look forward to the next family corroboree.'

'You've such a way with words, John. Corroboree, indeed! I must go. Thanks for your letter. See you soon. 'Bye.'

'Goodbye. Don't frighten yourself by taking on too much.'

The last injunction echoed in her brain as she scribbled a note of thanks to Sasha and then started to look through her clothes. None of them seemed suitable for Aubrey's dinner party that night and in the end she telephoned to find out what Caro would be wearing.

'Has something happened?' said Caro breathlessly as soon as Lavinia had got through to her number.

'No. I was just ringing to make sure you're still expecting me tonight and find out whether you're going to be very smart.'

'Fairly. But not as much as black tie.'

'OK. I'll do my best. Who else is coming?'

'Examples of the more intellectual end of the hunting fraternity mostly.' There was an edge to Caro's voice that Lavinia did not completely understand.

'That sounds a bit daunting. Who are they?'

'A couple of hunting QCs. You've probably met them here already. Robert Brough, who does quite a lot of high-profile criminal cases and his wife, who hunt with the Fernie, and Annaliese Quavers from the family division and her husband. He's a banker. They have a house down in Somerset and go out with the Mendip Farmers whenever they can.'

'They don't ring any bells. I'm not sure that I can have met any of them.'

'Oh. Well, they're all four reasonably good company. We see quite a lot of them. Then we're going to have Frank Oxborn; not that he hunts, but at least he's an undivided supporter of Tom and, as Home Secretary, wields useful power.'

'And he's fun. I've always liked him, even before he was so nice to me the other day.'

'I know, and he's one of the few Home Secretaries Aubrey's ever had much time for. Since Felicia's in the country with the children at the moment, we thought we'd have Sally Anlaby to balance Frank.'

'Why her?' Lavinia hoped that she did not sound as hostile as she felt.

'Because she's a great party supporter. They all like her and tend to use her whenever they need a spare woman at important functions. She fits in everywhere and she's a fanatical hunt supporter, too, and a friend of Tom's. She has a lot of influence in a kind of Glencora Palliser sort of way.'

Lavinia said nothing.

'What's the matter?' asked Caro into the silence.

'Tom's never mentioned her to me and he's clearly seen a lot of her. I'd rather assumed . . .'

'I don't think so. Honestly, Lavvy. I wouldn't do that to you. I don't mean that Tom's never . . . you know. I seem to be getting myself into a hole here, and I probably ought to stop digging, but . . .'

'Yes, I do know what you mean.'

'But I don't think Sally's ever been one of them.'

'I'm glad of that.' Lavinia did her best to suppress her strong dislike of the idea of Mrs Anlaby and added with an effort: 'I'll be interested to meet her. I liked her parents.'

'They're lovely, aren't they?' Caro's voice was warm. 'If we had room, I'd ask them, too.'

'And who's going to balance me?'

'Didn't I say? Nicko.'

'What's up with Loveday then?'

'Off at some medical conference in Edinburgh. See you at about eight then. I must run. There's still lots to do.'

'OK.'

Lavinia went back to her wardrobe and picked out a simply cut, dark-green silk dress that she had bought for an important reception at the previous year's party conference.

Setting off for the dinner that evening in her incongruous Landrover, Lavinia felt absurdly nervous and could not imagine why. The problem could not be that she was going alone for she had been to lots of parties without Tom. Eventually, as she was trying to find a parking space, she pinned her uneasiness down to the old terror of saying the wrong thing and damaging his prospects.

She found a space and backed the heavy vehicle into

it, trying to force confidence into her mind. A large, glossy black car driven by a chauffeur eased past her and she recognized Frank Oxborn in the back seat. He had not noticed her. Momentarily amused by the contrast between her battered, muddy Landrover and the sleek official car, she decided to get going. It would be tactless to arrive later than the guest of honour. Taking care not to snag her extra-fine tights on any rough edges, she levered herself down from the high seat.

Caro opened her front door a moment later, looking harassed but unusually smart in burgundy velvet.

'Is something the matter?' Lavinia asked as she was almost pulled over the threshold. Caro made a face.

'Just that bloody Aubrey has got held up with some infuriating meeting and won't be here for another hour. It's nearly as bad as the days when he was still at the Bar.'

'I shouldn't worry too much,' said Lavinia, who had long ago got used to managing parties when Tom was delayed. 'Just start dinner whenever you were planning to anyway and Aubrey can fit in at whatever stage we've reached when he does get here. It'll only matter if it makes you uncomfortable and that infects the others.'

'It's not so much that as getting the talk going,' whispered Caro. 'For some reason it's awfully sticky. I'm hoping it'll be better when Frank eventually arrives. He usually perks things up.'

'I'll help. Is everyone else here yet?'

'No. Only the lawyers and Sally.'

'In that case, I can't understand why they're not well away. Barristers are usually such good talkers and she seemed frightfully chatty at Saltley. Anyway Frank's nearly here. I saw his car when I'd just parked. I'm only here ahead of him because his driver had to go round by the one-way system and I nipped in on foot. There's the bell. That'll be him. I'll just go in.'

Casting a quick glance at herself in the hall mirror,

Lavinia straightened her shoulders and opened the door of the formal beige-and-white drawing room. The sound of animated talk stopped at once, casting a different light on Caro's anxieties. Four unknown faces turned towards her and Sally Anlaby smiled and stood up.

She looked astonishingly tall and slender as she uncoiled her long body from the corner of one of the plump beige sofas. That evening she was wearing a short black dress that made even more of her taut figure than the clothes she had worn in Yorkshire. Her smooth fair hair was short and feathered around her pretty face, accentuating the prominent cheek bones and glittering almond-shaped eyes. She was wearing the diamond solitaires in her ears again. Lavinia wondered bitchily who had bought them for her.

Slowly the others followed suit and got to their feet. Lavinia tried to put every negative thought out of her head and smiled at them all.

'Caro's just letting in Frank Oxborn, and she told me to introduce myself. Sally, I've almost met, but . . .' She turned to the barristers and their spouses. 'I'm Lavinia Medworth.'

Robert Brough advanced and gripped her hand firmly as he introduced first himself, then his wife, Charlotte, then Annaliese Quavers and her husband, Michael.

'It's a beastly time for you,' Michael Quavers said cheerfully. 'Bound to work out all right in the end, but beastly while it lasts.'

'Hellish,' she agreed. 'And it's going on so long. They said he'd be back within five days but it's more than a month now. I can hardly bear it. And almost the worst of it at the moment is worrying whether I'm making it worse for him.'

'In what way?' asked Sally Anlaby. Lavinia looked at her but could see nothing but concern in her lively face.

'Oh, stirring up all this feeling against the kidnappers and the loonier animal-rights people.' She smiled deliberately.

'But there's no point talking about it. I can't put the milk back in the bottle now. Talking of bottles . . .' She walked over to the drinks tray, that stood on a walnut table to the left of the white-marble fireplace and poured herself a glass of wine from a bottle keeping cool in a transparent perspex cylinder.

'Can I give anyone a refill?' she asked just as Caro brought in the Home Secretary.

He kissed Lavinia and Sally Anlaby, and waited to be introduced to the others. Having shaken hands, he sat down beside Annaliese Quavers and asked her politely about her present case by name. Lavinia, overhearing him through Robert Brough's sympathetic remarks about Tom, realized that Frank had been particularly well briefed about the people he was to meet. She wondered why.

'Have you had any response to your appeals for information yet?' asked Brough, soon after Nicko had arrived and Caro had offered everyone a second drink.

'I haven't,' she said, smiling at him. But I'm hoping that either the newspaper or the police will have. We've agreed that if anyone gets in touch with the paper all the information will be passed to the police. I won't be told anything until they've tested it out.'

'Fear of hoaxers?'

'Partly, but mostly I think the view is that the fewer times the information is repeated over the telephone the better really. Whoever took Tom in the first place must have had him under some kind of surveillance. We don't know exactly how sophisticated they are, or how well manned, but the police have decided that we must go on the assumption that they've got people watching me and listening to all of us all the time.'

As she spoke, Lavinia tried not to think what they might be doing to Tom, but she could not stop it. Her face felt as though it had been covered in plaster-of-Paris. She coughed and smiled to ease the tight muscles in her cheeks.

'I hate the thought that they might punish him because of something I've said or done. Or even . . . Oh, God.'

She rammed her left hand against her mouth to keep the words in. She knew that she had said far too much and wished that she could have kept better control over herself. It would be appalling to give way in public.

'It's most unlikely that they'll do anything violent,' said Brough, speaking more seriously than he had at first. 'After all, these people are not the Red Brigades. That was another time and another place altogether.'

'I know.' Lavinia collected herself as well as she could. She looked past him and saw from the expressions on the faces of the other guests that they had heard her impending hysteria. She smiled deliberately at Caro, who looked relieved and suggested that they go in to dinner.

She had taken immense trouble, Lavinia told herself as she struggled to pretend that everything was normal, to provide food that would require the minimum of last-minute adjustment and serving. They started with a salad of artichoke bottoms and broad beans and went on to a large casserole of pheasant cooked in cream flavoured with pickled walnuts.

Aubrey arrived, full of graceful apologies, just as Caro was offering second helpings of pheasant. He took a plate-ful from her and carried it to his place at the head of the table between Sally Anlaby and Annaliese Quavers. No-one was indiscreet enough to ask what he had been doing.

Lavinia, who felt as though her emotions had been scoured of all the furring-up of years, noticed how the atmosphere changed. A certain ease had gone and with it some kind of sincerity. People started to talk in speeches, as though with a Medworth in their midst they would have to answer for their views, when they had been talking about real things that mattered to them in whatever words came to mind.

She turned the ideas over and over in her mind, while making polite but meaningless comments whenever anyone said anything to her, and she was not distracted until she noticed the way Aubrey was leaning towards Annaliese. There was something about his expression, some hint of intimacy or even possession, that made her glance towards the other end of the table.

Caro was sitting with a smile on her face, apparently listening to Frank Oxborn on her right. Someone who did not know her might have thought her unconcerned, but her smiling lips did not move and her gaze was fixed on the wall behind Frank. It looked to Lavinia as though Caro were exercising every scrap of endurance she could muster.

Those bloody Medworths, Lavinia exclaimed in silence. She had never heard any gossip about Aubrey on the family grapevine and had assumed that he, alone of the siblings, had managed to stop himself philandering. His closeness to Annaliese, and Caro's concealed distress, suggested that he had merely been better at preventing the news getting out.

By the end of dinner Lavinia was so angry with his increasingly obvious devotion to Annaliese that if it had not been for her sympathy for Caro she might have walked out of the house. Instead, she talked as brightly as she could and whenever she caught Caro's eye, tried to show solidarity.

When everyone had finished eating the tangerines and picking off small bunches of grapes from the piles in the vast majolica fruit dish, Caro smiled around the table and stood up. Lavinia remembered that theirs was one of the few houses left where the women left the men to post-prandial port at even informal dinners and obediently followed Caro towards the drawing room. Caro stopped at the stairs down to the basement kitchen. 'Will you go on ahead while I get the coffee?'

'Why don't I do that?' suggested Lavinia. She thought that Caro looked as though she were on the edge of breaking down into visible unhappiness and did not want to overset her by saying the wrong thing. But she did want to help, and offering to fetch the coffee was the only thing she could think of doing.

'No, it's all right,' said Caro brightly. 'I know where everything is, and I'd quite like a . . . some time to myself. Will you just see to the others for me?'

'Yes. Are you all right?'

Caro shuddered, grimaced and then nodded before plunging down the basement stairs to brew the coffee. Lavinia sighed and gathered herself together to do as she had been asked.

In fact, it was not difficult. Annaliese Quavers and Charlotte Brough had taken advantage of the pause in the party to go to the lavatory and Sally Anlaby was alone, standing in front of the fire, warming the backs of her legs. She smiled nicely at Lavinia when she appeared in the doorway.

'My parents are so anxious to see you when you've got a spare minute,' she said. 'When I told them I was meeting you tonight, they were frightfully jealous.'

'That's nice! In fact, I spoke to your mother this morning and I'm going to see her tomorrow. I liked her – both of them – so much. You are lucky to have parents like them.'

'I know.'

There was a pause, during which Lavinia tried to pluck up her courage to ask a direct question.

'Is there something I can do for you?' said Sally eventually.

'You could tell me something, if you would.'

'Of course.'

'How did you meet Tom in the first place?'

'At Number Ten,' said Sally, frowning slightly. 'There

288

was a musical do, oh, about a year ago, and I'd been put next to him at dinner. It was a slightly lugubrious evening, but when we found that we shared a passion for hunting the whole thing perked up. It was Tom's ecstatic descriptions of the country round Saltley that made me look around there when I needed to move. Didn't he tell you?'

Lavinia shook her head. 'But there's nothing particularly surprising about that. We have to be apart for such a lot of the time that when we are together there's always a colossal amount to talk about.'

'I'm sure. Can I, in turn, say something to you?'

Lavinia was not certain that she wanted to hear it, but she could hardly refuse. She nodded. Sally looked uncharacteristically tentative.

'It's just that he talks of you with such admiration that . . .' She smiled, clamping her lips together. Her eyes looked full of a kind of regretful uncertainty. 'I've seen you watching me, suspecting me, judging me, and I just wanted to say that you don't have to. I don't want to sound presumptuous, but we're just friends.'

Lavinia found that in her mixture of embarrassment and gratitude she could not stay standing up without shaking. Luckily she was near one of the beige sofas and she subsided into it, feeling as wobbly as a boxer whose legs have collapsed under him after a particularly heavy punch to the head.

'I'm sorry,' she said, looking at her feet and noticing for the first time that the pink-and-beige needlework rug Caro had bought in Portugal years earlier was coming unravelled at the edge.

'It's all right,' said Sally, looking down at Lavinia's head. 'As a widow, I'm well accustomed to that suspicion, which is why I understood it so easily, but I'm not looking to take anyone else's husband away from her. You must believe that.'

'Oh, God! You're making me feel worse and worse.'

'Don't worry. I know how difficult it is when you're stuck in the constituency, particularly when . . .'

'When your husband has had at least one highly publicized affair.'

'Exactly.'

'Did he ever talk to you about that?' Lavinia flushed as she asked that question, and once again privately accused herself of prurience.

'Yes.'

'Oh.'

'Do you want to know what he said? It's not frightfully interesting – or very private.'

'All right. Thank you.'

'He told me that it was a remarkably small thing to have aroused so much interest in so many people, and completely irrelevant to the way he performed his job.'

'As you say, not very interesting,' said Lavinia after a moment's struggle in which she thought of the hurt the 'little thing' had caused her, the children, Teresa Somercote herself, and probably Tom too. She struggled for mastery over her feelings, but when they threatened to overtake her, she covered her face with her hands. 'I just don't understand why, if it was so unimportant, he did it at all.'

Lavinia felt strong hands on her wrists, pulling them down. Sally squatted on the rug in front of Lavinia, her long legs in their fine black tights bent into inverted V-shapes. Even at that moment Lavinia noticed that there was only the smallest possible bulge either side of Sally's knees; there was no flab on her thighs at all. Lavinia felt middle-aged and fat and very dowdy in her knee-length green silk.

'Because it comforted him in the loneliness and anxiety that are part of the life of any MP with a far-off constituency. That's all. Really, Lavinia. That's all. It was a little thing.'

Lavinia shook her head, but before she could say anything they heard the others returning. Sally stood up straight and swaggered back to the fire, but, as the other three women bent over the coffee tray, she looked back with such compassion that for a moment she seemed exactly like her mother. Lavinia's mistrust seemed ludicrous and she hoped that Sally could feel her gratitude as easily as she had felt the earlier suspicion.

Chapter 19

Lavinia had promised to see Ben Wroot early the following afternoon to give him some more exclusive 'loving thoughts' about Tom. Shaken as she had been by the sight of Caro's humiliated distress at dinner, and by her own surprisingly direct conversation with Sally Anlaby, Lavinia did not want to talk about her relationship with Tom to anyone, least of all a journalist. But a deal was a deal, and until Tom was back she was going to need the *Daily Messenger*'s co-operation. Carefully dressed in a severe black suit that was supposed to put up a barrier between herself and the rest of the world, Lavinia made sure that she had her tape-recorder in her bag and set off, rehearsing Coué-like exercises as she sat in the tube train. Every day in every way Tom's release is getting nearer and nearer. Every day in every way I'm getting tougher and tougher. Every day in every way Tom's release is getting nearer and nearer.

Wroot was waiting for her in Niccolino's café and it soon became clear that she was going to need every bit of real or pretended toughness she could muster. He said he had had more than enough loving thoughts already and that what he wanted Lavinia to talk about that morning was her reaction to Tom's adultery and why she had forgiven him.

When she refused to say anything at all, Wroot turned nasty and tried to goad her into giving him something quotable. He told her that it had been well established that political wives will put up with almost any public humiliation from their unfaithful husbands because they don't want to lose their perks.

Lavinia had heard and read several versions of the theory already. As usual she was tempted to say that, like a lot of the other political wives, she was bored rigid by official entertainments and detested the House of Commons and everything it had taken from her and her marriage. She would have traded what perks there were for a bit of ordinary family life any day.

Sitting in the café, watching Wroot pile gross amounts of sugar into his cup, she said none of it. In fact, hiding behind a polite smile, she merely shook her head and said nothing at all about anything.

'Think what the paper's doing for you,' said Wroot, clearly provoked by her stubborn silence. 'And what we could do to you once we decide we've had enough of you as a heroine.' He laughed. 'We've set you up and we can bring you down just like that. Don't think we won't.'

'I don't,' said Lavinia, 'but you, the editor and the paper itself will all look ridiculous if you start bringing me down before you've succeeded in the campaign to get Tom out and once he's back I don't care what you do to me.'

'You know how I told you I'd manage to find some good pics of you looking like an angry bag lady?'

'I remember,' said Lavinia coldly as she sipped her sugarless coffee.

'Good. Well I've been digging and I've found some corkers. Want to see?'

'Not very much, thank you,' said Lavinia, remembering several photographs of herself that made her look at least four times fatter than she was and virtually demented. She took the tape recorder out of her bag and laid it on the table between them.

'I've still got the cassette of your superbly frank

confession that truth means nothing to you when you're manipulating stories into the kind of titillating drama you think your bored readers enjoy. Just think about a banner headline in the *Sun* or the *Mirror* or one of your other competitors, quoting your contempt for your readers.'

'You'll never find a journalist who'd do the dirt on a colleague,' he said contemptuously.

'Want to bet? I can imagine that rival editors, under circulation-raising pressure, might well go for it.'

'That's blackmail.'

'That's right,' Lavinia agreed cheerfully. 'Just the sort of thing you do when persuasion has failed. Now let's get on with it. I'm due in South Kensington at four-thirty.'

Eventually they hammered out three hundred words that were enticing enough for him and revealed as little as she could manage. By the time they had agreed on the final sentence, each disliked the other intensely.

As Lavinia walked to the tube station to catch a train to South Kensington, she wished she had time to go home for a bath to scrub off the feeling that she had been prostituting herself. She had told Wroot nothing of her real feelings for Tom, or her doubts about him or herself. The subject of Philip had never been raised, and her real character was as much hidden from the readers of the *Daily Messenger* as it had been from everyone else. And yet she felt as though she had sold something important.

She was also afraid that she had made a powerful and mischievous enemy. Once Tom was home, Wroot might make real trouble for him. Pushing her money into the automatic ticket machine, Lavinia told herself that nothing – absolutely nothing – mattered except Tom's safety. The future could take care of itself.

When Elizabeth Trewhitt opened the door of her house and saw Lavinia standing on the step, she said at once: 'You look marvellous. Quite different. Come on in and get warm. I do hate this weather, don't you?'

'Yes, it's horrible,' said Lavinia, agreeing automatically. She was so surprised by the compliment that she hardly noticed the room into which Elizabeth was leading her. All she saw was that it was large and light, with french windows leading to a tiny formal garden and that there was an old-fashioned tea table drawn up before the fire.

Lavinia took in none of the details then, but she felt the atmosphere at once. Almost as distinctive as the mixed scents from the fire, a pile of cinnamon toast on the table and white hyacinths growing in green bowls on the windowsills, the goodwill and freedom in the room seemed to surround her and draw her in. As the clamour that had been building up in her head began to lessen, she smiled.

Elizabeth put her white head on one side and examined her guest in silence. There was warmth in her faded eyes. 'Now, do help yourself to something to eat,' she said eventually, 'while I make the tea.'

She scooped tea leaves from an antique caddy into a silver teapot and added water from a matching kettle, which had been simmering over a spirit lamp.

'I didn't know anyone still had tea like this,' Lavinia said with pleasure as she obediently took a plate and a piece of cinnamon toast.

'I'm not sure anyone else ever does. Now tell me how you are and why you're looking so much better than you were up in Yorkshire.'

Lavinia choked on her toast. 'I can't imagine,' she said when she could speak again. 'I'm not sleeping much; eating is tricky; I'm tormented about Tom; and worried all the time that the things I am trying to do to help may in fact be harming him. I ought to feel ghastly and yet in a way you're right. Something is better. I can't think what, though.'

'It looks to me as though you've let something go

that was dragging you down,' said Elizabeth lightly as she stirred the tea and then poured some into delicate Rockingham cups. Her right hand shook slightly as though the silver teapot was too heavy for her. When she had put it down again, she handed one cup to Lavinia. 'There's milk or lemon. And you ought to eat something else. You must need food if you haven't been eating much.'

Lavinia accepted the tea and obediently took a piece of shortbread, but she put it down untasted on her plate. Looking at her elderly, once-beautiful hostess sitting in the lovely room with an air of complete serenity, Lavinia felt a sudden passionate envy.

'May I ask you something, Mrs Trewhitt?' she asked before she could stop herself.

'Of course. What is it you want to know?'

'How did you become so – there just isn't an English phrase for what I mean – so *bien dans votre peau*?'

To Lavinia's delight, Elizabeth laughed, suddenly sounding infinitely younger than she either looked or was. She put the finger and thumb of her left hand on the loose skin of her neck and pulled it out.

'Having so much skin these days, my dear, and all of it so slack, may have helped me to be at ease in it.'

Lavinia laughed with her and took a small bite of the shortbread. Discovering that it tasted wonderful, she ate the whole piece and took another. For the first time in weeks she felt hungry.

'I know that isn't what you meant,' said Elizabeth, not laughing any longer, 'and I wasn't always at ease. For a time I was miserable in the kind of slight but grinding way that a lot of people seem to think is normal. Then I became actively unhappy.' She looked at Lavinia and added carefully: 'As I rather think you have been.'

'I can't . . .' Lavinia said and then stopped.

'You don't have to say anything about it.' Elizabeth

poured more tea into their cups and then put the heavy pot back on the table and sat staring down at her arthritic hands. After a while she looked up again and said frankly: 'But you don't have to be unhappy either.'

'That sounds as though it's within my control,' said Lavinia grimly, twisting her engagement ring round and round her finger.

'I think you might find it is. I did. You see, once I'd understood what it was that I had been doing to make myself unhappy, I found out how to stop.'

'You?' Lavinia was so surprised that her voice came out in a kind of squawk. 'Sorry. But wasn't it other people who'd been making you miserable?'

'Not exactly.' Elizabeth smiled but Lavinia could not bring herself to respond. She waited, half-angry and half-afraid.

'I'd always thought it was until it struck me that no-one was actually trying to make me miserable – quite the reverse in fact. They would all have infinitely preferred me happy.' She laughed. 'For one thing, I'd have been much easier to live with.'

'Maybe,' said Lavinia indignantly, 'but they were doing things that stoppped you, weren't they?'

'Yes, but don't you see the difference?'

Lavinia shook her head.

'Only the things they did were theirs.' Elizabeth took a minute piece of fruit cake and broke off a corner. 'The feelings were mine, and that meant that I could change them.'

'I don't understand.' Lavinia felt a sickeningly familiar mixture of shame at her own stupidity, anger at being made to feel it, and absurd panic, as though she were about to be punished for her failure to understand. Not only her skin, but also her eyes, felt hot. All the ease and freedom she had sensed in the room had gone. She might almost have been confronting Flavia at her most aggressive, and without any of the defences she had collected around herself. She tried to pull herself together.

'Understanding takes two,' Elizabeth said with such gentleness that it was clear she had understood Lavinia's distress. 'If I can't make myself clear then you could not understand, however carefully you listened. It's not your fault.'

'Nor yours,' said Lavinia with difficulty hanging on to the knowledge that she was an adult and had no reason to be afraid of Elizabeth. She wrenched a handkerchief from the sleeve of her sweater and blew her nose.

'Exactly. That's what it's all about.'

Lavinia's shoulders sagged. 'But you can't mean that no-one is ever to blame for anything they do,' she cried out in frustration, thinking not only of the kidnappers, who were obviously to blame for what had happened to Tom, but also of Tom himself, his mother and the rest of the family, and everything they had made her feel throughout her married life.

'No. That's not what I meant either,' said Elizabeth, reaching for her teacup. 'In the old days I was very much afraid of what other people could make me feel. You see, I hadn't understood that if I could stop being afraid of them, they would stop being frightening.'

'I don't understand.' Lavinia finished the tea in her cup as she tried to make her brain work for her. 'I do see that if you're not afraid then there can't be anything frightening you, but what can you do about it if you *are* afraid – or unhappy. Pretending you're not doesn't work. I've tried it.'

'No, you mustn't pretend.'

'Then what do you do?' The anger was becoming clearer in Lavinia's voice as it overtook the silly panic.

'I wish I were better with words,' said Elizabeth in tacit apology. 'Listen, Lavinia, I think it helps if you can work out precisely what you feel: not just the general misery, but the individual constituents of it.'

Lavinia put her cup carefully on the table, as though she could not trust herself to hold it any longer without throwing it on the floor, and turned to face Elizabeth.

'How?'

'I can only do it by tasting my feelings.' Lavinia brushed some imaginary crumbs off her lap with an impatience that was only too obvious. She was about to make herself apologize when Elizabeth added: 'When you take a mouthful of some unfamiliar dish, if you taste it carefully enough, you can work out what the different ingredients are. Do you see?'

'So far,' said Lavinia, managing to smile politely. 'You mean like distinguishing the surprising lemon peel in your shortbread from the butter and sugar?'

'Exactly. Now, do the same for your feelings. Work out what all the different flavours are. If you can do that, you can begin to understand. You see, if you're like me and tend to be afraid of other people, you will probably find that you've been blaming them for that, or been angry or perhaps even wanted some kind of revenge. And if you're the conscientious, sensitive person I think you are, you'll feel ashamed of yourself, and the shame will join the anger and the fear in dragging you down. If you can get rid of the fear, which was almost certainly unnecessary in the first place, all the rest will go and you'll be free. D'you see what I mean?'

'It sounds so easy,' said Lavinia when she had swallowed the last of her shortbread. She felt better. 'But I can't believe it's as simple as that.'

'Oddly enough it is – or it was for me once I'd seen how it all worked. And when I'd stopped expecting the things I'd found so frightening, they stopped coming. It was as though something in the way I had reacted made people do and say the very things I most dreaded.'

Lavinia's eyebrows twitched back across her nose and her forehead creased. 'It all sounds to me as though you're blaming yourself for everything that had made you unhappy.'

'Does it? Then I've put it badly. I didn't blame myself; I just stopped blaming other people.'

'I wish I thought I could be as happy as you,' said Lavinia as the old French clock above the fire struck five. Before her hostess could comment, she quickly asked about the clock and they talked peacefully about antiques until they had finished tea.

Later, when she got up to go, Lavinia thanked Elizabeth and then added abruptly: 'I'll try this tasting lark of yours.'

Elizabeth's face lit in a smile of extraordinary delight as she stood up and took Lavinia's hand between both of hers. 'You do that. Thank you for coming to see me. Don't lose touch, will you?'

Lavinia smiled too, and shook her head. She took the tube back to the Elephant and Castle and emerged in the orange glow of the street lamps that had been lit while she was underground. For once she hardly saw the muddle of ugly buildings or broad roads full of noisy, thrusting traffic as she tried to work out what Elizabeth had meant. The ideas seemed even more slippery and impossible to grasp than when she had been explaining them.

But I am not stupid, Lavinia said to herself, feeling her teeth grinding together like the heaviest of millstones. I am not.

Then she tripped over a lopsided paving stone and almost fell. As she straightened up, seeing the damage the rough stone had done to the toes of her good London shoes, she remembered promising to try to taste her feelings and grimly set about it.

After a while she began to separate the love she felt for Tom from the fear of what he had always been able to make her feel when he refused what she wanted to give him or withheld what she wanted from him. And then she found that she could distinguish other feelings, too.

She began to see that she had long ago assumed her unhappiness must be his fault but had been unable to bear to accept that. Fighting her urge to blame him, she had tightened herself up to withstand it and to bear the misery without letting him know how bad it was.

Glimmers of understanding began to flicker in her mind. If Elizabeth were right and the unhappiness had not been Tom's fault in the first place, and Lavinia was beginning to see that it might not have been, she could simply give up the battle and all the tension, the guilt and the anxiety it had brought with it. And if all that went, she might even be able to believe him when he told her that he loved her and simply accept that his way of expressing it was different from hers.

Could it really be as easy as that? she asked herself as she reached the corner of West Square. And then she remembered where he was and what might happen to him, and how he might never be able to tell her anything again.

As she turned into the square she saw a police car parked outside her house, forgot her dignity and her high-heeled shoes, and ran fast across the square. The rear passenger door opened as she reached the police car and a uniformed officer got out, putting her cap on as she straightened up.

'Mrs Medworth? I'm Inspector Waters. I have a message from Superintendent Chorley. Shall we go in?'

Lavinia stood where she was, her lips apart, neither speaking nor breathing. It felt as though her brain had shut down and nothing was happening within her skin.

'Mrs Medworth?'

'Yes. Sorry.' She shook her head violently as though to shake her brain back into working order. 'What sort of message?'

'Good news. Shall we go in?'

'How good?'

'Very good.' She spoke kindly and slowly but very firmly as though to an idiot: 'Have you got your keys?'

Scuffling in her bag, Lavinia found that she could not even see properly and so she simply held the bag out to Inspector Waters. With a slight smile, she took it, found the keys without difficulty and handed them back to Lavinia, who managed to select the right ones and even to get them to undo the locks in the front door and turn off the beeping burglar alarm. She leaned against the dark-blue-striped wall, breathing heavily.

'Now tell me.'

'They've got him back and they're on the way to St Michael's Hospital in York now. Three men and a woman are in custody.' The inspector looked down at the plain steel watch on her wrist. 'He should be just about arriving at the hospital now.'

'Why a hospital? Has he been hurt?'

'I don't know any details, but I understand it's a question of checking him over rather than dealing with any specific injury.'

'When did it happen?'

'About three-quarters of an hour ago. Superintendent Chorley will fill you in with all the details. I've got a number where he can be reached. Here.' She held out a small piece of paper. 'Mrs Medworth, can I make you a cup of tea or something? I think you ought to sit down.'

Lavinia shook her head again and then wiped her hands over her face. 'I don't know what . . . Yes, of course, do have some tea. Come along.'

She led the way along the dark passage to the kitchen and dropped into one of the pine chairs, leaning her elbows on the table so that she could rest her head in them. Holding it up seemed more than her neck could manage on its own.

'Are you all right?'

'I feel sick. Oh, God!' Lavinia got up and clamped her

302

left hand across her mouth as she ran to the lavatory. Saliva pumped itself into her mouth. She only just got there in time and knelt on the grey-lino floor, retching and sobbing. Eventually the spasms stopped. With what felt like the last remnant of her strength she pulled the plug and then took a yard or so of lavatory paper off the roll to wipe her face. She did not feel as though she would be able to move again, but the sour smell of sick mixed with the faint pungency of bleach was so horrible that eventually she had to get away.

Pushing herself up from the floor, she dropped the crumpled paper into the lavatory, pulled the plug again and looked at her face in the small mirror over the basin. Her eyes looked huge, surrounded by messy make up, and beneath the blusher and the powder her skin was very pale. She rinsed out her mouth, washed her face and eventually went back to the inspector, who was patiently sitting at the table with a mug of tea in front of her.

'Sorry.'

'It's not surprising. Shock takes us all in odd ways. Even good shocks. I helped myself to milk.'

'Good.' With a memory of Philip's persuading her to eat toast and marmalade to help with the first shock of Tom's disappearance, Lavinia took a tin of biscuits from the cupboard and offered them to Inspector Waters, who shook her head.

Lavinia poured herself out some tea and saw that her hand was no longer shaking much. As she ate a chocolate-and-ginger biscuit, she caught sight of the inspector's face, looking at her as though she were exhibiting signs of some rare disease, and made herself smile.

'I'm all right now, just talking to myself. Tell me again everything you know about Tom.'

'Very little, I'm afraid,' said the inspector, but she repeated everything she had already said, found the sheet of paper with Chorley's mobile telephone number, which

Lavinia had dropped, and wrote on it the name of the hospital where Tom had been taken.

'Now, what are your plans, Mrs Medworth?'

Lavinia thought she must be mad and said: 'I'm going up there, of course. It'll take me about five hours, perhaps more at this time of day with all the rush-hour traffic on the way to the M1. I'll call Chorley when I get there.'

'I don't think it would be wise for you to drive alone in this state. Is there someone I can call for you?'

As though on cue, the telephone rang. Automatically Lavinia got up to answer it. 'Mrs Medworth? Ben Wroot here. Is it true?'

Lavinia covered the mouthpiece with her hand and turned to say over her shoulder: 'It's the press. The *Daily Messenger*. Am I allowed to tell?'

'Yes.'

'It's true that he's out,' she said into the telephone. 'I don't know any more. I've only just heard. I'm going back to Yorkshire now. I'll ring you when I know more. I'm grateful for what you've done.'

'We'll get you up there. Don't worry. You shouldn't drive on your own after a shock like that – however welcome.'

Lavinia found herself laughing. 'That's what the police have said, but I suspect your motives are different. I can't . . .'

'I won't ask you anything on the record until we're there and you've seen him. But you're ours, Mrs Medworth. We've bought you with the campaign and we need the first pictures.'

Suppressing rage, feebleness and the familiar sensation that she had made a Faustian pact that would have horrible repercussions she could not even begin to imagine, Lavinia said: 'I don't feel strong enough for any of this at the moment.'

'It's all right,' answered Wroot, sounding almost kind.

'I won't hassle you. But you need to get up there and we need the first pics. It's in both our interests for me to have you driven up there. You pack a bag and I'll be with you in about twenty minutes.'

Lavinia was left with an empty line. She replaced the receiver and turned back to Inspector Waters.

'That's that, then. The *Daily Messenger* will be driving me up. God knows what I'll do about the Landrover.'

'There'll be time for all kinds of practicalities later. Might I borrow your telephone?'

'Yes, of course. I must go and pack. Oh, and leave a note for the cleaner. And I ought to telephone Aubrey, at least. No, perhaps that can wait.' Muttering to herself, she left the kitchen.

Chapter 20

Half an hour later, still not quite sure what was happening to her but with the sensation of relief beginning to prevail over the shock and the horror that she had been trying to keep pressed down throughout the time of Tom's maximum danger, Lavinia lay back in Ben Wroot's car and closed her eyes. Through her lids came the rhythmic, relentless, almost brutal flashing of headlights from the other side of the motorway.

I'll see him soon, she said to herself. He's not dead. He's not even injured – or not physically anyway. He's safe now. There is life beyond the horror after all. Hang on to that. He is all right.

Wroot and the photographer in the back seat talked at intervals during the long journey. They stopped once at a service station for more petrol and cups of black coffee, but even then Wroot kept his word and asked Lavinia nothing about Tom or what she felt. She was grateful and hoped that he knew it, but she did not want to say even that. It felt as though if she did not keep in every word the whole lot would spill out in an ungainly, dangerous flood. Her own fear of what the words might be – or tell her – was at least as sharp as her need for discretion in the face of a tabloid journalist.

They had almost reached York before her mind cleared

enough to think about the children. She knew she should have rung their schools even before she set out from West Square. And there was Philip. She did not know what she was going to do about Philip and she did not think it would be fair to talk to him until she did know. Someone in the family, probably Aubrey, would have been told about Tom's rescue and would pass it on to the rest. Philip would wait and understand why she was apparently ignoring him. But the children were different.

'Have you got a telephone in the car?' she asked aloud.

'It's beside you,' said Wroot, showing no surprise at her sudden return to communication. 'Feel free.'

'Thanks.' She had the numbers of the two schools in her bag and was soon talking to the boys' headmaster. He listened to what she told him in admirable silence, then congratulated her and promised to give the good news to both boys straight away.

'I expect they'll want to talk to you. Shall I tell them where you are and give them permission to phone?'

'Better not yet,' said Lavinia. 'I'm on my way to the hospital. They'll have all sorts of questions I haven't got the answers to yet. Would you just tell them that he's safe and that as soon as I can I'll ring them?'

'Certainly, Mrs Medworth. I am really glad – for you and for them. They've both handled themselves well, but Rory's been remarkably mature. You should be proud of him.'

'Thank you,' said Lavinia, hardly able to speak. 'I am. Goodbye.'

She took a moment to compose herself and then rang Tammy's headmistress, who was equally calm and sympathetic. Once Lavinia had put the telephone back in its cradle and closed her eyes again, it seemed only about twenty minutes before Wroot stopped the car.

'Here we are,' he said unnecessarily.

Lavinia did not even thank him. She simply picked

up her bag as soon as the car stopped, pushed open the door and ran across the wet road to the lighted doorway. Inside she took a moment to orientate herself in the noise and the crowds and then headed straight for the casualty reception desk. While she was waiting in the queue, she felt a hand on her arm and looked round to see Ben Wroot's face smiling at her. There was enough superiority mixed with the amusement to make her want to slap him.

'He's not here, Lavinia. He's in a room upstairs. Come on.' Wroot led her away from the casualty department and took her up to the fourteenth floor of the modern tower. When they emerged from the lift, the place seemed as crowded as a rush-hour station. There were police in uniform; journalists, photographers and television crews; and plenty of people who seemed to be no more than interested passers-by hoping for a little drama.

Wroot looked over his shoulder to check that his own photographer was still following and piloted Lavinia through the crowd. They were stopped at the entrance to the ward and Wroot stepped back to allow her to explain herself. A moment later Chorley appeared and took her to Tom. She did not notice – or care – that he had stopped Wroot from following her.

From outside the door of a dimly-lit room, Lavinia saw Tom sitting up against a pile of pillows, attached to a monitor of some kind. He was very thin and had obviously not been allowed to shave often since he had been taken. His hair was long and filthy, and he was scratching his scalp in an absent-minded way as he talked to someone out of her sight. There were marks of tension and exhaustion on his lined, yellowish face; his eyelids were thickly swollen and the eyes themselves looked painful, but he was alive, clearly sane and his face at least was unmarked by scars.

She went through the door. Tom was talking to two tough-looking young men in civilian clothes, one of whom was taking notes, but he saw Lavinia at once. His face seemed to loosen. He did not smile, but she did not need anything more than that tiny relaxation to know that he was glad she was there. She remembered his stifled calling out to her on the first tape from the kidnappers. Ignoring everyone else in the room, she walked forward until she was standing close enough to touch him.

He grabbed her hand and clung to it. She brushed the hair, lank and greasy as it was, out of his eyes and let herself feel all the yearning and terror of the past weeks, and her almost unendurable relief that it had ended.

'Tom,' was all she said and even that was almost more than her voice could manage without wobbling.

'Yes.'

She tried again, smiled and licked her lips. All she produced was a croak.

'I'm all right,' he assured her. Then he did smile.

'Are you sure?' Her voice worked adequately after all.

He nodded and swallowed. 'There's lots to say, isn't there?'

'Yes, but not here, perhaps.'

'No. And we've got time now.'

'Yes. Did they hurt you?' She hated herself for the clumsy banality of the question, but her need to establish some connection with what had been happening to him and how he felt – without actually asking such a Wroot-like question – was urgent.

'Not much.'

'Thank God for that, at least.'

He used his free hand to rub his face. 'They were a bit . . . physical at the beginning, but the worst was the dark and the emptiness.' He clamped his lips shut for a moment. 'And the not speaking.'

Someone else made a movement and Lavinia remembered that they were not alone. She looked round and smiled apologetically at the waiting men. Tom's hand, still gripping hers, seemed much more important than

309

any of their official status, notebooks, tape recorders or anything else.

'Would you like a chair, Mrs Medworth?' said one of the young men, pushing one forwards. He added to Tom: 'Shall we finish this later, sir?'

'Do you mind?'

'Not a bit. We'll all clear off for a while and get a cup of tea.'

Soon they really were alone and then Lavinia bent so that her face rested against Tom's.

'I'm too foul to kiss,' he said into her ear.

'That couldn't matter less.' She lay against him, breathing and feeling his heart pumping under her. Then she suddenly straightened up. 'Am I hurting you?'

'The reverse.' As she lay back across his chest, he let go her hand at last and put both arms around her. 'Oh, Lavvy, I've needed you.'

'Thank God, Tom. Oh, thank God.'

Neither of them tried to work out exactly what it was for which she was thankful.

'Did you read my letter?' he asked much later when she was sitting in the chair.

'Yes, and I've written several answers, all clumsier than the last. I'm sorry. I . . .'

'Don't. I've rewritten that letter so often in the last weeks. The more I've thought about it, the worse it seemed. There's so much I want to . . .'

She put her hand gently on his lips.

'As you said, Tom, we've got time. You need to get over what's happened to you before we start talking about things like that.'

He grabbed her hand again, but it was with a quite different grip; even harder and nearly painful.

'Why? What are you going to tell me?'

'Oh, Tom, don't look like that. Just that I love you, that

310

I've got things so wrong in the past and . . . and *minded* about things that I shouldn't have, and yet not told you about the ones that are quite . . . that I think it was quite legitimate to mind about. I just don't want to pour all my feelings out over you while you're still shaky. That's all.'

'How's Philip?'

'What? I don't know. When I last saw him he was fine. That's about four or five days ago. Why?'

'Are you going to go off with him?'

'No. Oh, Tom. There was never any question of that. You haven't been sitting in the dark all these weeks, thinking that, have you?'

He stared up at her, looking heartbreakingly like Rory, and then his eyes slid away.

'Tom, listen: this is important. Compared to what I feel for you, the mixture of sympathy and affection I had – have – for Philip is trivial.'

Something of the urgency in her voice seemed to get through to him and he looked at her again. 'Truly?'

'Yes,' she said, watching him. Somewhere in her there was regret for the denial of everything Philip had meant to her, but he had understood so much that she believed he would have understood that, too.

Tom did not relax. After a while he pointed to his ravaged face and said: 'Is that because of this? Because you pity me and think I need treating gently?'

'No. It's because you are the most important thing in my life and always have been. You must know that.'

'How could I know? You never said.'

She frowned, wondering how he could not have known. Trying to practise what she had learned from Elizabeth Trewhitt, Lavinia tasted her feelings and her memories and remembered just how much of her life with Tom had been spent in her own head. Too many of the exercises in self-discipline, in trying not to burden him with her doubts, her anguish, her love, her needs, had been carried out in silence.

'Don't be angry.'

'I'm not,' she said, her heart wrenched with pity, love and sharp regret. 'At least, not with you.'

'Then who?'

'Myself; mainly for being such a fool. I ought to have told you, but I assumed that you knew. That's what I felt when I got your letter. "How could he *not* have known?" For some idiotic reason I seem to have believed that you'd be able to hear even if I didn't tell. It seems bizarre, looking back, but at the time . . .'

Her voice dwindled. She didn't mind that yet again she hadn't finished her sentence, that the words she needed hadn't come. All that mattered was that the security was seeping back into Tom's eyes and his hand was clinging to hers, no longer gripping her wrist.

There was a knock at the door and one of the young plain-clothes men came in and told them that the *Daily Messenger* people were agitating for photographs.

'We'll have to let them have some,' said Tom, sounding quite different from the shaky lover of a moment earlier. 'Given that I'm told they conducted the campaign that got me out.'

'Actually, sir,' said Chorley from behind the young man's shoulder, 'that was Mrs Medworth. But the prime means she used was that rag.'

'I did sort of promise Wroot an exclusive,' Lavinia confessed.

'Ironic, isn't it?' said Tom, sounding less tormented and fragile by the minute. 'Still, we live and die by the media. OK. Let them in. The rest can wait until the press conference. I can't answer questions. And I . . .' He clamped his lips shut and shook his head.

Lavinia stood at his side, holding his hand, while Wroot and the photographer came in for their reward.

'Look here, guys,' said Tom with a cheerful smile, 'I'd much rather be shaved and have my hair cut before you . . .'

'Not a good idea, Mr Medworth,' said Wroot at once. He sounded brisk but not uncivil. Glancing across at Lavinia, he nodded at her. 'At your wife's instigation we've stirred up quite a bit of rage against the people who took you. "Loony animal-lovers who hate people" and all that. It'll be more easily justified if we show you looking like death. Oh, sorry: tactless. But you know what I mean.'

'Yes.' All Tom's old, half-forgotten dry sense of humour was in that word and Lavinia felt her whole body lightening. She grinned at him and was flooded with delight when he grinned back.

'And if you could manage to look agonized, that would be even better,' said Wroot coldly.

Tom glared at him. The appropriately miserable photographs were taken and then some more cheerful ones. The camera's flash clearly hurt Tom's sensitized eyes, but he tried not to screw them up and wiped them whenever they watered. When the photographer had enough shots, Wroot took out his tape recorder and asked for comments. Tom efficiently dictated a few short sentences, saying how deeply grateful he was to his family, to the police, to the press, and to everyone who had had a hand in his release.

'May we know how that was achieved?' said Wroot, sounding much more sycophantic than whenever he was talking to Lavinia.

'The police became aware of where I was being held,' said Tom carefully, 'and took appropriate action. That's it for now. They'll tell you more at their press conference tomorrow when they've finished their mopping-up operation.'

'And how are you feeling?'

'Relieved. Tired, although I've done little but sleep for

the last five weeks. Grateful to be alive. And looking forward to getting back to normal life again with my family.'

'Will you be hunting again?'

'Certainly.'

'And you, Mrs Medworth?' asked Wroot, raising his eyebrows. 'What are your feelings?'

What do you think? said Lavinia silently.

'Happiness,' she said aloud with a sweet smile. The photographer's camera flashed again. 'To have my husband back is the best thing that's ever happened to me. And I, too, am deeply grateful to everyone who was involved in his release.'

'Thanks. Now, kiss him for the final shot.'

'No,' said Tom and Lavinia in unison. They compromised eventually with a photograph of the two of them holding hands and smiling at each other.

'Ugh,' said Lavinia as the camera was lowered again. The familiar sensation of grubbiness and selling something important returned, bringing with it threatening nausea. She worked to control it, determined not to disgrace herself in front of a man like Wroot.

'Got enough, Dave?' he said, watching her with interest.

'Yeah. Some corkers,' said the photographer, putting the lens cap back on his camera and stowing it in the huge bag that he slung over his shoulder. 'Are we off then?'

'Yes. Thank you both. We'll be in touch.'

They left and Tom let out a great sigh. 'Thank God for that. Lavinia, darling, I ought to finish with the police while my memory's functioning. I don't know what my subconscious will do to it once I've relaxed properly.'

'No, of course not. I'd better ring the children anyway and your mother, too. She's been . . . Well, we've all been desperate, but the last thing I want to do is worry you with our feelings now. Dearest Tom, I . . .'

314

'I know,' he said, and she thought that he did. 'You'll come back, won't you?'

'I will.'

She made her telephone calls and then waited outside his room with the detective who was to guard him for the next few weeks at least. When the plain clothes officers had finished their questions she went back into the room and sat at Tom's side until he had fallen asleep. Half-asleep herself, she pushed her aching body out of the chair at last and went down to the lobby of the hospital to call for a minicab to take her to the Dower House.

There she took a moment to switch on the heating and hot water, boiled a kettle to fill her hotwater bottle, and staggered upstairs to pull off her clothes. She dropped them on the floor and fell into bed. For the first time since Tom had been taken she slept the moment she lay down and did not wake for thirteen hours.

The next morning, before she had even washed or dressed, she telephoned Philip at the surgery. His receptionist told her that he was with a patient and asked: 'Is it an emergency?'

'No, nothing like that, but I would like to speak to him as soon as possible. When he's next free, could you please tell him that it's Lavinia Medworth and that I am at home at the Dower House. He has the number.'

She sat beside the telephone, waiting. Seven and a half minutes later it rang.

'Lavinia, thank God he's safe,' said Philip at once. 'Aubrey rang us yesterday evening. How are you?'

'Reeling. Happy. And longing to see you.'

'Are you?'

'Yes. I'm sorry I didn't ring you yesterday, but I needed to work some things out.'

'About why you and I can't ever be anything but in-laws?'

'Yes.' She breathed more easily at his instant acceptance

315

of what she had not even said. 'You've always understood everything. I can't think why I was afraid you might not understand this. I'm sorry about it, Philip. So terribly sorry.'

'You don't have to be, Lavinia. And of course I understand. I think I knew really that evening in West Square, and . . .' He broke off and she was conscious that he was making a tremendous effort.

'Philip,' she said, wishing that he were within reach so that she could at least touch him.

'And I suppose I knew anyway,' he said doggedly. 'All along really beneath the fantasies that you and I would go off and be happy somewhere together. As I said in that letter, I always knew you felt for Tom what I feel for Sasha.'

'Yes.'

'What's that line of Yeats's about the folly of comfort?'

Lavinia took a moment to untangle what he meant, but then she remembered the poem and said: 'Isn't it something like, "Oh, if she'd but turn her head, you'd know the folly of being comforted"?'

'Exactly,' said Philip. 'And Tom has turned his now, hasn't he?'

'I suppose he has. But it's so much kinder than that poem always sounds, and there's a lot more to this, too. Philip, I badly want to tell you the whole thing, but I know you haven't got time to talk now.'

'You're right about that: I must go. The waiting room's full of people. But I'm glad you did ring.'

'Thank you,' she said. 'What I haven't actually said yet is what I most wanted to say: that I shall always love you and be grateful that you were here. I hope, oh I do so hope that you can be happy again.'

'Are you?'

'I think I will be.' Lavinia thought of Tom's face when he caught sight of her in the hospital. 'No, that's a silly way to put it. Yes, I am happy.'

'Good. Well . . . No, I can't let you go like this however many patients there are outside. It matters too much and we've got such a lot to talk about. When am I going to see you again?'

'As soon as possible. I can't leave here until I know for sure that Tom is ready, but as soon as it's feasible, we'll be coming back to London. I'm not going to shut myself up in my tower any more.'

There was a pause and then Philip said: 'Will he mind if we meet?'

'I don't know, but it's too important for us to pretend about. I'll let you know as soon as I can when I'll be back.'

'Thank you. Lavinia . . .'

'I know.'

'Yes. And that's a help. Take care of yourself.'

When they had eventually forced themselves to say goodbye, Lavinia put down the telephone receiver and went to get the house ready for Tom's return. As she was hauling the Hoover out of its cupboard in the kitchen she thought of Flavia and stood with the coils of black flex feeling cold and heavy between her fingers.

There had been so much anger between them that it was going to be difficult to forge any kind of peace, and, if they did not, their enmity would make it even harder for Tom to return to normal life than the kidnappers had already made it.

She pushed the Hoover back among the brushes and buckets, flinging the uncoiling flex on top of it and angrily putting her shoulder to the door to force it shut. The telephone started to ring just as she was unlocking the front door. She stood with her hand on the Yale, pulled both ways, and eventually went back to answer the call in case Tom was trying to get hold of her.

'Mrs Medworth? John Chorley here. I thought you'd like to know at once that we now have all the kidnappers.'

'You mean there are more than the three who were holding Tom?'

'Yes. There was the organizer, too. A woman.'

'Sally Anlaby,' said Lavinia before she could stop herself.

'No. Mrs Medworth, I told you weeks ago that she could not possibly . . .'

'You told me she could not possibly have had a hand in the snatch,' said Lavinia grimly, remembering all her myriad suspicions of Sally, 'but that wouldn't have stopped her being the mastermind behind it all.'

'I hadn't realized you were so worried about her,' said Chorley, sounding much friendlier than he ever had during the days when there had been no news. 'You should have told me; I'd have reassured you at once. We know all about Mrs Anlaby here, and there's nothing for you to fear from her. Nothing.'

His voice was so kind that Lavinia needed to change the subject at once.

'How did you find them in the end? Was it really information received?'

'Yes. You were right about that. The *Messenger*'s reward tipped the balance. One of the men guarding your husband cracked. Fifty grand was just too much for his determination to protect the rights of foxes.'

'Thank God for that.'

'Yes. If I may say so, Mrs Medworth, you did very well indeed. It's unlikely that we'll ever meet again, but I am extremely glad to have had a chance to know you.'

'Thank you, John,' she said using his Christian name for the first time. 'For all you've done. And I'm sorry if I sounded . . . petulant at times or angry.'

'You were fine. Take care of yourself now. Your husband will have round-the-clock protection for some time. There's nothing more for you to fear. Goodbye.'

Lavinia locked up the house and drove slowly over

the moor to Saltley, once more able to enjoy it. The last of the snow had thawed days earlier and the sun, escaping from behind dark clouds, shone down on the dark-brown and green moor in widening rays that looked almost too painterly to be real. Saltley's grey-stone wall glinted when the light caught it and the pregnant ewes that ambled across the road in front of the car as she turned into the gates made her smile.

There were no strange cars on the gravel sweep outside the great house and she let herself quietly in through the front door. She was about to call out when she saw her mother-in-law and stopped in astonishment.

Flavia, the statuesque matriarch of the Medworth achievers, was on her knees in front of Great-aunt Elfrida's wheelchair. Flavia's head was buried in her sister-in-law's lap and her broad shoulders were shaking.

Elfrida's typically Medworth face was full of pity, but there was exasperation in it as well. After a while she seemed to sense an alien presence – or perhaps just a draught – and looked up. Seeing Lavinia, she put a finger to her lips and gestured towards the back regions of the house. Lavinia nodded and mouthed: 'Coffee?' Elfrida smiled without moving and Lavinia made her way as quietly as possible towards the kitchen.

There she washed up the crockery the others had used for breakfast, cleaned the coffee pot and refilled it, taking as much time as possible to give Flavia a chance to regain the control that had always been so important to her. Taking the coffee back to the Great Hall fifteen minutes later, Lavinia found Great-aunt Elfrida alone.

'Is she all right?'

'She will be,' said Elfrida casually. 'She was fine yesterday when we first got the news, but Tom telephoned her just now, and it was too much for her. Poor Flavia, she always was grossly over-emotional.'

The last sentence made Lavinia stare. She had never

heard anyone speak of Flavia with the sort of condescending pity she herself had been given so often.

'We all thought her analysis had cured it,' said Elfrida, staring into the empty fireplace as though she could see her past in the ashes, 'but whenever there's a real crisis she relapses.'

'I never knew she'd had analysis for anything except her own training.'

'It has always been kept quite quiet,' admitted Elfrida. 'My brother disapproved of the whole thing, but he was at his wits' end by then; she was causing such trouble and making him so miserable that the rest of us persuaded him to send her to a very well regarded man. The brother-in-law of an old friend of mine, in fact. It was fine as far as it went and she became very successful. But it didn't make her any happier.'

'No?' Lavinia was finding it hard to reconcile the Flavia she knew with the one Elfrida was describing.

'No. It simply made it possible for her to blame other people's neuroses for her difficulties; whenever she's been brought face to face with something she can't explain that way, she's collapsed.'

'I've never heard about any of this before,' said Lavinia, so surprised she could hardly take in what Elfrida was saying. 'And I've been living on her doorstep for the best part of fourteen years.'

'Perhaps you've been away whenever it's happened. Or else she's hidden it from you,' said Elfrida with a half-smile. 'That's more than likely. It's not something she'd ever willingly admit, particularly to you.'

'Why not to me? Elfrida, do you know why Flavia's always loathed me so much?'

The half-smile on Elfrida's strong, lined face was overtaken by an expression of astonishment almost as complete as Lavinia's.

'Don't you know? You've always been so amazingly

patient with her that I assumed you'd understood.'

'Quite the opposite. But it was so awful that I couldn't think what to do except ignore it. What did I do to her to make her hate me?'

Elfrida wheeled her chair round to get nearer the fire and held out her thin hands to the flames. 'I've always assumed that you reminded her of herself in the days before she had achieved anything, and I don't think she's been able to forgive you for that.'

Lavinia, who was unable to think of any way at all in which she was like her mother-in-law, said nothing. Elfrida glanced at her and saw what she felt.

'When my brother first brought her into the family she was very defensive about her lack of education and her inability to join in,' she said kindly, 'and she always fought to show the rest of us that she was as good as we were – which wasn't ever at issue as far as the rest of us were concerned.'

'No?' Lavinia had not known that she could sound quite so politely disbelieving.

Elfrida looked directly at her and said: 'Well, if she had made him happy it wouldn't have been.'

Lavinia began to feel sorry for her mother-in-law.

'I've never been quite sure whether she was trying to punish you for reminding her of the bad years,' Elfrida went on as unemotionally as though she were discussing some academic question that did not really matter, 'or to show the rest of us that there was absolutely no connection between you both by criticizing you at every possible opportunity.'

Hearing Flavia's heavy tread on the stairs, Elfrida stopped talking at once and wheeled her chair round again so that she was sitting at right angles to the fireplace. After a moment Lavinia went to stand at the foot of the stairs, waiting.

Flavia's face hardened as their eyes met. Lavinia forced

herself to hold out her hand. She could almost hear Elizabeth Trewhitt's quiet voice saying, 'Only the things they did were theirs. The feelings were mine, and that meant I could change them.'

'He's going to be all right, you know,' Lavinia said, trying to smile at Flavia as though she liked her and was not at all afraid of what she might say. 'I was there for hours last night and the doctors told me that there's nothing physically wrong that a careful diet, plenty of rest and exercise won't cure.'

'I never know whether it's crass optimism, lack of thought or simple ignorance that makes you say such ludicrous things,' said Flavia in her familiar tones of unassailable superiority. She ignored Lavinia's offered hand.

Tempted to turn away as usual, Lavinia made herself stand her ground. As she had discovered in London, she had a right to her own ideas and to their expression. She also had a duty to defend them. Reminding herself that Flavia could say what she liked but she could not actually do anything, she added: 'I was going to go on to say that the psychiatrist in charge of him wants to talk to me today to discuss the symptoms he's likely to show. Apparently quite often they don't appear for a while after the rescue, but it's almost inevitable that they will come and we need to be ready for them.'

Flavia bowed her head, whether in approval, acknowledgement or an attempt to hide anger, Lavinia did not know.

'He's going to need us both, Flavia,' she went on as gently as possible. 'And it'll be easier for him as well as for you and me if we can work together. I'll try to be tougher if you will try to forget that you think I'm a fool and have no right to be part of this family.'

She waited for a moment, but Flavia did not move.

'Well?'

When Flavia eventually looked up there were tears spilling over her eyelids again, but still Lavinia did not know what they meant. Trying to believe that it did not matter, she leaned forwards and, for the first time, kissed her mother-in-law's cheek. She smelled Flavia's newly washed skin and her toothpaste and recoiled from the intimacy that neither of them wanted.

'I'd better go back now,' Lavinia said as pleasantly as possible. 'There's a lot to be done at the Dower House. I'll ring you up as soon as I've heard anything.'

Flavia said nothing, which Lavinia thought was reward enough for her first major effort, but Elfrida wheeled her chair towards the front door so that she could pull aside the cracked leather curtain to let her out. As she passed, Elfrida touched her hand and smiled in secret approval.

Lavinia collected Tom from the hospital three days later, doing her best to pretend not to mind having to run the gauntlet of the journalists and television crews who were still camped outside the hospital, getting in everyone's way.

All the physical and neurological tests the doctors had done had proved negative and Tom had been cleared to leave. His eyes were better and had grown used to light again, but he still had dreadful headaches. He could not eat much and his sleep was badly disturbed. The psychiatrist had warned them both that it would be a long time before he was completely stable again.

As they reached the moor Tom wound down the car window to breathe in the damp air. 'D'you mind the cold?'

'No.'

'It's just that today's the first day I actually feel free,' he said not looking at her. 'They were good in the hospital and kind. Chorley's men, too. Even the bloody ratpack. But they were always there.' He laughed shortly. 'Odd.

For all those weeks in the various cellars I longed for a human voice, for a human touch, and then, as soon as I was surrounded by people again, all I wanted – more than anything – was to be away from people.'

'It sounds quite natural to me,' said Lavinia, driving slowly so that their arrival would not interrupt him.

'You know, you've changed,' he said.

'Yes, I think I have,' she said, thinking of all the things that Elizabeth Trewhitt had helped her see. 'D'you mind?'

'Quite the opposite. You feel easier.'

She laughed and felt another glorious surge of confidence. They never lasted long, but the growing certainty that they would recur was giving her a lot of private pleasure.

'Easier to deal with, you mean?' she said lightly.

'No.' There was a warming sound of amusement in his voice. 'Though that, too. You feel as though you're more relaxed, but it's not only that. Less angry, perhaps. What happened?'

'Lots of things. I don't think I was angry exactly; I'm not sure quite what I was, but I've begun to get a few clues.'

'I can see that we've a lot to talk about.'

At that echo of what Philip had said, Lavinia longed to be able to tell Tom all about it and about everything she had felt and said, but she knew that the time was not yet right for that.

'Yes. And, as you said the first night in the hospital, we've got time now. We don't have to rush anything at all. We can take time, can't we, Tom? Have you got to go back to work straight away?'

'Soon. But not straight away.'

She turned into the gravel drive and drew up outside the Dower House.

'Home,' Tom said and she felt like singing at the satisfaction in his voice.

Chapter 21

While Tom thought, walked and rode himself back into health, Lavinia wrote hundreds of letters. Together they had drafted a standard one that could be printed off the computer for all the supporters they did not know, but she wanted to write properly to their friends. As she re-read their letters and typed or wrote her answers, she came to have an extraordinary sensation of being surrounded by ramparts of affectionate support that she had never even imagined could be there.

One afternoon while Tom was riding with Flavia and the detective, she embarked on the last sack of unopened mail and found a letter addressed to herself and marked 'personal'. Not recognizing the writing, she opened it gingerly, afraid that it might be another of the horribly abusive anonymous letters that she still loathed reading. As she unfolded the letter a piece of paper fluttered out.

Seeing 'My dear Lavinia,' at the top of the main letter, she turned it over and saw that it was signed 'ET'. It took her a moment to work out that it must be from Elizabeth Trewhitt and then she read it properly.

My dear Lavinia

What wonderful news! I am so terribly glad about your husband's safety. I won't write any more about that

325

because no words could possibly match what you must be feeling and you hardly need to be told about that.

I hope that you find your way to happiness. From all sorts of things that you have said, I feel sure that you will.

Please come and see me again when you're in London – if you have time. Having met you now, I'd hate to lose the chance of knowing you better.

ET

P.S. I used to enjoy watercolours and I got out my old box to paint you a sketch of "the tasting lark".

Puzzled by the postscript, Lavinia reached out for the piece of paper that had dropped when she unfolded the letter and found a lightly coloured, insouciant sketch of a lark flying through a storm above a bleak, mountainous landscape towards a distant but sunlit valley. The bird's beak was wide open as it flew. When she remembered saying to Elizabeth, 'Well, I'll try this tasting lark of yours,' Lavinia laughed aloud.

Having propped the Tasting Lark against the teapot in front of her, she picked up her pen to write her daily letter to Philip, longing to tell him some of the things Elizabeth had shown her. Lavinia thought that if she could do that neither she nor Philip would have done any real damage to themselves or anyone else by admitting that they loved each other. For a long time she sat without moving as she tried to find the right words.

Eventually she thought she knew what to say and shook her pen to bring ink back into the nib. But before she could write anything Tom came home. He kissed her cheerfully and sent her up to have a bath, saying: 'You must've done far too many of those letters today; you're all stiff in the shoulders. Go and soak in hot water while I cook supper.'

'Really? Wouldn't you mind labouring while I wallow in hot water?'

'Not at all,' he grinned at her. 'I've decided that I'd better learn a few of your domestic skills since you've been so successful at politicking in London. Besides, I've already had a bath up at Saltley – and a drink with my mother and old Elfrida. I'm well restored. It's your turn. Go on. Up with you, Lavvy.'

Lavinia kissed him and did as he said. As she lay in the hot water, thinking about the life they might be able to live together in London when Tom was well enough to go back, she began to smell cheese and mustard and curry powder and wondered what on earth he could be cooking. When she eventually went down to the kitchen again, she discovered that it was cauliflower cheese in a wonderfully strong-tasting sauce.

They sat eating it at the kitchen table, with a lit candle between them, talking easily and falling just as easily into silence. They did not tackle any subjects of particular importance until Tom pushed away his empty plate and poured them both another glass of wine.

'Silence sometimes makes me panic still,' he said abruptly. 'That's really the main thing now. And it only comes on me sometimes.'

'Is that what disturbs you in the night?' Lavinia asked, having been woken several times as his hand descended on her face. He had always apologized, sleepily telling her that he was just checking that she was still there.

After a moment he nodded and then shook his head. She waited.

'I'm not sure. Perhaps. Although I have dreams too. They're nearly always about being gagged or causing some frightful trouble by talking too much and being punished for it.'

Lavinia thought about telling him how similar that was to her own waking nightmares. Then she decided that the last thing he needed to know at that moment was what she felt about anything.

327

'The silence was the worst thing about those weeks, far worse than the duffing-up at the beginning or the darkness or eating nothing but cold food and not a lot of that, or not being able to bath or even wash much.'

'I told Chorley that you wouldn't find any of that sort of thing too awful,' she said, briefly touching his hand as it lay relaxed on the table. He turned it so that he could hold hers for a moment. As his face relaxed he looked so like himself as a young man that she felt almost disorientated.

'I explained that no-one who goes hunting regularly would be floored by physical things,' Lavinia went on when she could speak easily again. 'But after everything that's happened, even I never expected you to be so calm. It's terrifically impressive, Tom.'

She looked at him carefully, checking that he really wanted to talk about it and was not trying to humour her. Her curiosity about what his captors had done to him and what he thought about it was almost overmastering and it had often made her feel ashamed. She sometimes asked herself if she wanted to hear that it had not actually been too bad so that she could let herself off worrying about him.

A little later, tasting her feelings as precisely as she could, she concluded that if there was a little of that, there was also a much bigger chunk of wanting to understand him better so that she could avoid hurting him with a clumsiness born of ignorance. Once more able to approve of her own motives, she stopped feeling in the wrong and let all her defensiveness go.

'I can see that it must have been hellish to be forbidden to speak,' she said as a prompt and to show him that she was genuinely interested.

'It was.' Tom laughed, but there was something forced about the sound. 'Perhaps the real horror was being forbidden to use the celebrated Medworth charm to bend

328

them to my will. And being left with no distraction at all from the thoughts, the nightmares . . .' He frowned. 'Anyway it's left me with a need to talk to you, in a way I'm not sure I ever have to anyone.'

'Not even Sally Anlaby?' Lavinia knew that she was taking a risk in raising the subject, but she did not believe that they would be able to talk in the way she thought he wanted while it was still unmentionable between them.

'Why Sally?' He sounded abrupt, almost angry. 'I didn't know you knew her.'

'I don't really, although I'm beginning to know her mother quite well. But Sally herself was at dinner in London one night at Aubrey and Caro's, and she talked to me about you then.'

'Did she tell you we've been lovers?'

'No. In fact she went out of her way to tell me you weren't.' Lavinia paused, watching Tom pick the crunchy brown cheese off the edge of the dish, and then added: 'I tried to convince myself that she was telling the truth.'

He sighed and wiped his fingers on his napkin. 'That's like her chivalry. She's not the kind to rock any marital boats, however hurt she may have been.'

Lavinia thought of how far they had come and wondered whether to suggest stopping for the moment, but before she could say anything, Tom went on in a voice she had never heard him use: 'I hurt her pretty badly, Lavvy.'

'Did you? How? Or why?' She tried not to frown, to keep her forehead smooth and her eyebrows loose.

'God knows whether it's why or how or if they're the same thing.' He licked his lips. 'It wasn't deliberate. But it happened.'

Lavinia began to understand what Teresa Somercote had meant. The difficulty of awaiting a description of Tom's love for Sally – and it clearly had been love of a kind – was eased by the sense of companionship he was giving her by talking about it. She thought of Philip and it seemed as though she ought to be able to accept the idea of Tom's love for Sally in the same terms as hers for Philip. But she could not quite manage to do it. She found that she hated Sally.

'Yes,' said Tom. 'After we first met, you see, we discovered that there were all sorts of connections between us. Not just hunting, but all sorts of sadnesses and fears, dilemmas and bits and pieces of history that we found we shared.'

'Seductive,' said Lavinia as kindly as possible. She did not feel at all kind, but she clung on to her conviction that reality between them was so important that she could not refuse part of it just because it reactivated old hurts.

'And then, about six months after we first made love, I found that she had sold her house in Dorset and bought one up here.'

'And you were angry.' It was not a question. Tom looked at his wife in surprise and then nodded.

'Yes, I was. Furious. Even at that stage it seemed unfair of me.' He stopped talking as though the confession of his irrationality – or unkindness – had become too painful. Lavinia found herself back in the primordial soup of her most muddled thoughts, unable for the moment to distinguish Sally's humiliation from hers; Sally's pain from Teresa's and again from her own. And Tom's from any of them.

'That was quite rough on her, wasn't it?' she said at last.

'It was that belated realization that made me begin to see what I'd been doing to you and me – even before the day I came up here. You see, she's so like me that it was easy to be with her – much easier in fact.'

'You mean than with me?' Lavinia hoped she did not sound as hurt as she felt. The fact that Tom was describing what she had found with Philip did not seem to help.

'Yes,' he said, looking at her honestly. 'And it wasn't

330

until later that I discovered that easiness isn't the point. Do you know what I'm talking about?'

'I think so, but tell me so that we're sure.'

'I've thought it all out, you see, sitting in the dark like that. I've come to see that I fell in love with you for all the things that you are and I am not. Then, a bit later when it got so difficult for us both, all I could think about were the things you weren't, the things that seemed to me to be so easy, so obvious, and in a way so important.'

'The things that Sally is?'

'Yes, those. And it wasn't until she began to assume that there was more between us than there was that I got an inkling of what it all meant. Then I started to remember why I had loved you in the first place, why I loved you still.'

'Ah, I see. Hence the bracelet.'

'Yes. Hence the bracelet. I could see straight away that it appalled you – and that hurt, too.'

As she turned her head away, Lavinia said: 'There's a terrifying pattern about it all, as though it had been arranged.'

'What do you mean?'

'It was the bracelet that sent me up to the tower and into Philip's arms that day.'

'And my finding you like that that pushed you into telling me what you felt at last?'

'Exactly. And so I have to be grateful to Sally?'

There was enough humour in Lavinia's voice to make it possible for Tom to say seriously: 'If you ever can. I must be, for I owe her a lot. But I owe you an infinitely greater amount and I always shall.'

'I don't think owing comes into it, any more than blame,' said Lavinia as she took his hands.

'And Philip?' he asked, looking down at them. 'Must I be similarly grateful to him?'

'I don't know. I am.' Lavinia looked at his face again and suddenly realized what he wanted to ask her. She said simply: 'We haven't ever actually made love. But he has given me a lot, Tom. He is not you and he could never be what you are to me, never, but I think that in some way I shall always love him.'

Tom looked at her then, took a deep breath, nodded and with difficulty said: 'That is your right.'

Later they went upstairs. After they had made love, they talked for most of the night. Between them they opened up the oubliettes into which they had dropped all the hurts they could not acknowledge and all the longings. It astonished Lavinia to discover how many of Tom's matched her own, and she almost wept at the thought of all the time they had wasted.

'Promise me one thing?' he said, waking her up again just as the first of the birds outside began to sing.

'What's that?' asked Lavinia, laying her head on his shoulder and letting her heavy eyelids close.

She was almost asleep again when he said: 'You won't stop being yourself, will you?'

THE END

DROWNING IN HONEY
by Kate Hatfield

A battered husband, a beautiful unhappy woman and a failed priest are brought together during a trial one cold, wet spring in the west of England.

Melissa Wraxall thought that she was happy – until she was summoned to act as a juror in a murder trial. In court she had to listen to accounts of a horrifyingly violent marriage, but while the life of the tortured defendant in the dock seemed far away from her own sweet, golden existence, with a ravishing house in Bath, her successful small business, her handsome husband, loving mother and supportive friends, Melissa began to hear disturbing echoes of her own life in the evidence which unfolded.

Suddenly, all the things which she had prized proved to be tinged with doubt and violence, and as the trial moved to its shocking conclusion she found herself having to judge her own actions – and those of the people she loved.

'A strong and compelling novel'
Elizabeth Buchan

0 552 14284 0

THE SECRET YEARS
by Judith Lennox

During that last, shimmeringly hot summer of 1914, four young people played with seeming innocence in the gardens of Drakesden Abbey. Nicholas and Lally were the children of the great house, set in the bleak and magical Fen country and the home of the Blythe family for generations; Thomasine was the unconventional niece of two genteel maiden aunts in the village. And Daniel – Daniel was the son of the local blacksmith, a fiercely independent, ambitious boy who longed to break away from the stifling confines of his East Anglian upbringing. As the drums of war sounded in the distance, the Firedrake, a mysterious and ancient Blythe family heirloom disappeared, setting off a chain of events which they were powerless to control.

The Great War changed everything, and both Nicholas and Daniel returned from the front damaged by their experiences. Thomasine, freed from the narrow disciplines of her childhood, and enjoying the new hedonism which the twenties brought, thought that she could escape from the ties of childhood which bound her to both Nicholas and Daniel. But the passions and enmities of their shared youth had intensified in the passing years, and Nicholas, Thomasine, Lally and Daniel all had to experience tragedy and betrayal before the Firedrake made its reappearance and, with it, a new hope for the future.

0 552 14331 6

CATCH THE WIND
by Frances Donnelly

It was the wildest time, the wickedest time, the saddest time – it was the Sixties . . .

The three lost girls – reflecting the intertwined lives of their mothers before them – found themselves trapped in a zany lifestyle of rock bands, drugs, flower people, and – in Daisy's case – something more dangerous. Daisy was new into London, fresh from the hippy trail of California. Somehow she found herself labelled with the new woman of the 60s image – free-wheeling, aggressive, sexually uninhibited. It was an image that was hard to lose.

Annie had found her own niche in London as a dress designer – but somehow she just didn't fit into the vibrant mood of the 60s. Shy, self-effacing, she was continually left behind when it came to men, and taken advantage of when it came to women.

But Alexia was the most bewildered of them all. With a neurotic mother who had dumped her at birth, with a sophisticated French background, and a suave, rich husband much older than herself, she was ripe for trouble. When rock star Kit Carson exploded into her life and she was thrown out by her husband, she could do nothing else but join the erotic, wild, sleazy lifestyle of a top rock band. For a while it was fun, then when she became pregnant she realised she had to take hold of her life if history was not to repeat itself.

The three girls, victims of the past, with old hang-ups, and old secrets shadowing their lives, finally united into a friendship that was to hold fast and carry them into a happier time.

The compelling sequel to *Shake Down the Stars*.

0 552 13313 2

A SELECTED LIST OF FINE NOVELS
AVAILABLE FROM CORGI AND BLACK SWAN

THE PRICES SHOWN BELOW WERE CORRECT AT THE TIME OF GOING TO
PRESS. HOWEVER TRANSWORLD PUBLISHERS RESERVE THE RIGHT TO
SHOW NEW RETAIL PRICES ON COVERS WHICH MAY DIFFER FROM THOSE
PREVIOUSLY ADVERTISED IN THE TEXT OR ELSEWHERE.

99565 7	**PLEASANT VICES**	*Judy Astley*	£5.99
13648 4	**CASTING**	*Jane Barry*	£3.99
13649 2	**HUNGRY**	*Jane Barry*	£6.99
99648 3	**TOUCH AND GO**	*Elizabeth Berridge*	£5.99
99537 1	**GUPPIES FOR TEA**	*Marika Cobbold*	£5.99
13313 2	**CATCH THE WIND**	*Frances Donnelly*	£4.99
99622 X	**THE GOLDEN YEAR**	*Elizabeth Falconer*	£5.99
14231 X	**ADDICTED**	*Jill Gascoine*	£4.99
99610 6	**THE SINGING HOUSE**	*Janette Griffiths*	£5.99
13872 X	**LEGACY OF LOVE**	*Caroline Harvey*	£4.99
13917 3	**A SECOND LEGACY**	*Caroline Harvey*	£4.99
14284 0	**DROWNING IN HONEY**	*Kate Hatfield*	£4.99
14207 7	**DADDY'S GIRL**	*Janet Inglis*	£5.99
14331 6	**THE SECRET YEARS**	*Judith Lennox*	£4.99
13904 1	**VOICES OF SUMMER**	*Diane Pearson*	£4.99
10375 6	**CSARDAS**	*Diane Pearson*	£5.99
14298 0	**THE LADY OF KYNACHAN**	*James Irvine Robertson*	£5.99
99561 4	**TELL MRS POOLE I'M SORRY**	*Kathleen Rowntree*	£5.99
99606 8	**OUTSIDE, LOOKING IN**	*Kathleen Rowntree*	£5.99
13934 3	**DAUGHTERS OF THE MOON**	*Susan Sallis*	£4.99
14318 9	**WATER UNDER THE BRIDGE**	*Susan Sallis*	£4.99
14296 4	**THE LAND OF NIGHTINGALES**	*Sally Stewart*	£4.99
99546 0	**THE BRIDGWATER SALE**	*Freddie Stockdale*	£5.99
99547 9	**CRIMINAL CONVERSATIONS**	*Freddie Stockdale*	£5.99
99574 6	**ACCOMPLICE OF LOVE**	*Titia Sutherland*	£5.99
99620 3	**RUNNING AWAY**	*Titia Sutherland*	£5.99
99549 5	**A SPANISH LOVER**	*Joanna Trollope*	£6.99
99592 4	**AN IMAGINATIVE EXPERIENCE**	*Mary Wesley*	£5.99
99639 4	**THE TENNIS PARTY**	*Madeleine Wickham*	£5.99
99591 6	**A MISLAID MAGIC**	*Joyce Windsor*	£4.99